Praise for Kathy Reichs

"Every minute in the morgue with Tempe is golden."
—*The New York Times Book Review*

"I love Kathy Reichs—always scary, always suspenseful, and I always learn something."
—LEE CHILD

"Reichs always delivers a pulse-pounding story."
—*Publishers Weekly*

"Each book in Kathy Reichs's fantastic Temperance Brennan stories is better than the last. They're filled with riveting twists and turns. No matter how many novels she writes, I just can't get enough!"
—LISA SCOTTOLINE

"Kathy Reichs continues to be one of the most distinctive and talented writers in the genre. Her legion of readers worldwide will agree with me when I declare that the more books she writes, the more enthusiastic fans she'll garner."
—SANDRA BROWN

By Kathy Reichs

Young Adult Fiction (with Brendan Reichs)

THE BONE COLLECTION

THE BONE COLLECTION

FOUR NOVELLAS

BONES IN HER POCKET
SWAMP BONES
BONES ON ICE
FIRST BONES

KATHY REICHS

BANTAM BOOKS ▸ NEW YORK

The Bone Collection is a work of fiction. Names, characters, places, and incidents are the products of the author's imagination or are used fictiously. Any resemblance to actual events, locales, or persons, living or dead, is entirely coincidental.

A Bantam Books Mass Market Original

Copyright © 2016 by Temperance Brennan, L.P.
"Bones in Her Pocket" copyright © 2013 by Temperance Brennan, L.P.
"Swamp Bones" copyright © 2014 by Temperance Brennan, L.P.
"Bones on Ice" copyright © 2015 by Temperance Brennan, L.P.

Published in the United States by Bantam Books, an imprint of Random House, a division of Penguin Random House LLC, New York.

BANTAM BOOKS and the HOUSE colophon are registered trademarks of Penguin Random House LLC.

Bones in Her Pocket was originally published in a digital edition by Scribner, an imprint of Simon & Schuster, Inc., in 2013. *Swamp Bones* and *Bones on Ice* were originally published in digital editions by Bantam Books, an imprint of Random House, a division of Penguin Random House LLC, in 2014 and 2015 respectively.

ISBN 978-0-399-59322-2
Ebook ISBN 978-0-399-59323-9

Cover design: Caroline Teagle
Cover image: © Tewan Banditrukkanka/Shutterstock

Printed in the United States of America

randomhousebooks.com

9 8 7 6 5 4 3 2 1

Bantam Books mass market edition: November 2016

For
Fred Weber
July 14, 1945–April 21, 2016

CONTENTS

BONES IN HER POCKET

CHAPTER 1

I clung to an upright as the Mule bounced and lurched, engine churning, parts rattling like a junker from the Korean War. Though the sky was overcast, it was still warm for October. I blew upward in a vain attempt to unstick hair from my forehead, unwilling to release my death grip on the four-wheel-drive ATV.

However I'd pictured an artist colony, the image definitely involved more numerous and better-maintained roads. This one consisted of dense forest, a cleared seam for power lines, and rough tracks spidering through bushy undergrowth. North Carolina meets Jurassic Park.

But I hadn't come to commune with nature, or to nurture the creativity of my right brain. I'd come to recover a corpse.

My plan for the day had been a nice run on Charlotte's Booty Loop, lunch with my friend Anne, and a crawl through the galleries in NoDa, the art district north of Davidson Street. I'd gotten as far as lacing my Nikes when the call came from my boss.

"It's Saturday," Anne had protested when I gave her the bad news. "Why can't it wait?"

"You want to talk details of decomp before lunch?"

"Don't they have cops for this kind of thing?"

"It's my case." As forensic anthropologist for the Mecklenburg County Medical Examiner, I considered unidentifiable human remains my domain. "A fibula, tibia, and two vertebrae were discovered at Mountain Island Lake a few weeks ago. Cops thought it was a missing person named Edith Blankenship."

"I heard about her on the news. College kid, right?"

"Grad student at UNCC." I referred to the University of North Carolina–Charlotte, my other employer.

"Not Edith?"

"Amelogenin testing indicated the bones came from a male," I said.

"I love it when you talk dirty."

"I still haven't ID'd the guy." John Doe was in a box at my lab. Case file: ME422-13. I'd requested a sonar scan of the cove where the bones washed ashore. Perhaps not needed now. Less paperwork. Small consolation.

Anne didn't congratulate me for my commitment to public service.

"The same guy who found the bones thinks he's spotted more."

"And you have to retrieve the rest of Mr. Tibia Fibula." Theatrical sigh.

"I might have time to meet you after."

"Be sure to wash your hands." Anne disconnected.

The Mule jogged left and shot downward through an invisible break in the trees, nearly tossing me headfirst out the open side. The guy at the wheel shouted over his shoulder.

"You good?" Slight accent.

"Dandy," I managed.

My driver was an art cowboy named Emmett Kahn, his term not mine. He'd greeted me an hour earlier with a smile and a bone-crushing handshake.

I guessed Kahn's age at somewhere north of sixty. Shaggy black hair, olive skin, lidded dark eyes, muttonchops the size of prime ribs. A successful art dealer, Kahn owned the three hundred acres through which we were taking Mr. Toad's wild ride.

"I call the place Carolitaly because the property's shaped like a boot. We're heading to The Toe." The last conveyed in capital letters. "Know much about Mountain Island Lake?"

I shook my head, jaw clamped. By the time we rattled to our goal, I'd need fillings replaced.

"The lake was created in 1929 to support the hydroelectric and steam stations. It's fed by the Catawba River and is the smallest of the three man-mades in Mecklenburg County."

"Big." All I could muster was caveman speak. Land large. Drive bumpy. Tempe rattled.

"That's why I have a caretaker. Skip handles security." Kahn tipped his head toward the block of cement riding shotgun. More Thud than Skip, the man was square in every sense of the word. Square shoulders, square back, brush cut that squared the top of his head. Aviator shades hid Skip's eyes, but I hadn't a doubt he was scowling.

"Skip's a cop with Gaston County. Helps to have local grease, you know?"

The Mule leveled, allowing a clear sight line to the eastern horizon. Clouds hung low, dark and bloated with rain.

Smoother ground allowed me to yell, "I thought this was Mecklenburg."

"County line runs through the middle of the lake.

My property spans both sides. My man Skip knew Mecklenburg had a bone lady and suggested I call down there."

Clever Skip. The CMPD had rolled it to the MCME. My boss had rolled it to me.

"Actually, I work for the medical examiner."

"You're a coroner?"

"Forensic anthropologist. I examine bodies too far gone for normal autopsy."

"Like floaters." Kahn's use of the term suggested way too much television.

"Yes. And the skeletal, mummified, decomposed, dismembered, burned, and mutilated."

"I've seen that on TV. You figure out how old the vic is. Man or woman, black or white. How they died, right?"

"Yes."

"You can do that with just four bones?"

"Fragments are tough," I shouted. "It's good you found more."

Something winged from a back tire and ricocheted off a boulder.

"We getting close?"

Kahn either ignored or didn't hear my question.

"So the more bones, the easier to catch a murderer."

"If it's murder."

I had my doubts. Mr. Tibia Fibula's cortical surfaces were smooth and bleached. Too smooth and bleached. I suspected they'd been around for decades. My money was on a washed-out grave. North Carolina has relaxed laws on private burial. In the Appalachians, it wasn't uncommon for Grandpa to end up in the backyard with Rover.

"Were all the bones found at the same location?" I bellowed over the roar of the engine.

"The first four washed up on Arch Beach. Want to detour over there?"

"Another time." An ominous rumbling juddered from the clouds. "And today's find?"

"At The Toe, facing the Meck side."

"The opposite shore of the peninsula," I clarified.

"When the river flooded last week the lake rose fifteen feet. The whole point was underwater, so the bag could have come from either side. Skip was checking out the damage when he saw it snagged on a tree. One whiff and he called me."

Bag? Whiff? Apprehension rippled a neural pathway.

"I thought you found bones."

Kahn beamed over his shoulder. "You insisted we call if we found anything else, so we did. We didn't touch a thing, so the scene's not compromised." Definitely too much crime TV.

Irritation battled uneasiness. Was this a goose chase? A colossal waste of my Saturday?

With a twist of the wheel, Kahn jerked the Mule ninety degrees, bounced down a hill, and stopped just short of the water. When the motor died, the silence was deafening. "Here we are."

I jumped out and surveyed my surroundings.

We were on a finger of land showing signs of recent submersion. Rippled soil. Scattered pebbles and shells. Mud-coated vegetation.

I looked a question at Skip. He gestured toward the lake.

Branches snagged my hair as I picked my way toward the water. Kahn and Mr. Loquacious waited upslope.

A dead fish lay on the muddy shoreline, guts ballooning like mushrooms from its belly. Surprisingly, few flies were availing themselves of the free lunch. Feeding elsewhere? Spooked by the coming storm?

I scanned the length of a pine tree lying half out of the water. Saw an oversized blue canvas bag ten feet out, its surface crawling with flies.

I turned to question my chatty companion. "You didn't touch the bag?"

"Nope." Skip could speak. "Smell was enough."

"How long since you found it?"

"Two, three hours?"

I pulled on gloves, the neural pathways now pinging fortissimo. Smell? Flies on old bones?

Thankful I'd worn rain boots, I waded into the lake. The men watched without comment.

Footing was awkward. The mucky bottom sucked with every step I took. The water rose, eventually topping the rims and spilling into the boots, soaking my socks and chilling my feet.

At mid-thigh depth, I reached the bag and a waft of odor.

Hopes of viewing watercolors with Anne vanished instantly.

The flies. The odor. Something didn't track.

I stared at the bag, debating. Call for help? Drag it ashore, then phone the lab?

Clouds pulsed with electricity on the far side of the lake. The rumbling sounded louder.

Screw protocol. No way I wanted lightning frying my ass.

After shooting pics with my iPhone, I leaned toward the bag and tugged. My balance wasn't good enough to free the thing.

I stepped closer. Calliphoridae bouncing off my face and hair, I yanked the handles from the branches on which they were snagged. The bag dropped with a smack.

Moving as quickly as my water-filled footwear allowed, I lugged my prize toward shore. Irritated flies trailed in my wake.

Skip helped drag the bag across the mud and up onto the rise. Water oozed from the canvas and poured from a six-inch tear on one side.

Back on terra firma, I took several more shots. Then I pulled the zipper and peeled back the top flap. Disenchanted, the flies set off for the fish. Sushi al fresco.

A skull stared out, orbits round and empty, as though startled by the sudden intrusion of sunlight. Hair covered the cranium and trailed the face like long, dark seaweed.

The body was clothed. Beneath the sodden fabric I could see remnants of ligament, a tag of gray-green tissue here and there.

That wasn't what froze my breath in my throat.

The legs were tightly flexed, the bones slender tubes running below the muck-covered denim.

Legs.

Plural.

No way this was Mr. Tibia Fibula.

CHAPTER 2

Skip helped load the bag onto the Mule. The jarring ride might cause damage, but I didn't want to wait. Lightning was streaking in earnest now.

Our return was subdued, even Kahn silent. At the compound, I picked up sufficient signal to make a call.

Tim Larabee, head pathologist at the MCME, was as surprised as I was. He'd sent me out fully expecting old bones.

Larabee asked if I could toss the bag into my trunk. Hell, no. I'd done that before. Once. The smell lingered in my car as long as I owned it. Maybe in my mind. Either way, I wasn't going there again.

Larabee promised a transport van.

We waited amid cabins more suited to the Alps than the Carolina foothills. Kahn explained that they contained studios for the use of visiting artists, but I saw no signs of another's presence. Skip said nothing.

After twenty minutes, Kahn excused himself to handle some business. I wondered if he planned to heads-up his lawyer. Skip stayed with me. Silent as ever.

"Mountain Island Lake sounds like they couldn't make up their minds." My stab at small talk.

"Mountain's that island in the middle." Chin-cocking the water.

"Must be deep."

"Six hundred and fifty feet. Lake's 3,300 acres, 61 miles of shore." Two sentences. Skip was on a roll.

"That's a lot of lake," I said.

"People in Charlotte drink a lotta water."

"Word of today leaks out they may switch to bottled."

Skip didn't appreciate my humor. "We haul in five or six bodies a year. Mostly drunk boaters. Some we never find."

Maybe *I'd* switch to Evian.

Kahn rejoined us, so I directed my questions to him.

"How many people have access to this area?"

"Only my family, my guests, and Skip. At the moment we have two artists in residence. We change the gate code when we think of it, but the place is large and, frankly, porous."

"Fenced?"

Kahn waggled a hand. Yes and no. "We share a boundary fence with the Duke Energy folks. But it's old and pretty much ignored, except by me."

"The Riverbend Steam Station?" I'd seen it driving in, a hulking set of smokestacks, brick boxes, conveyers, and tangled wiring that looked like something out of a post-apocalypse film.

"Yeah. It's a coal-fired power plant built in '29 when the lake was created. Riverbend was brought online to supplement the supply when demands for electricity were highest. The place is so decrepit and poorly maintained the locals are rabid. And the situation has gotten worse since Duke shut her down a few months back. Environmental groups are screaming that coal ash is leaking from the lagoons into the lake, suing for cleanup. We'll see how that goes."

"So anyone could access the peninsula? The Toe?" My gut told me the bag was a water dump, but I wanted my bases covered.

Kahn shrugged one shoulder. "Sure. Just blow off the NO TRESPASSING signs. This area used to be Hells Angels turf, so we still get bikers hot-rodding the trails, buzzing us in boats, that kind of thing."

"Any indications of recent entry?"

Kahn turned to Skip. "You good here?"

Skip nodded.

"Please phone when the van arrives." To me. "Let me show you something."

Before I could respond, Kahn circled a cabin and set off down a path barely visible in the underbrush. I followed.

"At Carolitaly we try to integrate art with nature." Kahn spoke as we walked. "Throughout the compound are living installations. Beauty in unanticipated places."

"Ah." I was clueless.

Five yards into the woods, Kahn stopped and arced an arm skyward. "Beauty in the trees."

A Plexiglas and metal capsule sat affixed to the branches of an oak ten feet above our heads.

"Let me guess. A space ship?"

"A vessel for the contemplation of space. A person seeking tranquility can sit inside and meditate. Glass allows light to enter, but enclosure prevents distraction, allowing one to direct one's thoughts inward."

"Ah." Modern art, not my thing.

Kahn continued toward a pine-needle-covered mound outfitted with a refrigerator door and port-hole. Wordlessly, he tugged open the door and directed me to look inside.

A buried pod held a round table surrounded by a curved bench. The walls, floor, ceiling, and furnishings were plastic, a warmthless, hospital white.

"Up to three people can survive underground for days."

Not this chick, I thought.

"There are thirteen of these on the property. Thirteen is the number for rebellion, apostasy, defection, disintegration, revolution."

A survivalist's wet dream.

"For a while now I've been seeing signs of a squatter at some of the pods."

"Any idea who?"

"Ever heard of monkey-wrenching?"

"Eco-terrorism."

Kahn nodded. Ran a hand over his jaw.

"The fellow you want to talk to is that wing nut, Herman Blount. Back in August, Blount posted some videos online threatening to blow up the Riverbend station. Then he went off the grid."

"You think Blount's gone to ground on your property?"

Kahn nodded glumly.

"If anyone's capable of violence, it would be Blount."

CHAPTER 3

When I entered the Mecklenburg County Medical Examiner facility early Monday morning, Mrs. Flowers, the receptionist, was at her post. As usual, her outfit was floral, her hair a perfectly permed and sprayed peach helmet.

I waved, crossed the reception area, and carded my way into the biovestibule leading to the autopsy suites and staff offices. "Biovestibule" is what you call a three-hundred-million-dollar hallway. Hot damn.

Our recently built, state-of-the-art, LEED-certified MCME facility still has that new-car smell. After decades in the old, refurbished Sears-Garden-Center-make-do quarters, everyone on staff is loving the new digs.

I headed to autopsy room four, one of a pair specially ventilated for aromatics: decomps, floaters, putrefied corpses. My stinkers.

As I detoured to my office to lock my purse in a drawer, Larabee appeared. In his off time, the chief enjoys long-distance running. A lot of it. The hours on the pavement have turned him into a lean and leathery Ichabod Crane in surgical scrubs.

"How'd it go at Mountain Island Lake?"

"Beat the storm." I straightened to face him.

"Joe said it rained like hell on the drive back. Wind almost knocked the van off the road."

Joe Hawkins has been a death investigator with the MCME since before Moses discovered clay.

"I didn't see Joe's name on the sign-in board. Where is he?"

"Out with pink eye. Do you mind working alone?"

"I mind it less than pink eye. Where are my bones?"

"In the cooler. Joe did prelim photos and X-rays, then left everything on the gurney."

"Busy weekend?"

"Not bad. One stabbing, an electrical death, and a murder-suicide. Nothing for you."

In our strange industry, that roster qualified as "not bad."

"Keep me looped in." With this, Larabee was gone.

Relieved I had no other cases, I snapped a form onto my clipboard, went to the locker room to change, then headed to the cooler. I hoped forty-eight hours of chilling had diminished the smell. Knew that wouldn't be so. At least not for long.

After wheeling the gurney to room four, I gloved and strapped goggles onto my head. Then I slapped a mask onto my face, and finished with a plastic apron tied behind my neck and waist. Fetching.

Ceiling-mounted surgical light on. Industrial-strength fan blades whirring. I was ready.

Joe had done a good job articulating the bones while still leaving them inside the clothes. After years assisting me tableside, he knows what I want.

The skeleton lay supine, with limbs slightly splayed. *Savasana* posture. Weird, but that phrase popped into my mind. Corpse pose.

The hair mass had sloughed from the skull during transport or handling. It lay to one side, filthy with rotting vegetation and other lacustrine debris.

I flipped on the light box. Joe's full-body X-rays revealed nothing extraordinary.

Back at the gurney, I paused, studying what remained of a person. Water is not kind to the dead. The bloat is grotesque, the smell nauseating. That phase had largely passed, leaving only bone and shreds of putrid flesh.

Yet this had been a human being. I felt the usual stab of sorrow. Hair always does that to me. Evokes the simple act of brushing, ear-tucking, tossing in a breeze.

Somehow my brain was channeled on yoga. It now fired an image, a class I'd recently attended. "Set your intention," the instructor had said. "There is power in your thoughts."

My gaze roved the body. I set my intention. A name. A final trip home.

Time noted on the form: 8:38 A.M.

I lowered the goggles, raised the mask, and began.

First I ran a magnifying lens over the clothing. Spotted a few short hairs, likely animal. Plucked and placed them in a plastic vial.

Next, using scissors, I cut up the center of the thin olive T-shirt proclaiming HAPPILY EVER RAPTOR, and spread the two halves to either side of the torso. The jeans took more effort, but eventually they, too, lay halved and peeled back on the stainless steel. When finished with the bones, I'd remove and examine the clothing more closely.

A skeletal inventory revealed every element present. Surprising, given the breach in the bag.

A nonprominent nuchal crest, smooth brow ridges,

and small mastoids suggested female gender. Pelvic traits were in agreement with those on the skull.

The cranium was relatively long and thin. The nasal bridge was low, the opening wide. I ran measurements through a software program called Fordisc 3.0. Every indicator pointed to African American ancestry.

Determination of age requires more minute examination. At birth, the skeleton is only partially complete. Throughout childhood and adolescence extra bits appear and attach to the ends and edges of bones. Components of the vertebrae and pelvis fuse.

The clavicle is the last to complete the process. I examined both, where they met the breastbone. Each had a cap firmly affixed to its tip, but a faint squiggly line told me fusion had occurred shortly before death.

I checked the arm and leg bones. The pelvis where the two halves met in front. The ribs where they attached via cartilage to the sternum.

To confirm my skeletal estimate, I pulled the postmortem dental X-rays from their tiny envelope and popped them on a light box.

Minimal wear on all occlusal surfaces. Root formation complete throughout the arcade. Every age indicator told the same story. Young adult.

A femoral measurement placed the woman's height at solidly average. Small muscle attachments suggested she'd been of slight to medium build.

I reviewed the data I'd entered onto the case form.

Female. Black. Twenty-three to twenty-seven years of age. Between five foot five and five foot eight.

I found the missing person file the cops had sent over with the first four bones.

Edith Blankenship fit the profile in every parameter.

I unclipped the photo and studied the subject.

A girl smiled from under a tasseled mortarboard, curly black hair framing her face. She wasn't pretty, wasn't homely either. Just plain. But the set jaw and straight-at-the-camera gaze conveyed confidence and determination.

The media had flashed the same image for a week or so. Until fresher crimes drew the attention of law enforcement. Until news coverage shifted to flooding in the Midwest. Then Edith Blankenship dwindled to tattered flyers posted on telephone poles in northwest Charlotte.

Edith's case was briefly reinvigorated by the Mountain Island Lake bones. Those investigating her disappearance were certain the file would shift to Homicide or move to the "closed" category in some other way. I'd dashed their hopes.

Had Edith finally turned up?

My mind shifted to PMI. Postmortem interval.

I checked a date. Edith Blankenship was last seen alive on September 8.

Fall had been unseasonably warm, even for North Carolina. The torn bag had allowed access to fish, turtles, and other aquatic scavengers. They, along with the normal spectrum of bacteria, had done their job.

My first impression, the level of decomp looked good for an early September immersion. But I'd need to verify.

I straightened, arched backward, then rolled my shoulders. I was again thinking yoga when my stomach growled.

The wall clock said 1:03 P.M. I was starving.

I removed my mask and tossed my goggles to the counter. Stripped my gloves and apron, balled them, and tried a layup into a biohazard can. Two points.

Quick hand wash, then I returned to my office. I

was fantasizing about a giant sub when the desk
phone rang.

I considered letting the call roll to voicemail.

Picked up.

Big mistake.

CHAPTER
4

"Thanks for sending a floater into my basket."

Charlotte Mecklenburg PD Homicide investigator Erskine "Skinny" Slidell had not been pleased by my call on Saturday. I'd fled behind the transport van, leaving him debating jurisdiction with Officer Skip. Junkyard dog vs. Jersey barrier.

"You're welcome."

"You tossed in the Unabomber for shits and giggles?"

"Have you found Herman Blount?"

"Oh, yeah. Prick looked like Saddam friggin' Hussein peering outta his spider hole. I'll let him sweat awhile, think about the good times out hugging trees. Then I'll grill him."

"I'd like to be there."

"How come that don't surprise me?"

The Law Enforcement Center is on East Trade Street, in uptown Charlotte. The drive took ten minutes.

Skinny met me on the second floor, beside a door marked VIOLENT CRIMES DIVISION. Behind it were Homicide and ADW, assault with a deadly. Blount was in the farthest of three interview rooms on the opposite side of the hall.

"Mr. Birkenstocks and lentils has spent the past six weeks underground. Smells like shit."

Coming from Skinny, this was a statement.

"What's his story?"

"Guy's got a beef with coal power. And hydroelectric. And logging, mining, farming, ranching, pesticides, the fur trade, animal testing, zoos, circuses, rodeos, McDonald's . . ."

"You've already questioned him?"

"Asshole hasn't shut up since I hauled his sorry butt outta his hidey-hole. Keeps grinding on about coal ash and arsenic and fish having trouble porking."

"Do you think Blount's a serious threat?"

"Your artist buddy was right about the videos." Slidell shook his head in disgust. "The dude with the squirrels growing on his face—"

I rotated a hand, indicating he should skip the comments on Kahn.

"Blount posted a bunch of boom-boom DIYs on YouTube. Going for an Oscar in dumbfuckery."

"Does he have a record?" I made a mental note to check out Herman Blount's stylings on sabotage.

"String of minors. Criminal trespassing. Vandalism. Destruction of property. Got busted for spiking trees about eight years back, did a bump with the feds. Caused $400,000 in damage to logging equipment. Dumb moob left prints all over the spikes."

"Any crimes against persons?"

"Iredell County cops like him for two nonlethal pipe bombs. One at a chinchilla ranch, another at a joint that offs dogs so surgeons can learn how to cut. The guy's slippery as goat snot. Nothing's sticking so far."

"This is only a prelim, but the bones in the bag look good for Edith Blankenship."

"Yeah?"

"Black female, early to mid-twenties. I'll need dentals for a positive."

"Any signs of trauma?"

"No. But I'm guessing she didn't zip herself in to go for a dip."

"You're thinking body drop?"

I nodded.

"Still don't mean murder. She could have OD'd, or had some other kinda accident, her pals panicked and off-loaded the body."

"Maybe."

"Why'd she surface?"

"As a corpse decomposes the body cavity fills with methane gas produced by bacteria in the gut. The bloating, helped by flooding, likely floated the bag."

"You're always so full of sunshine, doc."

"An experienced killer would puncture the gut and intestines, then weight the container so it stays down. Blankenship was amateur hour."

Skinny opened his mouth to comment. I didn't let him.

"Find anything linking Blount to Blankenship?"

"They're into the same save-the-Earth shit." Slidell pulled a small spiral from his jacket, spit-thumbed a few pages, and read. "Blankenship's enrolled in the environmental sciences master's program at UNCC. Before that she worked for Impact Watch, a non-profit that studies the effects of development on wildlife in western North Carolina. Their HQ is in Mount Holly."

"Right up the road from Mountain Island Lake."

I raised my brows. Skinny raised his.

"Who reported her missing?"

"Grandmother." Slidell's eyes dropped to his notes. "Ada Wilkins. Blankenship lived with her. Went to school one day, never came home."

"Who caught the case?"

"Hoogie Smith. He says Blankenship was a loner. Didn't work, no boyfriend, no besties. Father was never in the picture, mother was dead. He followed up what leads he had. Interviewed a few profs, Ada Wilkins, some of her neighbors. Wilkins admitted her granddaughter had taken off once before, after the mom died. The kid had no credit cards, nothing like that. Everyone figured she got fed up and legged it out of town."

"Cell phone?"

"Traced to a tower near UNCC the morning she went missing. Then the thing stopped working."

I knew what happened when the leads fizzled out. Blankenship's folder went into a stack with other MP files. Was buried deeper and deeper as the pile grew higher.

Slidell jerked the spitty thumb at interview room three.

"I don't want to spook this toad. You watch from two."

I did as directed. Sat at the table with my arms crossed.

In seconds a small monitor kicked to life and tinny sound began sputtering through a wall-mounted speaker.

Blount looked up as Slidell crossed the room. He wasn't what I expected. Surfer-dude blond hair, chiseled features, electric blue eyes. Save for the ratty beard, he looked more Christian quarterback then eco-saboteur.

And Blount had obviously seen some gym time.

Broad shoulders. Upper arms the size of utility poles. Washboard abs beneath a long-sleeved T.

Slidell took a seat. Placed a folder on the table. One by one withdrew pages. Positioned them neatly. Slowly read. Or pretended to. I knew the routine. Put the interviewee off balance by making him wait.

"I've done nothing. You can't hold me."

Slidell continued as though Blount hadn't spoken. After several unhurried moments, he finally laced his fingers and dropped his hands to the roll lapping over his belt.

"Here's what I'm asking myself, Herman. You good with that? Me calling you Herman?"

Blount only glared.

"Why does a guy with nothing to hide go underground?"

"Every day we're surrounded by cancer-causing high-voltage power lines. I go to earth periodically to give my cells a break from the constant bombardment of electromagnetic radiation."

"Mm." Slidell nodded, as though thinking about that.

"And it's peaceful."

"That why you sabotage utility companies? 'Cause they're frying your balls?"

"I don't sabotage anyone. But if I did, it would be a justifiable act of self-defense. The Riverbend Steam Station is poisoning people by dumping coal ash into the water supply. It should be stopped."

Stoked either by zealot fervor and/or lunatic fury, Blount's eyes blazed like two gas flames. Mesmerizing. I wondered if Edith had been caught in his spell.

"Ever think of suing?" Slidell, the voice of reason.

"The courts are useless. The government's complicit. Pollutants keep people weak and submissive."

"Explosives are much more direct." Skinny leaned forward to consult the file. "Like at Destin's Chinchilla Ranch and Arnett Labs."

"You have the wrong guy. I was never charged."

"You did a stretch for spiking a tree."

"A foolish youthful impulse. I know better now."

"So these outfits you target online. They magically blow themselves up?"

"Obviously I'm not alone in my views."

Blount held Slidell's eyes, confident, composed. But a blanching of his lips suggested pent-up emotion. Anxiety? Rage?

"Cop lost a thumb defusing the Arnett bomb."

"Small sacrifice compared to the animals they tortured."

"What about Edith Blankenship? She a small sacrifice, too?"

The quick segue was meant to catch Blount off guard. I watched his face closely. No reaction.

"Who?"

"Grad student at UNCC."

Blount shrugged one well-muscled shoulder.

"Maybe you two hooked up at Impact Watch. She Xerox your manifesto for you? You can write, can't you, Herman?"

Blount didn't rise to the bait. "Impact Watch is made up of lackeys. The government pats them on their heads, pretends to listen. The problems continue, nothing is solved."

"That what happened? Edith become a problem you had to solve?"

"You've found her?"

"Who said she was missing?"

"I read the papers."

"Where were you September 8?"

"I refuse to live by the structure of a calendar."

"Let me jog your memory, Herman." Skinny leaned in until his face was inches from Blount's. "On September 8 you uploaded your thoughts on how to demolish the Riverbend Steam Station."

Blount drew back to give himself distance. "I had a court appearance in Buncombe County. I was hours away. Check it out."

"You can take that to the bank. Who helped you make the video?"

"A tripod."

Slidell took another sharp turn.

"You and Blankenship pour valve-grinding compound into engines together? A little hit and run at Belvedere Logging last May?"

Blount shook his head in feigned disappointment. "You guys just don't get it. We're an army. We're fighting back. You can't wish us away. You can't bully us away." Now it was Blount who thrust his face forward. His next words were barely above a whisper. "We're everywhere."

Slidell didn't blink. I was surprised. By now he'd typically be going all bad cop.

"Was Blankenship one of your henchmen?"

"Edith Blankenship and her sort lack the guts to 'hench.'" Air quotes. "Protests and petitions will never stop the destruction. Action is needed."

"So Edith disagreed with your radical politics. Threatened to turn you in. So you capped her."

"Turn me in for what? Being able to handle a knife? To stalk prey without making a sound? To kill what I eat? Survival skills, detective." Blount sat back and arm-draped his chair. "Just stayin' alive."

Slidell clicked his tongue and pointed a finger. "College boy, right? Ivy League?"

"Dartmouth. So?"

"Pipe bombs 101. That on their fancy-pants curriculum? That what they taught you? To blow shit up?"

Again, the disappointed head wag.

"I learned that distrust of the government and belief in free speech aren't crimes. I learned that we humans face extinction because we're consuming the earth. That nature must be protected at any cost."

"Swanky talk for a guy we yanked out of a hole."

"I'm not responsible for the crimes of others, even if I applaud them." Blount's neon stare now seemed cold as ice. "You have nothing linking me to this Blankenship woman. We both know that or I'd be under arrest."

"Maybe yes, maybe no. But know this, you pompous little sack of shit." Slidell's voice was now hard as granite. "I'll find that link. And until I do, you can forget about death rays and tinfoil hats. I'm your worst nightmare."

Slidell gathered his papers and strode from the room.

CHAPTER 5

"What's your take?" I asked as Slidell lumbered up the hall.

"Guy's a nut job, but I can't arrest him for being crazy."

"Do you think he's lying?"

"Course he's lying. Everyone lies. About what? You tell me. I gotta kick him."

"Can you hold him on a trespassing charge?"

Slidell gave me his long-suffering, pouchy-eyed look.

"He'll go to ground again. You'll lose him."

"I won't lose him."

I knew Slidell couldn't detain Blount without grounds. And that he'd put a tail on him. Still, it was frustrating.

"I get a bad vibe from this guy."

"He's a loon, but he's not dumb. He knows I'll check with Buncombe County. The alibi's gonna hold."

"September 8 is the day Edith Blankenship went missing. We don't know when she died."

There was a long silence. Then Slidell said, "I need more. Get me cause and time of death."

"I'm on it."

Back at the MCME, I inhaled a tuna sandwich, knocked back a Diet Coke, then recostumed and returned to autopsy room four. The bones lay as I'd left them.

Rule of thumb. One week aboveground equals two submerged. But a whole lot of variables come into play.

I contacted the National Weather Service. My recollection was correct. The North Carolina Piedmont had experienced a very warm fall.

I called Duke Energy. Discharge from the Riverbend Steam Station raised temperatures in Mountain Island Lake to levels higher than normal. The water was reasonably oxygen-saturated. Aquatic life was abundant.

I reviewed what I knew about underwater decomp. The fat layers in skin expand, deforming a corpse within twenty-four hours. One week out, the flesh and connective tissue loosen and parts begin to fall off.

Packaging slows the process. But the bag that held Edith was badly torn.

Given conditions, and the state of the body, I estimated PMI at roughly four weeks.

Consistent with LSA for Edith Blankenship.

I entered the information onto my form, then moved on to cause of death.

Again, I started with the skull. No bullet entrances or exits. No radiating, depressed, or linear fractures. No cuts, nicks, or slashes.

The hyoid is a small u-shaped bone that hangs between the mandible and the larynx in the soft tissue of the throat. I examined Edith's for damage indicative of manual strangulation. Saw zip.

No surprise. In younger individuals, bone elasticity allows the hyoid to undergo compression without breaking.

I went to the scope and adjusted focus. Peered through the eyepiece.

Nothing on the right side of the bone. I shifted to the left.

And there it was. A minute fissure jagging the edge of the body where it met the wing.

I straightened, heart beating a little faster.

Edith Blankenship had been strangled.

I pictured the woman's last moments, body bucking, hands clawing, so desperate for air her nails gouged her own flesh.

Christ.

Shoving my anger to another place, I continued. Ribs. Long bones.

At the pelvis, I got my next shock.

Adhered to the belly side of the right innominate was a small gray mass. Using one finger, I teased it free.

As I probed, the outer casing split, revealing a jumble of delicate bones. A single tooth.

Heat fizzed in my chest. Had Edith been pregnant?

But no. The shapes were off. The half mandible was too oblong, the clavicle too sharply s-curved. Though tiny, the tooth looked fully formed.

I carried my find to the scope. Tweezed out bone after bone.

Was it a tumor? A teratoma gone mad?

Teratomas are tumors that can contain tissues or structures from any of the three cell types into which an embryo differentiates. Hair, teeth, bones. Rarely, a whole organ such as an eye or a hand.

Then realization.

What the hell?

Baffled, I collected the whole assemblage and laid it on a tray. Then I returned to the gurney.

The left innominate produced a second blob similar to the first.

I straightened, running scenarios through my mind.

I'd examined the victims of sexual sadists. Knew the depravity of which humans are capable. Had Edith been tortured? Had some sick bastard forced this obscenity inside her? What was the slang term? Gerbilling?

An idea tugged the sleeve of my consciousness. *Psst.*

What?

My eyes roved the sink, the cabinets, the stainless steel around me. Returned to the gurney. I looked at the skeleton. At the sodden attire bisected and splayed beneath it.

Frustrated, I rubbed circles on my temples.

Psst.

Edith's clothes? Lifting one tattered side of the T, I laid the fabric back across the ribs. Read the faded words.

Of course.

I lifted the leg and pelvic bones, scooched the jeans free, and cut away the back pockets. More gray masses. I opened and emptied each.

"Bingo."

I yanked off a glove and dialed Slidell. He actually picked up.

"I've got something."

"What?"

"Get over here. Now."

I disconnected.

I could have explained by phone. Skinny at the morgue would be much more amusing.

CHAPTER 6

The door opened. Slidell strode in and tossed an envelope onto the counter. A hint of BO competed with *l'eau de floater*.

"Lemme tell you. This guy Chou is a real wanker."

I pitied the hapless dentist, Dr. Chou. His morning had not been a good one.

Without comment, I popped Edith's dental X-rays onto the light box beside the postmortem shots Joe had taken. On one of the little black squares in each set, two snowy white caps sat atop molars. Restorations. I compared their positioning, their shapes. The root configurations.

"We'll need confirmation by an odontologist, but I'll bet the farm it's a match."

Slidell nodded, already all sweat and heartbeat. Decades on the murder desk, yet an autopsy room still set him on edge.

"Whatcha got that's so important?"

I showed him my Lilliputian osteology collection.

Slidell studied the bones, then his eyes rolled up.

"Rats," I said.

Grunting a comment I couldn't hear, he refocused on the tray.

"And voles, maybe a few mice." I indicated the gray masses, now disemboweled. "The bones came from these."

"And they are?"

"Owl pellets."

"What the hell?"

"Not what, whoooo. Come with me."

I led him to my office and logged onto a website using my laptop.

"Carolina Raptor Center?" Slidell sounded light years beyond dubious. "Like eagles and hawks?"

I nodded. "Raptors are amazing carnivores. They consume the whole animal—bones, organs, flesh. Kind of like you at a barbecue."

"You're a laugh riot, doc."

"Thanks. Owls are different from other raptors. They can't digest fur, teeth, bones, claws, or feathers."

"You got a point?"

"As indigestible materials pass through the digestive tract, the gizzard compacts them into a pellet that the owl regurgitates."

"You're showing me bird barf."

"I found two owl pellets in Edith Blankenship's pelvic cavity, below where her front jeans pocket would have been."

Slidell said nothing.

"She had four more pellets in a back pocket. I suspect she was researching owls."

"And hit this raptor center."

I nodded.

"You know where the place is?"

"Mountain Island Lake."

"Oh-nine-hundred tomorrow. I'll pick you up at your crib."

• • •

Slidell was twenty minutes early. I left my unfinished Cheerios and took my coffee in a travel mug.

Full-body latex is as appropriate for Skinny's car as it is for autopsy room four. Fast-food cartons. Cigarette butts. Remnants of old bagged lunches. I perched gingerly, minimizing contact with the seat and floor.

We drove north out of town on Route 16. Soon the high-rise condo and office buildings gave way to suburban homes and strip malls, then to fields and the occasional muffler shop, church, or barbecue joint.

Forty-five minutes out, Slidell turned from the highway onto a narrow two-lane. Nothing but shoreline, woods, and pasture. Here and there a startled equine, a boat access ramp.

Soon we saw an arrow pointing to our destination. Slidell hooked left into a gravel parking area and cut the engine. A sign warned PROTECTED BY ALARMS, CAMERAS, AND SHARP TALONS.

The Carolina Raptor Center was bright and airy, festive with photos and avian carvings. Eagle replicas hung from the ceiling. Baskets overflowed with tourist goodies—stuffed peregrines, owl key chains, T-shirts proclaiming BIRD NERD and GIVE A HOOT. On one wall a verdant mural depicted the life cycle of the red-tailed hawk.

"Hello!" chirped a septuagenarian with an astonishingly hot pink smile. "I'm Doris. May I help y'all?"

Doris looked like a character straight from *The Far Side*. Cat-eye glasses, bouffant gray hair, cable-knit cardigan with more pills than a Walgreens. Small but stocky. Fit.

Slidell flashed his badge.

"Oh my!" The woman pressed a liver-spotted hand to her heart, eyes darting left and right as if fearful of a SWAT team hit. "Is there a problem?"

"That would be Doris . . . ?" Slidell dipped his chin in question.

"Kramer. Doris Kramer."

Slidell pulled a photo from an inside jacket pocket. "Do you recognize this woman?"

"Of course. That's Edith." Doris frowned. "Such a puzzle. I'd never have believed she'd just leave us like that."

"She was a frequent visitor here?" I asked.

"Many of Professor Olsen's students do projects at the center. He brings a group every Tuesday afternoon. Edith loved our birds so much she stayed on as a hospital volunteer."

"Hospital?"

"More than seven hundred injured and orphaned raptors come to our facility every year. We're one of the few centers in the Southeast that rehabilitates the American bald eagle." If people really can beam, Doris was doing it. Then her face collapsed. "It's horrible that so many of these majestic creatures are hit by cars and electrocuted by power lines."

"Power lines?" I said.

"Electrocuted?" Slidell said.

Doris nodded solemnly. "Because their wing span is so broad they can touch two lines at once. It near broke Edith's heart. She'd sit hours in the ER with injured birds. She was on our ambulance team, too, responded to calls about feathered friends in trouble. But mostly she tended our residents."

"Residents?" Slidell's tone suggested fast-dwindling patience.

"We house over a hundred raptors that can't be released due to injury, amputation, or human imprinting. Visitors can observe twenty-three different species by walking our raptor trail."

"What did Edith do?" I asked.

"She cleaned cages, filled feeders, performed routine health checks." Doris laughed, a sound halfway between a hiccup and a cough. "I swear that girl liked birds more than people. Especially owls. They were her favorite." Doris's smile crumpled again. "I mean *are*." She shook her head. "Oh, dear. It's just so troubling."

A couple entered carrying a beagle puppy. Doris jumped as though tasered.

"Excuse me! Absolutely no dogs allowed!" Moving faster than I thought someone her age could move, she hustled the offenders back out the door.

I nudged Slidell. Pointed to a bulletin board beside a nest big enough to accommodate pterodactyls. A thumb-tacked flyer proclaimed "Fight Back At Duke Energy—Learn To Live Off The Grid." The contact listed was hermanblount2@gmail.com.

Doris returned to her counter, vivid lips smashed up into a scowl. "Really. There are signs everywhere. Don't people understand that dogs are dreadful for birds?" She rotated her upper arm to display a bruise, an eggplant arch curving the pallid flesh. "A dog bit me last week. Truth be told, I don't trust the creatures."

"Did Edith know a man named Herman Blount?" I tried to steer the interview back on track.

"Yes." Wary.

"Not a fan?"

"I can't fault Herman's love of animals. Though it's poor judgment to own a Rottweiler, any bird's worst nightmare. But he's a bit . . . extreme for my taste." Doris's eyes went wide. "Has Herman done something wrong?"

Slidell ignored her question. "How well did Blount know Blankenship?"

"He once brought in an injured barred. That's an owl. Edith helped nurse it. Poor thing didn't survive. Edith and Herman were both passionate about forcing power companies to make their lines safer for birds. And, well, if you've met him, you know. Herman isn't hard on the eyes." Doris flicked her brows in a "get my drift?" message that was quite unsettling.

"Did they spend time together?" I asked.

"I don't know." Shrug. "I mind my own."

Skinny went straight for the kill. "Is Blankenship capable of violence?"

"Like what?"

"Like screwing with power lines? Blowing stuff up?"

Doris looked away.

"What?" Slidell pressed.

"I don't want to speak ill. But that girl might do anything to protect her birds."

"Do you have any idea what might have happened to her?" I asked gently.

Doris looked at me blankly.

"Any tiny detail could be a big help." I smiled what I hoped was an encouraging smile.

"Judge not lest ye be judged." Mumbled.

"If someone has hurt Edith, we need to find out in order to bring him to justice."

Doris sighed. "No good ever comes from sleeping with a married man."

Not what I expected.

Ditto Slidell. "Edith was hooked up?"

Doris's hands started worrying the edge of the counter. "I've said too much."

"I'm gonna need a name." Slidell whipped out his spiral.

"Edith only mentioned him once, in the very strictest confidence. They'd fought, and she was upset. I think she realized he was never going to leave his wife."

"A name!" Barked.

"She was seeing her professor. Dr. Jack Olsen."

CHAPTER 7

Slidell asked a few more questions, then we returned to the Taurus. While gunning from the lot, he called the biology department at UNCC. From his end of the conversation, I guessed he wasn't getting what he'd hoped.

I was totally amped by the lead Doris had given us. Wanted to jump straight on it. Slidell had another target on his mind.

Minutes after leaving raptorville, Skinny parked in front of a squat building with a sign featuring a grinning pig in a puffy chef's hat. Lancaster Barbecue. I've never understood why BBQ joints put cheery smiles on the farmyard friends they serve up for lunch.

Entering was like crossing from Kansas to Oz, lackluster exterior yielding to NASCAR wonderland. Neon signs, antique gas pumps, vintage car paraphernalia adorning every surface, including the ceiling. A zillion TVs broadcast race reports in keeping with the stock car theme.

I didn't need a menu. Pulled pork sandwich, hush

puppies, slaw. North Carolina gold. Slidell was on the same page.

Our food had just arrived when Slidell's phone rang. He listened, said "yeah" a lot. I watched him scribble an address on a paper napkin.

"Olsen finishes class at two, usually heads straight home." Shoving the phone back into his jacket. Which was maroon polyester, a good choice given the sauce he was dribbling. "I'm thinking we drop by for a little chat."

I checked my watch. Just past noon. "That works."

"You know this jackass?"

"Only by reputation. We've never met."

Slidell wiped grease from his chin. Chins.

"Living-thing departments don't mingle with dead-thing departments?"

"Only when there's free food."

Slidell's understanding of academia is limited at best. I wasn't in the mood to explain the complexities of a major university.

"So what's the campus scuttlebutt on this guy?"

"Earnest type. Go-getter. No rumors about sex with students, if that's what you mean."

"How's this track? He and Blankenship get it on. She threatens to dime the wife, he caps her."

"Other than Doris Kramer's statement, we have no proof Edith and Olsen were involved."

Slidell made an indeterminate noise in his throat.

"Strangling's not like shooting a bullet or stirring poison into your boss's tea," I said. "It's hands-on, up-close and personal. So I agree. We could be looking at a crime of passion. Still, I like Blount."

"If Blount and Blankenship were birding pals, why kill her?"

"She has a change of heart, threatens to expose

him for something he's done? Maybe it's an accident? Who knows?"

But with homicide you have to know. Murder's not like B&E, extortion, or rape. With other crimes the endgame is clear. A murder investigation is always about motive.

Slidell's next comment suggested he was reading my mind.

"Killing's simple. Sex or money."

"Maybe their passion for birds bound their hearts in love."

"Who the hell you talking about, Blount or Olsen?"

Good point, Skinny. I'd tossed the comment out in jest.

"In my view, the easy answer is usually the right one."

Another good point. Though he couldn't have named it, Slidell was summarizing Occam's razor, a principle stating that the cleanest hypothesis is usually the correct one.

"And that would be?" I finished the dregs of my lemonade.

"Married guy enjoys a little poontang with young honey. Honey wants more. Honey ends up in a bag in a lake."

Though I agree with ol' Occam, Skinny's tunnel vision irked me.

I didn't doubt a fellow faculty member could kill. But Blount made my skin crawl. Something menacing lurked behind those cobalt eyes.

We paid our checks and rolled back toward Charlotte. Instead of continuing toward uptown, Slidell cut north onto I-85, toward the university, and navigated to a neat brick bungalow on a tree-shaded street lined with neat brick bungalows.

In the driveway, a tall, pale man with round horn-

rims and thinning brown hair was retrieving a briefcase from a Volvo that looked older than me. He
glanced our way when we got out of the Taurus.

"Jack Olsen?" Three feet out, Slidell badged him.
"Charlotte-Mecklenburg PD."

Olsen's face pinched with a mixture of fear and
relief. Anxious, but glad the waiting was over.

"Have you found Edith?" Shifting slightly, perhaps
to block the sight line to his front windows. Or from
them.

"Edith is dead." Skinny tried the shock approach.
"We dragged her body outta Mountain Island Lake."

Olsen's knuckles went white on the briefcase he
was pressing to his chest. "She drowned?"

"She was strangled, then stuffed in a bag."

Olsen's long, thin fingers went tight on the leather.
I noticed they were trembling.

"Blankenship was your student?" More statement
than question.

Olsen nodded. Swallowed.

"You seem pretty shook up, just being her prof,"
Slidell hammered away.

The owlish lenses turned to me. "Who's she?"

"Annie Oakley. Just answer my questions."

"I— I— Of course I'm upset. Edith was a very talented student. A very warm person." Voice fading on
the last.

"That why you killed her? She decide not to be so
warm anymore?"

I thought it impossible, but Olsen's face went
paler.

"God, no! What? What are you suggesting?"

"Edith threaten to tell the missus?" Slidell pressed.

"It wasn't like that." Barely audible.

"You ball her during office hours? Close the door,
take the phone off the hook?"

Olsen shot a look over one shoulder. More concerned about his wife than accusations of murder?

"I made a terrible mistake. I'm truly sorry. But I didn't kill Edith." Beseeching. "I cared for her."

"Nothing says caring like a screw on the blotter."

"We called it off." The whispered denials were growing more shrill. "Edith was OK with it."

"Teachers occupy positions of trust," I said. "Crossing that line is never OK."

"Edith was a grown woman. Not an undergraduate." Defensive. "I breached my marriage vows, but not my professorial ethics."

"She trusted you."

"She seduced me!" Practically a squeal. "She'd call at all hours, wanting help with a sick or hurt bird. Sitting alone together . . . late at night . . . things happened that shouldn't have." Another anxious backward glance.

"How long did these 'things' happen?" Slidell demanded.

"Nine months. But it was over before Edith disappeared. I barely saw her for weeks, then she ended it. I think she found someone else."

"Right." Skinny snorted. "Where were you on September 8?"

"I'd have to check my calendar."

"Or we could ask your wife?" I said.

Olsen adjusted the briefcase, as though to better shield himself. From us? From her? "What day of the week was it?"

"Tuesday."

Olsen's face brightened. "Tuesdays I teach from eight-thirty to one. Then I either hold office hours or come straight home. If that's all . . ."

"Yeah? A witness at the raptor center says you're there every Tuesday afternoon."

A shaky finger came up in a hold-on gesture. Behind the thick lenses, Olsen's eyes closed in thought. Opened. "Of course. In September we were still going out there. Now we do field observations at ARC, Animal Rehabilitators of the Carolinas. On Mondays. I'd forgotten."

"Our witness doesn't recall seeing you on the eighth. Or Blankenship. Says you both disappeared most of the time when you were there." Skinny wasn't letting up.

"Are you talking about Doris Kramer?"

"Am I?"

Theatrical sigh. "We didn't *disappear*. We would go into the woods searching for owl pellets. Edith was researching the impact of urbanization on the hunting patterns of owls. She was testing the theory that habitat destruction is forcing owls to become city dwellers, at greater risk of injury."

Slidell gave him the long stare.

Olsen's Adam's apple did another round-trip. "I won't be badgered. I've answered your questions. Shall I engage a lawyer?"

"You need a lawyer?" Slidell, never breaking eye contact.

"Jack!" Sharp.

We all turned.

An Asian woman was standing in the doorway. I guessed her age at mid-thirties, her height at maybe five feet. In kitten heels. At her side, coming almost to her waist, an enormous German shepherd was straining on a leash.

"Are you going to walk the damn dog?" Sharp as a marine drill sergeant.

"Be right there, sweetie." Olsen turned back to us, eyes pleading. "Please. I've done nothing criminal."

"Explain that to Sweetie."

Skinny strode toward the Taurus. I followed.

We drove several minutes in silence. Skinny broke it.

"Am I the only person on the planet don't own a dog?"

"I don't own a dog."

"You got that brown mutt looks like a bear."

Slidell referred to my estranged husband's chow.

"Boyd belongs to Pete."

"Yeah? What's up there?"

No way I'd discuss my marital status with Skinny. Or the fact that my ex was about to marry a thirty-something blond with a bra size larger than her IQ.

"I kinda like that dog. Not a drooler."

"Mm."

Several moments later.

"That Canadian cop still your main squeeze?"

Definitely off-limits. I hadn't seen or heard from Andrew Ryan in weeks, was pretty sure what that meant.

Again, my silence did not deter Skinny.

"The guy's OK."

"Not a drooler."

"Whoa. I touch a nerve?"

"Can we stay on topic? What did you think of Olsen?"

"Twerp's terrified of his wee little wife."

I couldn't disagree with that.

"Can't say I blame him. Sweetie seemed like a nasty piece of work. Think maybe she learned about Blankenship and ended the problem?"

"That woman couldn't strangle a Chihuahua."

"Anyone can strangle a Chihuahua." Slidell made a right. "What's your take? You think like these ass-clowns."

I *was* thinking, but not like an academic. Like a forensic anthropologist.

"Get me back to the lab."

"Yes, Miss Daisy."

My brain registered no surprise at Slidell's reference to a movie in which nothing blew up. It was busy gnawing on another idea.

CHAPTER
8

An hour later I was gloved and staring at the bones. The hyoid fracture pointed to strangulation as cause of death. After spotting it, I'd been distracted by the owl pellets. Now I wanted more.

One by one, I examined the neck bones, first visually, then under the scope.

C-1 and C-2 were intact. No nicks or gouges, no breaks, no jamming of the articular surfaces. C-3 told a different tale.

Edith's third cervical vertebra showed compression on its anterior-superior rim, and a hairline fracture where the right transverse process met the body. Good. But not what froze my breath in my throat.

Embedded in the fracture was a single red filament. Using tweezers, I teased the thing free and placed it in a small plastic vial.

Hot damn. Call Slidell? Not yet.

Back to the vertebrae.

C-4 through C-6 showed no signs of trauma.

The pattern made sense. In life, the hyoid lies directly anterior to C-3. The sparing of all vertebrae save that one suggested strangulation with a narrow ligature.

Then I looked at the last cervical and first thoracic vertebrae. Both had damage to their spinous processes, the projections visible as knobs running down the back of a living person. Both processes were fractured and displaced inferiorly.

I closed my eyes. Visualized the ligature looping Edith's throat. The movement of her head. Her torso.

My eyes flew open. Shot to the vial.

I hurried to phone Slidell.

"You may have been right about Olsen," I said when he picked up.

"How much did that hurt to admit?"

"The other Olsen."

Pause. "The wife?"

I explained what I'd observed in the bones. In the simplest terms possible.

"And?"

"Edith was strangled, probably from behind. The fact that trauma is limited to C-3 tells us the ligature was narrow, something like a rope or cord."

"But you're sayin' other parts of her back were messed up."

"Exactly. If her killer was of equal or greater height the damage would run roughly horizontal, front to back." I was greatly oversimplifying. "The presence of damage lower down on her back, and the nature of those injuries, suggest her upper body was yanked backward and downward. Hard."

No response.

"Edith was how tall?" I asked.

I heard paper rustle. "Driver's license says five-seven." Sharp intake of breath. "We're looking for someone short."

"Blount and Olsen are both six-footers."

Slidell did that thing he does in his throat.

"There's more. I found a red fiber embedded in the fracture on C-3. I'm sending it over to the lab, but I'm almost certain it's nylon."

Silence hummed for a moment.

"Nylon is a common component in dog leashes," I said.

This clue he got.

"Sweetie's shepherd was on a leash."

"A red one."

"Yeah?"

"Yeah. A leash makes an excellent ligature." It didn't need saying.

"I don't know. The woman weighs, what? Four ounces?"

"Eleven pounds of pressure applied to both carotids for ten seconds puts a person out cold. Rage, adrenaline, the element of surprise. It's a lethal combination."

"A woman scorned, eh?"

I heard a catch in Slidell's breathing, knew something was coming.

"Blount's in the wind."

I bit back "I told you so." "I thought you had eyes on him."

"The tail car lost him somewhere off Sample Road."

"Lost him?"

"Dickwad parked, then pulled a rabbit into the woods. My guys ain't Daniel Boone."

"Sample Road is out by the raptor center."

"Eeyuh. Even if Blount didn't do Edith, the asshole's guilty of something."

"You going to bring him back in?"

"We'll run him to ground. In the meantime, I'm

gonna round up the Olsens. Park them in separate rooms, see what they have to say."

"Keep me looped in."

After disconnecting, I gathered the vial and called for a tech to run it over to the LEC. Then I made a quick call to one of the hair and fiber guys, not optimistic, but hoping to schmooze a fast turnaround.

When done, I surveyed the lab, restless. I'd done nothing on the Mountain Island Lake John Doe since recovering Edith in her bag. Why not? Same lake. Maybe there was a connection.

I pulled the box from the shelf, knowing I'd get little from two leg bones and a pair of vertebrae. But I've always had goals.

Both vertebrae came from the lower spine. One was thoracic, one lumbar. Lipping on both was further advanced than I'd have expected, given the overall bone quality. Arthritis in a young to middle-aged individual. Interesting, but not mind-blowing.

I studied the tibia and fibula. Fully adult. The cortical bone was dense and healthy. The articular surfaces showed little wear and tear. A patch of remodeling on the lateral aspect of the distal fibula suggested healed trauma. Not a fracture, something affecting only the outer surface. A burn? An infection that spread from a soft tissue injury?

I was amusing myself, creating fanciful scenarios to explain my observations, when the phone rang.

"Brennan."

"It was Mrs. Peacock in the billiard room with the candlestick." Frank, one of the guys in trace.

"Seriously? You looked at my fiber?"

"No. But I've got a prelim on your hair."

I didn't make the link right away. Then I remembered. The short, nonhuman hairs I'd collected when first eyeballing Edith's clothing.

"Rodent, right?"

"Some. And some canine."

"Dog hair?"

"Six from the jeans are definitely dog."

"German shepherd?" Could we get so lucky?

His answer was not what I expected.

CHAPTER
9

Come on. Come on.

No go. I got Slidell's voicemail. Left a message. Disconnected and finger-drummed the counter.

Debated.

What the hell?

I googled for the number at the Gaston PD. Dialed. Made my request, wishing I had a last name. Listened to a number of clicks.

A voice I assumed to be Skip's asked for a message.

I hung up and drummed some more. Antsy. Ready to roll.

The dog hair on Edith came from two breeds, Rottweiler and cocker spaniel. Herman Blount had a Rottweiler. Blount was out of pocket.

Too agitated to sit still, I stripped off my gear and changed to street clothes. After leaving another less polite message for Slidell, I hurried to my car.

Traveling the now-familiar route to Mountain Island Lake, I considered how to find Blount. No way I'd tramp through woods peering into underground pods. I'd ask around, see if anyone knew Blount's habits, his hangouts. I'd start at the raptor center.

I reviewed facts as I drove. Edith Blankenship knew Blount. Blount was attractive, charismatic in a Charles Manson sort of way. Blount and Edith shared a love of birds and a hatred of utility companies that harmed them. Jack Olsen thought Edith had someone new in her life.

Blount cherished his freedom. Would he eliminate a person who threatened it? Or had it been a lovers quarrel? An accident? Eco-terror gone awry?

Other factors could account for the pattern of trauma in Edith's vertebral column. Blount could have crouched as he attacked. Perhaps they'd been underground, Edith trying to climb to the surface, prevented by a cord lassoing her neck. I'd been hasty to assume height differential was the sole explanation.

Irrationally, I slowed on Sample Road. Scanned the woods that ran up to each shoulder. As if I'd spy Blount in the shadows, loping like Bigfoot. I saw not so much as a squirrel. Too many raptors, I guessed.

At the center, I parked by an eagle totem and entered the building. A blonde in her teens was manning the counter.

There are two types of gum-chewers in this world. Those who snap, crackle, and pop with openmouthed abandon. Those who hate the sound of loud, spitty bubbles. Blondie and I fell into opposite camps.

I cut to the chase. "I'm looking for Doris Kramer."

"Gone today." Snap. "Weird. She, like, lives here."

"Do you know Herman Blount?"

"I've seen him." She grinned, jaw working like a radial saw. "Me likey."

"When?"

"With Doris. Twice last week. He seemed, like, intense."

"Any idea where I can find him?"

"Naw. I never talked to the dude." Pop. "Doris might be able to tell you."

"Do you know where she lives?"

"Up Sample Road, 'bout a mile. You can't miss the mailbox—it looks like an eagle."

Blount was last seen on Sample Road. Doris was uncharacteristically AWOL.

I thanked the girl and hurried out. If Doris had stumbled onto something tying Blount to Edith's murder, she could be in danger. If not, she might lead me to him.

I did another crawl along Sample, this time scanning for the postal eagle. Spotting it, I hung a right.

Half a mile down, the rutted, weed-choked drive ended at a seedy frame box that hadn't seen paint since Hoover took office. I parked next to a Corolla with a HAWKS LOVE ME bumper sticker and got out.

Three bowed steps led to a porch hosting a plastic table and a saggy armchair bursting its innards. I crossed to the door, instincts all prickly. Given Doris's carefully constructed appearance, the squalor felt wrong. A private shame, unintended for guests.

A note taped to the doorbell read "Broken. Please knock." I did. No response. I waited a moment and knocked again, louder. Nothing. I recalled the Corolla, the bumper sticker. Was pretty sure the car belonged to Doris. My concern mounted.

I took a moment and a breath to consider. Heard what sounded like muffled barking.

Doris won't like that. Odd, but that's what my mind sent up.

Circling the house, I spotted a structure about a hundred yards down an expanse of very dead grass. I set off.

Drawing close, I could see that the shed was leaning badly, barely maintaining contact with its cracked foundation. The boards were weathered, the hardware corroded and orange with rust.

To the shed's right, a dozen indentations rippled the earth. Something cold traveled my spine. I dismissed the sensation as paranoia. Every depression isn't a burial. And the hollows were too small to represent graves.

Still, I stepped gingerly, avoiding branches that might snap underfoot. Stilling keys that might jingle in my pocket.

Reaching the derelict building's nearest door, I didn't knock or call out. I tried the knob. It turned. I shoved. The door creaked back on its hinges.

I squinted into the dim interior.

My hands flew to my mouth. I tasted bile and felt tremors beneath my tongue.

CHAPTER
10

The stench hit first. An overpowering reek of urine and feces, like a wet blanket slapping my face and molding itself to my skin.

A few deep breaths, then I stepped through the door. The building erupted in sound. A cacophony of yipping, whining, howling, and barking.

My brain moved slowly, reluctant to process the horror my senses were taking in.

Rows of cages ran the length of the shed. Double-decker. Thirty, forty, maybe a hundred.

Jammed in each cage were anywhere from three to eight dogs, eyes crusty, snouts raw from contact with the rusty chicken wire. Many had obscene tumorous nipples hanging like stretched and distorted fruit from their bellies.

My heart splintered.

I'd read of them, opposed them on principle. But I'd never actually seen a puppy mill. Dogs living their entire lives in tiny prisons. No toys. No comfort. No love. No hope.

I looked down the row. Saw cockers, Yorkies, Rott-weilers, Labs. The larger breeds were in pens just three feet high, barely tall enough to allow them to stand or turn.

Doris Kramer wasn't a victim. She was a monster.

Sweat began trickling down my back. The interior temperature had to be ninety-five. How could any creature endure these conditions?

Knowing the barking would soon blow my cover, I reached for my iPhone. It wasn't in my pocket.

Panic threatened to overwhelm me. I'd left my mobile in the car. Who expected this?

I steeled myself not to bolt. Not to wrench open the cages and let the dogs run free.

If they could run. I suspected many could not.

Slidell is coming, I told myself. He'll get your message. He'll follow the trail. But when?

I inched toward the closest row of cages, murmuring soft, comforting sounds in my throat. Maybe words. Maybe not.

The dogs watched my every move, flies buzzing their ears and crawling through their matted fur. Wary. As I drew close they shrank back as far as their cramped quarters would allow.

The cages held no food or water. Feces smeared every surface and lay mounded where the walls met the floor.

Fury exploded white-hot in my brain.

Breathing through my mouth, I picked my way across excrement-coated concrete. Eyes followed me, sad, frightened, hopeful, lost.

The odor was so strong it burned my eyes and the lining of my nose. As I crept deeper into the hellish gloom, another scent joined that of shit and pee and filthy fur. A scent I knew well.

At the end of the first row of cages, a mound of dead puppies lay tossed on the ground. Sensing threat, a zillion flies lifted from the grisly heap in a buzzing black cloud.

Appalled and dismayed, I took a step sideways. And nearly tripped.

I looked down. A large, hairy arm obstructed my path. Connected to it was a large, hairy man. Below his head was an ominous dark pool.

Herman Blount's eyes were closed and his mouth was open. Blood ran from a gash in his forehead, across his temple, and into his hairline.

I crouched and pressed two fingers to his throat. Felt a pulse, faint but steady.

Had Blount made the same grisly discovery I had? Or was he involved, the animal-lover persona a ruse?

Above the baying, I heard a muffled scrape. Dog? Something else?

My eyes darted wildly. Took in a wheelbarrow, a shovel, a shelf filled with clippers, metal bowls, a tranquilizer gun, a box of orange darts.

Beside the shelf, a pair of wall pegs held leashes. A slash of color peeked from the middle of the tangle.

More stealthy scraping. A footstep?

I held my breath. Thirty seconds. An eon.

The barking had grown more furious, obliterating any possibility of separating sounds.

I scooted closer to the pegs. Saw a bright red leash hanging among the others.

Synapses fired.

Doris Kramer ran a puppy mill. Edith Blankenship wandered the woods around it. Doris stood no more than five foot two.

I had to reach Slidell. But how? Bolt and leave Blount?

The canine frenzy was compromising my ability to think.

Blount was bleeding. How bad was the wound? How long would he last?

Drag two hundred pounds of Herman to my car? Definitely not a goer.

In the corner of one eye I registered movement. A sudden shift of shadow and dimness.

My head whipped around. I caught a glimpse of ratty cardigan. Something snakelike winging past my eyes.

My hands flew to my neck. The snake settled over them.

Cells in my brainstem fired orders to shield my windpipe. Neurons in my cortex overrode them. My hands slid sideways to protect my carotids.

I heard raspy panting close at my ear. Smelled a mix of salty sweat and drugstore cologne.

A stocky torso slammed against my spine, tensed. The deadly cord cut deeper into the backs of my hands. Dug viciously into the flesh of my throat.

Black spots began to gather and cloud my vision. My lungs heaved, desperate for oxygen.

The neurons shouted another demand.

Do the unexpected!

Moving like lightning, I dropped to a squat. The sudden change of angle threw my attacker off balance. As she pitched forward, I expanded the lasso outward, rolled to my back, and kicked out with both legs. One boot connected with bone.

A feral cry.

Doris hit the concrete.

The dogs went wild.

I scrambled to my feet and clawed the leash from my shoulders. Tossed it sideways.

Outrage and loathing overruled any instinct to flee. I wanted payback for the helpless creatures watching with terrified eyes.

I swallowed to calm my heartbeat. To quell the fire in my throat.

"Just toss them out like last week's trash?" Gulping air. "How many puppies have you killed, you freak show?"

"You hurt my leg." Rubbing a shin.

"The cops are on the way." Please. "You're going down for a very long time."

She snorted.

"You're a cold-blooded killer."

"A couple of dead dogs? You know the penalties in this state for animal cruelty? A slap on the wrist and a warning."

Balancing with both palms on the concrete, Doris slowly rose to her feet.

I stood my ground, fingers gripping my sides to stop the shaking in my hands. She was right. Lax laws made North Carolina puppy mill central.

"How about murder?" Rage hardened my voice. "You know the penalties for that?"

"What are you talking about?" A little less confident.

"Edith Blankenship." Over the clamor, my voice was eerily calm.

With amazing speed, Doris pivoted and snatched up the tranq gun. I saw a flash of orange. Knew the weapon was loaded.

"That's a discussion you can have with Edith," Doris snarled.

I backpedaled as fast as I could. My shoulders slammed a cage. The occupants went wild.

I threw up my hands, images skittering in my brain. The ballistic syringe piercing my flesh. The immobilizing drug coursing through my veins. Doris approaching my unconscious body with the deadly leash.

As I stared down the gun barrel, a denser denseness formed up in the gloom behind my assailant. My face must have changed.

Doris turned. Gasped.

Blount arced the shovel in a roundhouse swing at her head. The blade connected with a sickening crack. Doris flew back and lay still.

Blount straightened. I caught a flash of blue stare below the mutilated brow.

Our eyes locked.

Blood pounded in my ears. Dogs bellowed around me. Would I now suffer the same fate?

"Let's find someone to care for these animals."

I needed no second invitation.

CHAPTER 11

Slidell visited me a few days later. I was at home, forced leave, Larabee's order.

"Nice scarf."

Doris's leash had turned my neck into a Monet landscape of purple and yellow. I was covering the bruises with a bandanna featuring test tubes and beakers, a giveaway from some forensics outfit looking for business. Geek chic.

"Souvenir?" Skinny gestured at the Rottweiler asleep on the floor.

"Temporary boarder." Hoarse.

After we'd fled the horror show and called the cops, Blount had activated an animal rescue network. A swarm of volunteers moved in as soon as CSS released the scene. Dogs were taken to veterinarians, shelters, and homes. Most would make it. A few would not.

In the chaos, the Rottweiler and I had bonded. She was with me until a permanent home could be found. Kind of a foster arrangement. I was calling her Edie, in honor of Edith. My cat, Birdie, was calling her devil incarnate, refusing to come out from under my bed.

"Got a present waiting in your cooler."

I raised my brows in question.

"Turns out Gaston Skip isn't a complete waste of oxygen. Two days ago he busted a biker trail-riding through Kahn's art-fart estate. Kid's shitting his shorts, gives it up without a fight. Claims he wanted a peek at the legendary Hells Angels well of lost souls."

Again the brows. Saved wear and tear on my throat.

"Seems there's an abandoned well on Kahn's property. Rumor has it the thing enjoyed regular intake in the eighties."

"Bodies?"

"No. Tricycles. Of course I'm talking bodies."

I curled my fingers in a give-me-more gesture.

"After Skip learns the kid's story, he goes shaft-diving, does some digging and rock-lifting, finds a bunch of bones."

"Seriously?"

"Seriously. I'm guessing it's the rest of your John Doe. Skip figures recent flooding washed out the four he found on the beach."

"Edith Blankenship?"

"Your gal Doris is looking at murder one."

"She's OK?"

"She ain't dancing no jigs, but she'll pull through."

"Motive?"

"Like I told you, door A or door B. Love or money."

Amazing what you can ask without using words. Now I relied on upturned palms.

"Both. The old broad was totally mental for anything with feathers. Her financials showed she was donating to a boatload of birdie outfits, including the raptor center. The puppies gave her extra liquidity to take the load off birds. Blankenship intended to shut her down."

We sat in silence a moment, thinking about that.

"We found Edith's phone wedged between two beams in the back of the shed. Smashed to shit. But the tech boys were able to recover some pics from the memory. Dogs, kennels, a pile of rotting puppies. The kid probably stumbled across the place, wanted evidence to blow a big friggin' whistle. Doris caught her and took her out."

"The leash?"

"Lab guys lifted a couple hairs, some blood. They're testing for DNA. They're also running comparisons on the red fiber you pulled from the vic's neck bone. It'll come back to Blankenship."

"Doris dumped the body?" Four words. It hurt.

"She's tough, but for that she needed help. She has a son, retarded or slow or whatever. Works part-time as a forklift driver at some warehouse. She muscled Blankenship into the bag, then called sonny. Told him to take his rowboat way out onto the lake and toss it. Said there were dead dogs inside. Made him swear not to open the zipper."

Sweet Jesus.

"Blount?"

"That ass-hat's gonna live, too. Turns out our little chit-chat set the guy off. Blount liked Blankenship. Was pissed the kid got whacked. So, caped crusader that he is, he goes snooping, stumbles across Doris's shit show. Poetic, ain't it? The old lady belts him with a shovel, he uses the same shovel to belt her back."

"The Olsens?"

"I'm guessing Casanova's investing in flowers."

"His wife found out?"

Slidell shrugged. "Not from me."

Way to go, Skinny.

"Emmett Kahn?"

"Investing in fencing. Oh, and you're gonna love this. He's commissioned one of his bohemian buddies to make a giant owl sculpture. Plans to call it *Essence of Edith*."

With that, he took his leave.

So my John Doe might be a fallen Hells Angel. Made sense. Arthritic lower back from years of bouncing on a Harley. Burned ankle from contact with a hot exhaust pipe.

I pictured Edith roaming the woods, eyes moving from the trees to the ground at her feet. Finding a pellet and slipping it into her pocket.

Not knowing she had but a pocketful of hours to live.

But I didn't want to think about death today. Finally take that jog around the Booty Loop? Go for a drive? Bad idea in a scarf. Ask Isadora Duncan.

Edie padded over and placed her chin in my lap. I rubbed her ears. She rolled big caramel eyes up to mine. Rotated the eyebrow whiskers above them.

I thought about the horror she'd survived. Feared the memories would stay with her always. As they would with me.

Still, she found love in her heart for humans. I hoped I'd always be like Edie. Given my line of work, I am sometimes pessimistic about my species. But I do understand. The good in humanity outweighs the bad.

Suddenly, I knew what to do with my day. I grabbed my phone and dialed a friend at *The Charlotte Observer*.

"Is there still time to get an op-ed into this Sunday's paper?" I asked.

"What topic?" she asked.

I told her.

"Deliver by five today, I'll see what I can do."

With Edie on my heels, I hurried to my desk, booted my laptop, and typed a headline:

**OPT TO ADOPT—
STOP THE HORROR OF PUPPY MILLS**

AUTHOR'S NOTE

As a forensic anthropologist, I see the malice humans cause one another. As the owner of five rescue animals, I'm distressed by cruelty to all species. Occasionally, these paths intersect.

Early in my career, on a warm Monday in May, a heartbreaking case arrived at my lab in Montreal. Police recovered a burlap bag on the shore of a small lake in southern Quebec. It contained bones and a pair of bricks. My job was to determine if the remains were human.

They weren't. These were the skeletons of four puppies. The helpless creatures had been bagged, weighted down, and drowned.

Thoughts of those puppies stayed with me for a very long time. I imagined their terror as the water closed around them. Their desperate attempts to escape. To breathe.

I am a tolerant person, but animal abuse is a sin I cannot forgive. And nothing is more abusive than a puppy mill.

A puppy mill is a "factory farm" for dogs. Some are legal, some not. Government regulation is lax, if it exists at all. The "crops" are raised in cages. Females are bred as frequently as possible, and discarded when no longer fertile. It's a life with no joy, no love, no hope. The dogs are sick, starved, and sad. They have never played on the grass or run through a field.

Thousands of people buy dogs from puppy mills annually, most believing they are getting their pets from a responsible source. Inhumane breeders seduce buyers into "puppy love," either in pet stores or through online photos. The Humane Society estimates there are ten thousand puppy mills across the country. Collectively, they sell two million to four million puppies each year. My home state of North Carolina is one of the worst offenders, requiring no inspections and having no laws governing breeders' sales.

You can help prevent animal abuse. Here are eight things you can do to stop the horror of puppy mills:

- **Adopt your next pet.** The perfect pet is waiting for you at one of the thousands of shelters and rescue groups across the country. If you want a particular breed, you can locate one by contacting a breed-rescue organization.
- **Don't buy a puppy online or from a pet store.** If you buy a puppy, you're most likely supporting the puppy mill industry. If you must buy, please do your research to be sure your puppy isn't from a mill.
- **Take action against pet stores that sell puppy mill dogs.** Ask pet store owners to consider switching to a humane business model. If the store refuses to change, hold a peaceful rally or start a letter-writing campaign.
- **Advocate for stricter breeding laws.** Write or call your city, county, state, and federal officials and

ask them to take these issues seriously. Constituent feedback influences legislators. To help change your city, county, and state laws, sign up to receive action alerts from Voices for No More Homeless Pets at support.bestfriends.org.

- **Speak out in your community.** Write to the editor of your local newspaper about puppy mills keeping their animals in unacceptable conditions.
- **Elect animal-friendly candidates.** Ask candidates if they support regulating commercial breeders and what they would do about puppy mills. Let them know you support stricter puppy mill regulations and that you vote.
- **Raise awareness and/or donations.** Organize a walk, conduct a bake sale or car wash, or set up a table at local events to raise awareness and funding for animal rescue and breeding regulation.
- **Don't give up.** The fight against puppy mills and inhumane breeders has been going on for decades. Things won't change overnight, but there has been progress. If you educate just one person about the horrors of puppy mills or persuade just one person to adopt rather than buy, you've made a difference.

ACKNOWLEDGMENTS

I owe many thanks to the following: Rejine and Andreas Bechtler for welcoming me to their beautiful property; the Carolina Raptor Center for answering my many questions; and Kerry Reichs, daughter and fellow author, for her incomparable research skills and creative feedback.

SWAMP BONES

CHAPTER 1

March. Barely spring, yet the unseasonable Florida humidity made me feel like I'd disembarked from my flight into a Rottweiler's mouth. For the hundredth time since arriving, I berated myself for choosing the Everglades as a vacation destination. My hair was giving me a big thumbs-down.

I had no way of knowing at that point that lank locks would turn out to be the least of my worries. That my vacation would quickly descend to a dark and grisly place. But not yet. My first hour in the glades, I was just hot and bothered.

The Daniel Beard Research Center had been a missile site during the cold war and looked like it, despite now being painted a garish flamingo pink. The color really made the National Park Service logo pop. Pushing through the door, I applauded the overzealous air-conditioning. My sweat-slicked skin instantly goose-bumped up, but my limp ponytail was too far gone to rally.

I crossed the public area and headed toward the business side of the building. A woman behind a scarred wooden desk tracked my approach. Beige hair, beige skin, coral mouth. A stern expression said she took her gatekeeping duties seriously. Really? The South Florida Natural Resources Center needed protecting?

"Dr. Tempe Brennan." Cheerful as I could muster. "I'm here to see Dr. Robbin."

"I don't have you down as a visitor." Never breaking eye contact to consult a list.

I smiled disarmingly. The gatekeeper did not.

I kept smiling doggedly until my opposition broke and said, "Bird lady's in Lab B." Swiveling a clipboard to face me. "John Hancock."

After signing, then staring into a beady camera eye that produced a visitor's badge, I proceeded down the hall, a tiny image of my unsmiling face stuck to my breast. Wall-stenciled arrows got me to Laboratory B. Through the door's small rectangular window, I spotted a petite brunette bent over a stainless steel gurney.

I knuckle-tapped the glass, and the woman looked up and squinted. With recognition, she lowered her mask to reveal a mile-wide grin. Glad to see me or amused at my wilted appearance? The woman beckoned with a gloved hand.

The lab smelled of chemicals and decay, a familiar blend evoking thoughts of work, not sun and sand. Fortunately, this errand wouldn't take long—I was just stopping to pick up the keys to my hostess's house. The latest Jodi Picoult novel waited in a beach bag in my carry-on. Goodbye winter shoes, hello flip-flops.

"Tempe!" Lisa Robbin shot forward to embrace me, a gesture that, given her size, landed her head somewhere around my midsection. I did the awkward quick-squeeze thing non-huggers do.

"Sorry I couldn't meet you at the airport as promised. I know it's a hassle to cab all the way out here. But I just received a record number of packets." Lisa's hand fluttered toward the examining table, which contained seven lumps resembling compressed, dehydrated roadkill.

Dr. Lisa Robbin was for the birds, not just by name but also by mannerisms and calling: She was head of the Smithsonian Feather Identification Lab, and a pioneer in forensic ornithology. She and I had met while consulting on a case in South Texas. A bus carrying an exotic bird smuggler and his booty had gone over a cliff and exploded in flames, incinerating all those on board. I'd taken the human bones. Lisa had taken the talons and beaks.

Not as bizarre as it sounds. Lisa and I both analyze the dead too compromised for normal autopsy. In her case, necropsy, since her subjects are nonhuman. We work the skeletal, mummified, decomposed, dismembered, mutilated, or, in the bus crash recovery, charred to a crisp.

As a forensic anthropologist, I am a specialist in the human skeleton. I study the bones of the visually unrecognizable and the unidentified, searching for indicators of age, sex, race, and height. I observe peculiarities and anomalies. Anything to give the remains a name and, if necessary, a manner and time of death. Frankly, I'm not sure what Lisa does with her birds.

We'd bonded over the bus crash victims, passing bone fragments back and forth, human to me, avian to her. I liked her. After I'd returned home to North Carolina, and Lisa to Washington, D.C., we'd maintained contact, "birds of a feather" in maledominated fields.

"I'm so glad you're here!" She tipped her head,

quick and sparrowlike. "I know we'd talked about a visit but wasn't sure you'd ever make it."

My concept of vacation usually involves Bahamian blue water, ocean breezes, and a whole lot of sand. But Lisa's re-invitation had hit my inbox during a perfect storm of frustrations: An argument with my department chair at UNCC. A run-in with a testy prosecutor concerning my report on his homicide victim. Dietary issues with my cat, Birdie, that meant new carpeting in the parlor. A blown timing belt on my Mazda during rush-hour traffic.

It was that last one that did it. After two hours inhaling eau de I-77 waiting for AAA, out of boredom I hit the travel app on my iPhone. Life lesson on why you don't impulse-plan vacations. Rage booking can lead to swamps and leeches instead of waves and beaches.

"Calgon, take me away. To a predator-infested swamp," I half joked.

"Aw, c'mon. The Everglades rock. You've never seen such a gorgeous variety of native birds."

I knew increased knowledge of Florida's indigenous feathered friends was coming my way. Guessed life would have continued just dandy without it.

"I have all kinds of fun planned." Lisa really did chirp. "And when I have to work, you've got full use of my car."

"I thought your normal beat was up in our nation's capital," I said, allowing my carry-on to slip from my shoulder and drop to the floor.

She laughed. "I came to Florida to avoid the humidity in Washington, D.C."

"Seriously?"

"No. I jumped at the chance to do something other than bird strikes."

"There's an avian labor issue? Crows won't fly until they get lunch breaks during the workday?"

"Bird contact with airplanes." Rolling her eyes at my lame attempt at humor.

"Ouch."

"Exactly. The birds never win."

"I thought you identified feathers in the Smithsonian's anthropological collections."

"Feathers on ancient masks and clothing constitute a small part of what I do. But the Feather Identification Lab has interagency agreements with the Federal Aviation Administration, the Air Force, and the Navy. Most of our work involves bird strikes."

"They occur that frequently?" Add avian kamikazes to my growing list of travel concerns.

She nodded. "Birds put US Airways flight 1549 in the Hudson River. Even Wilbur Wright had a bird strike. Last year our team processed over forty-five hundred samples. Around eighteen a day—even more during spring and fall migration."

"Good lord. How do you manage to keep that pace?"

She threw a look toward her "packets." "Smaller samples. We rarely get complete bodies. Sometimes I'll get whole feathers or some bones, but often my sample consists of nothing but a smear wiped from an aircraft exterior. What we call a snarge. With a snarge, cataloguing only takes an hour."

Snarge. Ornithologists get all the fun words.

"We partner with a lab to analyze the DNA."

"And the point is?"

"If we can ID the species that are the culprits, an airfield can adjust."

"How?"

"Move a pond, stop spreading grass seed, do what it takes to make the environment less attractive to that particular species. Since most bird strikes occur on takeoff and landing, managing the airfield's immediate area can go a long way toward reducing risk."

"How many airports does the Everglades have?"

"None that concern me. I'm here on a different project."

I must have looked confused.

"The birds here are victims, not perps." Again gesturing to the remains. "The Everglades has a Burmese python problem."

"Pythons. As in alarmingly large serpents?" I wouldn't call it a phobia, but I'm not overly fond of snakes. Slithery moves. Cold creepy eyes. You can't trust something that doesn't blink. "I didn't know pythons lived in Florida."

"They're recent intruders. Many escaped into the swamp in 1992 when Hurricane Andrew wiped out Homestead, the nearest town, which was once a hub for breeders and importers. That's where my place is, by the way. Homestead's a mostly agricultural southern suburb of Miami, stretching between Everglades National Park and Biscayne National Park."

"At least it wasn't idiot pet owners releasing exotics into the wild."

"There's that, too. Morons who think constriction is cuddly and buy pythons as pets. Except when little Squeezy hits twenty feet he isn't so lovable anymore. The disenchanted owner dumps him in the Everglades and drives away. Upgrade for the snake. Not so good for the rest of the glades population."

My gaze roved the packets. Okay. The lumps looked a little bigger than what a jet engine would leave behind.

Lisa kept talking.

"Since Burmese pythons are threatening to become the top predator in the Everglades, the National Park Service has asked for help in identifying at-risk birds."

I looked at the dried masses on the table.

"You're examining the stomach contents of a python?"

"Twelve pythons, to be exact."

"That's a lot of dead snake."

"The National Park Service hunts them. They're trying to get a handle on the problem."

"You necropsy every snake?"

"I don't. Dr. Aaron Lundberg does. He's a park ranger and wildlife biologist over at NPS. As the bird expert, I just get the stomach contents, sometimes a section of intestine."

"What's Lundberg hoping to learn?"

"Everything. Growth, health, diet, reproductive behavior. I'm focused on preferred snack foods." With gloved fingers, she gently pried apart one of the smaller dehydrated masses. Other than a beak, a talon, nothing solid remained, just a matting of hair and feather parts. "That used to be a wood stork. *Mycteria americana*. Stood forty-five inches tall, with a wingspan of sixty to sixty-five inches. It's endangered."

"Jesus."

"Mature Burmese pythons eat maybe once a month, then hunker down to digest. Metabolism occurs quite rapidly."

"Meaning you don't usually get bones?"

"Not unless the snake is caught right after it has ingested. I mostly rely on feathers."

I leaned closer for a better view. "I don't see any feathers on this one."

"Birds have two types of feathers—vaned, which form the outer layer, and down, which lie underneath the vaned. For this recovery I'll use magnification to view the downy parts. They carry distinct species characteristics. Mites, the amount and distribution of pigment, the node shapes. Differences in feather microstructure set bird groups apart. It'll take a little work, but I'll nail this baby."

"I have no doubt."

Lisa glanced at the wall clock. "I'll need ten minutes to finish up here. Then I'll take a break and get you on your way." She hooked a thumb at the fume hood. "I save the easy cases for last. Those over there aren't so tidy but they've got more to work with. Literally. Meat, feathers, bones. Have a look."

While Lisa resumed prying apart the goodies on the gurney, I crossed to the fume hood. The smell of putrefying flesh was much stronger up close. Five specimens lay arranged in chronological order. Each was labeled with a field number and site name, and with GPS coordinates indicating the location of its recovery.

These masses were more oozy and less homogeneous than the lumps on the table. In some I could make out individual vaned feathers and small bones. In one, a furry ringed tail. I picked up a probe and teased a bone out of a packet labeled #1032-27 BIG CYPRESS. Yep. Raccoon. Next one was fox. I was feeling smug.

"I'll introduce you to Aaron while you're here." Lisa's words came out muffled by her mask. "He's quite a character."

"The only introduction I want is to a big cheeseburger." I hadn't eaten since leaving home for the Charlotte airport, five hours ago. It was early for lunch but I was starving.

I shifted to #1976-32 BOGGY KEY. Saw one fragment of bone. Recognized it as bird.

The fourth carcass was that of a decent-size doe. Mother of God. That was one ambitious snake.

The final set of remains showed more advanced decomp and smelled far more rank. I breathed through my mouth as I bent over #4715-59 HARDWOOD HAMMOCK. Black feathers. Raptor beak. I was going with vulture.

As I straightened, a tiny segment of bone caught my eye. The shaft was wrong for bird, the outer tube too thick in proportion to the hollow interior.

Definitely not avian. I peered closer. Noted the patterning on the bone's outer surface.

My heart tossed in a few extra beats.

What?

Tightening my grasp on the probe, I poked deeper into the putrefied thing that had once been a bird. Into its stomach. Saw undigested skeletal elements. Apprehension climbing, I extracted several.

"Almost done!" Lisa sang.

Grabbing a long pair of tweezers, I pulled bones until I had a small pile.

Breath suspended, I rolled each this way and that, noting anatomical details.

And felt a rush of adrenaline shoot through my body.

CHAPTER 2

So began the vacation that never was. I told myself I'd soon be snorkeling in Biscayne Bay. But on hearing what I'd found, Lisa had extracted a promise that I stick around until she handed this off to the authorities.

I looked like an oversize scarecrow in Lisa's tiny borrowed lab coat. The thing hit me mid-thigh and mid-forearm. The gurney had been cleared of everything but #4715-59 HARDWOOD HAMMOCK. The bird carcass lay to one end, my grisly discovery to the other.

Once again, Lisa and I were positioned on opposite sides of our subject, handing off bones to the correct expert. Taking shape in front of me was a small human foot. Eight phalanges, three metatarsals, a fragment of calcaneus, and one partial cuneiform. I estimated we'd recovered roughly one third.

"Here's the last." Lisa handed me another item teased from the turkey vulture's gullet. "It's remarkable how much a human metatarsal resembles a *Cathartes aura* tarsometatarsus."

"And how these bad boys possess the appetite of Hannibal Lecter," I said.

"And the smell of a teenage boy's sneakers."

I passed on the obvious foul fowl joke. Hunger headache was joining my list of discomforts. Unfair, but I blamed all my woes on the Everglades.

I was tightening the alignment of the foot bones when the door opened and three men strode into the room. The reinforcements we'd called for had arrived. The waft of male sweat gave the putrefaction a run for its money.

The largest of the trio wore a brown uniform bearing a Miami-Dade Police Department logo. A plaque on his shirt gave his name as T. Yellen. A gold sheriff's department badge declared Yellen's rank to be that of sergeant or higher. A bad mustache evoked the seventies. A substantial belly suggested a love of fast food.

The other two wore green park rangers' uniforms. One was short, with Earl Grey eyes behind rectangular, silver-framed glasses, and a seriously lopsided haircut. I could see him cruising a farmers' market in a tie-dye and Birkenstocks, an NPR tote over one arm. I guessed he was the wildlife biologist, Dr. Aaron Lundberg.

The other guy was too tanned and too groomed, and had a "stud legend in my own mind" demeanor about him. Black hair. Blue eyes. A physique that filled his uniform nicely. On his chest was a Department of the Interior badge identifying him as Scott Pierce, Everglades National Park Law Enforcement.

Lundberg, the biologist, and Yellen, the sheriff, were arguing, and appeared to have been at it for some time.

"Pythons do not attack humans," Lundberg said,

frustrated, as though he'd repeated the statement again and again.

"Goddammit, Aaron. Your friend here says she's got an eighteen-foot snake with human parts in its belly." Yellen looked red-faced and grim. "I've been dreading this day since the damn things first started appearing."

"Didn't happen," Lundberg insisted.

"I've seen these bastards down hundred-pound gators and deer. They can sure as hell handle one of us." Yellen sounded equally fed up with the debate.

"The chance of that happening is less than your chance of being struck by lightning while winning the Powerball." Lundberg finger-jammed his glasses upward. They immediately resumed their spot low on the bridge of his nose.

"The news loves to tell me about kids getting squeezed to death while they sleep," Yellen argued.

Lundberg spoke slowly, a teacher addressing a dull student. "Those are cases of escaped domesticated snakes attacking the first small prey they encounter. In the wild, we've recorded only five or six unprovoked python-on-human attacks. Only one resulting in a bite. None resulting in an attempt to wrap."

"One of these buggers tries wrapping me, its head is going straight up its ass."

So far Pierce had said nothing. Like those of a spectator at a tennis match, his eyes swung between Lundberg and Yellen. He leaned against one wall, arms crossed, more arranged than relaxed.

Yellen flapped a hand at Lisa. "You, missy. You called this in. Did this python eat somebody?"

"The foot bones came from the vulture."

Three sets of eyebrows shot up.

"The turkey vulture ate the human remains. The python ate the turkey vulture," Lisa expanded.

"A bird killed this guy?" The sheriff sounded a galaxy beyond dubious.

"Or girl," I interjected. Everyone ignored me.

"Turkey vultures scavenge on carrion," Lisa explained. "They rarely, if ever, kill prey themselves."

"How'd a bird find a corpse in a million-mile swamp?"

"It stank." Lisa stated the obvious.

Yellen's response was to hip-plant his hands and scowl. "The bird eats the vic, the snake eats the bird. Where's the bloody old lady who swallowed the fly?"

Perhaps she'll die winged into my mind. Not bad, Sheriff.

"Goddammit, this is a jurisdictional nightmare. There's flying and slithering and who the hell knows where the whole mess started? Could be Dade, Collier, Broward, or Monroe." Yellen pronounced the last *Mon*-roe, emphasizing the first syllable of the county's name. "Could be the park boys."

Pierce spoke for the first time. "The snake was caught near Hardwood Hammock. That's outside the park, south of Broward, in Metro." He used the slang for Miami-Dade County.

"So I'm the lucky asshat," Yellen said.

"You've got jurisdiction, Tom, but considering it's a mobile crime scene, NPS will cooperate fully."

Yellen's jaw tightened. "Who says we've got a crime at all? The damn foot could have come from a graveyard."

"No," Lisa said. "Turkey vultures prefer fresh corpses. Though they might wait for the skin to soften for easier consumption, they avoid putrefied meat. The victim wasn't dead long before the vultures fed."

Lundberg's face paled slightly. He swallowed. "And

the python couldn't have eaten more than a day or two before it was captured. The vulture is barely digested."

"Slow your roll." Yellen raised two palms. "There's still no reason to jump to violent crime. Could be a fall, a drowning, a heart attack. Folks die a million ways to Sunday out here."

"It's a crime," I said firmly. "Homicide."

This time every face swung toward me.

"And you would be?" Yellen looked me up and down, likely taking in the lank hair and ill-fitting lab coat.

"Dr. Temperance Brennan."

"Dr. Brennan is a forensic anthropologist from North Carolina," Lisa added. "She spotted the human bones."

"Tom Yellen." Yellen proffered one beefy hand. "Sheriff out of Miami-Dade Hammocks district office."

"I'm a colleague of Phil Evans." I named the Miami-Dade County forensic anthropologist I knew through the American Academy of Forensic Sciences.

"You used to be," Yellen said. "Evans died last month. Heart attack."

Jesus. There's blunt, but this guy was off the chart. Not knowing what to say, and feeling bad about Evans, I said nothing.

Yellen looked at Lisa. "And you would be?"

"Dr. Lisa Robbin, Smithsonian ornithologist. I'm assisting Dr. Lundberg with his python research."

"Uh-huh," Yellen said. "Let's get back to the foot. What makes you think we got a homicide?"

Using my probe, I singled out the calcaneus and cuneiform. "These are tarsals. When articulated, they lie close to the point where the foot bones and the lower leg bones meet." Overly simplistic, but close enough for this crowd.

"The ankle?"

"You can think of it that way." Using the probe's tip, I pointed to a series of gouges and striation on the superior surface of each tarsal. "These marks were made by a chain saw."

There was a long dead silence. Yellen broke it.

"You sayin' this foot was sawed off?"

"Yes."

"Why?"

"I can't answer that."

"You're sure?"

"That I can't answer?"

"That it was sawed off!" Exasperated.

"I am."

"Sweet lord on a bicycle. I've got a sawed-off foot that was eaten by a bird that was eaten by a snake, and no clue where the crime went down or who the vic is."

"Was," said Lisa.

Another silence followed. This time I jumped in.

"You can tell a lot from a foot."

Yellen's eyes rolled up to mine.

"While I can't definitively establish gender without DNA, these bones are small and the muscle attachments aren't overly robust, suggesting female. A smaller than average female, in fact."

"Could it be a kid?" Pierce asked. Children eaten by snakes—bad for park publicity.

I picked up the third metatarsal. "This bone shows evidence of a stress fracture."

"Not a kid," Yellen said.

My opinion of the sheriff rose a hair.

"Correct. There are two main types of metatarsal fracture: acute, due to sudden loading, and stress, due to overuse. If muscles become strained, they're no longer able to lessen the shock of repeated impacts. When this happens, the muscles transfer the stress to the bones. This can create small cracks or fractures." Again an oversimplification, but sufficient in this context. "The most common stress fractures result from high-impact sports, like distance running. It's rare to see them in children."

"So how old are we talking?"

"I'm limited in making an estimate because I've got mostly phalanges to work with. Toe bones."

"Yeah, yeah." Yellen curled his fingers in an impatient "Go on" gesture.

"I'll need an X-ray, but the bone quality looks good and the joints show no arthritis or remodeling. And I see no evidence of recent epiphyseal fusion." I referred to the growth caps at the ends of each bone. "Together, these features suggest young adult."

"That's it?"

"I'd say somewhere in the range twenty to thirty. A small, active woman, maybe a runner."

Something crossed Yellen's face. Recognition? Before he could speak, his mobile rang. With a nod, he stepped out of the room to take the call.

"I've taken what measurements I could," I said, peeling off and tossing my gloves into a biohazard bin. "Someone can enter them into the Fordisc program for assessment of gender and ancestry. But, given what I had to work with, the results will be virtually meaningless."

Lundberg and Pierce stood mute.

"See you back at the house?" I asked Lisa.

Before she could reply, Yellen thundered back into the room. His face was grim. And he was looking at me.

CHAPTER 3

I clung to my seat as the airboat jounced across the water, still unsure how I'd been talked into the excursion. On board with me were Yellen, Lundberg, and Pierce. A uniformed Miami-Dade officer was piloting the craft.

Yellen's phone call had brought news of more human remains. I'd explained that I was in Florida on vacation. That I'd only stopped by Lisa's lab to pick up a key. I'd practically yanked my bikini and Picoult novel from my suitcase as Exhibit A. Fruitless.

Yellen had waved off my objections. He had a dismembered human body. Evans, his forensic anthropologist, was on the wrong side of dirt and I was not. Before I knew what had happened, I'd been deputized.

While I was being driven to the dock, Lisa had headed out for lunch. My empty stomach did not appreciate the irony.

Our boat was a flat-bottomed aluminum six-seater with an elevated driver's chair at the back. Behind the driver's platform was a large propeller engine en-

KATHY REICHS · 94

closed in a protective metal cage. The thing looked like an oversize desk fan.

"You have to use an airboat in the Everglades because a submerged propeller won't work in shallow marshes," Lundberg shouted, close to my ear.

I nodded, unwilling to bellow. Even with mufflers, the propeller was incredibly loud. The upside: No one could hear the protests coming from my belly.

"This is called the Shark River Slough." Lundberg's arm arced to take in the scenery. "It's the primary source of water to Everglades National Park, and lies both inside and outside the park boundaries. You've probably heard it called the river of grass."

Though I hadn't, the description was apt. A sea of brown and green saw grass stretched as far as the eye could see, here and there carved by the occasional meandering waterway. The sky was an immaculate Carolina blue, dotted low above the horizon with fluffs of cumulus cloud.

Having no need to stick to the cuts, our boat whizzed unimpeded across the top of the vegetation. Despite the grim task that lay ahead, I thoroughly enjoyed the feeling of flying.

"We're headed to Hardwood Hammock." Lundberg seemed compelled to continually explain. "It's just beyond the park to the north. Where the hunt is taking place."

"The hunt?" That got my attention.

"The Python Challenge. It's a contest run by state Fish and Wildlife. Prizes for the most killed, for the longest, that sort of thing."

Yellen, to my right, overheard and shook his head. "Idea right outa the mind of a hormone-addled fourteen-year-old gamer."

On that point, Lundberg appeared to agree with Yellen. "The hunt goes for thirty days and draws participants from all over the country—this year there are sixteen hundred. Two categories, professional hunters in one, and anyone that can pay twenty-five bucks and sit through a thirty-minute video in the other. In 2013, the amateurs and pros together caught sixty-eight snakes. Majority by the hunters."

That surprised me. I thought the total would be in the hundreds. "How many snakes are out there?" I yelled.

"Twenty-five hundred Burmese pythons have been removed from south Florida in the last ten years. Our best guesstimate is a current population numbering in the thousands, maybe the tens of thousands. And breeding rapidly."

Holy shit, I thought.

"The funny thing is these guys are endangered in their natural habitats of Southeast Asia, because of illegal poaching."

"No shortage here." Yellen's clipped comment was almost blown away by the rushing air.

"Definitely not. The federal government is desperately scrambling to control the population explosion in south Florida. In 2012, the Burmese python was added to the species list covered by the Lacey Act."

At my questioning look, Lundberg said, "It's the federal act used by the U.S. Fish and Wildlife Service to prevent and manage invasive species. It bans importation and interstate commerce of listed species, like the pythons."

The boat slowed a bit. I took advantage to ask at almost normal volume, "How'd they multiply so fast?"

"Burmese are generalists, able to adapt to a variety of habitats," Lundberg prattled on, unimpeded by the need to shout. "So they can be more invasive. Their offspring output is prodigious, and, uncharacteristically for snakes, mothers stay with their nests and brood their eggs."

I thought that was what I'd heard. Much of what Lundberg said was lost to the wind as the airboat picked up speed again.

"And the ladies are about as picky as one-legged whores," Yellen added. "One decides a boy python is hot, bam, you've got a brood."

"How big do Burmese pythons get?" Not sure I wanted to know.

"The Burmese is one of the largest snake species. In the wild, females can grow up to eighteen feet, males up to fourteen. In captivity some reach twenty."

Regular meals, I assumed. Didn't ask what unfortunate creatures that entailed.

"A south Florida water-quality maintenance crew just bagged their second eighteen-footer this year," Yellen said. "Dragged out of a canal in the hammocks, north of Tamiami."

"Hammocks?" I'd been wondering about the term since first hearing it.

"Hardwood hammocks." Of course Lundberg demanded more precision. "Little islands in the swamp. The hammocks provide dry broadleaf habitat a few inches above the elevation of the water."

"That's where we're headed," Pierce threw in.

"How long's the boat?" I cracked.

"Sixteen feet." Either Lundberg was deadpan or he didn't get the joke.

"You say pythons never attack humans?" Just making conversation. No reason I asked.

"One can never say never," Lundberg backpedaled. "But most prefer to avoid trouble, will withdraw if allowed."

"Yeah? What about the guy got turned into Flat Stanley last month?"

Lundberg leaned forward to shout past me at Yellen. "Precisely the stupidity I was talking about! That was a domestic. The result of improper handling. Burmese are one of the most docile of all pet snakes. Which they should *never* be."

"You blaming the vic?" Yellen yelled back.

"Pythons have an acute sense of smell, and the mere presence of food can trigger a feeding frenzy. You don't uncage a twenty-foot constrictor with a live chicken nearby!"

"What's their preferred prey in the wild?" I jumped in to defuse tension.

"Pythons are voracious and indiscriminate eaters, I will admit." Lundberg pointedly addressed his answer to only me. "The species is consuming indigenous mammals at an alarming rate, especially those that forage near water. Ninety-nine percent of the raccoon and opossum populations have disappeared from the park, especially the southernmost regions, where pythons have been established the longest. Rabbits and fox have vanished completely."

Bunnies? I was beginning to agree with Yellen.

Lundberg failed to notice my reaction. "Lisa has identified twenty-five different bird species in python guts, including the endangered wood stork. The mammals and birds are unaccustomed to being hunted by pythons, so they lack the appropriate instinctual defenses."

"Because the damn pythons aren't supposed to be here," Yellen snapped.

"Neither are New Yorkers, but we can't keep them out," Lundberg spat back. To me, "Some populations may actually be benefiting, like turtles. Without raccoons to eat their eggs, we'll be knee-deep in turtles in twenty years."

"Do pythons have no predators?"

"Alligators do some damage, but once the snakes get large, the gators are no match. In fact, the two species compete for the same resources."

"I've seen a python split itself open from eating a six-foot gator," Pierce offered from across the boat.

"The Burmese's only real threat walks on two legs," Yellen agreed.

"Yet you're not a fan of the hunt," I said.

Ycllen shook his head. "Rednecks wading into the swamp shooting at anything that moves?"

"We get an annual circus of boozed-out idiocy," Pierce agreed with the sheriff.

"If the yahoos aren't allowed to hunt in the park proper, which is python central, of course the snake count's gonna be skimpy." Yellen barked the criticism to Lundberg. His tone said the argument predated my arrival by a very long time.

Lundberg responded with vehemence. "What certain people fail to understand is how well camouflaged these creatures are. You release an enormous tagged snake and it vanishes in seconds. I'm an expert and I've stood one meter from a fifteen-foot male, tracking his radio transmitters, and failed to spot him."

I definitely did not want this man's job.

Lundberg steamed ahead, face now the color of uncooked beef. "Burmese pythons are ambush hunters. They can lie in wait underwater, hide under bushes, drop from trees. They strike suddenly, ingest their catch quickly, then conceal themselves to digest for a month. Even herpetologists have a hard time locating them. Forget the inexperienced." At last, Lundberg made eye contact with Yellen. "Most captures are made because a snake is crossing a road. And there are far more roads *outside* than inside the

park. And less protected wildlife to shoot by mistake."

Mental note. Don't wade. Don't linger under trees.
Don't walk through tall brush. Don't leave the boat
sounded good, but I doubted that was an option.

"Almost there."

I turned. The driver was pointing to a stand of
trees about a mile away. One of several similar stands
marching the horizon.

"Are we still in the Everglades?" I asked.

"This stretch isn't part of the national park,"
Lundberg said. "It's one of four state-run wildlife
management areas where the hunt is allowed."

Our airboat drew up and stopped beside a more
battered model with indeterminate wording painted
on the stern in faded script. We all scrambled over
the bow and jumped to dry ground.

The transition from marsh to shrub to forest was
abrupt. Within feet of the water's edge, we crossed a
thick ring of scrub vegetation and single-filed down
a narrow path through a canopy forest.

"Watch for sinkholes." Lundberg pointed out a
steep-sided conical depression containing an emer-
ald pool. "They're everywhere."

The temperature dropped in proportion to the
rise in humidity. Looking up, I could see only slivers
of sky through the intertwined foliage overhead. So
much for avoiding trees. But snakes were now the
lesser of my problems. Swarms of mosquitoes were
draining me of copious quantities of blood. The
bloodsuckers loved me.

Five or six minutes in, we reached a small clearing.
At its center was a bearded giant in Australian bush
gear standing over a dead gator. Together, we crossed
to him.

The gator wasn't huge, but it was big enough,

maybe eight feet from snout to tail tip. Its mouth was half open. The reptile's teeth grasped what appeared to be a portion of human pelvis encased in flesh that had rotted to the color and consistency of congealed oatmeal. The only indication the flesh had once been human was an obvious, if mottled and dented, belly button.

Yellen addressed the giant. "Howdy, Jordan."

Jordan nodded. Looked each of us over. Then said, "Didn't touch nothin' once I brought her down and saw what she had."

"You did right calling us." Yellen didn't move closer. "This lady's a doctor specializes in bones."

"Tempe Brennan." I stepped forward and held out a hand.

Jordan wiped a giant paw on his khakis and thrust it toward me. "My name's Dusty Jordan." My hand disappeared in a leathery grip.

"What happened here?" I asked.

Jordan looked at me like I'd asked the meaning of "soup." "I was huntin' python. Saw this gal dragging somethin' didn't look right."

"She's quite dead?"

"She won't hurt you," he answered, obviously missing my Monty Python reference.

I squatted and leaned close to the gator. A full minute passed with only the buzz of flies and the whine of mosquitoes.

When Yellen could take it no longer, he burst out, "Is it the same vic?"

"The pelvic features I'm able to see are consistent with what I observed on the foot," I said. But something else troubled me. "Would an alligator eat something that's already dead?"

"Yep." Jordan answered quickly, to Lundberg's annoyance.

"It's true." Lundberg felt the need to assert scientific superiority. "And alligators will drag prey around for a long time, days even. To protect the food from other gators. And to help break it up."

Yellen sighed. "Mother Mary in a handcart. We're going to need CSI. Could be body parts all over this hammock." He walked off to make the call.

I shifted to view the pelvis from another angle. "I'd field-estimate PMI at roughly nine days. That tracks with the remains recovered from the vulture." Python. Whatever.

A snuffle from the gator made me spring back and land on my ass.

"You said it was dead." More shrill than I'd intended.

Jordan gave me another look that said he questioned my basic intelligence. "I said she wouldn't hurt you. Can't kill a gator without the Hunting and Game folks classifying it as a nuisance. And this ole gal's just out here working her turf."

I scooted back slowly and carefully.

"Relax. She's tranqed." Jordan bounced a conspiratorial glance off Pierce. *Women.* "Dive right on in. She won't wake for hours."

"You're telling me to reach into a live gator's mouth?" I wasn't believing this guy.

"Duh-uh."

Lundberg addressed Jordan. "Anesthesia is an imprecise science. One must know weight to calculate proper dosage."

Jordan regarded the biologist with an insolent stare. "If I say the dude's out, she's out."

No one moved.

"Man." Jordan dug into a ratty canvas pack and withdrew a Coke-can-size capsule. "Ketamine-midazolam. Eight thousand milligrams."

Lundberg nodded slowly. "That should do it."

"Should?" I looked from Jordan to Lundberg. "Should as in lost digits and phantom limbs?"

Wordlessly, Jordan pulled on heavy leather gloves, reached down, and pried open the gator's mouth. The pelvis rose with the upper jaw. Unperturbed, Jordan stuck a finger between the tooth row and the human flesh, and shoved downward. The pelvis dropped to the ground with a soft *thunk*.

All eyes swung to me. The gator lay motionless, mouth held agape.

My gaze roved the pelvis. Like the foot, it was on the small end of the range for human adults. And I could see the disturbing feature more clearly now. The unsubtle gouging and splintering left by the action of a chain saw.

"Get me the scene bag," I barked, emotions churning inside me.

Lundberg jumped to respond. I withdrew gloves and a body bag, pulled on the former, then unrolled and unzipped the latter. Ready, I edged closer to the gator.

I was right. The body part was a segment of lower torso, including a partial pelvis and portions of soft tissue from the waist and upper groin region. Dotted lines of puncture wounding crisscrossed the decomposing flesh. Bite marks left by reptilian teeth.

Moving cautiously, I slid my hands under the torso and transferred it whole to the body bag. When finished, I checked the gator's mouth and dentition. A glance up to make sure Jordan had a firm grip on the jaws, then I carefully collected stray tissue and bone fragments that had detached from the main hunk. Extracting evidence from between razor-sharp teeth was like the extreme sports version of the game Operation.

I was about to call it quits when a glint caught my eye, there, then gone.

"Can you spread the jaws wider?" I couldn't believe what I was asking. What I was about to do.

Jordan widened his stance, flexed the gator's neck backward, and did as I'd requested. Remarkably, the beast offered no resistance.

Sunlight flashed again.

Inhaling deeply, I took a small surgical forceps from the bag, reached my arm in, elbow deep, and peered at the back of the dental arcade.

The thing was silver and wedged between two maxillaries. As I wiggled it free, the gator whipped her tail left, then right. I froze, but Jordan held the animal's head immobile with a hammerlock.

Yanking my arm free, I scrambled backward and, in a childish display of victory, held my prize aloft. Then I lowered and studied the object in my forceps.

It was a silver dolphin charm affixed to a loop via a short filigree chain. A chunk of decaying flesh clung to the dolphin's upraised tail.

Belly ring. A distinctive one.

My moment of triumph faded when I glanced up.

My four companions were staring at me with matching expressions of horror.

CHAPTER
4

Kiley James was a short, athletic python wrangler. Former marathoner. Liked by all. At least, all but one.

It wasn't a formal ID, but my companions had no doubt that I'd recovered her belly ring. The gloom was palpable.

Solemnly, we reboarded the airboat and headed east. This was no case for the natural resources center. Yellen had gotten permission to collect and transport the torso, and me, and we were going straight to the Miami-Dade County morgue.

The boat pulled to shore somewhere along Highway 997. We sat on a weathered dock and waited for the medical examiner van, which was en route.

"She was one of the best." For a change, Lundberg sounded subdued.

"You can't be certain of identity from a piece of jewelry." I wasn't trying to raise hopes. Just being precise.

"The kid liked belly shirts." Yellen was terse.

I swatted a mosquito. Not to think ill of the dead, but the idea of exposing unnecessary skin in this habitat seemed lunacy. Then I berated myself. Facts before conclusions. Stop assuming the victim is James.

Our group had diminished, Yellen having directed his deputy to Jordan's airboat to ensure its owner found his way to the Hammocks district station. Jordan had protested vehemently, to no avail. Yellen didn't say it, but the man was now a suspect. Turned out Jordan knew James. And he'd "found" her body way out in the middle of nowhere. Yellen would be negligent not to bring him in.

And I'd be negligent to rely on personal effects to establish a positive ID. Many others probably owned the same belly ring. Or the ring could be unconnected to the body. Or James might have lost hers, sold it, or given it away.

And the thing just happened to end up in a gator's mouth with a mangled hunk of torso?

Small. Active. Woman. My own words whispered across my brain. Kiley James fit the profile in every respect.

"Has anyone talked to James recently?" I asked.

Lundberg shook his head no. "Kiley would camp in the glades for the duration of the contest. She was just like the pythons she hunted—you only saw her if she wanted to be seen."

"She'd be required to deliver her bounty, wouldn't she?" I persisted.

When the biologist nodded, midafternoon sun flashed off his lenses. "Any capture must be dropped off within twenty-four hours at one of several stations, along with a completed data sheet and GPS coordinates for the harvesting location."

"Maybe her GPS notes will help pinpoint her last field location."

Yellen shot me a scathing look. "This ain't my first rodeo, doc lady."

"Wouldn't mean diddly. The kid covered a lot of ground."

I jumped when Pierce spoke because he did it so rarely. I'd forgotten he was slumped against a piling behind me.

"Most snakes are brought in alive, but Kiley didn't mess around." Lundberg sounded totally miserable. "She'd euthanize in the field then move on. I've never seen anyone else deliver three kills in twenty-four hours."

"Mating season." Pierce crossed his outstretched legs, dropped his chin onto his chest, and, I assumed, lowered his lids. Couldn't see his eyes behind the dark Maui Jims.

"When did she last check in?" I persisted. The investigation was not my turf. But I'm impatient by nature and the wait was making me churlish.

"You'd have to check with FWC, the state fish and wildlife commission," Lundberg offered. "The contest is their show. But it couldn't have been that long ago. She'd have had bounty to register. She was leading the pack. By a good margin."

My guess was nine days.

"Who'd want to kill her?" I switched tack.

Yellen gave a humorless snort. "Only about fifteen hundred people."

"Tell me about her."

Yellen turned his aviator shades full on me. I held his stare. On the road above us, a pickup rattled by, belching black exhaust.

Finally, the lawman sighed. "For a little lady, James packed quite a punch. She was determined to win the whole damn shooting match."

"How much cash is involved?"

"With private sponsors sweetening this year's pot, the prize tops out at thirty thousand dollars."

"That's a lot of money." And a lot of motive.

"You bet your sweet ass it is." Yellen's thoughts were obviously traveling the same path as mine.

"With that many hunters out in the swamp, wouldn't people be falling all over each other? Someone must have seen her."

"Well, hell. Wish I'da thought of that." Yellen's sarcasm did nothing to calm my nerves. "You sayin' I should have my boys canvas the entire gun-and-machete redneck family reunion?"

Lundberg interpreted. "As an FWC python permit holder, Kiley could harvest snakes in several state-managed areas. Her FWC permits were as broad as one can possibly obtain. She was also on the Nature Conservancy's Python Patrol, and was one of the volunteer agents participating in the Everglades National Park's python program. The latter permit holders are authorized to use our roads and trails to look for snakes."

"So she could hunt anywhere."

"No. Harvesting for the FWC challenge isn't allowed in the national park." Apparently Pierce had been awake and taking in every word. "She could only collect in the park for us."

"And we don't call it 'hunting' in the park." Lundberg hooked air quotes. "Funding restrictions disallow use of the term."

Before I could respond, an ME van, a cruiser, and a Miami-Dade crime scene truck pulled to the shoulder above us. After a short briefing, the two CSS techs boarded the airboat for the trip to the hammock. Pierce and Lundberg joined those going to the Hammocks district station in the cruiser. Yellen and

I secured the torso in the back of the van in a small plastic tub and climbed in.

The ride passed in silence. Despite our grim mission, I was looking forward to a visit to Miami's famed ME facility. I'd been there on previous occasions and knew it to be the Taj Mahal of morgues—23,000 square feet of shiny and modern, including a grand total of fifteen autopsy stations. When we arrived, I was the first out of the van.

A lab-coated death investigator named Elvis helped us log the remains in to the computer, then led us to a separate "decomp" building behind the main morgue. We were assigned one of the two autopsy rooms, down the hall from a cooler large enough to accommodate seventy-five bodies.

I knew the fridge storage size because Elvis was a frustrated tour guide at heart. By the time we'd gathered around the autopsy table, I also knew that, along with the four main coolers, the facility could store as many as 555 bodies. Why 555? Exactly the capacity of a 747 jumbo jet.

You've got to love Florida's sense of mortality. And the state's willingness to pony up funding for a state-of-the-art death investigation system.

Elvis even found a lab coat in my size.

I'd barely slipped it on when a staff pathologist stepped into the room. Jane Barconi. We'd met, but I'd never worked with her.

Splatter on Barconi's lab coat and apron suggested she'd been interrupted while cutting and slicing and weighing. The look on her face said she was not happy about it.

While Elvis took the torso off for X-ray, I told Barconi the little I knew. The hammock. The gator. The belly ring. The possible ID. The directive from her boss, the chief medical examiner, that the remains come to the epicenter of the morgue bureau.

Barconi listened without comment, then, when Elvis returned, she peered at the contents of the tub. Her tight expression tightened even further. Relaxed slightly when I assured her I could work unassisted.

After gloving and masking, I transferred the remains to the autopsy table.

Yellen stood in a corner, expression impassive, thumbs hooked in his pockets. Impressive. Many cops can't stomach the autopsy room. Especially if the vic is a decomp.

So I began.

Using a scalpel, I gently teased tissue from the exposed innominate, one of three bones that compose the pelvic girdle, and the only one present. It was soon evident that the iliac crest, a crescent-shaped sliver of bone topping the hip blade portion, was not fully fused. I made a note and moved on.

As I worked, I'd periodically glance at Yellen. He didn't pester me with questions. Just observed, silent but attentive. I was actually starting to like the guy.

At some point Elvis returned again. I heard the sound of X-rays popping onto wall-mounted illuminators but didn't stop to look.

Thirty minutes of careful cutting and tugging revealed the pubic symphysis, the point at which the right half of the pelvis joins with the left front and center in the lower abdomen. I found a magnifying lens and leaned close.

The small oval face had deep furrows running horizontally across its surface. This, along with the condition of the oval's border, confirmed the age estimate I'd jotted down based on the iliac crest.

The shape of the oval, along with that of the pubic element and the portion of sciatic notch that re-

mained intact, confirmed my preliminary statement
with regard to gender.

I sat back and lowered my mask. Rolled my shoulders to loosen tight muscles. Then turned to Yellen.

"The victim is female, aged eighteen to twenty-
four. Small stature. Probably in good health at the
time of her death." Before being dismembered and
scavenged by a gator.

"Nothin' that says it couldn't be James."

"Agreed. But nothing that says conclusively it is."

"So what *are* you saying?"

"The remains are consistent with the biological
profile of Kiley James."

"And the foot?"

"Features I observed on the torso are consistent
with those I observed on the foot. For a positive ID,
both sets of remains should be submitted for DNA
sequencing."

While Yellen scribbled in a small notebook, I
walked to the light boxes and worked my way down
the X-rays Elvis had taken. Saw the partial pelvis
glowing white inside the gray mass of tissue. Some
lumbar vertebrae. The bottommost ribs.

At the last in the series, I stopped in my tracks.
Using a finger, I counted, not touching the film.

"Hmm."

Yellen's head snapped up. "What?"

"Most people have twenty-four ribs. The first seven
pairs are called true ribs because they attach to the
sternum via cartilage. The next three are known as
false ribs because they share a common cartilagi-
nous connection to the sternum. The eleventh and
twelfth pairs are called floating ribs because they
don't attach to anything in front."

I glanced at Yellen to see if he was following. He
was.

"Some individuals lack a pair of floating ribs, others have a couple extra. It's an uncommon anomaly, but not rare."

"Does missing a set cause problems?"

"No. Twenty-two ribs are sufficient to protect the organs. The condition is a harmless variation. Nothing you'd notice in a person walking around."

He waited.

"This victim is lacking a pair of floating ribs," I said. "If Kiley James has antemortem X-rays on file somewhere, they could help to confirm identity."

"I'm gettin' medical records. Anything else?"

I snapped off my gloves. "Unfortunately I can't give you cause or manner of death based on what was recovered. But I can state with certainty that this victim was dismembered with a chain saw."

A beat passed. I remembered Yellen had known this woman, and liked her.

"Ante or post?" was his reply.

"Post." Small comfort.

"Around here, chain saw doesn't narrow the suspect pool much."

"If you can locate the saw, I might be able to match the blade to damage on the bone," I said. "Or, better than that, recover tissue or blood from its teeth."

"You'd better stick with me then," Yellen said.

Vacation? Whatever. In for a penny, in for a pound.

After thanking Elvis, then reporting to Barconi, Yellen and I set out. A short drive brought us to the Hammocks district station house, decidedly less shiny digs than the ones we'd just left. Small tiled lobby. Front intake desk. Corkboard filled with the usual posters and flyers.

When we entered the rear working area, a male voice could be heard protesting loudly from an interview room.

"This is horseshit! You're costing me valuable hunting time!"

Yellen went straight to the room and opened the door. I followed, but held back a safe distance.

When Jordan saw Yellen he pounced. "What the hell's going on, Tom? One of your yokels just read me my rights."

At Yellen's nonresponse, Jordan popped to his feet. "No way I'm taking the fall for this. I called the freakin' thing in!"

"Just settle down." Yellen gestured two-handed for Jordan to resume his seat.

Jordan hesitated, then dropped back into his chair. With a sullen shake of his head, he thrust both feet out under the battered table before him, his bulk making it appear miniature.

I slipped in and pressed my back to the wall beside the door.

Jordan glanced at me, then refocused on Yellen. "This is shit, man. Kiley and me are buds. You know that."

Unconsciously, I noted that Jordan used the present tense.

Lunging forward at the waist, Jordan pulled his cellphone from his pocket, jabbed a few buttons, then placed the device on the tabletop so Yellen could see an image on the screen.

Yellen viewed the picture, then handed the phone to me.

On the left was a pretty blonde, straight teeth, turquoise eyes, a smattering of freckles across a tanned nose. No makeup. The all-American girl straight out of a J. Crew catalogue.

The girl held the neck of a snake easily three times her body length, firmly, behind the jaw. Beside her, Jordan held the tail. Both were beaming. The girl looked Lilliputian compared to her companion and the reptile between them.

"So?" Yellen was unimpressed.

"That was our winning python from last year's contest. We snagged the prizes for both the longest and the most caught." His voice cracked. Desperate, he looked to me for understanding. "Kiley's like my sister." His eyes bounced back to Yellen. "We're the best python wranglers and we make the best team."

"That why she dumped you to go solo this year?"

Jordan's face flamed. Clearly Yellen had poked a raw wound. "She didn't dump me, dickhead."

"How about the fact she was kicking your ass in the contest?"

"I'm catching up. Besides, I'm not in it for the money. Neither is she."

"Why the split then?"

"I dunno. She was acting all weird before the contest. Secretive. Always going out alone."

"And that pissed you off."

Jordan spread his big hands on the tabletop. Stared at them, as if puzzled by their uselessness indoors.

"When's the last time you saw her?" Yellen pressed.

"At the launch of the hunt," Jordan answered without looking up. "She vanished into the glades the second the gun went off."

A full minute of silence crammed the small room. Yellen let it continue, hoping Jordan would feel compelled to fill it. He didn't.

"Tell me about finding the body." Yellen used the interviewer's trick of quick-changing topics.

"Look. It's not me you should be grilling." Agitated, Jordan drew back his feet and shifted his weight in the chair. It creaked ominously.

"Yeah?"

"Yeah. You know as well as I do."

"Remind me."

"The damn poachers. Kiley's obsessed with poaching. Won't ever let it go." Jordan's eyes rolled up to Yellen, then shifted to me. "She has secret cameras, tree blinds where she'll sit for days watching. She keeps a journal—a weird little spiral-bound notebook shaped like a leaf. She writes all kinds of stuff in it. The idea of killing animals for commercial gain, her words, drives her nuts. She hunts pythons because it helps protect the ecosystem."

"How nuts?" Yellen prodded.

"Whaddya mean?"

"Would she confront the poachers herself?"

"Maybe. She won't rest until she sees every last one of 'em in jail. She's succeeding, too. Getting 'em fined, charged." Jordan jabbed a finger at Yellen. "Find the poachers and you'll find who hurt Kiley."

Yellen regarded Jordan a moment. Then, "I want your statement on paper."

Back in the hall, Yellen asked, "You a size seven foot?"

"Close enough." WTF?

"Wait here."

He disappeared into a back room, then returned and tossed me a pair of rubber hip waders. Fetching lime green.

"Let's go."

CHAPTER 5

We were headed west on Route 41, the Tamiami Trail. The sun was shooting long tangerine rays straight into my eyes. I squinted and guessed the time at 7:00 P.M. Quick check of my phone said 5:49. Tracker I was not.

For some reason Yellen was feeling expansive. "The Miccosukee are an officially recognized Native American tribe, with a reservation split over three areas in Broward and Miami-Dade: Alligator Alley, Tamiami Trail, and Krome Avenue. We're headed to Tamiami, the largest. Most tribal operations are handled there."

I was about to ask a question, but Yellen kept talking.

"It's mostly two hundred thousand acres of wetland under perpetual lease to the South Florida Water Management District's Water Conservation Area 3A South. Legit tribal members have some rights to hunt and fish, catch frogs, farm, whatever."

I waited to be sure he was done, then said, "I've heard of the Miccosukee. The tribe was a sponsor in all three of NASCAR's national series—the Sprint

Cup, Nationwide, and Camping World Truck. It was big news when they pulled out for budget cuts."

At Yellen's surprised look, I shrugged. "I live in Charlotte. The city's ground zero for NASCAR." I'd once worked the case of a body found in a barrel of asphalt at the Charlotte Motor Speedway. "So why are we going to Tamiami?"

"To nail the bastard who killed Kiley James."

The rest of the drive passed in silence.

After forty-five minutes, we reached a long stretch of bald cypress log fence paralleling the south shoulder. What my daughter, Katy, used to call the pink had joined the ginger and peach now lighting the horizon.

The sunset lit a low canary yellow building with a palmetto thatch roof. A rustically lettered sign proclaimed WELCOME TO MICCOSUKEE INDIAN VILLAGE. A clutch of smaller chickee huts encircled the main building—raised structures with supporting posts, thatched roofs, and open sides.

I lowered my window. The air smelled of grass and algae and fish eggs in the wetlands. Of mud and petroleum. Of food cooking on a charcoal grill. My brain telegraphed images of fry cakes and pupusas.

"Any chance of scoring some home cooking?" Sampling native cuisine counted as a sort of vacation experience.

Yellen's tone was scathing. "What you'll score here is a nine-dollar hot dog and a five-dollar Coke. Maybe some gen-you-ine Indian beading and a hyped-up alligator-wrestling demo. Village is strictly tourist."

Yellen steered the cruiser through the gate and parked before a building whose sign identified it as the Miccosukee Restaurant. As though cued by a coach, my stomach did an Olympic-level growl. I looked a question at him.

"Knock yourself out. We ain't punching a clock."

I scampered in, emerged minutes later with fry bread and an apple. Couldn't bring myself to eat the gator bits. Still. Any port in a storm. Swamp.

Across an expanse of grassless soil, Yellen was talking to a tall man with mahogany skin and black hair curling from under a raffia cowboy hat that had seen better days. There was a lot of arm flapping, then Yellen nodded and returned to the cruiser.

"Fry bread?" I offered as we climbed in.

No response. Suited me. It was my first real meal of the day.

"Didn't show up at work." Yellen's comment sprang from a conversation we hadn't had.

"Sorry?"

"Alligator wrangler. Cypress was scheduled. Didn't come in."

"Cypress?"

"Deuce Cypress, one of a zillion Miccosukee Cypresses. Including the last tribal leader."

"Is Deuce's nonappearance suspicious?"

"Not necessarily. The Miccosukee are generally a solid bunch. Got business sense. They own a casino at Krome Avenue, does good trade. Got 'em a new school, police force, clinic. Even a gym. Members get a cut of the profit, stay out of trouble. 'Cept maybe with the IRS or booze."

"But?" I'd heard one in Yellen's tone.

"But every community has its whack jobs. Miccosukee has the brothers Cypress. Rootin' tootin' shootin' moonshinin' rednecks, and proud of it."

"And poachers."

"That's the word on the street."

A canal ran along the right shoulder of the road. I watched it slide by the passenger-side window. Here and there gators were catching the last of the day's sun on one muddy bank or the other. Everyone tanned in Miami.

A short while after leaving the village, we turned north across a crude wooden bridge. "Road" would be an exaggeration for the bumpy, muddy track that followed.

For a full ten minutes the cruiser's tires jolted from one soggy rut to another. Dense vegetation brushed the side panels. It seemed the swamp was trying to swallow us whole.

"These guys really live off the grid," I said.

"You got that right. No AC or phones. Just fishin', gator huntin', marijuana smugglin', animal poachin'. The simple life."

Yellen cut right onto a barely visible track that made the previous one look like a superhighway. Tree canopy obscured the sky, making it seem as though dusk had suddenly won out.

The track ended in a bare clearing fronting a weathered stilt house with an adjacent chickee hut. A mud-spattered pickup sat out front. Past the house I could see a bronze glint of water. Marsh, I was guessing.

The property was overflowing with junk. Rusted-out cars. A clothes dryer that hadn't been manufactured in the last three decades. Aluminum lawn furniture. A stack of window air-conditioning units. Sawhorses. Cinder blocks. Plastic sacks filled with treasures I didn't want to imagine.

When Yellen cut the engine, the stillness was almost total. Birdsong. The *tic-tic-tic* of the cooling car.

We waited a moment. No signs of human activity. No breeze.

"You hold back behind me," Yellen cautioned, alighting.

I must have looked alarmed.

"They're generally not violent, but they don't take to strangers."

Take to strangers? Yellen watched way too many westerns. I said nothing, just followed him.

We were walking toward the house when two shots rang out. I hit the dirt. Yellen didn't. Just regarded me with amusement.

I stood and brushed soggy leaves and mud from my front.

"Redneck hello" was Yellen's only comment.

More gunfire, followed by laughter.

"Deuce!" Yellen barked.

The laughter stopped.

"Get your ass out here."

The screen door banged open and a dog came barreling out onto the porch. Brindle, snarling, the fur on its spine standing straight up. Pure junkyard.

My heart jumped to my throat, but this time I took my cue from Yellen. He held his ground. So did I.

A scruffy human emerged from around the side of the house. Sinewy, bearded, a Remington twelve-gauge gripped two-handed in front of his chest. Pure swamp.

For a moment we all looked at each other. I took in more detail. Bloodshot eyes. Inked forearms. Bulge of tobacco under the lower lip. Denim and camo that had never known laundry detergent. I guessed Deuce's age around five years north of high school dropout.

The dog ran to Deuce, tongue dangling, eyes hard on us. Deuce shot it a butt-kick accompanied by a nonchalant "Get on, Rooster." The dog yelped and slunk away. I didn't try to hide my disgust.

"Lose the shotgun, Deuce." Yellen spoke.

"Don't have to. Standin' my ground."

"Where's your brother?"

"Ernie!" Cypress shouted, eyes never leaving Yellen. "Sheriff's here wanting to invite you to the prom!"

A younger version of Deuce appeared. Mirror image except for the addition of a stud in one ear and a faded Little Feat concert tee instead of camo on top.

"Where's Buck?" Yellen made no effort to mask his impatience.

"Buck ain't here," Deuce said.

Yellen waited.

Deuce shrugged. "Ain't my brother's keeper."

Ernie made an odd giggling sound and looked to Deuce for approval.

"Kiley James was found dead in the swamp." Yellen didn't mince words. "Murdered and dismembered. And the trail leads right here."

"What the hell?" Deuce looked like someone had slammed him in the chest. "White woman dies and you blame the Indian?"

"Save it," Yellen said. "As I recall the little lady tuned Buck up with a bottle after he groped her at Alligator Ron's last summer."

"She's a bitch." Deuce's eyes flashed angry and black. "She's the one done the assaulting."

"Self-defense ain't assault, Deuce. That big brother of yours has a temper and a fondness for Jimmy B. Not a good mix. Bought him more than one night in my jail."

"What's your point?"

"Where is he?"

Deuce only glared.

"Word is Kiley was about to nail y'all for poaching."

"We ain't poachers." This from Ernie, who was still smiling. Deuce shot him a look.

"We got rights to hunt and fish." Ernie went on, barely audible, and now looking at his boots.

"Not on park land, you don't." Yellen was ignoring Ernie, talking only to Deuce. "Maybe Kiley caught you upping your bounty count with illegal kills."

Deuce's face crimped in scorn. "You talking 'bout the staties' Python Challenge? We ain't into that honky shit."

"When's the last time you saw Kiley James?"

Deuce shrugged. "Been a while, I reckon."

Ernie's eyes stayed glued to his footwear.

"Word is Kiley had pics that could put y'all behind bars."

Deuce shrugged again. He was good at it. "Can't have pics of what ain't happened."

"I'm thinking maybe Kiley came by pointin' fingers. You made the problem disappear. Be pretty easy way out here in the swamp."

"Screw you," Deuce said. "There's poaching goin' down all right, but it ain't Cypress."

"You got a chain saw?" Yellen switched tacks.

"What?" Surprised.

"Do. You. Own. A. Chain. Saw."

"Naw, man."

"Who's poaching then?" And again.

Yellen's interview tactics weren't rattling Deuce. "Maybe Kiley James. Ever think of that? Maybe it was her playing dirty tricks."

"Lady sure as hell didn't kill herself."

Deuce seemed to roll that around in his mind. Which I was beginning to suspect was sharper than his appearance suggested. Finally, he spat, "You know the real victims?"

Knowing the question was rhetorical, Yellen didn't respond.

"Pythons. And gators. Greedy pricks in Miami don't give a rat's ass where the skins come from. Long as they can make their fancy shoes and belts."

"Who are you talking about?" Yellen asked.

For the first time, Deuce looked uncomfortable. "All of 'em."

"The people you sell to."

Deuce nodded.

"You're saying the fashion houses buy illegal?"

"Not all."

"Which?"

"Shoulda asked Kiley. She was the one all cozied up to their hoity-toity asses."

"What's that supposed to mean?"

"I'm done here."

Yellen was about to push for more when his mobile sounded. Pointing a "Stay put" finger at Deuce, he stepped away.

Deuce and I eyed each other.

What the hell?

"Why were you shooting?" I asked.

Deuce just glared. Ernie smiled. I noticed that Ernie had a soiled gauze bandage taped around one finger. Defense wound? Knife? Chain saw?

"Hurt yourself?" I gestured at the bound digit.

"I got my tat." Ernie sounded like a kid excited by a new bike. "Show her, Deuce. Show her yours. Blow her mind." To me, "Mine will be just the same when it heals."

Deuce held out his hand and shot the middle finger. Underneath the nail, in ink, was a circle sliced top to bottom by three lines. On each side, within the larger circle, were three concentric curved lines. I recognized the symbol from the Miccosukee village.

"Jesus. Is that a tattoo under your nail?"

"Yep." Said with macho pride.

"Miccosukee tradition?"

Ernie started giggling.

"Just our clan. Takes a pair, know what I'm saying?"

"I'm eighteen." Ernie sounded pumped.

I looked to Deuce for explanation. "We get 'em when we turn eighteen and can gator-wrestle for the village. You hammer the fingertip, wait for the nail to fall off, then ink the bed. Nail grows back. Tat for life."

"Hammer the nail." Ernie giggled again.

Dear God. I couldn't imagine the pain. And the long-term wound way out here in the swamp.

"Keep it disinfected and bandaged," I couldn't resist warning him.

Hearing footfalls, I turned. Yellen was jamming his phone back into his pocket and hurrying toward us. His face could have served as an image to accompany the definition of grim.

To Deuce he said, "You tell Buck to drop by the station or I'm coming to haul his scrawny ass in myself." To me, "Let's roll. I'm taking you home."

"I'll go home when I'm ready." I was plenty ready, but I don't like being told what to do.

"Your call." Yellen turned and walked toward the cruiser. "But you're doing another autopsy first thing tomorrow."

Necropsy. Not autopsy. I'd explained the difference to Yellen, but he wasn't "interested in semantics."

I've examined victims lacking both arms and legs before, but none that had been born that way. My current subject was a sixteen-foot Burmese python, weighing 130 pounds and measuring eight inches in diameter. Except for the midsection, which showed a large bulge.

Lisa and I had risen at dawn. Over a breakfast of cold pizza on her terrace with its "angle your head just right" slash of canal view, we'd discussed possible motives for the James murder. The list had been longer than the snake.

There was tension among the python hunt contestants. Tension between the once-a-year amateurs and the full-time professional wranglers. Tension between the legal hunters and the poachers.

Then there was Kiley James herself. She'd been acting secretive and suspicious. She'd dropped Dusty Jordan as her python hunting partner. She'd had a violent encounter with Buck Cypress. Perhaps she'd tipped a poacher that she was on his or her trail.

After our healthy morning meal, Lisa had gotten a lift to her lab, generously leaving me her car. By eight I was back at Miami-Dade. Elvis waved as I passed the bustle of activity in autopsy one. I picked up that a car had been dredged from a canal, and there'd been decomps inside. No problem. Instead of Elvis, I needed Aaron Lundberg by my side. Today I was playing a supporting role to his leading man.

Yellen had issued a requisition to Fish and Wildlife. All reptiles captured in the vicinity of Hardwood Hammock were to be taken to the morgue and presented to Lundberg and yours truly. Since human remains were involved in the homicide we were trying to solve, the head pathologist didn't object, as long as the snakes were no longer breathing. A qualifier I enthusiastically applauded.

"Yellen was smart to order the roundup." Lundberg hadn't stopped talking since I'd arrived. "FWC is working assembly-line style—one person making incisions, another examining stomach contents, a third studying sex organs."

We'd rolled a gurney end to end with the autopsy table to accommodate the full length of our subject. Even knowing the snake was dead, I'd had to gird myself to touch it. Irrational, I know. But creatures without eyelids creep me out.

Still, I felt sorry for the snake. It hadn't chosen to be born in trigger-happy Florida rather than Southeast Asia.

"It looks alive," I said.

"There are two ways to ethically euthanize a python." Lundberg handed me one end of a retractable tape measure. I held the little metal tab at the tip of the snake's tail while he stretched the working portion to the end of its snout.

"By chemical injection or brain destruction." Lundberg jotted a number, then looped the tape around the snake's midsection and jotted again. When done, he glanced up.

I must have looked appalled.

"Like all reptiles', the python's central nervous system is tolerant to low oxygen and low blood pressure, so the brain can remain active for up to an hour after decapitation, allowing the snake to experience pain. To minimize suffering, you want immediate loss of consciousness and brain destruction."

Lundberg took a Nikon from the counter and began snapping pics, all the while maintaining the flow of his lecture.

"For challenge participants, we recommend using a captive bolt or a firearm. A captive bolt works like a gun, where compressed air drives a steel bolt into the animal's brain. FWC officials euthanized this catch by lethal injection."

"He was captured in the same location as the python containing the turkey vulture and the foot?" I asked.

"She. Yes. Just yards away. Pythons aren't territorial, so you can find more than one animal in close proximity. Especially during mating season."

Lundberg circled to my side of the table and snapped a series of close-ups. At his direction, I repositioned the case marker for each.

"This female would have attracted multiple males to the vicinity. What we call a breeding aggregation."

"How does one determine gender?"

"With most snakes you can't tell just by looking. You have to probe, or open them up to observe the genitalia. But pythons have vestigial organs in the pelvic girdle, left over from a time their ancestors had hind limbs. Look here, on either side of this vent." He set down the camera and pointed a gloved finger to tiny spurs toward the tail end of the beast. "The small size indicates that this is a female. They'd be larger in a male."

A female who would have cared for her young. Again, I felt a wave of sadness for an animal that had died through no fault of her own.

"Based on the size of the bulge, I'd guess she was bagged shortly after the swallowing process was complete."

"How long does that take?" I dragged my eyes from the telltale little spurs.

"A python can swallow a good-size mammal or bird in about twenty minutes."

"Does the catch ever get away?"

"Not likely once they have it in their mouth. The prey is dead by the time it's swallowed. A python strikes fast, then immobilizes the kill with its teeth while wrapping it with body coils. Death is by asphyxiation."

I could think of nothing to say.

"It's a remarkable creature," he said.

But a dead one. I swallowed. "I'm surprised the bones we've observed haven't been more damaged."

"Constriction doesn't actually crush bodies or break bones. That's Hollywood. Constrictors squeeze just tight enough to prevent the prey from breathing, but not tighter. Death is fast—three to four minutes."

"Then they do that jaw unhinging thing?"

"More media hype. The jaws aren't attached in a mechanical way. Long tendons and muscles connect the upper and lower jaws."

Lundberg leaned close and observed the snake's

right eye, then its left. Made a note on the form on his clipboard.

"The lower jaw is composed of two separate bones to enhance the snake's ability to manipulate large intake." He looked up, slashing light from the overheads across his lenses. "Snakes swallow prey headfirst so the limbs will fold in. Then they work it down the throat into the stomach with rhythmic muscular contractions."

"How does the snake breathe during all that?" Despite myself I was becoming interested.

"It has a special tube in the bottom of its mouth that stays open to one side to allow air inhalation. Shall we get to it?"

"We shall."

For my benefit, Lundberg spoke aloud as he made notes on marking patterns, pigmentation, nasal form, tail shape, old and recent wounds, abnormalities, and overall physical condition. Then, using a hand lens, he searched for external parasites such as ticks and mites. I had to agree with Yellen. There was little difference between an external in a necropsy and one in an autopsy.

Finally, Lundberg was ready for the internal exam. It'll be the longest, skinniest Y incision ever, I thought.

Together, Lundberg and I flipped the subject ventral side up. Then, using a scalpel identical to the one I'd used the day before, he sliced the length of the belly. Before examining the organs, he observed and then removed and weighed the glossy yellow layer underlying the skin.

"Fat's a good indicator of health. It can also signal that a female has had a clutch. A Burmese doesn't leave her eggs to hunt. While brooding, she survives off stored fat. Recent mothers have little of it left."

Again, the ping of grief. Crap. This was almost as bad as working a homicide vic.

At last, the organs. Lundberg went through his routine, excising, observing, then recording size, weight, color, and consistency, instructing as he went.

I let his words roll over me. I was waiting for the big event.

And then the stomach.

"When it comes to the gut, you see a rapid drop in pH after feeding." Lundberg was still rolling. "A steady maintenance of a very acidic pH during digestion, and a rise in pH upon completion of gastric breakdown. At which time acid production ceases."

"Making for quick digestion."

"In this case, hopefully not quick enough."

With one slash, Lundberg detached the stomach, lifted and placed it to the side of the snake. Using the scalpel tip, he sliced the outer layer and splayed the sack open.

A stench filled the room. Liquid oozed onto the stainless steel.

As Lundberg teased free the stomach contents, I scanned each chunk. Several appeared to be bone. I poked and prodded. Scraped off gastric sludge with my scalpel.

In less than a minute I knew. More than a vulture and a gator had found human chow to their recent liking. This python had also dined on Kiley James.

Most of the flesh was gone, eaten away by stomach acid, but I could see portions of at least twenty to thirty bones. Small ones. Likely more hands and feet. Not the upper torso I'd been hoping for, but definitely parts of a human skeleton.

"Snakes don't normally eat carrion." Lundberg's brow was furrowed above his silver frames.

"James was dismembered with a chain saw. There's no way she was alive when this snake consumed her."

Lundberg sighed. "The more we learn about snakes, the more we realize how little we know. The Burmese in particular are very adaptable. I suppose there's nothing to say they wouldn't eat a fresh carcass. They definitely take advantage of wounded prey."

We spent another twenty minutes tweezing bones onto a tray, which Lundberg then handed to me. I shifted to the sink and carefully cleaned away tissue and flesh. Details emerged. A joint surface. An articular facet. A portion of shaft retaining a nutrient foramen.

A tiny fizz of electricity sparked in my chest. What?

I sorted the bones into piles, starting with the smallest, moving to the largest. Finger. Toe. Wrist. Ankle. Ulna. Radius. Early projections pointed to a pair of hands, a lower right arm, and one foot.

At one point, Lundberg approached with another tray. "Hair and fingernails."

I heard the rattle of metal on metal but remained focused on the task of arranging bones. Before long I had assembled two complete hands. Then the distal portion of a right forearm.

As I took and recorded measurements, the fizz grew stronger. The bones were surprisingly large for a petite woman.

I turned to the foot. Arranged. Measured.

Knew something was wrong.

"Where's the James file?" Keeping my voice even.

"On the desk in the anteroom."

I retrieved the folder and flipped pages until I found the entry I needed.

The fizz blossomed into full-blown dread.

CHAPTER
7

"The foot does not belong to Kiley James," I repeated.

"You're sure?" Yellen asked for the third time, as if hoping my answer might change.

"Unless she had one size five, one size twelve, and they were both left feet, yes."

"What the blazes?" The sheriff's mutter was to himself.

"That's all I can tell you for now."

Yellen pinched the bridge of his nose. "And why can't you go back at it?"

"We got bumped." More repetition. "A fisherman found what the cops think is a child missing since last week. In a lagoon. The media's going berserk. That postmortem takes priority."

We'd been hustled out of autopsy room two by the chief medical examiner himself. Jane Barconi had caught the case. Her taut expression had made yesterday's seem downright relaxed.

I was delivering the news to Yellen in a corner of the staff kitchen. The lobby and parking lot were swarming with press.

"They needed the decomp room. Our snake exam got pushed to the bottom of the totem pole," I said. Again.

"What *can* you tell me now?"

Very little. I'd realized what I was seeing only minutes before the mêlée broke out.

"Rough measurements suggest a medium-size male."

"Goddammit." Yellen sounded furious, as though somehow I were the root of his problem.

"I'll know more once I can get back in." For clarification, I added, "When they've finished autopsying the little girl."

"I have body parts poppin' up in the bellies of every critter in the swamp, and I've got to cool my heels until who the hell knows when?"

"Any new intel on Buck Cypress?" I asked, mostly to distract him.

Yellen sighed. "Still MIA. We hauled Deuce into district. Genius managed to cough up a name. If there's nothing going on here, you might as well come along while I follow up."

We cut through the throng outside, heads lowered, eyes down. A few journalists recognized Yellen and shouted questions. A few cameras and mikes swung his way. He ignored them. Being a stranger, I drew no attention at all.

"Where to?" I asked, buckling my seat belt.

"Every woman's dream. Shopping."

"Hilarious."

A short ten blocks brought us to Miami's Design District. Art galleries and overpriced lofts jockeyed for square footage with designer boutiques and Korean clothing shops. Women's apparel, jewelry, and handbags sparkled in every other store window.

"Ritzy," I observed.

"Didn't used to be," Yellen said. "Until the Koreans worked their magic this district was nothing but vacant warehouses, boarded-up buildings, and thugs. Drop by back in the eighties, you'd get jacked. Now it's the swankiest five-block stretch along I-95."

Most of the merchandise looked light-years beyond my price range.

"What neighborhood is this?"

"Wynwood. Real estate's way upmarket." Yellen depressed his turn indicator. "District's half fashion, half artsy-fartsy. There's a minute of industry over along Fifth Avenue, textile and fashion. But it's mostly boutiques."

Yellen made a left, then a right. I waited for him to elaborate.

"Deuce Cypress fingered someone he says buys from the poachers. It's a label run by four sisters. Esther, Eun, Edie, and Evette Eugene. Name on their birth certificates is actually Yoo-Jin, pronounced the same. Some kind of reality TV wannabes with a fashion line specializing in skins. We've got an appointment with Esther at their fancy-pants boutique."

Yellen winged onto Second Avenue and pulled to the curb in front of a cool, modern storefront composed almost entirely of smoky glass. EUGENE was emblazoned on the window in sleek white letters.

The sleek and white theme continued inside with white mannequin busts, carpet, walls, and trim. The only contrast was provided by huge black-and-white photos. In each, four Asian American women pouted affectedly.

To the right of the entrance, a half dozen safari-chic dresses hung like works of art in a gallery. Facing them, on the left, was menswear in understated tans and taupes. A discreet sign designated the clothes as COLLECTION ARTISANAL FOR WOMEN AND MEN. Front and center, exquisitely tailored snakeskin and alligator-skin bags, belts, and shoes lay on pedestals arranged on white acrylic tables. I discreetly checked a tag or two. Yep. Way out of my range.

No matter. The merchandise left me cold. I've never felt right about putting on the hide of another creature. And my recent close encounters with pythons and gators made wearing reptiles feel especially distasteful.

"Good morning?" The woman was anorexically slim, her tone more question than greeting. Middle-aged paunchy sheriffs were probably not her typical clientele.

Yellen badged her. "Got an appointment with Esther Eugene."

"This way." Cool and gracious, devoid of emotion.

The woman, I assumed a salesclerk, led us through a door at the rear of the showroom. The photos continued down a narrow hallway, dark-haired, dark-eyed beauties pouting or flirting every ten feet.

The clerk stopped at an open doorway and gestured for us to proceed.

The office was, you guessed it, uniformly white, providing maximum contrast for the woman in the tight snakeskin print dress. She had porcelain skin and short black hair bobbed to her jawline. Fake lashes looked like centipedes crawling her upper lids.

The woman sat behind a creamy French secretary desk, chin resting on one upraised palm. The elegant pose suggested someone interrupted while deep in thought.

"You must be Sheriff Yellen," she purred. "Esther Eugene. Please come in." Tipping her head ever so slightly and elevating one perfect brow. "And you are?"

"Tempe Brennan." I kept it short.

"May I offer you tea?"

Seriously? Sheriff Crotchety looked like the chamomile and biscuit type?

"I've got a witness says you buy illegally harvested animal skins." Yellen arrowed straight to the point.

Esther placed a delicate hand on her chest. The nails were long and painted fire-engine red. "Oh my goodness! That's totally untrue." Every move seemed rehearsed. Artificial. "My sisters and I would never engage in unlawful activity. We pride ourselves on maintaining the very highest of ethical standards. We are absolutely committed to the concept of sustainable fashion."

I recognized the buzz phrase for what it was. Doubted she understood the concept. Doubted she understood the concept of concept.

Yellen cut off Esther's melodramatics. "I'm not here to arrest you for buying poached skins. I'm investigating a homicide."

Esther's brows rose as far on her forehead as the Botox allowed.

"You know a young woman named Kiley James?"

Esther's gasp was off the stage and out the theater door. "Kiley is dead?" The hand fluttered to the perfectly matched crimson mouth. I noticed that it trembled.

"What do you know about her?" Yellen stayed on point.

Esther plucked a tissue from a flower-shaped holder on her desk and ran it carefully under each eye. Back to character, mascara intact. "We recently signed Kiley to be the face of our brand. We're launching a huge advertising campaign for the python line, centered around her. An enormously expensive one."

"First I heard of Kiley being a model." Yellen was skeptical.

"That was the thing!" Esther clapped her hands, grief momentarily forgotten. "We wanted a real wrangler, not a model. When we saw Kiley at last year's hunt award ceremony, we had to have her. Kiley was so real! Pretty face, and a figure that could wear clothing." Coy tip of the head. "If you catch my meaning?"

Yellen waited for Esther to continue.

"We were just about to sign a male wrangler when we found her. But not one single applicant had a story like Kiley—little woman wrestling snakes bigger than herself, better than men? We didn't let up until we'd convinced her to be the face of Eugene." Self-satisfied look. "When the price is right, everyone eventually says yes."

"So what's this ad campaign?" Yellen asked.

"The theme is extraordinary." Esther ran her free hand horizontally through the air, as if mimicking a theater marquee. "Ugliness into beauty. Isn't that brilliant? Turning the greatest threat the Everglades has ever known into something positive and beautiful."

"Shoes?" Blurted before I could stop myself.

Esther drew a juddery little breath, then straightened her shoulders and eyed me with distaste. "Making people feel good about themselves puts positive energy into the universe."

"How 'bout you put some positive energy into this interview and tell me the last time you saw Kiley James?" Yellen's tone was sharp enough to chisel granite.

Esther considered. Or made a show of doing so. "It would have been two weeks ago. We were going over the shooting schedule. She said she'd be out of pocket for a while." A red-tipped finger rose in the air. "But, you know, come to think of it, she did seem distracted."

"How so?"

"I'm not sure. I just sensed she wasn't paying attention." Hiccupy little laugh. "Kiley was always a moral little spitfire, refusing to wear certain items, but she was particularly . . . challenging at our last meeting." Spoken with synthetic warmth.

"Challenging?" Yellen bounced Esther's word back to her.

She paused. Then, "Kiley had a strong sense of justice. She was highly principled. And extremely particular."

"Do you think that could have gotten her killed?"

Esther didn't hesitate. "I suppose. If she angered the wrong person."

"Any wrong person you have in mind?"

"No. I mean, competition for the modeling contract was fierce. Some applicants were very unhappy when we went with Kiley out of the blue. People want to be connected to we Eugenes." She preened. "It didn't sit well that she swooped in at the last minute and got the job. But I can't imagine anyone becoming violent because they weren't chosen."

"I'll need a list of names," Yellen said.

"Of course. Will there be anything else?" The woman was now eager to see us gone.

"We'll let you know."

Esther rose. "This is just so distressing. What will we do?"

"Reopen auditions." Mean, but I found the woman repugnant.

Esther maintained a carefully grieved expression as we walked through the door.

Outside, the mid-morning temperature was already in the high eighties. And the humidity was going for a personal best. Even for Florida.

Yellen started the car and cranked the AC. "You get any message from—"

"No." I cut him off. "With a child homicide, Barconi's going to take her time."

Lips pursed, the sheriff shifted into gear. He knew, was just impatient.

"Where now?" I asked.

"Your favorite place on earth."

He pointed the cruiser south toward Everglades National Park.

CHAPTER
8

"Please don't tell me there's another foot," I said as we drove.

Yellen's look said he wasn't in the mood for humor.

"I've got a deputy working to find Kiley James's journal. We've searched her house and her car. No luck. Lundberg says she had a locker at the rangers' station. I want to check it out."

We were retracing the now-familiar drive south through Homestead. We'd turned right on Ingraham Highway toward the park entrance when Yellen's mobile rang.

"Sheriff Yellen." As he listened his mouth bunched even tighter than before. "I'll head over there now. Get me Scott Pierce."

He disconnected. Seconds later his phone rang again.

"Thanks for getting right back to me. Listen, I'm on my way to search Kiley James's locker at the rangers' station."

I could hear a tinny voice on the other end of the line. Couldn't make out the words.

"Yeah, she had a locker. Brain Trust Lundberg just

told me last night. I have a warrant, but I've gotta get back to district. If Doc Brennan brings the paper, can you toss the thing then get her home afterward?"

The buzzy staccato sounded again.

"I owe you one." Yellen ended the call.

To me, "Change of plans. Dawn raid on a Florida City meth lab spat out a tweaker that's my favorite for a series of arsons. I'll drop you. Scott Pierce will get you home."

"My car's at the morgue."

"Just tell Pierce where you want to go."

A few minutes later we pulled up to the main entrance of Everglades National Park. Yellen drove past the visitors' center, and down a road behind a sign that warned PARK RANGERS ONLY BEYOND THIS POINT. The squat frame building at the end served as a rangers' station. The flag in front looked as limp as I felt.

As I got out, Yellen lowered his window. I circled to his side of the cruiser.

"You'll get to that foot ASAP?" he asked.

"As soon as I can." I meant it. No one was more eager to finish this than I was.

The window rose with a hum and Yellen was gone.

I climbed the steps and entered the rangers' station.

Unlike the visitors' center, the place was stark and functional. Desks and filing cabinets dotted the room, chosen for function over form. A collection of rescue equipment was stacked to my left, and a handful of park radios were propped in chargers to my right. At the back of the room, a stuffed alligator wore clown-size sunglasses and a University of Florida cap.

A green-uniformed woman occupied a desk near the door. Her name tag said H. FLORES. Dark brown hair knotted at the nape of her neck. Harry Potter glasses. A face that was neither friendly nor unfriendly.

"I'm looking for Scott Pierce," I said.

"And you are?"

"Temperance Brennan."

Flores made a call, listened, disconnected. "Sorry. No answer."

"He must be on his way," I said.

"You can cop a squat over there." Flores pointed to a collection of plastic chairs that looked decidedly uncomfortable. They were.

Five minutes passed.

I read the warrant. Kiley James had been assigned locker 53.

I drummed impatient fingers on the unyielding armrest. Eyed a wall clock that told me three more minutes had passed. I told myself I'd wait fifteen. Inspected my nails. Studied the park maps and pictures of local wildlife adorning the walls.

At fourteen minutes fifty-five seconds I popped to my feet and crossed to Flores.

"I have a warrant." I held up the judge's paper. "If you could point me to the lockers, I'll get out of your hair."

She looked at the paper and nodded. "Okay, locker room's down that hall, fourth door on your left."

"Tell Pierce where I've gone when he gets here."

"Will do."

I turned the knob and entered. The room was square, with linoleum underfoot and fluorescents overhead. Beige metal lockers lined three walls.

Movement to my right startled me.

Scott Pierce seemed equally surprised at my entrance. "What're you doing here?" he asked, frowning.

Odd. Pierce had gotten a heads-up from Yellen. He should have been expecting me. "I've got the warrant for Kiley James's locker." I produced the document again.

"Great. I'll take that." Reaching out. "You can wait up front."

A tiny alarm pinged in my head.

"Thanks, but I'll stick around." Tucking the warrant back into my pocket.

Pierce's eyes bore into mine. They were dark. Unreadable. I realized I'd never seen them before. They'd always been hidden by dark lenses.

"This is my beat." Pierce gave what I'm sure he considered a lady-killer smile. Probably practiced in the mirror every time he shaved. "We do things my way."

"Yellen asked me to inventory the contents of the locker." Not exactly, but the arrogant prick was pissing me off.

Another long stare. Then, "Fine. But you look when I'm done. And touch nothing."

"I work with law enforcement in two countries." I issued an abbreviated form of a smile. "I know evidence collection protocol."

Before Pierce could reply, the door opened and a ranger walked in.

"Hey, Scott." The kid looked twelve, with shaggy blond hair and acned skin.

Pierce gave a curt nod.

"What's up?" the kid asked, oblivious to the tension. "You doing an inspection or something?"

For the first time, I noted that a number of locker doors stood ajar.

Pierce shrugged. "No clue. They were open when I got here. Probably maintenance."

The kid went to a locker, twisted the dial on a combo lock, and flipped the door wide.

Pierce and I both waited him out. Couldn't say why. Maybe respect for the woman whose belongings we were about to rummage.

The kid took something from his locker, slammed and relocked it, then left, calling over one shoulder, "Catch ya later!"

When the door closed, Pierce refocused on me.

"Locker number?" Glacial.

Again, I hesitated, wishing Yellen were there. Even Lundberg. Why the apprehension? Just because he was an asshole didn't mean he wasn't good at his job.

"Fifty-three," I said.

Pierce picked up a bolt cutter I hadn't noticed and crossed to the specified locker.

"Stay back." With an effortless move he severed one of the double prongs, maneuvered the lock free, and opened the door. His body blocked my view of the locker's interior. Intentional?

"Shouldn't you wear gloves?" I asked his back.

Without replying, he held up the pen he was using to sift through things I couldn't see.

A full minute passed, then he paused and looked over his shoulder. "Actually, I could use gloves. Do you mind? They're in the supply cabinet out in the hall."

Again the ping. Why couldn't Pierce get his own damn gloves? I wasn't his gofer. But I was on his turf. And clearly unwelcome.

"Sure," I agreed. Reluctantly.

"Grab a pair for yourself." Suddenly Mr. Congenial.

I went to the corridor, found the cabinet, and returned two minutes later. Pierce hadn't moved.

"Here." I held out a pair of green surgical gloves.

"Thanks."

As Pierce pivoted, took the gloves, and snapped them on, I looked past him to the locker's interior. A fleece jacket hung from a hook. A pair of flip-flops lay on the bottom. The shelf held sunscreen, a box of tissues, a hairbrush, and a small stack of magazines. I couldn't see what was stored behind the front row of items.

"There's not much." Pierce followed my gaze.

"The journal?"

Pierce shook his head. "Damn shame. I was hoping it might help catch this bastard."

I felt a twinge of guilt for my unkind thoughts. The guy was probably just doing his job.

"You want help with the inventory?" Pierce asked.

"Thanks." I dug a pen and small spiral from my purse.

Pierce called out articles as he removed them from the locker. I recorded each. In addition to what had been obvious at first glance, there were granola bars, a box of tampons, lip balm, dirty socks. Mundane stuff.

"Scott?" Ranger Flores's head was poking through the partially open door. "Can I borrow you a minute?"

"Be right back." Thrown to me as he followed her out.

I stepped to the locker and lifted the magazines. Nothing hidden below. Balancing the pile on one palm, I ran the fingers of my other hand along the locker's metal seams. Zilch.

What had I expected? Geo-coordinates for the journal's hiding place etched on the shelf? Notes secreted in a crack?

As I was replacing the magazines, the top three slid

to the floor. I bent to retrieve them, and spotted a corner of paper sticking from the pages of one. I tugged the paper, and two sheets slid out. One looked like a page torn from a magazine. The other was lined in blue, filled with girlish handwriting. Jotted letters and numbers, not sentences. Identical crease patterns suggested the two sheets had been folded together.

The doorknob clicked. I quickly slipped the papers into my notepad. A violation of scene protocol, but I wanted to examine them in private.

Pierce joined me and eyed the escapee magazines.

"Sorry." Chilly grin. "They slid."

A curt nod was his only reply. So much for conviviality.

Wordlessly, Pierce gathered and shook each fallen magazine. I watched, anxious. Nothing fluttered out.

Pierce set the magazines on a bench and straightened to face me. "That's it."

I nodded. "I'll get this list to Yellen."

Pierce studied me for a very long moment. Appeared to dislike what he saw.

I stripped off my gloves and tossed them into a trash bin.

"It's been real." I turned to leave.

"Aren't you forgetting something?" Pierce's tone stopped me at the door.

I turned, mind scrambling for an excuse to justify confiscating the papers.

Pierce dangled his keys. "I'm your ride."

I exhaled breath I didn't realize I'd been holding. "So you are."

CHAPTER
9

The call came shortly after we exited the park. Decomp room two was at my disposal until eight the next morning.

I left Pierce with a quick "Thanks for the ride." I didn't like him. All ego.

Once I was safely alone in the autopsy room, I used forceps to transfer James's tear sheet and paper from my notepad into a Ziploc. I studied what I could see through the plastic.

The first sheet was a page torn from a magazine or catalogue. It depicted a model, not James, wearing a pair of albino-python-skin pants. Nothing sinister there. I must have ripped out hundreds of magazine pages depicting coveted items. I noted the pants were manufactured by the Eugene sisters.

The second was the lined notebook page filled with handwritten letters and numbers that looked like some sort of code. Occasionally a word popped out. Old Ingraham. Pearl Bay. Buttonwood.

Did the words have meaning? Or did James have her own special shorthand? What did the number and letter sequences signify? Frustrated, I set the sheets aside. I wanted to study them more, but analysis of the second victim took priority.

I composed a text to Lisa, telling her to contact me should she need her car and suggesting dinner around 7:00 P.M. I'd been the worst houseguest in planetary history. On the other hand, it was Lisa who'd gotten me into this mess.

It was only after hitting send that I looked at my watch: 1:30. An on-time dinner was iffy, but doable.

I gloved, tied an apron at my neck and waist, then retrieved the second victim's bones from the cooler. Standing at the counter, I reviewed what I had.

Arranged on four trays were two complete sets of hand bones: ten each of the distal, middle, and proximal phalanges, ten metacarpals, and fourteen carpals. I also had a complete left foot, and a partial right forearm.

Moving two trays to the autopsy table, I started with the hands. As I touched them, I noticed a roughening of the subperiosteal surface at points. I ran a gloved fingertip over a metacarpal, then carried it to the dissecting scope. Fine pitting covered most of the cortical exterior. Magnified, the surface looked like a moonscape.

I straightened. Puzzled. The porosity wasn't consistent with aging, or with any disease process I could recall. Too uniform. Too minute.

The python? Call Lundberg?

That would result in a nine-yard lecture. I opted to begin with the font of all knowledge. Google. Shifting to the computer terminal on the anteroom desk, I began working the keys.

It took a lot of cyber-looping, but I finally hit pay dirt. An article in the *Journal of Herpetology*. God bless the Society for the Study of Amphibians and Reptiles.

I cut and pasted relevant sections into a document for future reference. Basically, I'd learned that pythons have cells in their small intestines that optimize the absorption of calcium from the skeletons of their prey.

That tracked. Absorption of calcium would cause degradation of bone.

I returned to the cooler and pulled a formalin-filled jar labeled with the case number assigned to the second of the two Hardwood Hammock pythons. After unscrewing the lid, I tweezed out the sample of small intestine that Lundberg had snipped. Dropping it onto a glass slide, I observed the specimen under high magnification.

Small white specks dotted the tissue walls.

I repeated the process with the sliver of colon. Saw the same inclusions.

Microscopic bone particles. The results of specialized cells absorbing calcium. The pitting on the human bone was a by-product of digestion in the python, not an indicator of disease in her meal. The added barrier of the vulture explained the absence of these indicators in James's foot bones.

Satisfied with my diagnosis, I resumed my analysis, running through the same steps that I had with James, and recording my observations. Bone quality was good. No arthritis. No recent epiphyseal fusion. Young adult. Early to mid-twenties.

Next, I examined the ulna and radius. Immediately, I spotted antemortem trauma. Both bones had been broken in two places. Spiral fracturing indicated a twisting force of high magnitude. Nevertheless, each fracture had healed with good alignment. Though there was no pin or plate, I guessed orthopedic surgery had taken place shortly after the injury.

Remodeling suggested a time frame of approximately two to three years before death.

I thought of possible scenarios involving such violent wrenching. An industrial accident? An athletic mishap? An aggressive attack? Though I came up blank, I was certain serious pain had been involved.

I examined the truncated proximal end of the ulna. Saw scoring and gouging. Felt that tiny electrical charge. Chain saw.

I studied the damage left by the blade. Though it looked identical to that on Kiley James's foot bones, chain saws are not subtle. I'd need the actual tool to determine if it had dismembered both victims.

What were the chances of two perps and two saws?

I knew in my heart the victims had been killed by the same doer.

But who was the second victim? How was he linked to Kiley James? Friend? Former lover? Competitor? I was determined to find out.

I accessed Fordisc on the morgue computer and entered the measurements I'd taken. The program gave me lots of charts and statistics. All of which agreed with a high level of probability. My unknown was male and Native American.

Oh yeah?

I went back over the bones. Found nothing I hadn't already noted. Frustration was starting to make me edgy.

I took a bone plug for DNA testing, but wasn't hopeful. What were the chances this guy was in the system?

Out of ideas, I returned the bones to their tray and placed it with the others on the counter. My gaze fell on the jar of organ samples. Noted what looked like scallops of plastic floating in the formalin. Using a fine mesh strainer, I collected a few and viewed them under the scope.

The scallops were fingernails and toenails. God bless keratin. The stuff survives just about every enzyme digestion throws its way.

I was adjusting the light when a discoloration on one nail caught my eye. I teased it free and cranked the magnification.

My breath froze.

A layer of flesh adhered to the back of the nail. Visible on it was a circle sliced top to bottom by three lines, three more concentric curves to each side within the larger circle.

Twenty-something Native American male. With a unique nail bed tattoo. And a history with Kiley James.

Hot damn. I had a name for my unknown.

I grabbed my phone and punched in a number. My call was answered on the first ring.

"I'd bet my ass the second vic is Buck Cypress."

I explained the inked nail. The Fordisc. Yellen already knew the connection to James.

"It's a positive?" The sheriff sounded almost upbeat.

"Not yet. But the vic also sustained a bad break of the lower right arm two or three years back. Looks like the fracture was treated by a professional. If so, there would be X-rays. If no one kept them, one of the brothers could confirm the break."

"Well shite in a bucket." Yellen exhaled. "Those knuckle draggers don't have a damn phone and I'm tied up with this firebug mess. Got no time to haul back out to the swamp right now."

"I can go."

I could hear chaos in the background. Agitated voices. Someone calling Yellen's name.

"Hold on." The air went thick, as though Yellen had pressed the phone to his chest.

"Sorry 'bout that." He was back. "It's a circus here. My doer may not have acted alone. What'd you say?"

"I'll go see Deuce. Confirm ID."

"By yourself? That's nuts."

"Why not?"

"You gotta ask?"

"This ain't my first rodeo," I said dryly, mimicking Yellen's comment.

"You've got balls, Doc, I'll give you that." A pause. Then, "I'll send a deputy out with you first thing tomorrow morning."

"Fine." It wasn't.

"Almost forgot. You'll love this one." Yellen made a throaty noise I took to be a chuckle. "Scott Pierce's name was on the list of applicants for the Eugene ad campaign. Pretty boy made it all the way to the final cut." A door slammed. The background noise level rose. "Hell, I gotta go. My deputy will call when he sets out."

Three beeps told me Yellen had disconnected.

Sonofabitch.

I didn't want to go the swamp tomorrow. I wanted to sleep in. Lie on the beach. Eat stone crabs with Lisa.

I looked at my watch. 5:30 P.M. Quick calculation. Forty-five miles, fast chat with Deuce Cypress, half an hour back to Homestead. If I left now, I could confirm ID and meet Lisa by 7:00. And tomorrow I'd be free. Finished. Done. On vacation.

Why the hell not? I'd been deputized. The boys and I had bonded over fingernail tats. They might dislike authority, but they weren't going to shoot a cop.

Impulse decision. I packed everything back into the cooler, grabbed Lisa's keys, and headed for the car.

I hadn't counted on Miami's rush-hour traffic. Or the brain-scorching glare of the setting sun. Or the geriatric way I navigated the dirt track.

By the time I pulled up to the Cypress brothers' shack it was almost 7:00. I dug out my phone to let Lisa know I'd be late. Cursed. No signal.

As dusk gathered and the light faded, I began to regret my impetuous move. Deuce and Ernie pose no threat, I told myself. And Buck is definitely not home. No worries. Ask about the broken arm and vamoose.

I got out of the car. Listened. No gunshots. No *tic-tic*ing from Lisa's Prius. Nothing but the croaking of frogs and the whine of mosquitoes.

I was debating my approach when the little bloodsuckers hit. That got me moving. Again cursing the swamp, I mounted the front porch and knocked on the screen door. It rattled against the jamb. No one appeared. I banged harder. Same nonresponse.

I hadn't considered that the brothers might not be home. I was slapping and scratching when my ear caught a sound that wasn't a night bird or some small hunting creature. I cocked my head and held my breath, trying to pinpoint the source.

Stepping from the porch, I circled to the spot where Deuce had appeared the previous day. Cautiously. I didn't want to alarm Rooster, the man-eating dog.

Same motif as out front. Heaps of rusting junk piled black and angular in the growing dimness. Tetanus appeared to be the greatest threat back here.

I picked my way around the rear of the house. Heard voices. Saw a muddy path leading toward water. Started down it.

Deuce and Ernie were lounging on rickety lawn chairs, eyeing the marsh and smoking. A whiff told me their roll-your-owns weren't tobacco.

"Yo!" I called.

Deuce's head swiveled as his free hand grabbed the shotgun leaning against his armrest. Ernie smiled in my direction.

On seeing me, Deuce's eyes registered confusion, then recognition. He peered over my shoulder, probably expecting to see Yellen. The sheriff's absence seemed to surprise him. His shoulders relaxed a micron, but the Remington stayed tight in his grip.

"What's up, lady?" he said, stubbing out his joint. Ernie continued beaming.

My gut clenched. I hate to deliver news of death. Especially death by murder.

Deuce read my face. "It's Buck, ain't it?"

"When did you last see him?" I asked gently.

"'Bout two weeks."

"Did your brother ever break his arm?"

"Sure!" Ernie piped up. "Gator chomped him really, really good."

"It was a lunge performance," Deuce confirmed. "Wrangler taps the gator on the nose. That day, the gator lunged early. Dragged Buck into a roll. Broke his arm and ripped him open palm to elbow. They took his sorry ass away in an ambulance."

Ambulance meant hospital. Hospital meant X-rays.

"Which one?"

"Kendall Regional."

"Does Buck have a fingernail tattoo like yours?" I knew the answer.

Ernie nodded enthusiastically. "Buck's the oldest."

"What happened to him?" Deuce's eyes had gone as dark as his tone.

"What he deserved." The voice came out of nowhere. Cold. Male.

My body tensed as adrenaline shot through me. Had I been wrong about Buck? Impossible.

Night changes your perception, your sense of distance and orientation. I couldn't tell how far away the guy was, had no idea where he stood lurking, watching us.

I peered into the darkness, heart banging, mouth dry. Finally, at three o'clock, I noted a flick of movement. There was a reshaping of the shadows at the edge of the forest. A flash of fair skin. The glint of an eye. Then Scott Pierce came into dim focus.

I glanced at the brothers. The expression on Deuce's face was unlike any I'd seen there before. The man was terrified.

I looked back at Pierce, every instinct on hyperalert.

"The Remington. Kick it over here."

Deuce tossed then kicked the shotgun toward Pierce, hands raised in submission.

"Pierce. You startled me." Though my tone was casual, my brain was whirling.

"My bad."

"A little outside your jurisdiction, aren't you?" I was pleased at the steadiness of my voice.

"Easy to get lost in the glades." Pierce kept his eyes on Deuce. "Easy to screw up."

"We ain't done nothin' wrong." Deuce's tone was half defiant, half pleading.

"You morons do just about everything wrong." Pierce stepped further into the clearing.

"Why are you here?" I demanded.

"Thought you might want protection."

I caught the glint of steel in Pierce's hand.

"Yellen sent you?" My mind was clicking at warp

speed. Disjointed pieces were sliding into place. The humiliation of losing an ad campaign. The jotted words that read like places in a national park. A photo of a python skin used by women fingered for illegal procurement.

"Sure did," Pierce said.

Except Yellen didn't know I was coming tonight. Had Pierce followed me?

"I'm good," I said. "Sorry you made the long trip for nothing."

More pieces. Hostile behavior at the rangers' station. Unsupervised time in the locker room.

"Can't have a city gal running around all by her lonesome. This swamp's a dangerous place." Pierce began walking toward us.

"Yellen's on his way," I lied, heart hammering against my ribs.

"Yellen ain't coming." Pierce called my bluff.

As the ranger cop drew closer, details of his appearance emerged. A flashlight in his waistband. A Glock in his hand. A deadly look in his eyes. The bulge of an object in his shirt pocket.

My flight instinct screamed for me to take action. I held my ground and squinted to make out the bulge. It was leaf-shaped. With a spiral along one side.

Sudden recognition.

Kiley James's journal.

"I'm leaving anyway," I said.

I had to get out of there. Pierce had murdered and dismembered Kiley James and Buck Cypress. I'd stumbled onto his secret. Now he wanted me dead.

I turned and started toward the car.

"That's not going to happen."

Pierce raised the Glock and pointed the barrel dead between my eyes.

CHAPTER 10

"What the hell are you doing, Pierce?" I held my voice steady, despite the gun pointed at my face.

"Taking care of a problem."

Deuce and Ernie were frozen in place. No help coming from that direction. My best tactic was to stall, look for an opening. Then what?

Whatever it took to survive.

"You killed Kiley James over a modeling job?"

Pierce looked surprised. Then irritated. "The gig was mine. She stole it."

"That justifies murder?"

"Revenge for the Eugene beat-down was just icing on the cake. Nosy bitch was into everyone's business. Taking her out was reward in itself."

"She discovered you were poaching."

Pierce's lips curled in a reptilian smirk. "Big thanks to Yellen for the shout-out on the journal. You understand why I had to get it first." He actually laughed. "But even I didn't know how useful it would be."

"What do you mean?"

"Miss Busybody had the number of every poacher

in the swamp. Proof, too. Places. Dates. Photos. Everyone except for me." He shook his head at the irony. "I didn't even earn an honorable mention."

To Deuce, he said, "But she was all over you and big brother. Recorded everything but the length of your dicks. Ole Buck shouldn't have pissed her off with his wandering hands."

"She'd have been onto you soon enough," I said.

"Life's all about timing." He shrugged. "She was here raging at Buck when I came to drop off a snake."

"Why'd you kill him?" Deuce's voice hitched. "Buck never done nothin' to you."

"Your brother was dumber than a bag of rocks," Pierce snarled. "James knew every detail of our setup. Buck's stupidity is forcing me to relocate my whole operation."

"Not to mention he saw you commit murder."

At my words, Pierce swept the Glock in an arc taking all of us in. "Start walking," he commanded, stabbing the barrel toward the woods. "Hands where I can see them."

We complied, arms raised. Mud squelched underfoot as we marched single file along a path tunneled over with dense broadleaf canopy.

It was now full night. The woods were thick and black. And alive with tiny sounds. I imagined all sorts of creatures going about their nocturnal business, invisible, annoyed at our passing. I heard water to my right but saw not a glimmer of reflected light.

I was following the two brothers, with Pierce directly behind me. His flashlight beam was a pale yellow oval probing the path at our feet. I sensed the Glock at my back. Felt bullets ripping through my spine, tearing my innards, shattering my ribs. Pictured my blood pooling on the ground. My body in some remote corner of the swamp, my friends and family never knowing what happened to me.

I could hope for nothing from my fellow captives. Ernie was childlike. And the fight had gone out of Deuce when I'd confirmed Buck's death.

Desperate, I tossed questions over my shoulder. "How are you going to explain killing us?" I expected no answer, but Pierce surprised me.

"I'm not going to kill you." I twisted my head to see him. Pierce's eyes were cold and hard in the dark recesses of his face. "You're going to kill each other."

"You're sick," I spat.

"They find this baby"—he tapped the notebook in his breast pocket—"they'll figure you died in a three-way shoot-out. Cypress boys take the fall. No shock. No tears."

"That'll never fly."

Pierce jabbed me roughly with the Glock. "Keep moving."

I pivoted and began walking again, as slowly as I dared without arousing suspicion. "Yellen will spot a staged scene in a heartbeat."

"How much scene do you think will be left by morning? It's the swamp."

"We found both Kiley and Buck." In my mind I saw the mangled remains. Forced myself calm.

"Fluke. Anyway, it's irrelevant. The swamp will take care of the corpses. If not, the journal will explain why they're out here."

Ahead, I could hear the steady slogging of boots. Sniffling I assumed was coming from Ernie.

"No need for the chain saw. Blood. Calluses. All that mess." Pierce sounded like the voice of madness. "Easy breezy."

Mosquitoes swarmed my face and feasted on my neck and arms. My mind ricocheted in a million directions. Turn and charge Pierce? Run for the trees? Make a break and dive into the marsh?

The woods were dark as a tomb. What time was it? Eight? Nine? Would Lisa phone Yellen when I didn't come home? Would he drive out here? How long would it take?

The path reached a clearing. Overhead, the sky was a black dome peppered with tiny white dots. No moon.

In the center of the clearing, a collection of cubes hulked darkly opaque against the slightly lighter backdrop of the dome. They looked like crab traps— wooden frames wrapped in finely woven chicken wire. Inside each crate I could see the silhouette of a coiled snake.

The heart of the operation. Stacked in threes and fours, there must have been two hundred crates.

"Anyone want to snuggle with a python?" Pierce's laugh was pure evil.

I felt panic rise like a white-hot heat.

Pierce again thrust the gun barrel between my shoulder blades. "Keep walking."

We passed through the clearing and picked up the track on the other side. Narrower now. Twigs and leaves grabbed my hair and clothing. Mosquitoes still gorged.

My eyes scanned continually, assessing, picking out nuances in the darkness around me. I noted a small gap in the trees ahead and to my right. My brain flashed an image. Steep conical sides. Sinkhole.

The width or depth of the hole was impossible to know, but somehow I had to take advantage of the break in vegetation without getting mired in the depression. I'd have only seconds. The plan was risky, but it beat certain death.

Deep breath. Tense to the balls of my feet, I forced

myself to wait until the optimal moment. When we reached the small breach, I two-hand-shoved Ernie into Deuce. They pitched forward and hit the ground in a tangle of limbs.

Not hesitating, I leapt right, hurling myself across the little depression. The sinkhole spring was maybe two feet across. I hit the far edge hard, knocking air from my lungs and causing them to spasm. Gasping, I tucked into a ball and rolled, relying on the downslope to keep me moving.

Behind me, shots rang out. Expecting fiery lead to rip through my flesh, I staggered to my feet and began running as fast as I could. Branches and scrub vegetation tore at my hair and sliced my skin. Roots and vines grabbed my ankles.

Distance. More distance. This was the mantra in my brain.

I ran on.

My heart hammered. Blood pounded in my ears.

Again, the crack of gunfire. More muted. Aimed in another direction?

A cry.

Another crack. A muffled thud.

Feet pumping, I chose speed over furtiveness. Far from quiet, I stumbled through the dark, snapping twigs, splashing mud, panting for air.

Spotting a stand of live oaks, I aimed for the largest and flattened my back against its trunk. Pain knifed both my sides. My lungs screamed for air. Sweat stung my eyes.

I struggled to slow my breathing and the thumping of my heart, all the while straining to listen for signs of pursuit.

Every sound seemed menacing. Was that wind or a snake slithering through leaves? A croaking frog or a gator testing its voice? A marsh bird or a clip snapping into a Glock?

I closed my eyes and tried to visualize the route I'd driven to the Cypress brothers' shack. Failed. Decided to continue in the direction I was headed, hoping to reach a canal or road. Placing each foot carefully, I set off again. Stealth my priority now.

Suddenly, the trees thinned and the ground dropped off abruptly. Realizing too late, I lost my balance and, arms pinwheeling, careened downward into knee-deep mud and brackish water.

End of the hammock. For the first time all night, I was grateful there was no moon. Feeling exposed, I slip-slid back up the bank and, making myself as small as possible, crouched to regroup.

"What the buzzard!" For the second time, a disembodied voice caused me to flinch.

A new round of adrenaline firebombed through me. I slid back into the muck, but the marsh grass provided little cover. Swim? The shore of the hammock curved sharply to my left. A short underwater trip and I could be out of sight.

"Don't move," the voice ordered.

Not Pierce, but who?

Trying not to show movement, I ran my fingers through the slime at my feet, groping for a rock, a stick, anything to serve as a weapon.

"You might as well holler 'Here, gator gator.'" The voice was male. Familiar.

"Jordan?" I hissed. Friend or foe? Why was he here?

"Who's askin'?"

"Tempe."

No response.

"The bone doc."

"What the hell are you doing in the swamp at night?"

Water rippled to my left. Close. I turned only my head, slowly. Saw nothing.

I was about to reply to Jordan, when something smooth and solid brushed my arm underwater. Something thick and long. Very long.

My heart leapt into my throat.

"Dammit," Jordan boomed. "You just cost me a sixteen-footer."

A tall shadow shaped up on the hammock and splashed toward me. A strong hand wrapped my upper arm and yank-lifted me up the bank.

"One more second and she'da gone for that crane." His words didn't penetrate. "I'da had her."

"Shut up!" I was desperate to quiet him.

"What kind of stunt are you tryin' to pull?"

"Listen to me right now." I thrust my face close to his and put all the force I could into a loud whisper. My intensity got his attention. "Scott Pierce killed Kiley James. Buck Cypress. Maybe all three brothers. Now he's trying to kill me."

"The NPS cop?" Dubious, but at a more subdued volume.

"Pierce is armed and crazy. Believe me or don't, but we need to move fast. Where's your boat?"

Jordan jerked a thumb over one shoulder.

"Let's go. Now."

Nothing gave Pierce away until the bullet hit Jordan. The big man spun, face contorted, then flopped into the water at my feet. I dropped, too, and huddled behind his bulk.

Pierce charged from the hammock, Glock leveled in two outstretched hands. I was preparing to dive when Jordan fountained up from the water, arm rising in one smooth move, a handgun aimed at Pierce.

Jordan squeezed the trigger. *Crack!* Pierce stumbled backward, a dark circle blossoming on his chest. Jordan held position, feet spread, gun steady, as the ranger cop staggered and fell into the marsh.

Serpentine ripples glided toward Pierce. Something dark and slender flicked below the surface and was gone.

Pierce flexed to lift his gun.

The gator struck.

Pierce struggled, but the animal lunged from the shallows and clamped its powerful jaws on the ranger's upper arm. The scream was high and piercing. And brief.

Pierce twisted and flailed as the gator dragged him deeper. Then the rolling began. I couldn't watch. I couldn't look away.

Desperate thrashing as the gator revolved a helpless Pierce over and over. Seconds. Minutes. An aeon. Then the marsh was quiet. The water dark and opaque, enveloping its terrible secret.

My eyes flew to Jordan. The wrangler stood frozen. I felt sick.

"Should we . . . ?" I let my question dangle.

"Out. Get out of the water." Jordan put a surprisingly gentle hand on my back and guided me up onto shore. His other arm was crooked inward at an odd angle. A river of black stained his khaki shirt, its origin in the region of the collarbone.

Jordan saw my pale face. My expression of horror.

"What could you have done?" he said quietly.

I had no answer.

"Enough for one night," Jordan said. "Let's hit that boat."

CHAPTER 11

"How was your day?" I called from the hammock when the patio door slid open.

Lisa dropped into a chair and kicked off her shoes. "In addition to python guts, I got a mallard that dive-bombed into a ranger's Ford pickup."

"Grilled duck for dinner?"

She laughed. "Let's stick with tacos." Her face grew serious. "How are you doing?"

Lisa had been fluttering over me ever since the Great Glades Gunfest.

"I'm peachy." I really was. I'd spent three days sleeping late, snorkeling, sunning on the beach, and lazing in the hammock, book spread open on my chest as I napped. Reading by osmosis. I'd even gone back to the national park to hike. Turns out an Everglades vacation isn't so bad.

"Want to talk?" she asked way too casually.

"Lisa, my only problem is a paper cut from a postcard for Katy." I held up a finger. "What do you want to know?" She'd waited three days to ask for specifics, giving me space.

"Everything. What happened? Why'd he do it?"

"Scott Pierce was poaching big time. Mega-irony. Kiley learned of it via the Eugene fashion sisters. The dolts put her in a pair of albino-snakeskin pants for a shoot. The skin had an unusual marking pattern. Kiley knew it came from a microchipped python that had been released in the national park."

"Wait. I thought the park service was trying to kill the snakes?" Lisa was confused.

"They chip-and-release some males during the breeding season, hoping the transmitter will lead them to mating aggregations where they can catch more snakes, especially reproductive females."

"Kiley actually recognized an individual python?"

"It was an albino with distinctive markings." I bet the Eugene sisters went batshit over the white-on-white hide. "Since pythons like to stay within fairly limited home ranges, Kiley knew the snake had to have come from the national park. Pythons can find their way home even when relocated twenty miles away." I was becoming quite the herpetologist. "The notes I found in Kiley's locker were a listing of the albino python's last transmitter coordinates."

"And harvesting from the park is illegal."

"Felony. Kiley was waging war against poachers. The main reason she took the modeling gig was to fund her crusade."

"How'd she finger Pierce?"

"Actually, the one she nailed was Buck Cypress. Using the albino's transmitter coordinates, she set up surveillance. Caught Buck on tape pulling a female."

"Buck worked for Pierce."

"Yes."

"Rangers are supposed to protect wildlife." Lisa's tone was a mix of repugnance and outrage. "Why'd he do it?"

"Same reason most people kill. Money. Pierce works

a python beat, knows that illegally traded skins are a billion-dollar annual industry."

"Seriously?"

"European fashion designers are rabid for snake-skin. In Indonesia, Malaysia, Cambodia, and Vietnam wild pythons are quickly becoming endangered."

"Which drives prices up. Which creates a black market."

"Bingo. The Eugenes bought local on the cheap. Not just pythons, either. Alligators, too."

The Miami Herald had run a front-page story covering the raid on the Eugene production factory. I'd particularly liked the above-the-fold shot of the four ladies shielding their faces as they hurried from a downtown cop shop. The caption read: "Snake harmers." One photo op the sisters would rather have skipped.

"Aren't there plenty of legal skins? From the extensive python hunting?"

"Not enough to make serious coin, legal or otherwise. Especially since hunters can't harvest in the national park."

"But Pierce was. Hunting in the park."

"More than that. He was capturing wild females and breeding them."

"Grow your own. Also illegal."

"Very. Breeding is prohibited by federal law. Violation carries up to five years of jail time."

"All these new laws to address the python problem." Lisa sighed. "It's a bit of closing the stable door after the horse has bolted."

"True. And the regulations create a perfect climate for illicit trade. Current breeders are grandfathered, but they can't transport or sell snakes across state lines. In Florida, ownership of a python requires a hundred-dollar annual permit. If the snake has a diameter greater than two inches, a tracking microchip must be implanted. Owners also have to prove their handling skills. The U.S. snake-loving community is huge, and the reptile industry trade association is up in arms, suing to overturn what they view as overly restrictive laws."

"Lots of incentive to go rogue."

"That and the moolah," I said.

"Pierce was in it for the cash. How did the Cypress brothers fit in?"

"They ran the day-to-day operations. Cops found cages full of breeding females and hatchlings on their property. The brothers fed, killed, and skinned the snakes. Had a setup for tanning—that's how they remove and treat the skins. Made the deliveries."

"Why'd Pierce kill Buck?"

"With Kiley, Buck, and Pierce all dead, it's hard to know for certain. Our best guess is that Kiley went to confront Buck. Pierce showed up, and she put two and two together. Pierce shot her, then did Buck to cover his tracks. Yellen's deputies found a chain saw in a shed on Pierce's property, blood and tissue in the blade. Guy's a sociopath."

"The good lookers often are." Lisa rose. "I'd better clean up. We've got to go soon."

I gave a thumbs-up. "Ready when you are."

Through the screen I heard a double chime.

"I'll get it. You go get ready." I rolled from the hammock and headed through the house to the front door.

There on the porch was Sheriff T. Yellen. "Howdy," he said.

I gave him a "Come in" gesture. Yellen followed me to the kitchen and perched unsteadily on a stool.

"Big week for you," I said. "Nabbed an arsonist

and a murderer, shut down a meth lab, and busted an illegal snakeskin op."

Yellen flapped a dismissive hand. "It's Florida. You headin' home soon?"

"Tomorrow," I said. I thought about the call I'd gotten from the ME in Charlotte. About the calls I hadn't gotten from Andrew Ryan. Wondered where he was. What we'd say to each other if ever he phoned.

Nope. Not tonight.

"They find Pierce?" I asked.

Yellen shook his head. "Not likely to. Gators drown their prey real solid. After the death roll, the ole boy probably jammed Pierce under a submerged log for marinating. He'll dine at his leisure."

All righty then.

"And the Cypress brothers?" I asked.

"Swamp rats are either too stubborn or too stupid to die. They lost a lot of blood, but they'll both make it."

Me too, I thought. I estimated I was a quart down due to mosquito consumption.

Yellen went on. "Ernie'll get a pass, 'cause of his limited thinkin' ability. He probably knew nothing about the murders, and wouldn't have understood the snake operation. Kid's got no criminal record. But Deuce'll serve time enough for the both of 'em."

"For murder?"

"Poaching and breeding. The killing's all on Pierce. I'll be thanking the next gator I see for saving the state the cost of a trial."

We were quiet another moment.

"Nice shirt." The pink and blue Hawaiian print stretched across Yellen's paunch like a tablecloth at a luau.

"Nice whirly-do you got going with your hair," Yellen snarked back.

"Gotta look good for my first rodeo." I grinned.

Yellen grinned back. Then held up four tickets stamped HOMESTEAD CHAMPIONSHIP RODEO. "Southernmost ropin' in the continental US of A. Consider it your paycheck from the great state of Florida."

"Will Jordan meet us there?" I picked up my purse.

"Yep. Got his heart set on riding a bull. Give new meaning to the name Dusty."

"Ready!" Lisa joined us, now in denim, a tee, and a cowboy hat. "Let's go watch us some wrangling!"

We trooped out into the soft Florida evening.

Not such a bad vacation after all.

AUTHOR'S NOTE

Swamp Bones was conceived during rush hour. As I fumed in my car, going nowhere, a story about the Smithsonian ornithologist Dr. Carla Dove and microscopic feather identification came on NPR. The piece caught my attention because, like me, the aptly named Dr. Dove was applying her dry, academic (or as TV *Bones*'s Agent Seeley Booth would say, "squinty") knowledge to real-world problems. Just as the fictional Dr. Temperance Brennan uses the skeleton to identify human victims, Dr. Dove was using her expertise to determine bird species from feather "remains." Both were catching culprits, in Tempe's case murderers. By classifying birds ingested into aircraft engines (bird strikes), Dr. Dove was helping the aviation industry build safer engines and arming airfield managers with habitat information to discourage avian use.

The NPR story focused on a different form of strike: birds as victims of ambush predators. Specifically, there's a Burmese python epidemic in the Everglades. The Burmese python, one of the largest snakes in the world, is native to Southeast Asia. So what are these giants doing in Florida? Not visiting the Magic Kingdom, I guessed.

An owner no longer wants his pet python. Hurricane Andrew rips through South Florida, releasing the inventory of zoos and exotic-reptile suppliers. Where do these creatures end up? The Everglades.

We may never be certain how the pythons got into the swamp, but it turns out life there agrees with them. Burmese pythons have established a large breeding population across the Everglades' 1.5 million acres. Estimates vary from a few thousand to 150,000 snakes. With their ability to produce up to a hundred eggs annually, and the absence of natural predators, that number will undoubtedly rise.

These guys are impressive. Adults average six to nine feet long, but can grow to twenty-two feet and weigh two hundred pounds. The largest captured in Florida clocked in at eighteen feet eight inches.

They eat well, too. The Burmese python is an "apex predator," dining on raccoons, rabbits, bobcats, wrens, ibis, herons, opossums, deer, and even alligators and panthers. In areas where they have existed the longest, raccoon populations have dropped 99 percent, opossums 98, and bobcats 87. Marsh and cottontail rabbits, as well as foxes, have all but disappeared. In 2012, the Burmese python was added to the federal law used by the U.S. Fish and Wildlife Service to prevent and manage invasive forms. The Lacey Act bans the importation and interstate commerce of listed species. In this case, sort of like closing the swamp door after the horse has already swum off (perhaps to avoid being python chow).

In 2013, the Florida Fish and Wildlife Conservation Commission offered a Python Challenge: Anyone with twenty-five bucks and a hankering to chase snakes could humanely capture and slay the invaders. The monthlong contest offered prizes for the most killed, the longest, the biggest, and so forth. Participants hunted in one of two categories: Licensed Wrangler (the pros) or Everyone Else. Nearly 1,600 hunters came from thirty-eight states, Washington, D.C., and Canada. How many snakes did this veritable army of trackers harvest? Thousands, right? Nope. Sixty-eight. The majority by the professional wranglers. Eighteen by one person alone, veteran permit holder Ruben Ramirez.

Deeming the experiment a success, Florida repeated the challenge in 2016. This time participants were required to complete an online training course and score at least 80 percent on a quiz. Over a thousand got their B-minus or better and showed up to bag snakes. Overall yield: 106 pythons.

Why was such a paltry take viewed as an achievement? Public awareness, for one thing. Also, we return to Dr. Dove. During both Python Challenges, Florida Fish and Wildlife ordered the necropsy of every snake captured. Here's the reason.

As the largest subtropical wilderness in the United States, Everglades National Park provides habitat for a wide array of walking, flying, and swimming creatures. Many are endangered: the manatee, the American crocodile, the Key Largo wood rat, the wood stork, and the Florida panther. Unaccustomed to being hunted by pythons, these animals and birds lack the appropriate instinctual defenses. Postmortem analysis of the pythons would help conservationists learn which species face the greatest threat of becoming lunch.

Feather fragments from python stomachs were bagged and sent to the Smithsonian's Feather Identification Lab. Dr. Dove identified twenty-five avian species in python guts, including the endangered wood stork.

Back to me, stuck in traffic. The morbid turn of my brain. Thinking, This is fascinating. Thinking, There's a story here. What if a necropsy turns up a bone that doesn't belong? What if it's human? I wonder what snake digestion does to human bone. I wonder how Tempe feels about snakes. . . .

Voilà, *Swamp Bones*.

To learn more about
the Everglades python problem, visit
myfwc.com/wildlifehabitats/nonnatives/python.

ACKNOWLEDGMENTS

As usual, I owe a debt of gratitude to others for their help on *Swamp Bones:* For her intriguing data about forensic ornithology, the aptly named Dr. Carla Dove, head of the Feather Identification Lab at the Smithsonian Institution. For his knowledge of pythons and all things Everglades, Dr. Skip Snow, retired Everglades National Park wildlife biologist. For his helpful information about National Park Service operations, National Park ranger extraordinaire Pete Lundberg. And I want to thank my daughter, author Kerry Reichs (*The Best Day of Someone Else's Life, Leaving Unknown, What You Wish For*), for bringing the story of pythons in the Everglades to my attention, and for her unparalleled research skills. Any mistakes or inaccuracies are, of course, mine.

BONES ON ICE

CHAPTER 1

The transport van backed into the receiving bay, dark and silent. Standard. Morgue vehicles have no need of flashing lights or screaming sirens. There's no urgency. Logos on the van's windowless side panels proclaimed: INTERNATIONAL MORTUARY SHIPPING. My daughter, Katy, would've dubbed the thing a rolling kidnap trap.

The doors winged open and two uniformed techs hopped out and circled to the back. The taller of the pair had a shaved scalp marred by angry nicks. The shorter had buzz-cut hair and full-sleeve tattoos starting on his forearms and spiraling up toward rolled cuffs.

The men moved quickly and efficiently, opening the rear doors, hauling an oblong cardboard air tray from the van, and transferring it onto a gurney. It landed with a grating *clunk*.

Snapping on latex gloves, I stepped forward. The carton's outer surface was stamped with three grisly words: HUMAN REMAINS. At one end, HEAD. The latter made me think of directions on a case of wine. THIS SIDE UP.

Shaved Scalp handed me a clipboard thick with paper. I skimmed a death certificate, a burial/transit permit, U.S. embassy international transport documentation, certification of noncontagious disease, an embalmment waiver.

Setting the paperwork to one side on the gurney, I used an X-Acto knife to slice the plastic binders, then eased off the carton's cardboard cover. Inside was a zinc-coated metal container.

I flipped the butterfly hasps to unfasten the lid of the transport coffin. It opened with a hiss and a puff of icy vapor. I pulled back a large subzero gel pack covering the contents like a chill blanket and searched for the body bag's ID data. The orange pouch was bunched, as if its occupant had been restless during the long journey home. After much rummaging, I found the tag, wiped frost from the plastic, and confirmed that the name and numbers matched those on the documentation.

"Will you wait for the container?" I directed my question to either tech.

Tattoo lifted a shoulder. "One use only."

"Seems a waste." Eyeballing the chilled metal box.

Another inky half shrug. "My granddad used one like it for storing fish that he caught."

Shaved Scalp shot his partner a look of annoyance. To me, "If that's all, ma'am?" Ready to go. Another corpse awaited. Another passenger who wouldn't complain.

"That's all. Thanks."

While Shaved Scalp started the engine, Tattoo closed the van's rear doors with a double *thunk* and climbed into the passenger side. Quick finger wave, and they were gone, leaving me alone with my frozen cargo.

Muscling the gurney through the bay doors, I was relieved to see Tim Larabee, my boss and Mecklenburg County's chief medical examiner, loping toward me. He moved with the wiry grace of a longtime runner. Read: marathon junkie.

"Where do you want me today?" I asked.

"Take her into five."

The new whiz-bang Mecklenburg County Medical Examiner facility, or MCME, completed in 2008 and LEED certified, boasts a shared refrigeration unit and four standard autopsy rooms. Two additional rooms are outfitted with special ventilation and disposal systems for postmortems involving decomps and corpses with potential for contamination. Number five was a "stinky" room and had its own cooler.

"Remind me why I won this lottery?" I wasn't panting, but I was close. My load was heavy and the gurney had a bad wheel.

Larabee regarded me, puzzled but not breaking stride.

"Forensic anthropology? Bones? Mummies? Decomps?" I cocked my chin at the freight I was pushing. "Does this fall into one of those categories?"

"Not exactly." Larabee did something with his lips meant to be a smile. "But, Tempe. You are the Queen of Ice and Snow."

My eyes rolled at the tired old joke. At the label derived from my parallel position as forensic anthropologist for the Bureau du coroner in the Canadian province of Quebec. Yes, I split my time between Charlotte, North Carolina, and Montreal. Long story.

The split, I might add, is truly a wide one. A chasm. Different language, different city, different lab, different justice system. And the big gorilla: different climate. When temperatures move into the sixties,

Charlotteans reach for jackets and gloves. Les Québécois break out their sandals and shorts.

North of the forty-eighth, death comes in ways rarely seen in Dixie. The hunter caught in the unexpected blizzard; the drunk staggering home from a bar; the underdressed driver leaving her broken-down car; the diaper-clad toddler wandering out into the night. Arctic winters mean hypothermia and bodies frozen solid.

Such cases usually don't require my expertise. Cold kills, but it also preserves. I catch the long-gone dead. The family submerged in a frigid lake since the 1950s. The skier mummified for a decade then coughed up by an avalanche. The student fallen into a ventilator shaft and freeze-dried for five winters. Enter the Ice and Snow Queen of balmy North Carolina.

"You know the reward for winning the pie-eating contest, right?" I asked.

Again, the long Larabee stare.

"More pie."

"They asked for you by name."

"So you said."

I pushed through the door into autopsy room five, bum first. As Larabee helped maneuver the gurney, I recalled our previous night's conversation. He'd caught me at the Peculiar Rabbit with my best friend, Anne Turnip. Friday night. Trendy restaurant. Planning a trip to the Turks and Caicos. Not thinking about Ryan. Not thinking about The Proposal. Good times. Larabee's call had not made my evening.

"We have an unusual case." I knew from Larabee's tone the news wouldn't be good.

"Unusual?" Dunking a mussel in wine sauce, then popping it into my mouth.

"Frozen."

I felt an urge to belt out a few lines of "Let It Go." Anne and I were in that kind of mood. Instead I asked about a recent MP. The cops liked the husband for the lady's disappearance, but so far no body. Perhaps wifey had turned up in hubby's subzero.

"Melissa McLaughlin?"

"No. This case involves an accidental death on Mount Everest."

I motioned to Anne that I needed to step away. The restaurant was packed and vibrating at runway decibel level. Obviously I'd misunderstood Larabee.

"Sorry, say that again?" Outside on the street.

"The victim is a Charlotte kid who died trying to summit Everest."

Many questions jockeyed to be first in line. "Nepal is a bit out of our jurisdiction." Or was it Tibet?

Larabee answered indirectly. "The family is . . . well connected. The mother, Blythe Hallis, is a friend of the mayor. And the police chief. And the governor. And . . ."

"I get it." I did. A billion Charlotte landmarks bear the Hallis moniker. A boulevard. A park. A school. An endowed chair at the University of North Carolina at Charlotte. Big bucks. Big philanthropy. Big political influence.

"What's the vic's name?" I asked.

"Brighton Hallis."

"How did she die?"

"It's unclear. There were no witnesses, but the presumption has been a combination of high altitude, hypoxia, exhaustion, maybe disorientation . . ." Larabee let the grim thought hang.

Flashbulb image. Ice. Snow. Vacant-eyed Jack Nicholson from the end of *The Shining*. Despite the warm night, I shivered.

Point of information. The Queen of Ice and Snow detests cold weather. And is not wild about heights. I can't imagine why anyone would want to climb any mountain. Ever.

"What's the PMI?" I was asking about postmortem interval. Time since death.

"Three years."

"Wasn't the kid ID'd in Nepal?" Tibet?

"Yes."

"So what's the problem?"

"The mother's concerned about chaos caused by the earthquake in Nepal. Thinks they'll say anything to move another body along. Wants ID confirmed locally."

"Shouldn't they hire a private—"

"By us."

A truck passed on the street, the driver grinding gears like a dirt biker gunning uphill.

"There's no question of foul play?" Stalling. Larabee had already answered that.

"No. It's a question of peace of mind. You wouldn't believe what was required to bring this girl's body back to Charlotte." Larabee paused. A hitch in his breathing told me something was coming that I wouldn't like. "Mrs. Hallis has requested, specifically and firmly, that *you* do the analysis."

"What? Why?"

"Because you're the best."

"Spare me."

"Should be a piece of cake."

Behind me, a couple argued loudly. Something about beer and a guy named Weed. Or maybe a guy with beer and weed.

My contrary side wanted to be free to plan a summer vacation with Anne. To buy a new swimsuit, maybe some snorkeling fins. I also had to get to Montreal. I didn't need extra work. Especially unofficial "do the mayor's wealthy friend a favor" work.

A woman passed, leading what might have been a poodle. Behind me the squabble ratcheted up. The girl was definitely peeved at someone named Weed.

It shouldn't be that difficult, my helpful side admonished. Dentals. Maybe prints. Match. Done.

Shit. I hated my helpful side.

"When does the body arrive?" Sighing with as much drama as the two at my back.

"Tomorrow, seven A.M."

Seriously?

"Don't worry." At my nonresponse. "I'll be up at dawn, too."

And here we were. At eight-fifteen on a Saturday. In autopsy room five.

"Full-body scan?" Larabee asked.

"Eventually. Do we have antemortem facial shots?"

"Candids. And dentals." Larabee handed me two envelopes I'd seen tucked into his breast pocket, one small and brown, one letter-size and white.

"I'm hoping for visual confirmation. If I can open the jaws, I'll compare dental X-rays. If I can access the fingertips, I'll take prints. Is she in the system?"

Larabee shrugged "who knows."

"Hopefully that won't be necessary for the prelim." I was optimistic about an eyeball ID. Hypothermics are eerily preserved, if bluish, at the moment they slip away. "Once the body thaws, I'll finish a complete analysis."

"Is that necessary?"

"I do the exam right or I don't do it at all."

Larabee accepted this. All or nothing is how I roll. "So today some, Monday some?"

A frozen human isn't like poultry you can zap and tease apart. If hurried, the body's exterior warms faster than the gut, allowing the outside to decompose while the organs remain rock hard. Evidence can be lost. A corpse must thaw slowly, at a steady thirty-eight degrees. Depending on size and weight, the process can last three to seven days. Larabee knew that, too.

"Let's hope she's skinny" was all I said.

"Right. If you need more information, contact Blythe Hallis directly."

"Will do." Fervently hoping no call would be necessary.

"I'll leave you to it." Larabee headed off to have a proper Saturday morning. Maybe to run to Cleveland and back.

After snugging the gurney parallel to the autopsy table, I toed the brake, crossed to the counter, and scooped up the envelope holding Brighton Hallis's dental X-rays. Sliding the contents onto a lightbox, I flipped the switch and arranged the small films by quadrants: upper, lower, front, back. The teeth appeared opaquely pale against the gray of the bone and the black of the background.

A crown on a first maxillary molar and fillings in two mandibular incisors glowed like dense white clouds in the surrounding enamel. I noted an odd curvature to the root of a second mandibular molar. A slight twist to one upper canine. No wisdom teeth.

Happy day. ID would be straightforward.

I crossed back to the metal transport container. Zinc. Good for temperature control, bad for X-rays. I used the wall phone to call for a tech.

While waiting, I masked and reopened the coffin. As before, chill damp air wafted out. Already it carried a hint of something familiar. Something sweet and fetid. Something inevitable. Oh so faint, but already sending out feelers.

On top of the orange body pouch lay a document noting gel pack replacement times throughout the long trip from Kathmandu, a protocol meant to ensure that a corpse remained frozen. International Mortuary Shipping was thorough.

I removed the paperwork and tugged free the gel packs, keeping one, chucking the others. When I'd finished, the body bag lay exposed. Lumps and sharp angles suggested the position of a hip, a knee, maybe a shoulder, a head. I gripped the zipper and tugged. It slid downward with a wet buzzing *whrrrp*.

Most victims of exposure die seated or lying down, perhaps having paused for a "quick rest." That might account for the lumps. Or might not. Other than the gel packs, I had no idea how these remains had been handled in recovery and transport.

The body lay on its side, frozen, curved in on itself. It was fully clothed in serious mountaineering gear, feet encased in bright red gaitered boots. Long strands of hair emerged from a stiff North Face cap. Brassy now, the color was probably once blond.

The sight sent an unexpected wave of melancholy through me. The colorful puffy sport garments conjured images of bracing air, flushed cheeks, youth, adventure. Not sudden death. They did not belong here.

With almost no flesh exposed, I could determine zip about the body's state of preservation. Impatient, I checked the time. Just after nine.

I assessed. The vic appeared to be tall but slender. There was little room in the container, but some manipulation was possible.

Hoping for a glance at the facial features, I grasped the downside shoulder and knee and lifted. Nothing. I tightened my grip, pull-shoved, and the corpse rotated with a soft pop and a rustling sound.

Nose to nose with the grotesque face, my spirits plummeted.

CHAPTER 2

In her pre-ascent photo, Brighton Hallis stood smiling in front of a snowcapped peak. Blond and athletic, she could have stepped from an ad for a Ski Vail campaign. Tan, confident, pretty enough.

The face in front of me was shrunken and stained a deep mahogany brown, the shriveled lips drawn back in a rigor grin. The lidless eyeballs stared at me, disconcertingly lifelike, beseeching. *How did this happen to me?*

There would be no visual ID. Worse, not a tooth remained. In a face otherwise unnervingly intact, the dentition was shattered. Save for an outside chance on the odd root configuration, the antemortem dental records would be useless. Brighton Hallis's charmingly crooked left canine remained as nothing but a jagged splinter.

The tech's arrival interrupted my colorful expletive. He didn't hear it. Or pretended not to. His name badge read J. Ortiz. I didn't know him. I wasn't that familiar with the weekend crew. Yay work-life balance.

After introductions and a brief strategy discussion, we got to work. Ortiz wasn't a talker; I like that in a tech. Together we transferred the remains from the metal container to the autopsy table, then eased them free of the body bag. While Ortiz set up the camera, I penned info onto an ABFO ruler that would act as both scale and photo identifier. Then he snapped pictures as I jotted observations.

For several minutes the only sounds in the room were the squeak of Ortiz's rubber soles and the click of the Nikon's shutter release. Then, "No paradoxical undressing."

At my raised eyebrows, Ortiz expanded. "I did some search and rescue in the Cascades, hikers and climbers lost during storms. Lot of them turned up with their clothes half-off."

Severe hypothermia causes a nasty divorce between body and brain. One short-circuits the other. Disoriented, victims may begin taking off their clothes. The behavior is referred to as paradoxical undressing. Misinterpretations have led more than one investigation down the wrong path, untrained personnel suspecting a sexual assailant instead of Mother Nature.

"Paradoxical undressing occurs in only twenty to fifty percent of cases," I clarified.

"Damnedest thing." Ortiz moved the marker and shot from another angle. "You're freezing, so you strip."

"The cause is unclear, maybe malfunction of the hypothalamus." That is the part of the brain that regulates body temperature. "Or loss of muscle tonus."

"That can make you want to show off some skin?" More repositioning and framing. More clicks.

I gave him the 101 version. "When you get cold, your muscles slow the flow of blood to your limbs. As you weaken, the muscles become exhausted, relax, and there's a sudden surge of blood. This creates a hot flash, which fools people into feeling like they're burning up."

"Some turned animal. We'd find 'em naked, dug into holes."

"Terminal burrowing." Absently.

Terminal burrowing, also called hide-and-die syndrome, refers to victims seeking small, enclosed spaces—hiding under beds, nesting in closets, digging burrows. Another agonal behavior not well understood. Another source of confusion for untrained law enforcement. A body in a wardrobe or trunk taken as evidence of foul play.

Hypothermia: accidental death masquerading as murder.

"Freezing seems a horrible way to go." Ortiz tossed that out unsolicited.

"It's probably like falling asleep." I might have been premature on my "strong, silent" assessment of Ortiz, although I didn't disagree with his statement.

Photos done, Ortiz put the camera away. "You want help stripping him?"

"Her," I corrected. Presumably, her.

"We've got a lot of intake, a four-car wreck out on I-77. But I can stick around if you want."

The failure at visual ID was disappointing. Ditto the absence of teeth. I shook my head. Reluctantly. I was going to have to do this the hard way.

"Go ahead," I said. "I'll call down if I need you."

"I'm here until four P.M." And he was gone.

I should be so lucky.

Before starting my long list of tasks for the prelim, I slipped out to grab a Diet Coke. Thus fortified, I cranked the AC as low as possible and began the most hated part of my job: paperwork.

Dropping onto the stool at the computer terminal, I logged into the network and opened a file. Larabee had assigned a case number: ME215-15. I filled in the date, my name as the investigating anthropologist, and various administrative data. Then I moved on to information about the victim.

Name: Brighton Hallis. Presumed.

I paused, realizing how little I knew about this young woman. Eye color? Height? Weight? Tattoos? Scars? Surgeries? I left all antemortem descriptors blank.

I had one fact. Brighton Hallis was twenty-four when she set off to climb Everest. Same age as my daughter, Katy. The death certificate reported this tidbit, and listed manner of death as "accidental." Meaning what? Hypothermia? Exhaustion? Hypoxia? Blunt trauma from a crack on the head? Botulism from a bad energy gel shot? A coil of rope in the library with Colonel Mustard? Frustrated, I sat back.

Had Brighton been alone at the end? In pain? Frightened? Had she thought of her family? Her best friend? Her dog? Or had death been quick, an odd noise, a change in air pressure, then oblivion?

I pushed these thoughts aside. Channeled scientist. The body would tell the story.

Abandoning the keyboard, I donned the tools of my trade: plastic apron over my scrubs, mask, goggles, fresh latex gloves. Thus garbed, I approached the remains.

The form on the table looked more like a gaudy pile of bundled laundry than a human being. I couldn't help but admire the quality of the North Face and Mountain Hardware garments. Three years' exposure in a harsh high-altitude environment, yet fabric damage was minimal. Macabre brand marketing, but impressive.

Slowly, I worked my way around the body, taking in detail, making notes. Not much to say. The victim liked vibrant colors. The clothes were expensive. When satisfied that I'd missed nothing, I took scissors from an under-counter drawer and began excising fabric in stiff swatches.

Down floated upward, then drifted to rest. I cut through red, yellow, lime green. Polar down jacket and pants. Gore-Tex. Fleece. Thermal long underwear. Layer after layer, like an archeologist digging through strata. No single item had been enough to protect her. Together, they'd fueled the hubris that she was armed against an environment antithetical to life.

Ninety minutes after starting, I reached flesh. Ninety more and the victim wore only her red boots, still frozen to her feet, impossible to dislodge.

In contrast to the dark, desiccated skin on the face and hands, the rest of the body glistened alabaster. And, now that it was unwrapped, I understood its twisted alignment. Brighton Hallis had died and frozen solid while seated, knees partly flexed, torso gently slumped, head tilted to the right, one porcelain arm angled across her chest. Defensive? Movement with her last breath? I suspected Hallis had hardened while leaning, one helpless arm dangling.

I studied her hands, stained and dry as toughened leather. There would be no prints until I rehydrated the fingers.

The lab phone rang. I broke free to answer.

"Brennan."

"Progress?" It was Larabee.

"Some." Not really.

Not the answer he wanted. "Is the body skeletonized?"

"No. The extreme cold protected against putrefaction. At that altitude, there's no scavenging."

"Not even bacteria? Insects?"

"The highest-altitude organism on the planet is a moss that can grow at sixty-five hundred meters. Above that, there's literally no life. Even if something could live that high up, the bacteria responsible for aerobic decomposition don't function below zero Celsius." No rodents, birds, bugs, or microorganisms. None of the usual companions to death.

"So she's intact." A reformulation of his first question.

"The protected parts of the body, yes. But the combination of frigid temperatures and high winds, with a UV assist, led to mummification of the face and hands."

"Like the Iceman."

There are numerous ancient and modern examples of bodies preserved in ice. The most famous is Iceman Ötzi, discovered in the Alps in 1991. Ötzi was so well preserved, he was first thought to be a hiker who'd succumbed to exposure the previous winter. Forensic analysis bumped the date of his passing to 3,300 B.C.

"Exactly."

"That case was extraordinary. They've catalogued his tattoos, ascertained his last two meals, where he grew up, how he was murdered. They've even sequenced his DNA." I'd rarely heard Larabee wax so enthusiastic.

"I'll have all of that by five," I said.

"Leave the report on my desk," Larabee deadpanned back, then disconnected.

I began a mental checklist of my next steps. Topping it was fluoroscopy, meaning a full-body scan. The victim's pretzel position would make that difficult. I elected to wait until she was thawed enough to lay her flat.

Fingerprints. Not easy on a mummy. Rehydration took time. I'm told I have many good qualities. Kindness. Generosity. Humor. Intelligence. Patience is not on the list. I detest waiting.

My stomach grumbled, suggesting I add food to my to-do list. I ignored the input, anxious to get on with what I could.

One hand was accessible. The leathery appendage looked like a workman's glove, at the end of a gypsum arm. Returning to the drawer, I selected a tool that looked like small pruning shears. Positioning the hooked blades around the thumb, I applied pressure to the handles. A lot of pressure. No go. It was like trying to cut through steel.

I considered my options. I didn't like them. That "patience" thing again. But I didn't see a way around it. I didn't want to damage the body.

With nothing left but the waiting, I returned to the dentition. Though I work with bone, I'm fairly competent with teeth. Still, complicated dental analyses fall to the forensic odontologist. Given that Brighton Hallis did not have a single intact tooth, she'd clearly be filed under "complicated."

The jaws were frozen in a half-open grimace. Grabbing a handheld magnifying lens, I adjusted the over-table light and peered in. I couldn't see the entire dental arcade, but one thing struck me as strange. The damage appeared uniform from front to back, on both uppers and lowers. Every tooth was toast from the gum line up. The result of a deadly impact? Had she face-planted into a rock during mountain removal? Or was a three-year wait in an unforgiving climate that tough on teeth?

Back to the computer. A Google search using the

keywords "freezing" and "dentition" revealed that scientists could now harvest and cryo-preserve stem cells from extracted adult molars. Interesting. But not helpful. Too edgy to sit, I left research for another time.

One potential source of information remained. Returning to the clipboard, I reviewed each piece of documentation more carefully. Every page was resplendent with official foreign stamps and indecipherable squiggles I took for Nepali. Tibetan? I had to look that up.

Nothing in the file to enlighten me concerning Brighton Hallis's last moments on earth.

My eyes fell on a phone number with a familiar area code.

Crap.

I braced myself. Then I picked up the handset and dialed.

A man answered on the second ring. Deep bari-
tone, full of smoke and grit. Or maybe the guy
was working on a polyp.

"Hallis residence."

"Mrs. Blythe Hallis, please. It's Dr. Temperance
Brennan calling." Delivered with full Katherine Daes-
see Lee Brennan Daughters of Dixie charm. My
mother is pure sugar and peaches on the phone. And
I was trying to contact one of her tribe.

"Please wait." Husband? Jeeves the Butler? I
couldn't tell.

I waited. Far too long for my already agitated
nerves.

"Dr. Brennan." The voice was female. A fusion of
cut crystal and Carolina honey. Yep. Mama's folk.
"I've been expecting you."

"Mrs. Hallis, I'm so very sorry about your daughter. We received the remains this morning." *They are
thawing as we speak.* I didn't say that. "Unfortunately, the dentition is badly damaged, a fact that
will complicate positive identification. I was hoping

you might have access to additional medical records or X-rays."

"Of course. Five o'clock today is good for me. Raleigh will provide you with details. Casual, of course."

No asking after my convenience. My preference of time or location. My desire to meet at all. A directive, a presumption of compliance, and she was gone.

A brief pause, then Raleigh was back on the line, dictating an address I knew to be in one of Charlotte's most expensive zip codes. Still couldn't slot the guy.

I hung up, conflicted. While I detest taking orders, I do appreciate telephone brevity. I decided not to dwell. It was my current mantra. Don't dwell on Ryan and his alarming proposal. Don't dwell on Mama and her cancer. Don't dwell on Katy and her deployment to Afghanistan.

My watch read four-ten. Unbidden, a hand floated to my hair. I couldn't see myself, but knew my hasty predawn topknot hadn't improved through the course of the day. And I'd opted to go sans makeup. So be it.

After rolling ME215-15 into the cooler, I hurried to the women's staff lounge and changed from scrubs to the jeans and knit top I'd thrown on that morning. Following a thorough washing of face and hands, I tugged the elastic band from the remains of my do, gave my hair a quick brush, two fast twists, a snap of the binder, and I was ready to go.

As I navigated my Mazda through the late afternoon sun, long strokes of light and shadow kicked across my windshield, flashing the city beyond like an old-timey movie reel. *Flick flick flick.* At first, small businesses and plants whose functions I couldn't imagine. Then the shops, restaurants, and steel-and-glass skyscrapers of Trade and Tryon streets. Johnson & Wales University. Bank of America Stadium.

South of uptown, I took Fourth Street through the heart of the medical district, past the colonial-red-brick-and-modern-box complex comprising Presbyterian Hospital. Shortly I was in Eastover, a neighborhood of stately residences surrounded by overprivileged lawns.

The Hallis home was set back from the street, down a long driveway swooping below oaks that could have gossiped about sightings of Robert E. Lee. After parking in front of elegant double wooden doors, I killed the engine and got out. The air smelled of wisteria and honeysuckle. Of American Express black cards, Italian espresso makers, fifty-year-old Macallan single-malt scotch.

The doorbell placement was so subtle it took some searching. Wasted effort. Before I could ring, the door was opened by a very large freckled man in a very large uniform. Pinstripe jacket, trousers, and tie. No gloves.

Question answered. Raleigh was a butler.

After inspecting my ID for so long I thought he was memorizing the content, Raleigh led me through a marble-floored foyer to a small office that had lost a battle with Laura Ashley. Floral drapes, chintz armchairs, embroidered pillows, desperately complicated rug. Wordlessly, he gestured an ungloved palm toward an overstuffed Regency something-or-other. I perched.

"Refreshments?"

"No, thank you."

"Madam will be taking refreshments."

"Lovely."

When Raleigh had withdrawn, with an unsettling

absence of sound, I inventoried the cluttered space. Felt anxiety rise at the proximity of a quadrillion fragile baroque decoratives. Arms tight to my side, I catalogued porcelain, crystal, wood so polished I could have used my reflection to apply eyeliner. An ornate clock marked time with the cadence of a hummingbird heart. *Tick tick tick tick*.

A large brown envelope lay on an iron and marble sidepiece so petite and scrolly I wasn't sure if it was a desk or an end table aspiring to more. An exterior stamp denoted X-rays.

Hearing the staccato click of footfalls, I glanced toward the door. The woman matched the room. Pale pastel Chanel suit. Oscar de la Renta kitten heels. Diamond the size of a Krispy Kreme donut.

It wasn't just the clothing. In a town changed by a four-decade infusion of big-money bankers and financiers, Blythe Hallis retained a commitment to old-style Southern feminine beauty. And did it well.

Though I knew Hallis's age to be north of sixty, her hair was a flawless ash blond; her pale, softly lined skin was a testimonial to years of sunscreen and wide-brimmed hats. Her body was slim and muscular, suggesting regular workouts with a personal trainer or at an upmarket Pilates studio.

My point, she looked good. Except for her eyes, which were gray and cold. Eyes that suggested she could serve you *sencha* in Haviland Limoges cups, smiling over the rim as you died from the strychnine in yours.

My hostess seated herself on a Queen Anne armchair, crossed her ankles with a steel magnolia elegance as natural to her as drawing breath. I couldn't help noticing the pantyhose. I endure them for weddings and funerals. Maybe. Hallis was wearing them in her own home.

"Thank you for coming."

I got straight to the point. "The ME is eager to settle this matter to your satisfaction, Mrs. Hallis. Any details you can share about your daughter's accident will be helpful."

Blythe Hallis was not a woman to be hurried. Or challenged. "It's after five. Raleigh is preparing tea."

Not a question. An expectation. I said nothing.

"Do you need a writing instrument?" A pointed look at my empty hands.

Not really in the mood to play "Who's Got the Bigger Ones," I dug in my purse for notebook and pen. I was about to begin posing questions when Raleigh appeared with a tea party setup that would've turned the Mad Hatter green. Hallis and I took a few moments pouring and stirring. Then she launched in. Showing who was in charge?

"Brighton was my wild child. And a very gifted athlete. She was good at all sports, but preferred those in which she could excel individually. Did you know she ran high school and college track?"

"I did not."

"She was offered scholarships, but of course that wouldn't have been appropriate." Hallis's tone implied that accepting scholarship money would have been akin to selling one's kidney on the black market. "But it was extreme sport that she truly loved."

"When did she begin climbing?"

"On a camping trip with her father and brothers when she was twelve. She was too young, of course, but I had no say." Long-suffering glance down at fingers curled motionless around her cup. "Brighton was just like her father. My late husband, Sterling, was addicted to the thrill of risk. His poison was speed."

I took a sip of the unwanted tea. Meaning drugs?

"Sterling would've been at the track every weekend

if other responsibilities hadn't kept him away." The cool gray eyes met mine. "It's a definition of insanity, don't you think? Driving in circles as fast as possible, never going anywhere?"

"Mm." Setting my cup on its saucer, the saucer on the table between us. Damn, that was good tea.

"My children were like that, too. Always running loops to get Sterling's attention with one daredevil antic or another."

"Did Brighton sustain any injuries that required medical attention?" Trying to get back on track.

Blythe placed her cup and saucer beside mine, delicately rotated the handle to an aesthetically pleasing position. Or she was being OCD.

"Everything's in there." She gestured to the envelope. "As you'll see, there were many ER visits. Of greatest interest will be a broken ulna and calcaneus."

"Thank you." I helped myself, placing the envelope beside my purse. "Is there anything you can tell me about the events on Everest?"

"Very little, I'm afraid. My daughter passed three years ago. As I understand it, she made the top and died just below the summit on her descent. She was twenty-four."

"You don't know the specific circumstances of her death?"

"I have only secondhand information. I was told that her climbing team had already descended. Bad weather moved in suddenly and there was much confusion." Delivered by rote. A story she'd told before. "The next day another climbing group discovered Brighton's body. They collected her personal effects and had them shipped to me. None of Brighton's team revisited the site."

It sounded callous beyond words. "No attempt was made to recover your daughter's remains?"

Wry twist to the delicately tinted lips. "Do you know anything about conditions on Everest?"

"The climate's not up to my standards." I regretted the quip as soon as the words left my mouth. But the woman's gracious superiority was grating as hell.

"Before ascending, every climber must choose a form of body disposal, opting for leaving remains in place, cremating in Kathmandu, or paying for recovery attempts—a fee that can be upwards of thirty thousand dollars." Another smile lacking humor. "It's also a form of madness, isn't it? Pursuing recreation that requires death disposition? We elected to pay for recovery, of course."

"Of course. Why did it take three years?"

"Mount Everest doesn't care about one's personal preferences."

Hallis took a sip of tea, again centered the cup on its saucer. Again adjusted the handle. Her face remained a mask of composure.

"The area above eight thousand meters is called the death zone. Bodies in the death zone are not recoverable." Eyes lowered. Concealing what? "Rough terrain and lack of oxygen make it far too dangerous. So Brighton remained where she was. Frozen in place. Observed and passed by each subsequent wave of foolish dreamers blind to reality."

"But something changed," I prompted.

"Are you aware there are more than two hundred bodies atop Mount Everest?"

She didn't expect a response. I didn't offer one.

"One section is called Rainbow Valley, named for the multicolored jackets and gear attached to numerous corpses strewing the slope." The gray eyes rose to mine. "Litter has become a real problem up there. In recent years, groups have attempted to clean the mountain and reclaim some of these poor, abandoned souls. Methods for this sort of thing have improved. I contacted one such organization, but Brighton remained out of reach. Until the recent earthquake. I assume you followed reports of events in Nepal? So heartbreaking."

I nodded. The disaster had been all over the news. Death toll over 8,500. A country of few resources devastated. The calamity had been *the* story. Until a fatal train wreck outside Philadelphia lured the media on to the next human tragedy.

Hallis continued. "I'm afraid it's a sad case of one person's misfortune being another person's gain. After the quake, local Sherpas identified bodies sufficiently shifted by avalanche activity to allow recovery. Brighton's was among them. I was happy to pay the bill."

"Your daughter was airlifted out?"

Hallis surprised me with a shard of a laugh. "Isn't it funny the things one learns in the course of necessity?" Deep breath. "Helicopters cannot function above Camp Two. The atmosphere is too thin for safe operation. Absent a life-threatening emergency, airlift to Kathmandu occurs only below Camp One. Cadavers taken from above that altitude must be strapped to canvas and lowered by rope and the body's own momentum, hand lifted over crevasses. At points, the angle is as steep as sixty degrees. The process takes six to eight Sherpas an entire day."

I pictured brittle, frozen bones jouncing down a rocky cliff on a fabric sled. It wasn't a forensically encouraging image. "Rough descent may have introduced further damage to the body," I cautioned.

"Not more than the ascent, I'd hazard." Devoid of emotion.

"I was surprised that the remains arrived at our facility still frozen. International law normally requires embalming."

"International Mortuary Shipping is a highly regarded enterprise. Their personnel were able to acquire the necessary waivers. If possible, I wanted Brighton to arrive home in the same condition in which she left the mountain."

And you are Blythe Hallis, I thought. Friend of the mayor, the governor, probably the pope.

"I'm confident that Dr. Larabee and I can confirm identity. Beyond that, I'm uncertain what our analysis will be able to determine. Three years is a long time in such harsh conditions."

Hallis's eyes locked on to mine. "I know you deal in physical rather than social science, but it's important that you understand how driven my daughter was. Of my three children, she was the most determined, and the cleverest. Once she was set upon a goal, nothing could stop her."

"Did your daughter have experience climbing other top-tier mountains?"

"Oh yes. Her ambition was to complete the Seven Summits. Do you know what that means?"

"Ascending the highest peak on each continent." There. I wasn't a total dunce.

"Brighton began immediately after college. She and Sterling plotted endlessly. Everest was going to be their crown jewel. She was halfway through the cycle when Sterling died unexpectedly."

"Racing accident?"

"Colon cancer. It devastated Brighton. After his passing, summiting Everest became her obsession. My daughter's trust fund allowed her to focus full-time on training. I tried to reason with her. Nothing mattered but that hideous mountain." Hallis blinked rapidly. The first crack in the façade?

I felt a stab of sympathy. A lost husband, a lost daughter. Offspring who'd preferred another parent.

"My point is that when Brighton was focused, nothing got in her way." Hallis had recomposed her face. "It astonishes me that a context as knowable as Everest could have defeated her."

Did the woman cradle the delusion that her daughter was incapable of error? Or was she implying something else? Something more sinister?

Hallis misread my look as one of disdain. "Please don't judge me, Dr. Brennan. I'm no fool. I don't believe my daughter was faultless. But climbing was her passion. She spared no expense on training and equipment. No one was more aware of and prepared for the risks. I simply need to know how she died."

I was confused. Was that the real ask? Point a finger elsewhere so her daughter's image remains unblemished?

"I can't make any promises," I said.

"All I desire is a thorough examination. If there's any indication this accident was caused by faulty equipment or poor instruction, I want to know."

Bingo. Lawsuit. How the wealthy deal with loss. My budding sympathy began to ebb.

"I promise we will do our best." I stood, slung my purse over one shoulder, and tucked the envelope under my arm. "My findings will be in my report."

Hallis rose, the Chanel showing not a hint of a wrinkle.

"I've arranged for you to interview Brighton's climbing team. Dara Steele, Cash Reynolds, and Damon James will meet you at Leroy Fox tomorrow at noon. I left venue selection to them." Her tone apologized for the lowbrow choice of one of my favorite gastropubs. "The bill will come to me, naturally. Feel free to ask them anything. In my experience, they won't offer."

Hallis's smile was accustomed to being returned. I didn't. The woman's assumption of submission was astounding.

"I'll check my schedule," I said.

"My friends and I are grateful for your efforts." No need to name the "friends."

One manicured hand came forward. We shook, Hallis not contacting a molecule more of my skin than necessary.

Outside, the sky was pink streaked with yellow, aiming for night. I stood a moment, listening to the whisper of wind in the ancient oaks. Taking in the smell of crocus nudging through earth newly released from winter's long grip. Enjoying the serenity of an early spring dusk.

Not knowing it was the last peaceful moment I'd have for some time.

CHAPTER
4

Sunday began with a white furry paw batting my nose. Birdie wanted breakfast. After a few ineffective elbow shoves, I gave up and hauled myself out of bed. Sleep hath no enemy like an unrelenting cat.

Bird's penance was to dine solo. I took my bagel and coffee outside to the patio, ignoring a voicemail I knew to be from Ryan. Face buried in kibble, the cat bore the slight with aplomb. Or didn't notice.

Around me, azaleas winked pink and white among the waxy green leaves of bushes planted years before I moved into Sharon Hall. The air was rich with the scent of spores and pollen, with the promise of life and allergies about to burst forth. Over the wall, a lone church bell called out to the faithful.

The sky was unblemished, the sun soft and warm on my shoulders and hair. It was a morning for hiking or biking, for gardening or reading a novel on a lounger. Not for mummified corpses and icy death.

The buzz of my mobile interrupted my thoughts. I answered and clicked off the ringtone silencer in one move.

"You missed a good time last night." Anne and I

had been invited to a dinner party at the home of a mutual friend. She'd gone, I'd bailed. After meeting with Blythe Hallis, I'd been too bummed.

"But I'm enjoying a great morning." Garbled by cream cheese and dough.

"What are you eating?"

"Bagel."

"How's the corpsicle?" Never subtle, and not totally sober, Anne had phoned the previous evening demanding the whole story. Naming no names, I'd given her the bare bones.

"Frostier than a Greco-German economy summit," I said.

"Good one." Anne and I liked making up outlandish similes. It was a game we played.

"Strained," I said.

"A bit."

For a moment, empty air hummed across the line. I took another bite of bagel. Coffee. Anne spoke first.

"My view? Jumping out of planes or scrabbling up precipices is batshit crazy."

Amen to that.

"It's still sad," I said. "Life shouldn't end at twenty-four. But I agree. I don't see the point of deliberately endangering yourself for a rush. Hang gliding. Crocodile bungeeing. BASE jumping. Ice climbing."

"Buying sushi from a street vendor in Tijuana."

"Why do it?"

"Costs less."

"I mean extreme sport." Eyes rolling. Which she couldn't see.

"The thrill of the chase? The chase of the thrill?"

"More like a subliminal death wish. Did you know that the odds of dying in a random accident are three percent? The odds of dying on Everest are more than double that. This kid had everything. Now she's lying in a cooler with a tag on her toe." Close enough.

"Aren't you being a teeny bit hypocritical?" Anne needled.

"What?"

"You're always all clappety-clap for women who put it all out there."

"What are you talking about?"

"Amelia Earhart? Sally Ride? Diana Nyad?"

"That's totally different."

"Is it?"

The conversational twists and turns were making me dizzy. An effect not uncommon when talking to Anne. I switched tack.

"The mother claims all the daredevil antics were for Daddy's approval."

"Well blow me down. Do I hear shades of connection to young Tempe and her elusive mother?"

"Why is it you called again?" Mock annoyed.

Anne launched into a tale of a morning adventure involving a hose, a raccoon, and a badly bruised knee. I half-listened, chewing and inserting comforting sounds at appropriate points. Following a particularly long pause, I said, "Good for you."

"It was his ass or mine."

"Gotta run."

"Seeyalaterbye." I always appreciate Anne's speedy disconnects.

I raised my chin, eyes closed, to let the fast-warming rays bathe my face. In my mind I saw Blythe Hallis in her chic couture and designer makeup. Recalled her arrogance. Also remembered that moment when the mask slipped. Whatever her faults, the woman had lost a daughter.

I rose, massaging the waffle ironwork pattern imprinted on the backs of my thighs. There was little point in going to the lab. No way ME215-15 could be thawed yet. But what the hell? I'd give it a shot.

I stopped mid-step, mug and plate half off the table. Was that where Anne had been going? Was I driven? Was I like Brighton Hallis after all?

The MCME facility was deserted save for a minimal weekend crew, and humming with such absence of activity that every sound seemed to crack like gunfire. A puff of HVAC air hitting a vent. A door clicking shut. A phone ringing out of sight down a hall. I geared up, went to autopsy room five, and rolled Brighton Hallis from her chilly overnight resting place.

The porcelain skin had grown pallid and lost its gleam. I pressed a thumb into the flesh of one shoulder. Noted some softening. Encouraged, I tried flexing the right elbow. While far from supple, there was some give. Mimicking therapy Gran had undergone following knee replacement surgery, I massaged each limb, slowly, methodically, in my mind easing the body toward prone. Ninety minutes later, my headway could have been measured in fractions of microns.

"It's a start. You'll do better tomorrow." Rewrapping the girl on the table in plastic sheeting. "Soon we'll have you flat enough for Victorian sex."

Jesus! Did I really say that? Time to go.

Stripping off gloves, mask, and apron, I washed up and headed to Leroy Fox, a spot with several things in its favor: Good food. Easy parking. Proximity to home. Not part of the ladies-who-lunch set, I was pleased Blythe Hallis had left venue selection to others.

Bingo. A spot right at the door. Inside, the décor

was industrial chic meets locker-room manly. All around, balls of various sizes and shapes were dribbled and arced and pitched and scratched on screens sharp enough to beam satellite images from Mars. The hostess, a twentysomething in tight top and black jeans, whispered "Hallis" to her cohort, another twentysomething in tight top and black jeans. Smiling broadly, a mistake given the calamity that was her dentition, Black Jeans Two led me to one of a row of booths lining the back wall.

A man and woman sat shoulder to shoulder on one bench. Neither looked on speaking terms with thirty. Hearing my approach, they exchanged slicing sideways glances before facing me, expressionless. I took the woman to be Dara Steele. Him, I wasn't sure.

"Dr. Temperance Brennan." Thrusting a hand forward and flashing my most disarming smile.

Steele's grip was as limp as her straggly ponytail. Dropping her hand to her lap, she recoiled as though trying to mold her skinny frame into her companion's negative spaces.

"Cash Reynolds." The guy shook with more snap, but zero friendliness.

"May I?" Cocking my chin toward the empty bench.

Reynolds nodded, making as little eye contact as possible.

I slid into the booth, discreetly assessing the pair. Reynolds was big and muscular, probably used to being told he was good-looking. Dark brown eyes. Walnut hair carefully arranged to look carelessly disarranged. Toned forearms bulging from rolled chambray cuffs. Steele looked like a colorless scarecrow burrowing into his leftover air.

"Mrs. Hallis said I'd be meeting with three members of Brighton's team?" Inflection implying the question.

"Damon's late." Reynolds, one thumb working condensation on the side of his mug.

"As usual." Steele's pitch suggested she wasn't amused.

A waitress appeared at our booth. Yep. Tight top and black jeans. Hers were draped with a little apron tied at the waist.

"Who knows with Damon. We should order." Without querying my readiness, Reynolds asked for burgers and fries for himself and Steele, refills on their ginger ales. Showing he was a take-charge guy? Anxious to be gone? A self-focused prick?

Reserving judgment for the moment, I went with fried chicken, fried zucchini, and Diet Coke. What the hell? It was Sunday. And I hadn't had time to read the menu.

"Thanks for meeting with me." As though we'd gathered by choice. "I'd like to learn as much as possible about what happened on Everest the day Brighton died."

Again, the flicking eyes, the closed faces. And a whole lot of silence.

Seconds ticked past. A full minute. Another.

Alrighty, then. New approach. Side door. "How did you all meet?"

"SheClimbs Charlotte." Steele sounded, well, steely. "It's a women's climbing group."

Reynolds looked uncomfortable. And silent. Red burned high on each of his cheeks.

"Go on, Cash." Steele prodded. When Reynolds didn't comment, she did. "Brighton and Cash used to date."

"Christ, Dara. Let it go!"

Steele's eyes dropped and her body drew inward, like that of a chastened puppy.

"You and Brighton were a couple?" Directed to Reynolds.

"Briefly."

"On Everest?"

More silence.

"Depends who you ask," Steele answered cryptically. Reynolds studied his fork.

I was about to follow up when our waitress delivered enough food to feed a ninth grade. We took a moment with seasonings and condiments and dipping sauces. Then I asked, "Who else was on your Everest team?"

"Damon James was Bright's business partner," Steele answered, after a glance at Reynolds, who ignored her. "She knew Elon Gass from college. Bright began pulling together an Everest team, like, eons before the contest."

"Contest?"

"Reality show," Reynolds corrected. "*The Heights*. Like Anthony Bourdain's *Parts Unknown*, but about mountaineering. The production company was looking for a host. The climbing community was going apeshit."

"Brighton wanted to be cast?" To Steele.

"Who didn't? Get paid to wear cool gear, travel to amazing places, test out hotels and commercial guide groups, be a celebrity? Everyone was wetting their pants to get picked."

"Including you?"

Blank look.

"Were you hoping to be picked?"

One bony shoulder lifted ever so slightly.

"Like that was ever gonna happen." Reynolds's tone was harsh. I was definitely leaning toward the prick theory. "Right out the door, these guys loved Brighton. She was sure the gig was in the bag once she nailed the tallest mountain in the world."

"Bright convinced us we needed Everest to be serious contenders," Steele agreed.

"And now the field's wide open." Habit. My brain was already going to a dark place.

Reynolds shook his head. "Elon's their new golden boy. If he ever gets back from Russia."

Steele snorted. "Whatever. They can't pick the dude who turned back before reaching the top."

"Elon didn't summit Everest with you?"

"No. And now he's a finalist. Show's a joke."

It was the most emotion I'd seen from Steele. A sore point?

"So Brighton was your guide?"

"Are you kidding?" Reynolds mashed a fry into ketchup, downed it. "None of us is qualified to be a guide. We're Seven Summits people."

"The highest points on each of the seven continents." I repeated my nugget of climbing knowledge. But something had bugged me since the subject had arisen with Blythe Hallis earlier. I'd gophered around in my freshman-year world geography memories. "Aren't there only six? Africa, Antarctica, Australia, Eurasia, South America, and North America."

"Geologically, yes. Politically, no. Europe and Asia are considered separate, so you include Mont Blanc between France and Italy, and Elbrus, along Russia's southern border with Asia. It's actually eight, because you have to do two for the Oceanic continental mass. Kosciuszko is the highest point on the Australian mainland, but the Carstensz Pyramid of Papua New Guinea is technically taller."

Reynolds might be obnoxious, but he wasn't dumb. I started to ask a question, but he cut me off.

"The point is"—air jab with a fry—"that none of the Seven Summits are extreme mountaineering climbs. Even with the altitude challenges, Everest isn't technical. We thought we were trained and in shape."

"We really thought we could do it," Steele echoed.

"So what happened?" I was growing less patient with their skirting and dodging.

"Altitude."

"Go on." Bunching and tossing my napkin onto my plate. Which was largely empty now.

"We didn't really know what we were getting into. None of us were eight-thousanders."

"Pretend I don't read *Outside* magazine," I said.

"Eight-thousanders are the fourteen peaks in the Himalayan and Karakoram ranges with summits in the death zone."

"Altitudes at which there isn't sufficient oxygen to sustain human life." There. I knew that, too. Tough on humans. Above eight thousand meters, oxyhemoglobin levels plummet.

"We were all death zone virgins." As Reynolds answered, Steele shrank even more, eyes down, face still as a moth on a branch. I gathered she hadn't enjoyed her visit to the death zone. "Everything's a bitch above eight thousand meters. Breathing, eating, pissing, sleeping. Ever hear of HAPE and HACE?"

Reynolds used the acronyms for "high-altitude pulmonary edema" and "high-altitude cerebral edema." In lay terms, fluid in the lungs or brain. Triggered by oxygen deprivation, HAPE and HACE are the primary causes of death related to high-altitude exposure.

"Is that what killed Brighton?"

"What am I, a doctor?" The retort carried some strong emotion. Anguish? Guilt?

Flash of insight. "You weren't with her when she died. Neither of you."

From Steele, a haunted stare. From Reynolds, a nervous thumb working sweat on his mug.

I pushed my plate to one side. Sipped my drink. Let the silence stretch. Reynolds broke it first.

"You don't know what it's like up there."

"Tell me." Waving off the waitress who was heading our way.

"Everything's wrong—the air smells different, your clothes feel different, your food tastes different. *If* you can manage food at all." He paused, struggling, dissatisfied with what he'd just said. "At the top, your brain doesn't work. Taking one step feels like running a marathon."

"I had to walk around a dead body." Steele's voice floated like smoke from her shadowy corner. "My brain was telling me to cry, but all I could think about was getting up, getting down, getting away."

"Getting down is the hard part," Reynolds said.

"That's what got Bright." Steele.

"We've no idea what got Bright," Reynolds snapped, then refocused on me. "The last we saw her, we were going down and she was heading up."

"Why didn't you climb together?" I asked, nothing in my voice.

"Elon turned back at Kangshung Face. He was feeling awful." Steele's pale face was all eyes and trembling mouth. "We lost Bright at the top of the Hillary Step. She—"

Reynolds cut in. "That's a twelve-meter vertical face. The last challenge before the summit. Everyone has to ascend with fixed ropes, and it can turn into a bottleneck. But not that day." Reynolds swallowed. Drew a deep breath. "Bright was ahead of us."

"Always," Steele interjected.

"She stayed at the top to help another climber who was ascending behind us."

"We kept on and made the summit just before turnaround."

"Turnaround?"

"You have to head down by two P.M. or you can't make it back to camp by dark."

I nodded understanding.

"Above eight thousand meters you need supplemental oxygen all the time. You can't bivouac that high because you'll run out. We each had just enough to summit and return." Reynolds sounded defensive.

"We only stayed at the top ten minutes." Steele's saucer eyes were haunted. "No one stays longer than that."

"Dial back the drama, Dara." Reynolds gave a tight shake of his head. "On the way down we passed Bright, about a hundred meters below the peak."

"With a guide?" I asked.

"You kidding? We were too cool for guides."

The voice came down hard from outside our booth. Startled, we all turned.

The man was bearded and sinewy tall, dressed in jeans and a sweatshirt with the sleeves cut off at the shoulders. Holey tee underneath. Boots. Startling green eyes. Uninvited, he dropped to the bench beside me. Assuming this was the tardy Damon James, I slid left to make room.

Chilly nod to the new arrival, then Reynolds resumed his story.

"We used a semi-independent or 'supported' company, as they're called. Sherpas who provide tents, food, supplemental oxygen, fixed ropes. But no guides."

"Because we're badass and can get ourselves up and down unassisted." James was doing sardonic. Maybe his usual demeanor. "Bright's choice. Or *The Heights*'s choice." To me. "They told you about the climbers' Holy Grail?"

"They did." Back to Reynolds. "So Brighton should have been able to summit by turnaround? She had thirty minutes to go ninety meters." The length of a short home run. Three NBA courts. One football field.

Just three sets of eyes, staring.

James spoke first. "Doubtful."

"People don't understand." Steele, forward now, elbows on the table. "You're dizzy all the time. Your brain doesn't work. One morning I sat in my tent staring at boots for God knows how long, clueless which pair was mine. I had to rest twenty minutes between putting them on and tying the laces."

"Imagine climbing a thousand stairs, carrying fifty pounds of gear, breathing only through a cocktail straw," said Reynolds. "One step can take ten minutes. The rule is to never exceed sixty percent of your physical capacity."

"Which is near zero up there," offered James.

"The rule is to turn around by two P.M.," Steele repeated, moving toward petulance.

"Rules meant nothing to Bright." From James. "I tried to talk her into coming down with us but she'd have none of it. She was determined to summit. And absolutely certain it wouldn't take her past time."

"We should've made them turn around," Steele said.

"Them?"

"She and the woman she stopped to help," Reynolds said.

"You couldn't *make* Bright do anything." James, now doing scornful.

Something didn't ring true. "If Brighton was so focused on summiting, why did she stop to offer help at Hillary Step?"

"It was weird." Steele's voice trailed off.

"Weird?" I prompted.

"Bright always had to be first."

"Maybe she did have HAPE or HACE." Reynolds didn't sound convinced. "It's like being drunk. Causes you to make bad decisions."

"It might have been fine, but for the storm," Steele said.

"There was a storm?" Were these guys for real, or feeding me the plot from *Into Thin Air*?

"Squall." James corrected. "It came up fast and slowed everything down."

"We were half-frozen by the time we got to camp," Steele said. "My oxygen regulator was choked with ice. Cash was hallucinating and nearly wandered off the side of the mountain." Disgusted exhale from Reynolds. "We passed out in separate tents. It was after dark when Elon realized Bright hadn't come back."

Again, the feeling their story didn't track. "Nap time over, everyone's ready to share mountaintop selfies, and no one notices your ringleader's not there?"

"We had no idea she was in trouble." Steele was vehement. Too vehement? "She didn't radio. After passing her below the summit we never heard from her again. It made no sense."

"Another guide alerted our Sherpa." Reynolds picked up the thread. "Said the second late climber came down in bad shape, had to be escorted to Camp One and airlifted out. Damon wanted to go up after Bright, but it was impossible. We were exhausted, it was dark, and—full honesty—we lacked the skills to get the job done."

"We couldn't raise her on the radio. It was horrible." Steele was either genuinely devastated or an Emmy-class actress.

"Nature one, humans zero." James pantomimed marking a score sheet. "The next day, a Taiwanese group found her body in an alcove on the South Summit, about a hundred and fifty meters below the top. A couple of Sherpas tried to dislodge her but she was frozen in place. Not barely alive frozen, like Beck Weathers or David Sharp. Dead frozen."

Seeing my look, Reynolds explained the reference. "Sharp was a climber who got frozen to the ground while still breathing and had to be left. His body's now a trail marker, of sorts. Weathers, they genuinely thought was dead when they left him behind, but he somehow wandered into camp the next morning. They were able to get him off the mountain."

"Most of him. He left behind a nose, an arm, and most of his toes," James said. "But I saw the before pics. He wasn't so great-looking to begin with."

Jesus flipping Christ.

James rolled on, matter-of-fact. "Brighton was dead. There was nothing we could do. It was descend or die. Everyone knew the risks going in."

"What do you think happened to Brighton?" *Not barely alive frozen. Dead frozen.*

James shrugged. "She was either too exhausted or too disoriented to work the ropes down Hillary Step. She sat down to rest and froze in place. It happens." He paused. "She might have made it overnight if the temperature hadn't taken a nosedive. But it was just too fucking cold and she had too little oxygen."

Steele chimed in. "The other climber told the Sherpas that Bright insisted she descend Hillary Step first. Claimed she waited at the bottom but Bright never showed. Said she didn't have the strength or oxygen to go back up, so she headed to camp to find help."

"What was the other climber's name?"

Ten seconds of nothing.

"She was Italian, I think." Steele looked to Reynolds.

"No. Colombian."

"She was a solo climber," James said. "We didn't know her."

"You never tried to locate her? I mean later, after you were all down off the mountain?" These three were a piece of work.

"What was there to say?" Reynolds shrugged. "Bright was dead."

The new silence was broken by Steele. "I'm sorry but I can't keep kicking myself. It's been three years. Time to let it go."

By implied command, Reynolds swung his feet from under the table and stood.

Also rising, Steele said, "It was hard." Almost pleading. "You just don't know." Then, Reynolds in the lead, bodies not touching, the two strode toward the door.

"Ain't she a darlin'?"

My gaze swung to James. He was watching Reynolds and Steele, his face unreadable. But the venom in his tone was clear.

"You don't like Dara?"

"If anyone had motive to leave Bright on that mountain it was Dara."

I didn't see that coming. "Seriously?"

"Dara hated Brighton. As in, wanted to be her."

"What do you mean?"

"Stand by your man." The lyric half-sung, half-whispered.

"Dara wanted to be with Cash?"

James did something meaningful with his brows.

"She seems so passive."

"Passive as a coiled mamba until it takes off your face." At my look. "Fine. I shouldn't single Dara out. Everyone verbally loooooooved Brighton, but they were all trying to score something off her. Even me."

"Oh?"

"You know we were business partners, right?"

"Dara mentioned it."

"Bright came up with the idea to start a nonprofit to help Nepali Sherpa. Called it Bright Ascents. Hidden agenda: boost our profiles and make us reality TV worthy. I had the Everest connections but Brighton had the charisma. She was the star power with the rich friends. In less than a year she raised over a million bucks."

"Your role?"

"My handsome face and boyish charm." Getting no reaction from me, he went on: "I knew the climbing community. Could navigate Nepali red tape. If we ever started a project, I was going to grease the wheels. Until then, I was just along for the ride." Winsome wink. "Looking pretty."

"And a small salary?"

"Do you work for free?"

I dipped my chin, acknowledging he had a point.

"Elon Gass?"

"Poor Elon never had a dime to his name. Bright funded his trip. He owed her upwards of thirty thousand dollars."

"Pretty steep for a walk up a mountain."

Too late I realized my bad pun. James ignored or failed to catch it.

Derisive expulsion of air. "And that's the budget version, ma'am."

"Depends on how you count costs." My reply was acid. Brighton Hallis had paid the highest price possible.

James scooched right and stood in one quick, controlled move, all angles and knees and sharp shoulders. A long meeting of our eyes. Then, "There's no love lost between Dara and me. My view? She's not the brightest bird in the cage. But she's got one thing right. You weren't there, you can't judge. Brighton put herself at risk and 'paid the price.'" Air quotes like angry little hooks. "Hell, she put the whole team at risk. We all could've died. I'm sorry she's gone, but it wasn't our fault, and I refuse to feel guilty just because she was a pretty blonde with the last name Hallis. Case closed."

With that, he stalked off.

In a short forty-eight hours I would learn how wrong they all were.

CHAPTER 6

It was Tuesday before my informal "knee therapy" yielded results. At 10:47:22 EST, I was finally able to fully extend Brighton Hallis's right leg. I checked in with Larabee.

"You're doing fluoroscopy?" His muffled voice told me he was shoulder-snugging the phone, doing something else.

"Yes."

"You'll have to work alone."

"Fine." It wasn't.

"Ditto if you're ready to roll her for prints."

"I think the fingers are thawed enough to rehydrate."

"Any thoughts on what happened to her?"

"Hypothermia, hypoxia, HACE, exhaustion, exposure, head trauma . . ." I ticked off the lineup of suspects. "A brain scan may be in order if you want to nail specific cause of death." Soft tissue and organs are Larabee's department.

He grunted and hung up. Or dropped the phone. Hard to tell.

Suited and gloved, I organized my approach. Prints

first. Then radiography. Then. I wasn't quite sure about the next then.

Maneuvering free the accessible hand, I clamped the shears around the thumb and squeezed firmly, using both palms as before. The blades slowly bit into the desiccated flesh. Severed the bone. The thumb dropped to the table with a soft *thup*. I repeated the process with each finger. When finished, my palms felt bruised inside their layer of latex. But five partial digits lay on the table, dark and hard as petrified twigs.

I placed a stainless-steel bowl in the sink and filled it with a tissue-enhancing solution, the kind used by morticians to plump up Grandpa or Aunt Dee. After submerging the digits, I stepped back and stared, "watched pot" style. Pointless. The process would take hours, perhaps even days.

On X-ray, superimposed bones can be difficult to interpret. Horizontal bodies are easier to sort. Applying cautious but steady pressure, I eased the bent figure toward a supine and fully extended posture. Not easy, but I got the job done. Except for the boots, which were still frozen solid, giving new meaning to the expression "died with her boots on." For now, they had to stay. Cursing inwardly that every tech was tied up elsewhere, I wheeled the body out of autopsy room five and down the hall to X-ray.

Fluoroscopy is a type of real-time imaging in which X-ray images are sent to a monitor. Overly simplistic, but you get the idea. I hoped a full-body scan would reveal any abnormalities, trauma, or evidence of disease in the skull, skeleton, musculature, or gut. The technology would also allow me to make hard copies of specific views that might prove useful for comparison to Brighton Hallis's antemortem medical records.

After rolling the gurney next to the apparatus, which looks sort of like an open-air MRI or CT setup, I muscled the body across onto the platform, head and shoulders first, followed by legs and booted feet. Then I donned a lead apron and radiation glasses, set the dials as I'd seen scores of technicians do, and stepped to the viewing monitor.

A lot of whirring. A few clicks. Then showtime. The arm hooking over the body began its slow journey from the head to the toes, firing images as it progressed. A constantly changing panorama in grays, blacks, and whites lit up the screen.

Watching the inside of Brighton Hallis pass by, my heart sank. The skeletal trauma was beyond my worst fears. Clean breaks and jagged edges suggested that a lot of fracturing had occurred postmortem. I wondered what the hell had happened in the course of the dislodging, ride down the mountain, airlift, and overseas flight. I repeated the scan twice to take it all in, knowing that separating antemortem from perimortem from postmortem injury would be a bitch.

Irritation flared. *Piece of cake,* Larabee had said. Right. Mummified and distorted face. Shriveled hands. No teeth. Shattered bones. I felt a stab of a headache behind my left eyeball. A stab of guilt. The girl in that X-ray unit hadn't asked for this, either. Focus on the job.

Basics first. ID. Having a full body, I'd been able to take a proper height measurement. Sixty-eight inches, subtracting for the boots. Muscle development suggested small male or large female.

The pelvis, though in several more pieces than it should have been, remained articulated by flesh. I noted a broad sciatic notch, wide pubic bones, and a

U-shaped subpubic angle where the two pelvic halves met in front. Good female traits.

That and the gray smudges that were her uterus and ovaries. And the vagina I'd noted when the body was undressed. What we in the business call anatomical "clues."

The proximal and distal ends of the long bones showed no gaps or indications of recent epiphyseal fusion, the medial clavicle maybe a trace. Given the stage of skeletal development, I jotted an age range of seventeen to twenty-five. Consistent with Brighton Hallis's known age at death.

Race. Always the puzzler. Pale skin and fair hair straight down to the roots suggested Caucasoid. But death can play strange games with pigmentation. Narrow zygomatics and a nonglobular cranial shape supported a conclusion of European ancestry. The rest of the facial architecture told me little.

Why? The facial distortion hadn't been due to freezing alone. Along with the dental trauma, both maxillary bones and the lower nasal cavity exhibited breakage in a fairly circumscribed pattern. My first guess was a deadly face-plant on an unyielding surface, probably a conical rock or gorilla hunk of ice. Interpretation was complicated by the fact that the facial damage was superimposed over an area of fracture at the back of the skull.

After forty minutes at the monitor, my notes read: Female, probably white, age 17 to 25, hair blond, height 5'8". The bio profile was consistent with Brighton Hallis, but not enough for a positive ID.

Confident that would come via the medical file, I popped Brighton Hallis's antemortem X-rays onto a row of wall-mounted lightboxes and thumbed the switches. Slowly, I walked from plate to plate, taking in detail. In addition to the broken ulna, I spotted a healed stable fracture of the left calcaneus. Not much else of interest.

Back to the monitor. Within minutes, I found an opacity suggesting the old healed ulnar break. Or thought I did. There were now multiple fractures of that forearm, impacting both the ulna and radius. And overlying bones and tissue prevented an unobstructed view. Pressing a button to make hard copy, I moved on.

Not a chance of getting a peek at the feet. Millet Everest Summit GTX mountaineering boots had enough metal in their components, fasteners, and lining to make X-ray impossible.

Frustrated, I arched my back and rolled my shoulders to ease the tension. Maybe antemortem ulnar fracture. Maybe Caucasoid traits. It seemed this body was determined to vex ID at every turn. I was going to have to do it the old-fashioned way. Boil and deflesh, then eyeball the bones. Piece of cake my ass.

I snagged a cuff of my glove and checked my watch. Almost noon. A quick Diet Coke and egg salad sandwich, then I returned, rolled a stool to the monitor, and began cataloguing and diagraming ME215-15's cornucopia of injuries.

The images on the screen showed superimposed road maps of diverging, converging, paralleling, and crisscrossing bones and fracture lines. Read: a Wyeth-painted haystack jumble of skeletal trauma. My task was to sort through the damage and pull out the relevant.

The cranial trauma seemed to suggest two direct impacts, one anterior, one posterior. Okay. That worked with the theory of a fall. Maybe the head whipped on the neck, smacking both the face and back of the skull. Or maybe the blows were sustained while jouncing down the world's tallest rock on a canvas toboggan. As I watched the body cross the screen yet another time, my attention was snagged by damage near the neck, at the level of the third and fourth cervical vertebrae. I leaned in, staring, mind running a zillion explanations.

The wound appeared similar to a type often seen at the MCME. To injuries incurred in a form of violent death more native to urban contexts.

I took in more detail. Made notes. The right transverse process of each vertebra was displaced sharply downward. I saw no brittle edges or sharp, dry-stick splintering. No signs of healing. The fracturing definitely looked perimortem. But that wasn't what had my heart beating faster.

The damage was limited to one side, clustered tightly, and flowed with similar directionality. That suggested a single, penetrating blow. Perhaps caused by a fall onto something hard and sharp. Perhaps resulting in a punctured vessel.

Had I stumbled upon manner of death? Had Brighton Hallis fallen so hard that an object was forced deep into her neck? On falling, had her head whiplashed, striking both in front and in back?

But something cold and dark was slithering across my brain. What?

Warily, I prodded the source of my uneasiness. The prodding led to Ortiz.

No paradoxical undressing.

It doesn't happen every time, I chided myself.

It happens often enough, my brain insisted. Rob Hall, Scott Fischer, almost all the dead atop Everest exhibited some form of paradoxical undressing.

Still.

This woman died gloveless, my mind insisted.

Yet her outerwear was zipped to the chin.

If Brighton Hallis had removed her gloves, her exposed hands would have quickly become frostbitten. I hurried to the platform and studied the victim's remaining digits. Mummification was uniform. The fingertips weren't misshapen, blistered, or blackened.

In other words, I saw none of the typical signs of frostbite. Meaning blood hadn't been diverted away from her fingers prior to death. No hypothermia. Translation: She died quickly.

Over and over. Round and round. A fall? Tumbling rock? An equipment malfunction leading to hypoxia and disorientation?

Hallelujah. I was still at first base.

Then a thought. Hurrying to the computer, I pulled up the photos Ortiz had taken and entered into the ME215-15 case file.

There was Brighton, curved on her side, the polar jacket in place and in remarkable condition. More keystrokes. More photos. Underneath layers showing rips and tears. Cheaper fabric? Note to self: Examine the clothing.

Returning to the platform, I tucked the limbs and rolled the body onto its stomach. Under the harsh fluorescents, the back and buttocks looked dimpled and morgue white. Gashes in the pallid flesh bore witness to the woman's last rough ride down the mountain. One large abrasion lined up with the damage I'd seen on X-ray at the level of the third and fourth cervical vertebrae.

I found a handheld magnifier and brought the wound into focus. The abraded area was rough-edged, approximately two inches across, and shallow. Except at the centermost point. There it was deep. Very deep.

I leaned in closer.

My breath froze.

CHAPTER 7

My statement got pretty much the reaction I expected.

"Murder?" Larabee's brows were smacking his hairline.

We were three, cloistered in Larabee's office. Homicide detective Erskine "Skinny" Slidell of the Charlotte-Mecklenburg Police Department (CMPD) was gracing us with his presence, but zero patience.

"What the shit?"

I turned to Slidell. His slouching posture and outstretched legs mooted all benefit intended by the ergonomic seat under his substantial polyester-clad buttocks. I explained. Again. Slowly.

"I believe someone killed Brighton Hallis. Or incapacitated her and left her to die on the mountain."

"You called me over here 'cause some kid got whacked in China?" Even Slidell's orange socks looked pissed.

"Nepal." I'd checked.

"Whatever. It ain't my jurisdiction."

"She was twenty-four. And from Charlotte."

"She was stupid to go up that mountain. And stupid killed her."

"That is not what the X-rays suggest."

"The images are . . ." Larabee struggled for a word. Settled on ". . . conclusive?"

"The images are a mess," I admitted. "But once the bones are cleaned, they will show that Brighton Hallis suffered intentional perimortem injury resulting in death."

Larabee looked dubious. "With causation?" Meaning, did violence kill her before something less deliberate, like falling. I think.

"I believe the fracture patterning will show that the trauma inflicted on her either killed her directly, or unavoidably led to her death under the circumstances."

"According to that gobbledygook"—Skinny jabbed a thumb at the X-ray I'd just displayed—"the mountain or the Sherpas got in a few good whacks. My money's on a jury blaming Everest, not some moron crawling up its side."

"She didn't accidentally impale her neck on an ice pick or a tent stake or whatever." Terse. I'd been thinking about whatever. Come up with no good candidates.

"Ever heard of the perfect weapon?" Skinny's mouth mashed up at one corner.

I cocked a brow.

"Icicle. Perp stabs his vic, weapon melts." Slidell was dragging up an age-old crime scene riddle. "Poof. No evidence."

"An icicle would not have cut into the vertebrae."

"The detective has a point." In a rare move, Larabee sided with Slidell.

"Seriously? An icicle?"

"No, no. But it's quite a leap to homicide. A blow

from falling rock or ice might easily mimic intentional blunt or sharp force impact."

"I understand the biomechanics of fracture." A bit sharper than I intended. "And I appreciate that the death zone provides the perfect setting for concealing foul play. That's my point. The killer used knowledge of the mountain to his or her advantage."

"Say you're right. It don't matter." Slidell spread beefy palms. "Whatever went down, it went down in China."

"Nepal." Curt.

"I don't care if it was in freaking Neverland. It wasn't here. Not my turf. Not my problem."

"The perp is," I snapped.

Now the hand flapped, dismissive. Wait. Had Skinny gone for a manicure? "You ain't got shit."

Dial it back, Brennan. Calming breath. "Five went up, four came down."

"And a Sherpa or two and five hundred other yahoos who think freezing their nuts off makes for a good time."

Larabee jumped in, partly to keep the peace, partly motivated by the tower of files on his desk. "It's a bit of a stretch, Tempe."

"Agreed, but the X-rays show physical evidence of stabbing and blunt force trauma. There is soft-tissue evidence to contradict hypothermia as cause of death. And the perp may be right here in Charlotte." Blank looks. "It's a closed universe of suspects. Except for Elon Gass, who is expected back soon, Brighton Hallis's climbing buddies are all right here. I talked to three of them. You need motive? This trio is lousy with motive." I looked from Larabee to Slidell. "What's the harm in digging a little?"

"And we're done here." Slidell slapped the arms of

his chair and heaved himself up. With less effort and grunting than usually required? Had he lost weight?

"Detective. I can demonstrate that a Charlotte girl was killed."

"Call me when you can prove she was killed here." Tossed over one shoulder, heading for the door.

Images flashed in my mind. Brighton Hallis, radiant and youthful before a snowy peak. Alone and frightened as life drained from her in a bitter mountaintop wind.

Play the card? Cheap trick, but I went for it.

"I'm sure Blythe Hallis won't be too disappointed when I explain that the CMPD can't investigate her daughter's murder. Did you know she's besties with the chief? He'll explain all about jurisdiction while she's keeping her checkbook safely in her purse at the next police fundraiser."

Slidell froze. Larabee's face swung to me, expression saying exactly how he felt about being caught in the middle.

"This is horseshit." Slidell's shoulders slumped. He held a moment, then turned, crossed to us, and dropped back into the chair. Which protested loudly.

"So what's your next step?" Larabee, resigned.

"The bones." I was going for the gold.

Larabee pinched the bridge of his nose with thumb and forefinger. "You want to deflesh the body."

Put that way, it didn't sound like I was on Brighton's side. "Just the parts that show trauma."

"How long will that take?"

"A while. But the end result will be worth the effort."

"Uh-huh. When you speak to Mrs. Hallis, spare her the details."

"Of course." I turned to Slidell. "What do you need from me?"

"All the dirt you have on your new pals."

"In my office?"

"Over lunch." Slidell again lumbered to his feet. "You're buying."

Slidell's choice of eatery didn't surprise me. The King's Kitchen is one of his favorites, topping Wendy's and Burger King by a hair. What did surprise me was his selection of salmon over the "Southern meat and three," his usual. I didn't ask. But something was up.

I went for a chicken salad sandwich. Filled him in between bites. To his credit, Slidell listened with little interruption. Then, "So this kid, Brighton Hallis, whistles her merry crew up Everest to make dead Daddy proud. They come down, she doesn't. Turns out she's stuck to the mountain like a tongue to a flagpole."

"At that altitude, a person freezes in place within an hour." Ignoring Slidell's unsettling simile. "One climber, David Sharp, stopped to rest in a place called Green Boots Cave, so named because of the *other* dead climber inside."

Slidell's fork paused, butter beans halfway to his lips.

"More than thirty climbers passed by as Sharp sat immobile and hypothermic. By the time someone realized he was still breathing, it was too late to pry him loose. Had to leave him to die. Now he's a guidepost along the route."

The beans made it into Slidell's mouth. Didn't slow his speech. "You say your vic was dead before she hit the snow."

I nodded. "One way or another. With her injuries, she wouldn't have survived a descent down the mountain, even if she wasn't dead when her killer left her."

"That don't equal murder." Still resistant? Or playing devil's advocate?

"You need to talk to Hallis's climbing team. They're like a motive vending machine. Pick your flavor." I spoke around a mouthful of cornbread. Complimentary upon request. Mind-blowing upon ingestion. "Maybe I'm misreading them, but no one seems to be mourning Brighton's passing."

Slidell summarized what I'd told him. "So the boyfriend maybe wants to move on. The girlfriend wants the boyfriend. The college pal owes a chunk of change. Everyone's dying to be a star. And the business partner looks like a creep."

"Okay. Maybe Damon James doesn't have motive," I conceded. "But he has a name like a bank robber."

Skinny ignored my joke. "All sucking the Brighton Hallis teat."

"As far as I know, she underwrote only Gass's trip. But I'll bet my grandma's china everyone benefited from her trust fund."

"Coin is what gets most folks clocked," Slidell agreed. "Not to devalue sex and drugs."

"And you're right. Everyone wanted a piece of the reality show action."

"I'll run down this Gass character." Skinny wiped his mouth and inspected the napkin. "What kind of assclown calls a kid *Eee*-lon?"

"He's on some sort of expedition in Russia. Supposedly back soon."

"I'll put the screws to the three stooges first, see if something shakes loose." Pushing back from the table, he tossed a "Thanks for the grub" over his shoulder and left.

I paid the bill, leaving extra for the soup kitchen supported by the restaurant, then headed back to the lab. En route, I phoned Blythe Hallis. Hands free. Gotta love Bluetooth.

Raleigh answered, as before asked me to wait.

"Ms. Brennan, you have news?" Blythe Hallis's overly long vowels glided like silk across the line.

"We've completed a full-body X-ray on your daughter. As I feared, the damage caused by recovery was extensive."

"I'm confident you'll overcome."

"I did notice some anomalies." I paused to gather just the right words. "Based on certain injury patterns, we believe your daughter may have been the victim of foul play." Not quite fair to use the plural pronoun, but I did.

Nothing but a sharp intake of breath.

I made a left, then a right. Pulled into the MCME lot. Finally, Hallis spoke, voice modulated as always. "Are you suggesting someone intentionally harmed my daughter?"

"It's a theory I will have to verify with more detailed analysis of the bones."

More silence. Then, "And how may I be of help?"

"To study the skeletal trauma more closely I must—"

"Do what you need to do. An open casket was never an option. But please. No more defacement than necessary. Is there more?"

"You mentioned that a Taiwanese climbing team collected Brighton's personal effects and returned them to you." Perhaps a clue lurked among the tools of her trade. Right. And what were the chances she'd kept them all this time?

"I have the box. But it will take some time to have it brought out of storage."

"I'd like to examine those items."

"With the exception of a necklace, I've removed nothing." In a quieter voice. "Funny, but we always hope, don't we?"

"Yes, ma'am." Hope what? It was all a mistake and Brighton would come home someday? Evidence existed that would spur a large legal settlement?

"One last thing." I always hate making this request. It sounds so final. "Would you be willing—"

"You'd like a DNA sample." Hallis was way ahead of me.

"Yes, ma'am. The queue for analysis can sometimes be long."

"Would you prefer a cheek swab from me or a sample of Brighton's hair?"

"If you have a brush that was used solely by your daughter, that would be perfect."

"Can you use a cutting from when she was young?"

"The hair has to retain the root bulb, I'm afraid." Has to have been forcibly removed.

"I will have her brush ready for you tonight."

"I'm in my car now. Is there any way I could swing by in fifteen minutes?"

A beat of hesitation. "Yes."

With that she was gone and Raleigh was back. We arranged for me to pick up the hairbrush immediately and return for the box from Everest after six. The diversion added no more than fifteen minutes to my drive.

Entering the lab, I tossed a quick greeting to Mrs. Flowers, the receptionist, and hurried to autopsy room five, eager to collect samples from ME215-15 for DNA sequencing. After suiting up, I cut specimens from the untouched digits, placed them in a vial, and marked the cover with the case number, the date, and my initials. Then, as a precautionary backup, I plucked several strands of hair, with root, and packaged them in the same manner.

That done, I added the Ziploc containing Brighton Hallis's brush and phoned Slidell. Detective Delightful didn't answer, so I left a message asking that he collect the samples and deliver them to the CMPD forensics lab. Results wouldn't come with TV crime drama dazzling speed, but turnaround times in Charlotte are far faster than average. This case wasn't high priority, so I expected a report in a matter of weeks.

Next, I checked an erasable board hanging in the hall. My lucky day. Joe Hawkins was on duty. The best death investigator on staff.

A quick call, and Hawkins came up from the morgue. I explained and demonstrated what I wanted him to do.

"You want me to make a cast of the stab wound located in the back of the neck near cervical vertebrae three and four." He pointed it out. "And take those two vertebrae out and clean them."

"Yes."

"Then you want me to reflect the scalp and face so you can examine cranial trauma, especially near the nasal-maxillary areas in front and the parieto-occipital areas in back. That about it?"

"Ink and roll her." I considered. "While you're at it, dissect out and clean the right ulna and left calcaneus. And go ahead and take X-rays of them. Could be useful if ID becomes complicated." As in, you can't get readable prints. "Can you manage all that today?"

Hawkins checked his watch. "Maybe."

"Perfect."

"What do you want me to do with the scalp and face?"

"Would removing them intact be too difficult?"

Hawkins gave me the long Hawkins stare.

"Place them in a formalin solution. If the tissue has to come off in sections, I can deal with that."

Hawkins tipped his chin in the direction of the sink. "The fingers are rehydrated?"

"Ready and waiting." I'd tested. The mummified flesh had puffed up nicely.

"Priority?"

"Skull, postcranial bones, cast, X-rays, then prints."

Ever taciturn, Hawkins just nodded.

"See you later!" Big smile. Wasted. Hawkins was already on the move. I left him to his grisly tasks.

Changing to street clothes in the staff lounge, I was pumped. Progress! I balled my apron and shot a J into a biohazard bin, my shoulders doing a jazzy little dance. But at my office door, my exuberance fizzled a bit.

Bones would be boiling. Prints would be taken. Samples would be submitted for DNA sequencing. What to do? My momentum stubbed its toe.

As I stepped through the door, my eye fell on a magazine I'd been looking at for research lying open on my desk. On an ad for Millet Everest Summit GTX mountaineering boots that I'd been checking out. My gaze drifted to a local insert on the facing page.

Try it! a tiny voice urged from some corner of my mind.

No way.

Fieldwork.

Yeah. Right.

Might help your analysis.

Valid point.

Scared?

What the hell. I'm the Queen of Ice and Snow. I

243 · BONES ON ICE

had time to kill and yoga pants in my trunk. I tore
out the flyer and headed for my car.

Minutes later, at my destination, I wasn't so sure.
Was even less sure as I powered through double glass
doors into an overly bright lobby with way too many
posters.

"Hello!" a perky broomstick with a bouncy bob
and sun-leathered skin greeted me from behind a reception desk. The patchouli tsunamied strong as I
crossed to her. "Welcome to Inner Peaks Climbing
Center!"

More and more, I was regretting my rash impulse.

"Are you here to climb?" Overly cheery.

No. I'm here to learn neurosurgery. I nodded.

"First-timer?" Wide, sincere eyes.

"Yes."

"Great! Over eighteen?"

"Yes." Last time I was eighteen "Stayin' Alive" was
a new release. I didn't add that.

"Our first-timers package includes a day pass, harness, shoes, and gri-gri lesson."

"Gri-gri?"

"An assisted braking belay device."

"I'll take the package."

"Great! You'll need a qualified belayer—that's the
person handling the ropes—to help you climb. Got a
friend?"

"Not today."

Earnest frown. "I'm not sure. . . ."

"I've got this, Amy." The voice came from behind
me. Familiar. I turned.

Damon James, chest stretching a tee to its tensile
limits, the Inner Peaks logo centered on front. Sleeves
razored off at the shoulders.

"Dr. Brennan, I presume." Boyish laugh. Like he'd
practiced in the mirror.

"Moonlighting?" I stepped back. For some reason, the guy made me want to run for the showers.

A shrug. "My former business pipeline's a little frozen right now."

My breath caught. Was the asshole referring to Brighton Hallis?

James drew an arm across his waist and tipped his head. "So you get Prince Charming."

"Great!" Chirped from Amy. "Please sign the waiver, we'll swipe a credit card, and away you go!"

"Great." James raised his eyebrows at me.

"Great." I raised my eyebrows at James.

After signing and paying, I trailed my belayer, whatever the hell that was, into the inner sanctum. In the gear room, James sorted through brightly colored straps and ropes, selecting and handing me some that, to my eye, were indistinguishable from others.

"How's it hanging with Brighton?" he asked, casual as hell, crouching by a bin overflowing with metal clasps.

"I'm not at liberty to discuss an ongoing case."

"Fair enough." He stood, holding the climbing equivalent of bowling shoes. "I watch TV. I'm hip to how cops roll."

I frowned. James couldn't know Hallis had been murdered. Why mention cops?

"All set." Quick jerk of the head. "This way."

The main climbing gym looked like the love child of Mars and Tim Burton. Fake rock escarpments curved upward, their ochre walls speckled with modular grips resembling brightly colored wads of leviathan chewing gum. All around, people in ropes and helmets dangled in various stages of ascent and descent.

James led the way to a fairly straightforward "cliff." "We'll start simple."

Have I mentioned that I dislike unprotected heights? My heart was already inching up my throat.

I slipped into the climbing shoes, then James flopped me about like a rag doll, affixing harness, ropes, carabiners, gri-gri, and helmet. When finished, he assessed his handiwork, again shot the practiced grin. The contrived boyish-charm thing was wearing thin fast.

"How's your upper-body strength?" Still grinning.

"Decent."

"Let's find out." James began issuing instructions, his style methodical and concise. "Climbing's as much about your hands as your feet."

I listened. Whatever his personality, the guy knew his stuff.

A final check of my gear, then he pointed out the route.

I wiped sweaty palms on my pants then stepped to the wall. Curtain time.

"On belay?" I called, following the script James had provided.

"Belay on," James replied.

"Climbing," I said.

"Climb on."

A moment passed. Another. I hadn't moved.

"Climb on," James repeated, tone not mocking, but close. Deep breath, then I reached to find purchase and hauled myself up.

My form wasn't pretty, but slowly I worked my way up the rock face, pits damp, heart hammering, totally oblivious to the passage of time. To anything outside the rhythm of grasp, pull, step.

I was close to the top when a high shriek echoed somewhere below me. A cacophony of sound followed. My adrenaline-stoked fingers flinched, my grip faltered. I fell.

I felt air whoosh past my ears. Was bracing for impact when the rope tautened, snapping me around wildly. My body slammed the wall. I scrabbled for a handhold, a toehold. Clung, gasping, not looking down.

"Dr. Brennan." Pause. "Dr. Brennan." Calm. "Please look at me."

I opened my eyes. Saw serpentine green ones. Level. I risked a glance toward the ground. Saw that I was two feet above it. Trembling, I released my grip, and eased onto terra firma.

"I'm sorry." James raised his hands, apologetic. "I got distracted by the kids." He indicated a mushrooming gaggle of children flowing in from outside. "You okay?"

I nodded, not trusting my ability to speak. The same thing had distracted me. But still.

"I haven't lost a climber yet." Lame attempt to lighten the mood.

"I'm fine." My voice was squeaky, my knees rubber.

"Ready for another try?"

"I'm good." Wiping a shaky hand over my face.

"You know what they say about getting back on the horse."

"I've got to go." Glance at my watch. Five-thirty. I'd never make it to Blythe Hallis by six.

"You definitely got the hang of it fast. Must have a primo instructor." James was back to cocky and smiling. "You sure?"

"I'm sure." Crazy, but somehow the invite felt threatening. Funny how raging adrenaline distorts one's perception. "Thanks for the primer."

"I'm really sorry," James apologized again.

"It's no big deal," I assured him.

"Duty calls?" The reptilian green eyes, measuring. Prying?

"More like a hungry cat. I'm edging into tuna-or-pay time."

James stepped close, morphing from stillness to motion so quickly I had to steel myself not to recoil. Another practiced grin as he unclipped my harness and helped me free. Then we moved toward the lobby.

"It's good to push yourself," James said as we went through the door, his body so close to mine I could smell his sweat and the onions he'd had with his lunch. "It's not good to push others."

What the hell?

"Bright's death hurt a lot of people." Pausing in the narrow hallway, one hand on the lobby door. "So did her life. Dredging up all that baggage will just cause trouble."

"What are you saying?"

He thought a moment. Or appeared to. When he answered his voice sounded different, deeper. "It may have been better if she'd stayed where she was. Nothing good will come of bringing Brighton down off that mountain."

With an aggressive shove James pushed through the door. In the lobby he was all sunshine again. "Y'all come back and see us now, hear?"

"Don't keep the light on for me."

Hurrying out, I felt the small hairs rise on my neck. Cooling sweat? Or the pressure of steady eyes watching my back?

CHAPTER 8

In my dream, I was belly-sliding down a sheer preci-pice, fingers clawing but catching nothing but air. Below, a hollow-eyed Brighton Hallis was position-ing herself to catch me, arms frozen to her sides. Above, two pairs of eyes were peering over the cliff's edge, one green and one gray, both cold as a grave. A song floated from somewhere far off, blurry and in-distinct.

As I edged into consciousness, the lyrics crystal-ized into Neil Young singing "Harvest Moon." From my nightstand. A squint at my iPhone yielded two bits of information. It was damn early. Slidell didn't care.

"What's up, Doc?"

"Apparently I am."

"The freeloader's back from Russia. I'm meeting him for a chat. Any interest?"

"Give me fifteen." I disconnected and rolled out of bed, shoulders suggesting that the previous night's hot bath had been insufficient to placate overworked muscle groups. I popped two Advil and hurried to get ready.

Twenty minutes later, I climbed into what normally constituted a rolling biohazard zone. To my shock, Slidell's Taurus was cleaner than I'd ever seen it. No trash. No fast food reinventing itself as mold. No reeking footwear.

"Wow. Spiffy floor mats. Someone die in here?"

"I also got a new eject button, if you have issues."

I bit back a retort. Watched a pine tree air freshener do a trapeze act on the crossbar of the rearview mirror. The cloying spruce odor made my nose itch. But it beat the usual stench packing Slidell's car.

"Did you reach out to Steele and Reynolds?" I asked.

"Boris and Natasha? Annoying as boils but harmless, especially him. Don't see either as the doer."

"James says Steele is a nasty piece of business. Timid on the outside, hard as nails at the core."

"Motive?"

"She wanted Reynolds. And she wanted her shot at stardom."

Slidell waggled his head, weighing the notion. "I could buy that the little mope could be a sleeper. But it don't matter. They're alibied up the wazoo." Slidell made a left, an impatient gesture toward a pedestrian in the crosswalk. "All three claim they were together. Say they left the summit way before Hallis arrived."

I described my encounter with Damon James and the wall. Left out the embarrassing tumble. My hallucinations of menace. "Maybe check James's finances."

"Gee, I never would have thought of that."

Nope.

"I'm seeing him later. And I can assure you, the guy ain't thrilled. Want to come?" Slidell's idea of a peace offering?

I thought of the malignant green eyes. "Thanks. I'll pass. Did you get the DNA samples?"

"Already delivered." Slidell made another turn. We were now in a burgeoning hipster area called Third Ward. "And, while some of us were logging beauty sleep, I also called Catawhatsis."

"To the literate, it's Kathmandu. Capital of Nepal."

"Right. I think they use tin cans and string for communication over there. Forty-eleven numbers and hours bouncing around, I finally connected to a constable in Lukla."

"You actually phoned?"

"I like to hear a guy's voice."

Slidell's skill set does not include the use of computers. He typically leans on subordinates to run prints or enter info into databases. I let it pass. "Lukla is the nearest real town to base camp. It's big enough to have an airport."

"It also has a clown named Raj with jurisdiction over Everest. Must be lonely. I thought I'd have a birthday before he'd let me off the phone."

"Comparing notes on modern crime?" I could imagine the conversation, felt sympathy for Raj.

"Aside from what they charge climbers?" Sarcastic snort. "But, yeah. The guy wouldn't shut up. Sounded mostly like Wild West stuff—prostitution, drugs, petty theft, drunken brawls. Oh, and news flash: A lot of oxygen tanks walk off on their own."

"But no murder?"

"If you don't count abandoning the lame and disabled to freeze to death."

I counted it. Though I'd never been there, I couldn't imagine walking past a dying human being.

"So what did you learn?" Other than the deficiencies of Himalayan telecom.

"I wanted the story straight from the Sherpas who were with Hallis at the end. Not gonna happen. One died of HACE the following year. The other bought it in the avalanche of 2014."

"Tough life up there."

"And, it would seem, short."

"So that leaves only the climbers."

"And they're sticking with their stories." Slidell turned into a lot fronting a silver dining car that looked like it had chugged straight out of the 1950s. A neon sign proclaimed Mattie's Diner. "Let's see what *Eee*-lon has to say."

The restaurant's retro interior matched its vintage exterior. Stools lined a long counter on one side; red vinyl booths with miniature jukeboxes filled the wall opposite.

The sole patron was a man sitting alone in a booth. He was small, with scruffy dark curls and black-framed glasses that looked about the same era as the place he'd chosen for breakfast. On seeing us, he raised a hand. We crossed to him.

"Thanks for coming to 'my office.'" Gass stood to greet us. Up close I could see that his face was dark with stubble. Not the "groomed to look ungroomed" style so fashionable of late. The "I haven't bothered with a razor in some time" style.

Slidell and I shook hands with Gass. I slid into the booth and scanned a menu that offered, among other temptations, the Hunka Hunka Burning Toast and the Ya Might Be a Redneck Breakfast Plate. Just what I needed. More artery-clogging Southern fare.

A waitress in a black Eat At Mattie's tee, leather shorts, and Doc Martens plunked three mugs of coffee onto the Formica. Waited expectantly. I wondered what she'd do if I asked for tea.

"Hey, Carla," Gass greeted her.

"Usual?" Carla shifted her weight. A fairly impressive maneuver. Gass nodded.

Carla turned heavily mascaraed eyes on me.

"Nothing, thanks."

Slidell also stuck with coffee. Added Sweet'N Low. When Carla retreated, he went in hot.

"Someone took Brighton Hallis off the board on Everest. You know who?"

All color drained from below the dark stubble. "What? You mean, like, killed her?"

Slidell said nothing. Gass looked to me. Back to Slidell.

"You're joking, right?"

"You think it's funny?"

"No. Of course not." Bobbing Adam's apple. Eyes jittery behind the thick lenses. "Why? I mean, how?"

"Chop to the neck. You know anything about that?"

Gass gulped his coffee. Winced, as though scalded. "I thought she died of hypothermia." Faintly.

"Apparently not."

"But who would do that? She was by herself."

"Was she?"

Gass shook his head. "I don't know. I never made it above Kangshung Face. I was afraid of exhaustion and turned around." Fingers to his lips, testing for a blister. "Most climbing deaths come from human error. Fatigue, ascending too slowly, ignoring the signs of altitude sickness, refusing to turn around. I freaked, I guess. Wasn't going to let that happen to me."

"Easy to turn around on someone else's tab." Slidell was hitting hard.

"What's that supposed to mean?"

"Little Miss Trust Fund footed your bill."

"I didn't ask her to do that." Voice rising. "She insisted. Said she owed me for getting her through college."

"How much?"

Gass looked up, as though receipts might be affixed to the ceiling. Back to Slidell. "An Everest pass runs $25,000 per, but we got a group rate. $70,000 for seven—five hikers, two Sherpas. A fully guided expedition runs upwards of $65,000 per person. A trip like ours, with support but no guides, tops out around $30,000."

"So you owed Hallis thirty K?" Slidell was verifying what James had said.

"A little more. Everything costs, man. Your gear, your flight, your yak. Oxygen is five hundred dollars a bottle and you need six to summit. Each group chips in for base camp. Brighton was a champ at fundraising but everyone had to pony up."

"Except you."

"I could've paid!" Shooting forward in his seat. "I secured sponsorship before we left. When she changed her mind at the last minute and switched from a guided to an assisted trip, everyone thought it was because of me. But it wasn't. The sponsorship would've paid. Going the cheap route was Brighton's call."

"What kind of sponsorship?" I was curious, suspected competition was stiff. Gass didn't strike me as a mountaineering poster child.

"The Sure Foot Society. They've been incredibly supportive of my Yeti research."

Slidell's mug paused in midair. "Your what?"

"The abominable snowman. Bigfoot," I translated.

"I prefer Sasquatch." Prim. "Or Yeti. The creature is indigenous to the Himalayas of Nepal and Tibet. For me, the trip was less about scaling Everest, more about gathering proof."

"Proof."

"Of the creature's existence. I'm a cryptozoologist." Gass referred to a pseudoscience centered on the search for animals whose reality is questionable: Bigfoot, Loch Ness, Chupacabra. "I specialize in megafauna cryptids."

"And you thought you'd run into Bigf— Sasquatch on Everest?" Was the guy for real?

"A sighting would have been incredible, but I was mostly compiling evidence. Interviewing locals, examining fur samples, scat, possibly finding a snow-print. Most print discoveries occur between six and seven thousand meters. So you can see why summiting wasn't my priority."

"Naturally," I said. Slidell was taking in our exchange, mouth hanging open.

"Many have found physical evidence over the years. In 1960, Sir Edmund Hillary retrieved what he claimed was a scalp. Reinhold Meissner diaried that he killed a Yeti in 1986. A Japanese trekking guide reported a sighting as recently as 2003. They're out there." Vehement. "You can believe it. They are out there."

As are you, I thought. Way, way out there.

Slidell rolled his eyes but, to my surprise, remained relatively reserved. "So where's this sponsorship money now?"

"I used it to pay for my trip to Russia. Yeti sightings are emerging from a remote region of the southwestern Adygea Republic. Video and plaster casts of footprints. Amazing stuff. I had to investigate."

"Brighton disappears, so does your debt." Slidell leaned back, pooched out his lips, and folded his arms. "Maybe worth greasing a few climbers' palms for the sake of an alibi."

"What?" Aghast. "No! I told you. I tried to pay Bright back before we left the U.S. She refused."

"Got proof?"

Carla returned and placed eggs, bacon, and grits in front of Gass. Filled our mugs. Headed toward the kitchen.

"There's an email." Gass stared at his food as though he had no idea what to do with it. "Honestly, I wish she'd taken the money. Bright wasn't as liquid as people thought. Her trust was locked up tight. I don't know how she managed her champagne and caviar lifestyle off the small distribution she got each year."

"Wasn't she pulling a salary from her nonprofit?" I asked.

Gass gave a short cough of a laugh. "Bright Ascents? What a joke. Bright needed me to carry her through sophomore econ for a very good reason. Bright Ascents sounded sexy, funding medical care for Sherpas and cleaning up the mountain. But the operation was a disaster. A shell game."

"It pulled in over a million dollars its first year," I said.

"Maybe in promises. But the cupboard was bare. Damon was a saint."

"James wasn't getting paid, either?"

"Only in handshakes."

"What about *The Heights*?" Slidell jumped in. "TV can be a cash cow."

"You bet your sweet ass!" Behind the stubble, red flamed his cheeks. "Sorry. Language. I'm in the final eight. The producers are really interested in my Yeti angle."

Figured. Katy once forced me to watch an episode of *Here Comes Honey Boo Boo*. Crazy makes for good reality TV.

"Word on the street says Hallis had the gig wrapped up." Slidell.

"Maybe according to her." Diffident sniff.

"Maybe that's why someone wanted her gone. Maybe you."

Gass tipped his head, slashing a dotted line of overheads across his lenses. "You're barking up the wrong tree, man. I wasn't being considered because of my climbing skills. I was in the running for my Yeti slant. I'm the guy who never made it near Hillary Step. And I've made no bribe payments to co-conspirators. Talk to people who know me. Climbers at Camp Four. Search my bank accounts. I'm an open book."

"You can take that to the bank. Anyone else on the mountain maybe wanted the *Heights* gig? Or had a beef with Hallis?"

"Part one is easy. Everyone wanted the *Heights* gig. But I doubt anyone was plotting murder to get it. Up there, all your energy goes into surviving. You stick with your group. You huddle in your tent. There's no swapping email addresses." Gass considered. "As to hostility, no. No opportunity. The only person I saw Bright talk to, other than us, was a solo climber from somewhere in South America."

"The woman she helped up Hillary Step?" I asked.

"Hell-o? I never made it that far. I only noticed her once, at Camp Three, didn't pay much attention because I was worried I was getting HACE."

"Did you catch the other woman's name?" I asked.

"Sorry. I think Damon joined them. I never talked to her." Gass abandoned his eggs. Laid down his fork. Seemed to go deep into thought. Deep into another time.

Slidell and I exchanged glances. Waited.

"On the mountain, you're one-dimensional. You

exist as a jacket color. A shape. A stereotype. The Japanese in the red cap. The dude with the Canadian flag. The Australian with the lavender boots. Bright was the American blonde in the lime-green jacket. To me, that woman was just the girl talking to Bright."

Gass's eyes reddened. He whipped off his glasses and swiped them angrily with the heels of his hands. The first sign of grief I'd seen.

"Sorry." Repositioning the specs. "I never got to say goodbye. Bright was just . . . gone. Killed by the Nepalese government."

"'Scuse me?" Slidell's tone was razor sharp. "You talking a serious suspect?"

Deep sigh. "Everest isn't being regulated rationally. There are no prerequisites for climbing experience, no rules covering who can be an outfitter. Any fool can hang out a shingle. One guide from Connecticut Photoshopped a fake summit for creds and has since abandoned three clients at the top. He claimed they were beyond help, but he didn't report the situation for two days!" Gass was winding up for a topic that was clearly upsetting for him. "And no one does anything! It's like open season for high-altitude death."

"You think some con did in Hallis?"

"No. Crap, I don't know. It's hard to imagine mustering the energy to kill anyone up there. Just wait and the mountain will do it for you. A blizzard, a rockslide, a crevasse, an avalanche. That bastard's the perfect crime scene. Sorry."

"Maybe the abominable snowman did it." Slidell snapped his notebook, pocket-jammed it, and got to his feet. I stood.

"The Yeti is a peaceful creature." Gass, craning up at us.

"Yeah, well, leave him to the Russians for now." Slidell's parting words. "Stick around town."

Gass, voice solemn, eyes unreadable behind the tilted lenses. "Bright was my friend. She could be tough, but I loved her. The others, not so much. I want to help if I can."

Slidell flipped some bills onto the table and I followed him outside. We rode without talking until he dropped me at my car. I knew the reason for his silence. Though squirrelly, Gass seemed believable. So we hadn't a single viable suspect. If not Sasquatch, then who?

At the annex, I got straight behind the wheel. Eager to examine the bones, I gunned the engine and fired toward the lab.

Where the body would deliver its second bombshell.

CHAPTER
9

As it turned out, I got back to the lab much later than I'd planned. Mama phoned. Which required a series of calls back and forth with my sister, Harry. Which meant I had to go inside. Then I discovered that I was out of cat food. A trip to Petco. Back home. By then I was hungry and decided to stop for a quick taco.

When I finally arrived at the lab, Hawkins had left. But he'd followed my instructions with his usual precision.

In autopsy room five, Brighton Hallis's face and scalp floated in a large glass jar, flattened, lidless eyes staring through the murky fluid in which they were submerged. A hunk of white silicone rubber sat on a tray on one counter. A collection of bones and cranial fragments lay on another, drying on towels. Beside the bones was a stack of three-by-five color prints. Beside the prints, a fingerprint card.

In the cooler, ME215-15 was chilling on her gurney, prone, covered in blue plastic sheeting, which I flipped open. The skull was angled up, forehead tight to a rubber headrest, stripped of flesh to the level of the neck. The bone looked pale yellow, the suture lines squiggly dark in the artificial light. On the neck, a deep gouge and tiny white flecks marked the spot where Hawkins had painted his casting material.

I wheeled Brighton Hallis out of refrigeration. Then I turned on the fans. All of them.

After gloving, I examined the area of damage in the neck region. A shallow track angled downward from the skull base toward the gash overlying the third and fourth cervical vertebrae. I considered its form and depth. Studied the photos Hawkins had taken. Then I walked over and picked up the cast.

The thing looked like the beak of a petrel seabird. I closed my eyes, willing an idea to form in my mind. An image. A link.

Nothing.

I laid the thing down and returned to the body.

The second area of trauma was on the skull, with impact blows to both the front and back. This one was easier. Or maybe it was because this injury involved bone. My turf.

I started with the back. On the ectocranial surface of the right parietal, three inches superior to the lambdoid suture, was a classic example of a depressed fracture. Concave center, radiating cracks, the full Monty. But something was off.

Puzzled, I found a hand lens and brought my eyes close. With the damage magnified, I could see what was actually going on. What I'd mistaken for a single depressed fracture actually showed two points of impact. Fractures radiating from the second impact ran up to, but didn't cross, fractures radiating from the first. That meant two separate blows to the back of the head.

I thought about that. About the size and shape of the concavity. A brick? A paddle of some sort?

I circled the gurney and, using two hands, rotated the skull so that I could see the face. What was left of the face. The damage to the nasal-maxillary region was extensive. The bones were shattered in the region below the nose, the teeth virtually obliterated.

I returned the skull to its original position. Thought about two blows to the back of the head. About the anatomical location of the anterior and posterior injuries. The picture was not one that I'd expect from a fall. Unless Hallis lost her balance and cracked headfirst onto a rock. Then backward. Twice. Or a giant bird dropped two boulders onto her skull.

But she wore a helmet. Unless she removed it.

Or someone did.

Holy crap!

A bird!

Neuron-fired recollection. A quick fumble through a cardboard carton. Faded clothing. A headlamp. An ice axe. Bright blue rope.

I dropped the lens and shot back to the counter. Picked up and angled the cast this way and that.

Holy flying crap!

I raced to my office, grabbed the box I'd collected from Blythe Hallis, rummaged wildly, finally yanked out the object I sought. Pulse going double time, I pumped back to autopsy room five and positioned my prize side by side with Hawkins's cast.

The resemblance hit me like a punch. The Grivel Quantum Tech ice axe was a perfect match for the beaklike shape of the silicone rubber. For the wound in Hallis's neck. And the handle could easily have created the damage to the skull.

Could have been used to knock out the teeth?

Hot damn! Though I knew my informal comparison would never hold up in court, I was certain I'd found the weapon that had killed Brighton Hallis.

KATHY REICHS · 262

I dialed Slidell. Got voicemail. Left a message.

Two calming breaths, then on to the vertebrae. Gross observation showed greenstick fracturing, uniform staining, and no remodeling, indicating that the stab wound to the neck was definitely a perimortem injury.

Next step, reassembly. Not the whole skull, but the relevant sections. Using good old Elmer's and toothpicks, I started in. Yeah. Low tech. And tedious. Especially when the head has not been removed from the body. But I had promised Blythe Hallis. No more mutilation than necessary.

By ten-thirty my back was screaming and my vision was blurring. I'd had it. But I'd reconstructed enough to get a pretty good picture. After snapping an autopsy diagram onto a clipboard, I began sketching in detail.

When finished, I knew what had happened to Brighton Hallis, if not the specific sequence. A stab wound to the neck. Repeated blows to the face and dentition. Two blows to the head. And the angling of the posterior damage suggested that the ice axe had penetrated at roughly a forty-five-degree angle. Given the size and shape of the weapon, and the victim's height, if standing at the time of the attack, I estimated the assailant's height at somewhere between sixty-five and seventy inches. Fantastic. Slidell would have a field day with that. Only Sasquatch could be crossed off the list.

I paused, visualizing the one fuzzy photo taken during recovery of Hallis's body. Not crystal clear, but the slope appeared to have been moderate, with very few rocks.

I stepped back, considering. An ice axe to the neck. Multiple blows to the face and back of the head. I was unsure which injury killed her, but certain of one thing: Brighton Hallis's death was not accidental.

I stripped off my gloves and dialed Slidell. This time he answered.

"A little payback, Doc?"

I had no inkling what that meant.

"I call you at dawn, you call me at night when I'm catching some hoops."

While I'm busting my ass in an autopsy room. Without apologizing, I explained what I'd found.

Slidell made a noncommittal sound in his throat. In the background I could hear the frantic sound of play-by-play coverage.

"Ever think maybe the kid offed herself? Dove from a ledge?"

"Where the hell did that come from?"

"Your vic was in trouble up to her tits. I started digging into Bright Ascents, found a trail that led to Bert Malle over in Financial Crimes. You know him? He's that asshat wears—"

"Why financial crime?"

"Your golden girl was engaged in some good old-fashioned embezzling. Fraud guys were about to pop her when she split for Everest."

"But she was wealthy." This didn't make sense.

"*Eee*-lon was right. Her trust had a leash tighter than a—"

"Meaning?" Not up to a raunchy Slidellism.

"The kid was spending way beyond her means. Mostly on Everest."

"How much went missing?"

"About a mil."

"Roughly the amount Bright Ascents took in."

"It was a small charity with a lot of dumb donors."

"No one caught that the money wasn't going where it was intended?"

"It wasn't like contributors were hopping over to China to check on progress."

"Nepal." Jesus. Why did I bother? "What about Damon James?"

"Hard to say. Malle didn't have a handle on James. Looks like Hallis kept her cards pretty close to her chest."

"They're sure it wasn't mismanagement? Gass said Hallis had no head for business."

"They claim their evidence is solid. Despite the Hallis name, the kid was facing prosecution. Question was when, not if."

"Where's the money now?"

"Hadn't thought of poking down that hole."

Dead air.

I slammed down the handset and rubbed my eyes. Which felt like someone had lit them on fire. Time to go.

As I packed away the photos, bones, and cast, my gaze fell on the detached face pasted to the inside of the jar.

Uh-oh, that tiny brain-corner voice whispered.

What? Was I missing something? Or was it just fatigue?

I viewed the flat, lifeless features through the liquid and glass. The boneless nose. The shriveled lips. The elongated ears.

The tiny voice drew in its breath.

The ears? I looked more closely.

Sweet God in heaven!

As before, I flew to my office. This time I pulled out an envelope and jiggled a photo out onto the blotter. A blond young woman smiled in the sunshine under an immaculate blue sky.

I grabbed a lens and brought her face into focus.

Son of a bitch!

Fingers trembling, I logged onto the Internet and googled for more images of Brighton Hallis. Page after page popped up. I clicked through them.

Son of a freaking bitch!

In every shot in which her ears were visible, Brighton Hallis wore earrings. Studs mostly, but also loops and a few dangly numbers. It wasn't her taste in jewelry that had my heart banging. It was the undeniable fact that Hallis had pierced ears.

The mummy in the cooler did not.

Back to room five. To the lightboxes. To every X-ray I'd made into hard copy. I stared at the pickup-sticks jumble that contained within it the record of Brighton Hallis's youthful calamities.

Or did it? I'd been so focused on cause of death, I'd neglected the question of ID. Taken it for granted. Violated my own first rule.

Time to fix that.

Pulling on fresh gloves, I picked up and studied ME215-15's right ulna. Then I carried the bone to a magnifying scope, leaned into the eyepieces, and adjusted focus.

At sixteen, Brighton Hallis broke her arm while racing BMX. I searched the entire shaft, looking for gross evidence of an old healed fracture. Saw none. Only damage that was recent and postmortem.

My scalp tingled.

At eighteen, Brighton Hallis jumped into a quarry, hit bottom, and cracked her heel. I repeated my actions with the calcaneus.

No fracture line. No remodeling.

I checked the X-rays Hawkins had taken. Not a hint of old injury on the foot or arm bone.

I stood, eyes burning, the undeniable truth slamming home. The woman on the gurney in the cooler was not Brighton Hallis.

• • •

"What about DNA?" Slidell and I were back on the phone. The sports announcer was still sounding frenzied. Surprisingly, Skinny wasn't taking off my head.

"I'll phone in the morning, plead extraordinary circumstances. But I doubt that'll do any good. Fingerprints are a better bet."

"Call me when you have something. *Tomorrow*." Slidell hung up.

I drummed agitated fingers on my desk, recalling my earlier statement to Slidell. *Five went up, four came down.*

Was it true? Was Brighton Hallis still on Everest? If so, who was the unnamed guest in our cooler?

One candidate popped to mind right away.

The mysterious solo climber of confusing South American origin. The woman last seen with Brighton Hallis? I checked my watch. Checked the Internet, source of all knowledge. Kathmandu was ten hours ahead of Charlotte. Morning. Business hours. I picked up the landline, already hearing Larabee's lecture about fiscal restraint.

Slidell was right about both the quantity of numbers and the switching required to reach a knowledgeable official in Nepal. I finally got one in Chitra Adhikari of the Nepal Ministry of Tourism, Mount Everest permit and statistics office.

Chitra's English was limited, but eventually we do-si-doed into useful territory. In 2012, his agency issued thirty permits to expedition teams comprising 325 climbers. A veritable conga line up the mountain. They also issued nineteen unguided, or solo, permits.

"Can you fax me a list of those names?" I asked.

Chitra could. "Two thousand twelve, very bad year. Eleven people die on Everest."

It took a lot of repetition and word searching, but in the end I learned that seventeen climbers were airlifted alive to Kathmandu that season. Only one on May 20, 2012. The day Brighton Hallis died.

"Viviana Fuentes." The name sounded odd with Chitra's lilting accent. "Solo climber. Very sick."

"Did she survive?"

"Big puzzle. Woman disappear."

"On the mountain?"

"No. After. Helicopter fly woman to Kathmandu Medical College Teaching Hospital. So sick, carried on stretcher. Doctor arrives, patient is gone."

"She was dead?" Wanting to be clear.

"No. She walk out."

"She could walk?"

"Maybe she not so sick at lower elevation. This happens. Maybe she confused. This also happens. No one knows."

"Then, nothing?"

"Not quite nothing." I could almost hear his smile. "Chitra, he a curious guy. I call a friend in Immigration. Learn someone using Viviana Fuentes's passport fly from Kathmandu, Nepal, to Santiago, Chile." I heard paper rustle. A lot of it. Then, "That happen on June 5, 2012."

After thanking Chitra, I disconnected. Thought. Rubbed my temples. Thought some more. Then I hit the keyboard.

The images weren't as numerous, but they were there. Praise the Lord for social media.

A woman smiled at a camera from the deck of what looked like an Alpine ski lodge. Her blond hair was a little shorter, her frame a smidge stockier. Otherwise, the resemblance between Viviana Fuentes and Brighton Hallis was startling. I clicked more images. The two could have been twins.

I learned that Viviana Carmen Fuentes was born in Santiago, Chile, in 1987, a year before Brighton Hallis entered the world. She attended the University of Santiago and, after graduation, worked as an independent software consultant.

I learned that Viviana's resemblance to Brighton Hallis went beyond the physical. An avid climber since her youth, she'd attained brief notoriety at age nine as the youngest person to summit Ojos del Salado in the Andes. Viviana was taught to climb by her father, Guillermo Fuentes, an accomplished mountaineer in his own right. Fuentes Sr. died in a storm on Denali when Viviana was fifteen.

I learned that a charitable website linked Viviana's summiting endeavors to Alzheimer's fundraising efforts in honor of her afflicted mother. Viviana's Facebook page boasted that Everest would complete her Seven Summits. Surprisingly, the page went silent after 2012.

I also learned that Viviana Fuentes was dead.

Fuentes fell while attempting to summit Aconcagua, a mountain she'd successfully climbed in the past. The accident had taken place four months earlier.

I don't trust coincidence.

A new series of Google searches yielded what I needed. I again checked the clock. Revisited the time conversion site. Mendoza, Argentina, was one hour ahead of EST. Far too late to call at that hour. And far too late for me to still be working.

Frustrated and exhausted, I logged off the computer. I'd never hit so many twists in one case. As I drove home, questions swirled in my overwrought, overtired brain.

Had Brighton Hallis swapped identities with Viviana Fuentes? Why? To avoid prosecution? Had the trade been made willingly? Was Viviana Fuentes the woman lying in my cooler? If not Fuentes, who? And whom had the killer intended to put there?

CHAPTER 10

I was back at it early. Before making calls, I educated myself about Aconcagua. Located in Argentina, east of the Chilean border, the 6,900-meter peak is the tallest in the world outside the Himalayas. Though technically an uncomplicated climb, Aconcagua sees multiple casualties each year, and holds the dubious distinction of having the highest mountain death rate in South America. The most recently recorded was that of Viviana Fuentes.

Aconcagua also happened to be one of the Seven Summits still on Brighton Hallis's bucket list. A theory was congealing in my brain.

"Couldn't resist, could you?" I reached for my phone and dialed a lengthy string of numbers. Listened to a harsh international *brrrrppp.* "Had to make Daddy proud."

Another *brrrrppp,* then a woman answered speaking shotgun Spanish. "Centro de Visitantes del Parque Provincial Aconcagua."

I replied in Spanish, considerably more slowly.

"Yes, please may I help you?" She shifted to flawless English.

Fine. My Spanish was rusty. Taking the hint, I rolled with her and stated the reason for my call.

"Let me find the dossier." I heard the squeak of a drawer. Flipping. Shuffling. Actual paper files. "Ah yes, so tragic. Ms. Fuentes purchased an unguided, high-season Valle de la Vacas permit."

"Can you explain that?" *Por favor.*

"Of course. The park has two entry points and multiple climbing options. Permit prices vary depending on the season and whether a trip is guided. Ms. Fuentes intended a solo ascent along the Direct Polish Glacier. It is our most difficult route."

"How difficult?"

"The Direct Polish Glacier is secluded and significantly more challenging than the Ruta Normal. It has fifty- to seventy-degree snow and ice gradients requiring technical ice mounting skills, protection, and roped climbing. Few climbers choose this path. Ms. Fuentes did. Her résumé qualified her for such a permit." More shuffling. "According to our records, she entered the park at Pampa de Lenas station on December twenty-eighth."

"How many others were on the mountain during the period of her climb?"

This time keys clicked. "Three groups were up the Polish Glacier when Ms. Fuentes entered the park. We registered one other new climber that same day. An American. He ascended solo."

"Do you have the name of the other climber?"

"I have aggregated data with numbers and nationalities. Individual permits are filed by name rather than date. To match them up requires hand-sorting through records." She sighed. "If you leave contact information, I will phone you back."

I accepted her offer and provided my mobile number. "I'd appreciate the names of anyone summiting around the same time as Fuentes."

"According to the aggregate data, no one else checked in for the Polish Glacier until December thirtieth, when a German team began the trek up."

"The Germans found her body?"

"No. When Ms. Fuentes didn't return within an expected time, a ranger went looking. The German crew reported seeing a male climber descending solo, but never encountered Ms. Fuentes. It is presumed she perished shortly after summiting."

"Do I understand correctly? Rangers track the climbers?"

"Formally, there is no monitoring on the mountain. Permits are valid for twenty days. Climbers are encouraged to carry radios. If concerns are raised, a ranger will deploy."

"In Ms. Fuentes's case, concern was raised by . . ." I let the question hang.

"Pace is dictated by weather and ability. Most climbers arrive at the park acclimatized and ready to proceed. From the ranger station at Pampa de Lenas, it's a two-day trip up to base camp. It's another day to Camp One, and another to Camp Two. Summit day, departing from Camp Two, should take no more than twelve hours."

I did the math. Nine to twelve days.

"So the ranger went looking after two weeks?" I hazarded.

"Exactly. He located the body on January sixteenth at an altitude of sixty-four hundred meters, in a deep channel. It appeared Ms. Fuentes had fallen to her death. The remains were retrieved and transported to authorities in Mendoza."

"How was identity confirmed?"

"Identity was never in question." Puzzled. "Ms. Fuentes was carrying her permit and her passport."

"Do you have the number of the Mendoza morgue?"

I scribbled the information, hung up, and immediately punched in more digits. Minutes later I was connected to Dr. Ignacio Silva of the Cuerpo Médico Forense, Morgue Judicial. Again, I started in Spanish. Again the reply came in English. Well, muchas friggin' gracias.

"I remember the case." Silva's words were music to my ears. "It is a great pity when such a young woman dies."

"Can you describe Ms. Fuentes?" Barely breathing.

"Caucasian female, blond, approximately one hundred and seventy-three centimeters in height."

More quick math. Sixty-eight inches.

"Fit, no signs of disease or abnormality. Of course, there were significant injuries resulting from her fall. The drop was estimated to be a minimum of twenty meters."

"Did you take X-rays?"

A moment of hesitation. When Silva spoke again, there was a very slight edge to his perfectly honed English. "Due to budgetary constraints, there are times when we must make difficult decisions. I deemed X-ray unnecessary in this case. It was clear to me that the victim had died as a result of a fall followed by exposure."

Shit.

"Next of kin had no reservations?"

"Sadly, there really were no next of kin. Ms. Fuentes had a mother who was institutionalized with advanced Alzheimer's disease. But identity was never in question." He paused. "We did take fingerprints, for our records, before cremating the body."

"Is there any way you could share those?" Masking my excitement.

"Certainly. Provide an email address and I'll send you images."

Silva was true to his word. And efficient. Minutes after we disconnected, my inbox pinged notice of an incoming message. I opened the file and took a quick look. Then I sat awhile. Thinking and sipping coffee.

When that approach triggered no hundred-watt lighting up over my head, I pushed from my desk and went to make hard copy of the image Silva had sent. When the machine spit out its product, I checked the detail. Each dark little oval was full of loops or swirls or arches or whatever.

On to autopsy room five. I looked at the cast. The isolated bones. The card showing the prints taken from the mummy in the cooler. I lay Silva's prints next to those obtained by Joe Hawkins.

Considered.

Quick call to Blythe Hallis. Decision. I dialed Slidell to explain what was winging his way. And what I needed.

"Get someone to run them through AFIS."

I was asking that the prints I was sending be input into the FBI's Automated Fingerprint Identification System.

"The guys in the lab ain't gonna like it."

"Then you do it."

"What're the chances she'll be in the system?"

"She could be." It was a long shot, but I was hoping.

"Eeyuh."

"Look, only law enforcement can submit prints to AFIS."

"No shit."

"Tell them it's for me."

"That should do the trick."

It did. Or maybe it was Slidell's captivating personality. Ninety minutes later I had my answer.

I leaned back in my chair. Stunned. Not really believing.

I'd learned from Blythe Hallis that Brighton had interned with the National Park Service during her college summers. And I knew the AFIS database includes prints of individuals employed by the federal government. My long shot had paid off. One of the candidate "matches" generated by the search was Brighton Hallis.

Brighton Hallis had indeed perished atop a treacherous Seven Summit peak. But not on Everest. And not in 2012.

Brighton Hallis had died four months ago on Aconcagua. She'd been autopsied and cremated under the name Viviana Fuentes.

More phone time with Slidell.

"You're saying Brighton Hallis offed Viviana Fuentes to steal her identity?" Slidell sounded as though I'd suggested the outlawing of soup.

"The physical resemblance is remarkable. If they'd switched outerwear, it could easily fool the casual observer."

"I change jackets all the time. My ma still knows it's me."

Skinny had a mother? I stored that away for future consideration.

"Neither of the women encountered a KA after Brighton's death." I used cop lingo for known associate. "A woman wearing Viviana's jacket was airlifted to Kathmandu and subsequently disappeared. A woman wearing Brighton's jacket and gear was found by strangers, frozen to death. People see what they're told they see. And in Viviana's case there was no one to raise questions."

"What the flip does that mean?"

"Her only relative was a mother with late-stage dementia. Fuentes worked as a software contractor for herself, alone, from home." Slidell tried to interrupt. I rolled on. "And even if someone did raise questions, there was no body to exhume."

"How'd Hallis get Fuentes's passport?"

"Unguided climbers carry their own. Brighton probably helped herself when she switched gear."

"The two were pals?"

"I found nothing to suggest they'd met before Everest. It could have been a crime of opportunity. Brighton saw her chance to start a new life with a new name and a cool million. Took it."

Slidell made that throat noise he makes.

"That late in the day, they'd have been the only climbers foolish enough to remain that high up. It explains why Brighton loitered at Hillary Step, waiting for Fuentes."

"Not to help her, but to bash her." Slidell was coming around. "So Hallis arranges to be alone up top with Fuentes, takes her down with an ice axe, cracks her skull, maybe twice, smashes her teeth, switches gear, and skips on down the mountain with a fake Spanish accent, a new name, and a feigned case of the dizzies."

Not bad, Skinny. "Yes. The location of the head trauma is consistent with an assailant matching Brighton's height and weight."

"Risky business."

"So's prison."

"But Hallis is now toast?"

"Ash, actually. The body was cremated."

"Sonofaflyingbitch."

"Yeah."

For several seconds silence hummed across the line. I broke it.

"The only other climber up that route that day was a guy. I'm trying to track him down to see if he remembers seeing Viviana along the trail."

"What do you need from me?"

"See if you can find a connection between Hallis and Fuentes before Everest. Any evidence of collusion or premeditation. See if Hallis got sloppy after Everest. Slipped. Contacted someone. Used an old bank account. Got arrested for jaywalking. Anything to prove Hallis was living the good life in South America after 2012."

Clearly Slidell didn't share my enthusiasm. "Not sure the point. They're both history."

"Justice for Viviana Fuentes," I said.

"This ain't gonna make Blythe Hallis happy."

"But it will make her go away. And it puts a solve on your score sheet." Both persuasive arguments for Slidell.

After we'd disconnected I ran through everything I'd learned in the last few days. Got snagged on something Elon Gass had said.

I think Damon joined them.

Damon James had met Viviana Fuentes. Had talked to her and Brighton at Camp III. Might he have something to contribute? I looked up his number and dialed.

"Yeah." Distracted.

"It's Dr. Brennan."

"What?" I could hear a lot of commotion in the

background. Kids. A whistle. A dull echo that sounded like a train.

I repeated myself, louder.

"Sorry. I'm at my other glamorous job." James barked an admonition to someone named Brian. "At the Whitewater Center." I assumed he meant the U.S. National Whitewater Center, a state-of-the-art kayak and rafting facility on the outskirts of Charlotte.

"You're into kayaking?"

"They also have climbing and bouldering tours. I— Hey! Ease back!"

"I have a few quick questions. . . ." I began, but he cut me off.

"Put it down. . . . Now!" To me: "I can't talk in this chaos, and there's another busload of third graders showing up any minute. Can we do this after I clock out?"

Damn. "Sure."

He hesitated. "Actually, I caught a ride with another instructor today and she had to split to collect a sick kid. Any chance you could pick me up?"

Was he serious? The place was halfway to Mount Holly. Still, I wanted information. Nothing more to do here. Favor curries favor, blah, blah, blah.

"What time?"

"I'm done at eight. Drive around to the employee gate in back. It's never locked."

Three beeps indicated he'd disconnected.

CHAPTER
11

The rest of the day passed at the speed of continental drift. I ran a few errands. Did some paperwork. But my mind kept seeing fractures, prints, mummified tissue. Kept looping through theories. It was a relief to finally steer my Mazda into the remnants of rush-hour traffic at seven o'clock.

Forty-five minutes after setting off, I was at the U.S. National Whitewater Center. I parked as instructed and followed a sign pointing out the employee entrance. I'd almost reached the gate when my phone rang. Sang.

"Temperance Brennan."

"Dr. Brennan? It's Paola Rossi."

Total blank. "Excuse me?"

"At the Centro de Visitantes del Parque Provincial Aconcagua."

"Of course, Señora Rossi. I'm sorry. The connection is poor."

"I found the name you wanted."

"That's so kind of you." I began digging one-handed in my shoulder bag, looking for paper and pen. Stopped when Rossi spoke again.

"Can you repeat that?" Stunned.

Slowly and clearly she restated the name. "Damon James. He was the other climber ascending Aconcagua's Direct Polish Glacier route on December thirtieth. Mr. James listed his place of residence as Charlotte, North Carolina, United States."

Pulse humming, I thanked Rossi and disconnected. Around me, dusk was fast yielding to night. The lot held few vehicles. I heard no voices, no sounds of activity.

In my brain, disparate facts were snapping into place. Damon James was Brighton Hallis's business partner. *Snap.* Damon James had talked to Viviana Fuentes on Everest. *Snap.* Damon James had been on Aconcagua.

I dialed Slidell. Got voicemail. Left a message explaining my whereabouts and asking for a call back.

More snapping. This time questions.

Was James dirty? Had he and Hallis acted together to embezzle from Bright Ascents? Had he killed Viviana Fuentes on Everest? Why? To help Hallis switch identities? Were James and Hallis lovers? Did they have blood money stashed in some secret offshore account? Had James killed Brighton Hallis on Aconcagua? Why?

A woman in jeans and a bright green U.S. NATIONAL WHITEWATER CENTER tee approached. Smiling warmly, she held the gate open for me. I hesitated.

Jesus, Brennan. The slalom team trained for the freaking Olympics here. The place is probably crammed with people. Go. Find the creep.

"Thanks." I passed through the gate.

While crossing the grounds, I reviewed what I knew about the center. What I'd learned online before heading out. I'd never visited.

Four hundred acres, adjacent to the Catawba River.

Nonprofit. Training facility for the serious athlete. Recreational facility for the not-so-serious. Rafting, kayaking, canoeing, zip-lining, hiking, mountain biking, and, apparently, rock climbing.

I entered to the right of the main building. Registration, guest services, rentals, conference center, snack bar, gift shop. A few women sat outside under umbrellas at iron tables. Soccer mom types—Lululemon yoga wear, Jack Rogers sandals, Tory Burch shades. They played on iPhones, bored, waiting for progeny.

Beyond the building, a steady flow of people were exiting the main gate toward the general parking lot. A sign on an exterior wall provided two important facts. The last "put-in" was at 7 P.M. Closure was at 8 P.M.

I entered guest services and asked for Damon James. Was directed outside, to a towering fauxstone V jutting skyward beside the Upper Pond. James was at the base, coiling ropes into a box. He straightened on hearing my footsteps, turned. Big surprise. Whitewater Center tee with the sleeves razored off. The guy was predictable.

"Good timing." James flashed the movie star grin. "Let's walk and talk. I have to do a sweep. Make sure no kids are hiding out."

Though James was relaxed, I felt my pulse pumping hard. I followed him to a paved path skimming along the bank of the simulated river. Signs warned walkers to stay five feet back from the water's edge. Zip lines threw looping shadows from overhead.

James walked so quickly I had to lengthen my stride to keep up. Now and then we passed a late straggler heading for the exit.

To hide my nervousness, perhaps my suspicions, I tried casual conversation. "Is the circuit a complete loop?" Indicating the river. Not really caring.

He glanced at me, then nodded. "The water goes around two islands and forms multiple channels, but basically it's a big circle." He pointed to a landmass on our left. "That's Belmont Abbey Island. It's got a music venue and beer garden. Hawk Island's on the other side of Lower Pond. You'll see. It's wilder, has the obstacle and ropes courses."

"Mm."

"Tough crowd." James wagged his head. "How about this? You're looking at the largest and most complex recirculating artificial whitewater river on the planet."

"Impressive. And you teach here?"

"Seasonally. Rocks only."

We curved past tents on our right and a music pavilion on our left to a point where the wide Lower Pond stretched between us and the main center opposite. Pines towered above our heads and needles carpeted the ground at our feet. We were now the only people on the trail. Now or never.

"Elon Gass said you drew no salary from Bright Ascents."

James did a mock double take. "Well, well. I'm guessing the little lady didn't come out here for the pleasure of my company. I'm wounded."

"Were you paid?" asked the little lady.

James stared for so long I thought he wasn't going to answer. Then he surprised me. "I was supposed to get a salary. Didn't happen. I'm not really a delayed gratification kind of guy, but Brighton had a way of getting people to do what she wanted."

"The fund had a million bucks. Why didn't she pay you?"

"Guess we can't ask her."

"Did you know the police were investigating Brighton for fraud?"

"Not until your cop pal called me yesterday."

"What was the nature of your relationship with Brighton?"

"What are you getting at?"

"Were you together?"

"No. Nor were we thieves." Too pat.

Before I could poke at that, James spun and strode off at a pace even faster than earlier.

Momentary hesitation. Follow? Every neuron in my brain screamed no. I ignored them.

The river narrowed. The water now whirled and frothed in furious hydraulics. The sound was deafening.

"Tell me about Viviana Fuentes?" I shouted to be heard.

James wheeled on me, face a tight mask. "Let's not play games. What is it you really want to know?"

"What happened to Brighton Hallis?"

"What happened to Brighton Hallis? She got greedy, stole a million bucks, and left me holding the bag."

I said nothing.

"Shit was going to hit the fan after Everest." Spit so loud his neck muscles bulged taught. "And I was the chump about to be flattened by the Hallis Express."

"So you couldn't allow her to come down." My heart was going ninety. I knew I should back off, but couldn't stop myself. "With Brighton dead the investigation would go away."

James's chin hiked up, sending shadows slicing across his face. It was dark now, but a crescent moon was hanging above the tree line. And scattered floodlights kept the grounds from total blackness. When he spoke again his voice was ice. "When Brighton died on Everest, I had no idea that money was missing."

"You expect me to believe that?"

"I have an alibi, sweetheart. I was nowhere near Brighton when she bought it."

Every nerve tingling, I went for the kill. "Except Brighton didn't die on Everest. Did she?"

James regarded me, eyes glistening cool and green in the moonlight. Then, he startled me by chuckling. "You are fucking crazy."

"You knew of Brighton's plan to disappear. You were in on it from the start."

He circled an index finger at his temple. "Cra-zy."

"Tell me your version of events."

James crossed his arms. Spread his feet. "Imagine my astonishment when I spotted my former business partner, supposedly dead, coming out of the Aconcagua permit office in Mendoza, Argentina. Brighton Hallis, alive as a nasty rumor."

"What did she say?"

"She never saw me."

"You want me to believe that you both just happened to be in Argentina at the exact same place on the exact same day. Totally by coincidence."

"No. We'd planned the trip together."

"So—"

A chop of his hand cut off my question. "*Before* Everest. We'd scheduled our outings years in advance. After, when everything went sideways and no one was climbing, the trips were canceled. But Aconcagua fell on the anniversary of Sterling Hallis's death. For some fucked-up stick-it-to-myself reason I decided to make a pilgrimage in honor of Bright."

James's words were tumbling with fury now, carrying with them a note of madness.

"Go on."

"When Bright was gone, I went into the office and got the same permit she had. I knew her plan. I'd written the bastard. I trailed her every step, staying close behind, until I lost the benefit of crowd cover at Camp One. She spotted me. Son of a bitch, you should've seen her face. Pure terror."

"Continue." As unobtrusively as possible, I inched back a step. Why hadn't Slidell returned my call? Or had he? I couldn't risk checking my phone.

"The dumb bitch confessed everything. Her plan was to disappear in the icefall right above Everest base camp. The world would think she'd fallen into a crevasse when in fact she'd slipped down the trail and away to a beach in Goa or Rio."

"That's why she switched the Everest climb from guided to unguided."

"Made it easier to ditch me holding the bag."

"What about Viviana Fuentes?"

"Bad luck for Viviana, wrong place, wrong time. But that was pretty much Brighton. One lucky break after another."

Somewhere in the darkness, an owl hooted. I forced myself not to jump. "So it was a crime of opportunity?"

"I honestly don't know. Bright said it was. The resemblance between them was spooky." James was talking more softly now. I had to strain to hear. "Bright befriended Fuentes, learned her background. Saw a chance to walk into a new life and took it."

"Home free until she ran into you."

"Oh, she never gave up. That wasn't Bright. She tried to buy her way out."

"She offered you half."

"She did."

"You refused."

"Why would I do that?" Astonished. "What was

done was done. Fuentes was dead. We discussed our glorious life of shared wealth all the way to the top."

"You continued up the mountain?"

"Why not?"

This guy really was certifiable.

Or was I? Alone on a deserted path with an accomplice to murder. I put more space between us.

"Honest truth? Until the bitch transferred my share, I didn't want her out of my sight. Phones were useless at lower elevations. We had to get close to the summit to get an unblocked sat phone signal."

"She trusted you?"

"Of course. We were planning a long and happy life with our loot. She couldn't rat on me, I couldn't rat on her."

"But she died."

The reptilian eyes bored into mine. So flat they seemed to suck all warmth from the night. "Tragic, wasn't it? So close to the summit. Such a terrible accident."

Not just an accomplice. A stone-cold killer. The neurons again screamed a warning. This time I decided to comply. Too late.

In one lightning move James bent and charged. The impact of his shoulder knocked the breath from my lungs and catapulted me backward. I'd barely processed that I was falling when frigid, churning water closed over my head. I couldn't see. Couldn't breathe. Blood pounding in my ears, blind, I swirled with the current.

Kick! Fight!

I smashed into a boulder, winged off, spinning. My ribs screamed. My lungs burned. I tried to pull myself to the surface, but my waterlogged clothing dragged me down. Stars burst on the backs of my lids.

I forced my eyes open. Could see nothing but swirling brown chaos. Pulling with my arms, I angled my head in a direction I thought was up. I kicked. Kicked again, legs frantic, adrenaline firing through every fiber of my being.

Seconds seemed like eons. Finally my head broke the surface. I gulped air. Was dragged under again. Went wheeling. Fought my way back up.

I tried to get some bearings. To gain control of my flailing limbs. Failed. My body slammed another rock. Pain exploded up my back. Roaring filled my ears.

Then something. A shape in my peripheral vision. The pump house. I was being washed toward the filtration system.

My brain shot an image. Details taken in during my walk along the path with James. A narrow chute. Boulders forcing twelve million gallons of racing water through a three-foot gap. I was barreling straight for it out of control!

Before my mind could spit out a plan, I slammed the first boulder. Quickly pinwheeled to another. With animal desperation I struggled, finally managed to reorient my body. Despite the pain, I plastered myself like a barnacle to the rock's surface. Clung with every ounce of my strength.

The surging water pushed me hard toward the chute and the pump house. Straining against the flow, I clawed my way crablike around the rock's slippery circumference. Finally, I was able to heave my body topside out of the river.

I lay gasping. Too tired to turn my head. Too tired to look for James.

I don't know how long I stayed there before I started to shake. Cold. Shock. Both. Trembling, I rolled to my bum and sat up. Surveyed my state.

Soaked. Chilled. Possible fractures. No phone. No keys. But I was out of the water. And connected to land. Hawk Island.

On hands and knees, I crawled from the boulder to solid ground. Another brief rest. Then I rose on unsteady legs and headed for the nearest building. The pump house.

A man stood in the control room, doing something with switches and knobs. Denim overalls, look of surprise.

"Hi," I said.

The man's eyes went even wider, then dropped to the puddle forming at my feet.

"Do you possibly have a phone I can use?"

CHAPTER 12

"And then"—Anne flourished her fork for effect—"the damn rodent reached out a filthy paw, never breaking eye contact, and flicked my glass candle jar right off the patio table. Shattered into a million pieces."

"She didn't like the way you'd abused her man." I didn't point out that raccoons are not rodents.

"Maybe. It was some coon Bride of Chucky action. And those crafty buggers can get in anywhere. I slept for days with a bat by the bed."

I chuckled, then winced. Undirected, a hand went to my tightly wrapped torso. "Don't make me laugh."

Anne's look was a sympathetic question mark.

"Rib fractures take time to heal," I said.

"And the rest of you?" I knew she wasn't querying other physical injuries. Those had turned out to be minor. Even so, Slidell, the recipient of my pump house phone call, had insisted on ambulance transport. The sum total of my grievances included two cracked ribs, abrasions, and sore muscles. Seriously, seriously sore muscles.

"Right as rain," I said.

As if cued by my flippant response, my phone sang from below the table. I glanced into my open beach bag. The screen showed a caller with laser-blue eyes and wind-tousled hair. Surreptitiously, I hit decline. I'd tell Ryan all about the past few days. But not now.

"Here's to Isle of Palms." Anne lifted her wineglass and *chink*ed it against my ice tea. "Flat as a twelve-year-old." After a swallow of Chardonnay, she asked, "What'll happen to Damon James?"

"Hard to say." I pushed some lettuce around on my plate. Scored a crouton. The real reason to eat Caesar salad. "He didn't get far. After Slidell issued a BOLO, a CMPD cruiser picked him up at a gas station near Kannapolis. He's cooling his heels in the box right now."

"For murder?"

"Doubtful. There's no proof he killed Brighton Hallis."

"But you think he did."

I pictured cold green eyes. Remembered a bony shoulder slamming my gut.

"I do."

"Why did he do it? He had access to the money."

"Greed? Revenge? Rage? Feeling used can mess with a person's mind. So can the promise of a large sum of money. Maybe he wanted the whole pot. Maybe Hallis pushed him past the tipping point. Maybe it was a split-second impulse. Or maybe she just slipped." I didn't really buy the last option. "James is lawyered up and not talking. I wouldn't, either, were I in his shoes."

"But the asshole tried to kill you."

"They've charged him with assault and battery and attempted murder. He says I fell into the water. There were no witnesses. It's my word against his."

"So he walks?" Anne refilled her glass. To soothe her outrage.

I was outraged, also. Two girls dead in the most godforsaken places on earth. Fuentes on Everest. Hallis on Aconcagua. A good possibility no one would pay.

"James will definitely do time," I said. "There's a very patient, very determined crew over at Financial Crimes. They and the DA are working hard to ensure a conviction."

Anne nodded her approval.

I tilted my head to allow the offshore breeze full access to my flushed skin. "The paper trail is apparently a thing of beauty. Proving embezzlement was easy. So was tracking the missing money to James's Cayman Islands account."

"Dumb shit." Anne rarely minced words. Or held back.

I inhaled salt-laced air. Savored the roughness of Anne's beach house deck on the soles of my bare feet.

"How did Blythe Hallis take the news that her little angel was a crook?"

"As you'd expect," I said. "Composed, ever the lady." I thought a moment. Added, "She insisted on paying for Viviana Fuentes's burial in Santiago, next to her father. She's also making good for every penny of the stolen money."

"Really?" Anne took another sip, then settled back, legs up, ankles crossed on the railing.

"Same nonprofit. Same mission. New name. Vivi's Fund. Dara Steele and Elon Gass are going to run it."

"Out of the goodness of their little snake hearts." Anne chortled at her own joke. She did it a lot.

I shrugged. "Guess we'll have to watch *The Heights* to find out."

"Pass. If I want to observe narcissism in high places, I'll tune in to C-SPAN. How about a beach walk?"

"You're on."

She rose and carried our plates to the kitchen. I lingered. Wondering. Had Damon James been right? Or had something good come from bringing Brighton Hallis down from Everest?

Yes, I decided. Definitely yes.

Viviana Fuentes was mourned, if only by me. Lying safely beside her beloved father, she would not spend her eternity as a macabre landmark in a top-of-the-world death zone. It wasn't much. But it was something.

"Let's hit it." Anne had reappeared wearing a hat the size of her table.

We stepped out into the Carolina sun. Wind teasing my hair, sand caressing my toes, I felt the frozen knots of frustration begin to thaw.

AUTHOR'S NOTE

Bones on Ice was inspired by a story I read in the fall of 2014, describing more than two hundred bodies frozen in the so-called death zone of Mount Everest. The body of the legendary mountaineer George Mallory has remained intact on the peak since 1924. Others have evolved into more recent climbing landmarks, such as "Green Boots Cave," or "Rainbow Valley," named for the multicolored down jackets and climbing gear of corpses dotting the hillside. I was horrified and fascinated, and couldn't help wondering what would happen if one of those bodies came down and revealed unexpected secrets.

I immersed myself in researching the triumphs and perils of high-altitude climbing and began to write. This story was nearly complete when tragedy struck on April 25, 2015. A magnitude 7.8 earthquake hit northwest of Nepal's capital, Kathmandu, killing more than 8,000 people, injuring 23,000 more, destroying thousands of homes, and flattening entire villages.

An avalanche triggered by the earthquake slammed into Mount Everest base camp, killing nineteen, making it that mountain's deadliest day ever. Dozens more were injured and hundreds were stranded above base camp, futures uncertain.

On May 12, 2015, a second earthquake, magnitude 7.3, rocked Nepal, bringing further loss and destruction.

I stopped writing, uncertain. I didn't want to exploit such a tragedy. At the same time, I more than ever wanted to share the stories of Everest. I'd been touched by the heartbreaking losses and the triumphant victories.

I decided to complete this work to honor those lost, and to direct attention to organizations providing disaster relief, and to groups dedicated to improving long-term conditions for the indigenous communities of Everest.

Sherpas are a Nepalese ethnic group numbering around 150,000. They are renowned for their climbing skills and superior strength and endurance at high altitudes. They are essential to any Everest outing, acting as guides and porters, doing everything from carrying loads to setting up camps. They secure the climbing routes, fix lines, ferry supplies, and conduct clients to the top of Himalayan peaks. They also face the highest risks.

Devastation in the wake of the earthquakes is severe. Nepali relief efforts continue, and financial support is desperately needed. If you have been moved by the news, please visit the websites of these worthy nonprofit organizations:

ActionAid USA: act.actionaid.org/usa/nepal -earthquake-emergency-appeal

International Federation of Red Cross and Red Crescent Societies: ifrc.org/en/news-and-media/ news-stories/asia-pacific/nepal/earthquake-in -nepal-68486

Nepal Red Cross Society:
  ammado.com/nonprofit/155815
Oxfam International:
  oxfam.org/en/emergencies/nepal-earthquake

Nepali Sherpas serve as the bedrock of an industry with the highest mortality rate in the world, and do so for a fraction of the pay received by Western guides. Conditions in the region are harsh. Many worthy groups strive to ameliorate the Sherpa standard of living. Please visit the websites of the following nonprofits:

Himalayan Trust: himalayantrust.org/donate
The Juniper Fund: thejuniperfund.org
Sherpa Education Fund: sherpaedfund.org
Sherpa Healthcare Nepal:
  sherpahealthcare.org/index.php/donation

ACKNOWLEDGMENTS

As usual, I owe a debt of gratitude to others for their help on *Bones on Ice*. My daughter, the news junkie and author Kerry Reichs, has an unerring ability to see the stories behind the news. She read an article about bodies used as landmarks in the death zone of Mount Everest, researched high-altitude climbing, and brought me a "killer" story idea. I want to thank my assistant Melissa Fish for her unflagging enthusiasm and diligent research on any project I hand her.

Carson Sprow at International Mortuary Shipping was patient and thorough in walking me through the bureaucracy and details of shipping frozen remains from Kathmandu, Nepal, to Charlotte, North Carolina. Chuck Henson of the Charlotte-Mecklenburg Police Department good-naturedly fielded my questions on jurisdictional matters of international crime, no matter how bizarre. The editorial comments of Jennifer Hershey and Anne Speyer made the work infinitely stronger.

To prepare for this book, I immersed myself in the stories of those who climb. Credit for my newfound knowledge goes to *Into Thin Air,* by Jon Krakauer; *The Climb,* by Anatoli Boukreev; the website of noted mountaineer Alan Arnette; and numerous on-line articles and blogs that share their authors' personal experiences.

The dangers of climbing the tallest mountain on earth are legion, yet generation after generation responds to the siren song of Mount Everest. My story could not exist without theirs, so I tip my hat to all those determined to summit an impossible peak "because it was there."

FIRST BONES

CHAPTER 1

I sat with my chair drawn close to him, an icy heat hovering below my sternum. Fear.

Through the sliding glass door came muted hospital sounds. An arriving elevator. A rattling gurney or cart. A paged code or name. In the room, only the soft rhythmic pinging of sensors monitoring vital signs.

His face looked gaunt and greenish gray in the glow of machines tracking his pulse and respirations. Every now and then I glanced at a screen. Watching the lines jump their erratic zigzag patterns. Willing the pinging and jumping to continue.

Surgical Trauma Intensive Care Unit. So cold. So sterile. Yet a human touch: a stain shaped like Mickey's ears on one rail of the overcomplicated bed. Funny what you notice when under stress.

A sheet covered him from the neck down, leaving only his arms exposed. A pronged tube delivered oxygen to his nostrils. A needle infused liquids into a vein in his right wrist. The arm with the IV lay tucked to his torso. The other rested on his chest, elbow flexed at an obtuse angle.

I watched his sheet-clad chest rise and fall. Somehow his body looked smaller than normal. Shrunken. Or was it an illusion created by the fish-tank illumination?

He didn't move, didn't blink. In the eerie light, his lids appeared translucent purple, like the thinly peeled skin of a Bermuda onion. His eyeballs had receded deep into their orbits.

Hollywood's dramatic death scenes are a scam. A slug to the body destroys roughly two ounces of tissue, no more. A bullet doesn't necessarily drop a man on the spot. To kill instantly, you have to shoot into the brain or high up in the spinal cord, or cause hemorrhage by hitting a main vessel or the heart. None of those things had happened to him. He'd survived until a late-night dog walker stumbled upon him, unconscious and bleeding but still showing a pulse.

The wee-hours call had roused me from a deep sleep. Adrenaline rush. Shaky clawing up of the phone. Then the heart-hammering drive across town. The argument to talk myself into the STICU. I hadn't bothered with polite.

Death by firearm depends on multiple factors: bullet penetration deep enough to reach vital organs, permanent cavity formation along the bullet's path, temporary cavity formation due to transfer of the bullet's kinetic energy, bullet and bone fragmentation. All of those things had happened to him.

The surgeons had done what they could. They'd spoken gently, voices calm through the fatigue, eyes soft with compassion. The internal damage was too severe. He was dying.

How could that be? Men his age didn't die. But they did. We all did. America was armed to the teeth and no one was safe.

I felt a tremor in my chest. Fought it down.

Uncaring death was about to punch a hole in my life. I didn't want to consider the coming weeks. Months. We had done so much together. Fed off each other physically, emotionally. Despite the occasional aloofness, abruptness. The arguments. The unexplained retreats. The exchanges weren't always pleasant, but they spurred the process, helped us accomplish more than either of us would have managed solo. Now the future looked bleak. Unbearable sadness wrapped me like a shroud.

He'd been a good man. Capable. Devoted to his work. Always busy, but willing to listen, to provide feedback, sometimes outrageous, sometimes sage. Forever in motion.

I thought of the hours we'd spent together. The shared challenges. The identification of issues and approaches toward solutions. The painstaking attention to detail that could knit together a comprehensible whole from fragments. The shared sense of accomplishment in uncovering answers to perplexing questions. The mutual frustration and disappointment when no solution emerged.

I'd seen so much death. Corpses whole and partial, known and unknown. Lives ended in every conceivable manner. From the very old to the very young, male and female. At times cause was apparent, at others a puzzle requiring prolonged assessment and all my acuity. He was my greatest resource.

Throughout my career I was often the bearer of heartbreaking news. The changer of lives, informing anxious next of kin that their loved ones were dead. He'd been there. Or listened to my telling. Death was a constant in my work, and now death would put an end to this cherished partnership.

I looked again at the man in the bed. All was past. There would be no future.

The door opened and a nurse entered, rubber soles noiseless on the immaculate tile. She was short and round with ebony skin that gleamed in the monitors' reflected light. A badge on her scrubs said v. SULE.

Nurse V. Sule smiled, a quick upward flick of her lips, then patted my hand.

"He is having morphine." Accented English. Rich, lilting. "He will sleep long. You go, hon. You have a coffee."

"I'm good," I said.

Another pat, then Nurse V. Sule began checking fluid levels and dials and tracings. I scooched my chair to the wall and sat back down. I'd been in it for hours. Ever since he was wheeled into that room.

I watched Nurse V. Sule. Her movements were quick and efficient, but at the same time strangely graceful. I thanked her when she left.

The chair was uncommonly comfortable as hospital furnishings go, armed, padded, willing to tilt slightly if I leaned back. I wondered if seating of this type was specially selected for rooms hosting those facing vigils of long duration. For visitors helping usher in death.

I gazed at the rising and falling sheet. My vision blurred. The final breath would soon be drawn.

Exhausted, and overwhelmed by sorrow, I stretched my legs, angled my head back, and closed my eyes.

Just for a moment.

CHAPTER 2

Years earlier.

8:07 A.M. Wednesday, December 17.

The knob rattles. I feel a subtle pull of air, note the time, and look up, curious. It's winter break and the building is deserted. The entire campus is deserted. Who could be coming into my lab?

The door wings back and two men stride in. Uninvited. Both are tall, maybe six feet. One is thin. The other is not thin. Both are in their mid-thirties.

I'm annoyed at the interruption. I've been on the anthropology faculty at the University of North Carolina–Charlotte a single semester, my employment contingent upon having a PhD. The junior member of my doctoral committee has recently informed me that he won't be signing off on my dissertation. Not only did the jackass refuse to read my opus during summer break, now that he has read it he's demanding the inclusion of another trait in the statistical treatment.

The borrowed collection I'm examining is due to be returned in three weeks. Spring term looms and course outlines, lectures, and exercises must be prepared. I've yet to hang tinsel or purchase a single gift. So, yes. I'm not in a ho-ho-ho mood.

The heavy man has cop stamped on his forehead. Which, being greasy, matches his hair. Brown corduroy jacket, butt-shiny polyester pants, Kmart tie, kiss-my-ass swagger.

The thin man looks like an antonym in more ways than weight. Designer suit, silk tie, custom shirt, Italian leather shoes gleaming like soup. His hair is artfully arranged to disguise its erosion from his scalp.

I lower my mask but don't rise. The men cross to my work table. Kiss My Ass takes the lead.

"Where's Doc Becknell?"

"I'm Dr. Brennan." Premature on the title, but soon enough. If I can shake this pair and get back to scoring foramina. "Can I help you?"

"We need the doc."

"And you gentlemen would be?" Laying down my magnifier.

Kiss My Ass yanks a badge from his belt and holds it out for inspection. The leather fob is so new it still smells of cow.

"Congratulations on the promotion, Detective Slidell."

Slidell's chin cocks up and his lower lids crimp.

"Fresh off the press," I respond to his unasked question, then turn to his partner.

"Detective Eddie Rinaldi. We're sorry for the intrusion, ma'am."

"Where's Becknell?" Slidell demands.

"Unavailable."

"How 'bout we get her on the horn and make her available."

"That would be difficult."

"We live in difficult times."

"Dr. Becknell is on sabbatical," I say.

"Meaning?"

"She's away." I suspect this Slidell is oblivious to the ways of academia.

"Away where?"

"North Azraq, Jordan."

"Doing what?"

"Excavating. The site is Epipaleolithic, early Kebaran down to Acheulean. Also some lower Levallois-Mousterian layers." Half making it up, knowing the guy's clueless. Bitchy. But Slidell's arrogance isn't playing well with me.

"Dandy."

"Indeed."

Slidell's eyes hold on mine, then drop to the table.

"What's that?"

"Prehistoric cremains."

The eyes roll up, still irritated over my newbie crack. Maybe the archaeo-jargon.

"Burned bone," I explain.

"Who's the vic?"

"A girl who died in her teens."

"How?"

"Her heart stopped beating."

"You're funny."

"I try."

"So you do the same bone-whispering mojo as Doc Becknell?"

"What is it you want, Detective?" The clock is ticking. And I don't like this man.

"I've got a crisper needs a name."

"Excuse me?"

Hearing the disgust in my tone, Rinaldi jumps in.

"Let me explain, please. A physician named Keith Millikin vanished about a week ago. Dr. Millikin ran a street clinic off Wilkinson Boulevard, a one-man operation providing low-cost health services for indigents, the homeless, street kids—"

"Junkies and deadbeats."

I ignore Slidell. So does Rinaldi.

"When Dr. Millikin failed to open his office for five days running, one of his patients, a gentleman named Louis Grimm, filed a missing persons report."

I wait. Rinaldi doesn't continue.

"Go on." Guarded. I suspect where this is headed. Slidell opens his mouth, but his partner hushes him gently with a raised palm. I notice that Rinaldi's fingers are long and graceful, his nails buffed, his cuticles neatly trimmed.

"Dr. Millikin lived in an Airstream off Highway 49, down near the South Carolina line. Yesterday, getting no response from the police, Mr. Grimm persuaded his brother to drive him to Dr. Millikin's home. To make a long story short—"

"Which you ain't."

"—Mr. Grimm observed smoke damage to the rear of the trailer, found the door unlocked, and entered." Rinaldi sounds like he's reading from an incident report. "The trailer's interior was gutted by fire. Spotting remains among the debris, and feeling the authorities might once again ignore him—"

"Grimm bagged the bones and hauled ass to the morgue. Apparently he and his brother watch a lot of *Quincy*."

Though I know little about death-scene recovery, that doesn't sound good. I say nothing.

"The arson team will be heading there soon. From Mr. Grimm's account, a kerosene heater may be involved."

"Corpses ain't sausage. Smoking don't improve 'em." Slidell thinks he's quite a wordsmith. Again, I ignore him.

"I'm a bioarchaeologist. I don't do forensic work." Not admitting to the tiny skeleton I once examined at the request of an anthro grad student who is also a cop. Those images still haunt me.

"A charred stiff's a charred stiff," Slidell says.

"This 'charred stiff' "—hooking air quotes around Slidell's callous turn of phrase—"died two thousand years ago. A medical examiner won't be issuing a death certificate. An insurance company won't be paying beneficiaries."

"So why bother?"

"Archaeologists work to piece together humanity's past." Now I'm defensive and spouting boilerplate. "To reconstruct the complexit—"

"And a few eggheads in ivory towers give a shit."

"I believe interest in human evolution is much more widespread than that." Cool. How could I explain my love of bioarchaeology to this dolt? My passion for understanding people who inhabited the earth long before my birth? For learning of their accomplishments, their failures, the minutiae of their lives? The connectedness I felt when touching their bones?

Slidell shoots me a brief, pitying glance. Then he tries a different tack. A good one.

"Doc Becknell ain't so wrapped up in the past she don't care about the living."

That hits home. Still, I can't spare the time. But is work pressure the sole reason for my reluctance? Or is something else operating? Fear of inadequacy?

"Dr. Becknell has training in areas that I do not," I say.

Slidell laughs, a mirthless little snort. "Horseshit."

Heat flames my cheeks. I bite back a retort.

Rinaldi tries to defuse my anger. "That didn't come out the way my partner intended."

I say nothing. I think, Horseshit.

"Skinny means he's confident you possess the skill set required to ID this man."

"Skinny?" Slidell is far from that.

"Erskine."

Slidell glares. I store the nickname for future use.

"Dr. Millikin has family?" Against my will, I feel myself drawn in.

"A son. In Wisconsin." Rinaldi pauses, cop instincts triaging what is safe from what must be withheld. "Dr. Millikin was a loner. And, by all accounts, an odd duck. But his patients say he was a kind and generous man."

"You speak of him in the past tense."

"Dr. Millikin's patients insist that he would never willingly abandon them. A burned body has been found in his home." Rinaldi's brows float up. What remains to be said?

"Millikin was a whack-job, Millikin was a saint. It don't matter." Slidell, caring only about closing a file. "Until someone says otherwise, I got a John Doe in a cooler with a tag on his toe. If he still has a toe."

"Once more, with feeling. I don't do police work."

"You could."

Easy, Brennan.

"I'm very sorry. But I haven't the time right now."

"You got time for people haven't breathed since John the Baptist was handing out towels."

"Colorful image."

"I try." Slidell fires back my own quip. Though obnoxious, the man isn't dumb.

Slidell crosses his arms and gives me a hard green stare. I give it back. His fingers drum an impatient staccato on one brown corduroy sleeve. Several nails wear dark crescent caps. I refuse to consider the nature of the grime.

Around us, things hum quietly. The overhead fluorescents. The HVAC. The motor in the ancient storage fridge.

"If you'll excuse me." I rise.

The fingers drum faster. It's clear Skinny is used to getting his way.

Seconds pass. No one moves. No one speaks. Then Slidell fires one last volley.

"Guess the little lady ain't ready for prime time."

"Really, Detective." Calm. I want to reach out and stuff the Kmart tie down his chauvinist throat. "You can do better than that."

A bell trills, dismissing students far away on beaches and slopes.

Slidell's arms drop to his sides. His shoulders roll back. His lips part, but Rinaldi jumps in.

"May I say one last thing?"

I nod.

"Keith Millikin was an educated man. A physician. Had he chosen, he could have led a very different life. Taken cruises, driven Porsches, played golf at the club. He did none of those things. He lived in a trailer and treated the people whom society has kicked to the curb. The poor and forgotten. Should we forget him?"

Sonofabitch.

I make a decision that changes my life.

CHAPTER 3

The Mecklenburg County Medical Examiner facility is located in uptown Charlotte. The drive takes twenty-two minutes. That's where my mind is. Tallying lost time like a taximeter tallies up miles.

Using Rinaldi's directions, I find the place, a brick box with all the architectural whimsy of a Stalinist bunker. Signs tell me the MCME is at one end, satellite offices of the Charlotte-Mecklenburg Police Department are at the other. Parking is easy. The building is surrounded by enough asphalt to pave Orlando.

I kill the engine and get out of my VW Bug. The sky is clotted with clouds that are serious about rain. The wind is sharp.

I mount a few stairs and approach a window to the left of double glass doors. A woman is behind it. She is blond and probably living on a high-carb diet. Her cardigan is a shade of yellow that nails the daisies in her shirtwaist dress. A chain loops her chest, connecting the button to the buttonhole side.

I press my faculty ID to the window. The woman studies it so long I think she's memorizing the content. Finally satisfied, she gives me a big wide smile. Her teeth aren't great.

The lock buzzes. I enter a small vestibule and continue through a second set of doors. To the left stretch Cardigan's command post and four work carrels. To the right, groupings of upholstered furniture and wooden tables. Magazines. Plastic plants. The universal waiting room motif. Today, no one is waiting.

Cardigan greets me. She's younger than I thought. Too young for the severe perm and sweater clip.

"Welcome, Dr. Brennan." Vowels broader than juleps and grits. "I'm Mrs. Flowers."

We shake hands. Mrs. Flowers's grip could maybe crumple a tissue.

"Dr. Larabee is expecting you. I'll let him know you've arrived."

"Thank you." I assume Larabee is the ME.

"Please make yourself comfortable."

I sit facing the carrels. Only one shows evidence of use. Stapler, pens, stacked folders. A framed picture of Joe DiMaggio.

Behind Mrs. Flowers's desk is a mountain range of gray filing cabinets. Opposite the cabinets, on the far wall, is an erasable board divided into a grid. Numbers and dates fill some of the cells. Abbreviations I don't understand.

I assume the digit-letter combinations represent cases. Suicides, homicides, accidents, flukes. Deaths that have earned tickets to Y incisions. One entry has been designated ME1207. The code also incorporates the year. The letters *Sk-b* have been penned into one of the squares. I suspect this is the man I am here to inspect.

The meter ticks a long ten minutes. I wonder if Slidell is having success acquiring the antemortem records I've asked him to gather. If he's found a forensic dentist to look at them. I wonder if Rinaldi is learning anything from Millikin's neighbors.

Finally, a man hurries toward me with long, lopey strides. His limbs are sinewy, his torso lean inside blue surgical scrubs. I stand.

"Dr. Tim Larabee." He doesn't offer a hand. Fine with me. The bloodstains on his chest aren't reassuring.

"Temperance Brennan."

"I apologize for the delay. I have a gunshot case open on the table."

"No problem."

"Thanks for agreeing to pitch in." Larabee's gaze is intense. There's an air of coiled energy about the man.

"I don't know how helpful I'll be."

"You'll outperform me. My knowledge of bone is minimal. Ready?"

I nod. Pick up my purse and backpack.

Larabee leads me to the secure side of the operation. The "dirty" side. His Nikes make little squeaks when we cross from the carpet onto tile. My heels click softly. We turn down a corridor, pass several doors, stop at one with a plaque that says AUTOPSY.

"You're set up in here. I'll be over there." Indicating an identical door with an equally grim plaque. "This one's outfitted with special ventilation." In case I miss the meaning, he adds, "For odor. Joe Hawkins calls it the stinky room. He's my death investigator."

I can think of no response.

"I doubt you'll need it. There's almost no soft tissue." Larabee points to a door farther down the hall. No signage. "The locker room's there. We don't have women's scrubs, but a man's small should fit."

"Sexy."

Larabee looks at me, uncertain if I'm serious.

"Joe is away on a pickup, so I'm afraid you're on your own. He's set out forms, cameras, Dr. Becknell's kit. X-rays are on the counter. If you need anything, just ask."

With that he's gone.

I go to the locker room and change out of my street clothes. By rolling the cuffs and cinching the waist string I make it work. Pant legs flapping, I cross to the stinky room.

ME1207's intake form contains little information. A case number. A brief description of the remains, of the circumstances surrounding their arrival at the morgue. Slidell and Rinaldi are listed as investigators.

The room has one autopsy table, which is outfitted with an adjustable overhead light. Counters with cabinets above and below, a sink, a scale, a dissecting scope. Lots of gleaming tile, glass, and stainless steel.

A Nikon and a Polaroid sit on the counter. I check. Both are loaded.

Next to the cameras is a small metal suitcase with butterfly hasp locks. Assuming this is Becknell's "kit," I thumb the clips and lift the lid. Inside are the familiar tools of my trade: calipers, brushes, magnifiers, a diagram of sub-adult dental development, a list of equations for calculating height from long bones.

I search drawers, eventually find items to accessorize my fetching ensemble. Paper apron and mask. Latex gloves. I pass on the plastic goggles.

The cardboard carton on the table once held cornflakes. The number written on its lid matches that on the form and on the erasable board.

I shoot 35-millimeter prints, backups with the

Polaroid, then pop the X-rays onto wall-mounted light boxes. Each film makes a sound like a tiny thunder roll.

I hit the switches and, plate by plate, study the images. See a skull, other glowing white shapes I recognize as bones and teeth. Densely opaque blobs that could be dental restorations. I haven't a clue about the nature of the gray matrix.

I find a plastic sheet and spread it across the autopsy table, don my protective gear, and open the carton. My heart sinks.

The brothers Grimm have done a good job of separating decedent from Airstream. The box, half-full, holds mostly bone, little debris. The gray jumble turns out to be bits of charred carpet and fabric not easily detachable from the remains.

The brothers Grimm have done a lousy job of estimating the volume of a burned human being. And a lousy job of keeping that human being intact. Accompanying the skull are limb bones, all broken, the left half of a mandible, and a hunk of pelvis. Discoloration ranges from black to gray to white, suggesting varying degrees of exposure to flame. Eyeing the paltry postcranial assemblage, I know major parts are missing.

Slowly, gingerly, I begin transferring elements. Some are brittle and leave scatters of ash on the blue plastic sheeting. A few retain remnants of tendon or muscle cooked hard and leathery as beef jerky. A smell like cinders and charred meat permeates the air.

Eventually, a patchwork skeleton lies with arms and legs spread, torso sparse, hands and feet unrepresented. Though the skull has survived relatively intact, the face is badly damaged, and every dental crown is missing from the maxilla and mandible.

I center the skull on a rubber ring for stability. It stares at me with empty black orbits.

I begin my examination. My pulse settles. Grudgingly, I admit that Slidell is right. My skill set is dead-on.

I observe the orbital ridges and rims, the nuchal crest on the occiput, the hunk of pelvis, which includes the right pubic and sacroiliac areas. I measure the diameter of a decapitated femoral head. I record gender as male in my notes.

Enough of the right pubic symphysis remains to observe the articular surface. Two fragments of rib are complete to their sternal ends. Two isolated molar crowns, each showing moderate wear on its occlusal surface. I check the X-ray, see completed molar roots in the mandibular fragment. I record age as thirty-five to fifty.

With my ancient dead I don't address the question of race. But I know the markers. I observe a narrow nasal opening and tight cheekbones. Little projection of the lower face. A parabolic dental arcade. I write *Caucasoid* in my notes. Add a question mark. Erase it.

There is sufficient femoral shaft to calculate height. I measure, do the math, add the estimate to my profile. Five eight to six one. The range is broad and I anticipate Slidell's scorn. But the bone is incomplete and I'm unsure of the amount of shrinkage due to burning.

Still, Slidell will be pleased. The remains are compatible with what he and Rinaldi have told me about Keith Millikin.

But something bothers me. I know cremation of a human corpse takes an hour and a half at a thousand degrees Fahrenheit. Ballpark. The Grimm brothers reported minimal damage to the outside of the trailer. Yet Millikin is toast. I wonder how long the fire burned undetected. I know body fat can provide fuel after other combustibles have been depleted. I make a note to ask if Millikin was obese.

And something else is not right. The brain is roughly 75 percent water. With temperatures high enough and exposure long enough, that water turns to steam. The steam expands, causing separation along the sutures, cracking, sometimes explosion of the skull.

Millikin's head shows no thermal fracturing. Why?

I rotate the skull on its ring, studying every detail with a magnifying lens. Melted gunk coats the crown in back. Scrap by scrap, I tweeze it free. When the area is clean, I retrieve the magnifier. And feel an irrational flip in my gut.

I stare, breathing in the smell of ash and soot. I'm still staring, nose inches from the glass, when Slidell shoulder-barges through the door. His hair is flattened and separated into wet clumps. The corduroy jacket is mottled with dark splotches.

I glance at the clock: 12:14. The rain has started.

I set down the lens. "Detective."

No response. Slidell is seeing nothing but the burned man on the blue plastic sheeting.

"Did you obtain Dr. Millikin's dental records?"

He pulls an envelope from a pocket and tosses it onto the counter.

"Originals?" I have instructed him that copies are unacceptable.

"Yeah. Dr. Steiner's a real peach of a guy."

I imagine the conversation. Feel empathy for Steiner.

"Did you contact a forensic dentist?"

"None to be had."

"I'm not qualified—"

"So what's up here?" Hooking a thumb at the table.

I tell Slidell that the bioprofile is compatible with the descriptors he's provided for Keith Millikin.

He rolls that around.

"The victim is a white middle-aged male." I add this thinking he doesn't understand.

Slidell gives me a pained look, like I've said frogs can croak. Then the cop notebook comes out. A stub of pencil. He licks, then poises the lead.

"Shoot."

I outline my findings. He jots them quickly in some kind of shorthand.

"What else?" Without looking up.

I give him my height estimate.

"That narrows it to half the population."

"It's the best I can do with so much missing."

"What do you mean, missing?"

"Gone. Absent. AWOL."

"Burned up?"

"Or not collected."

"Like what?"

"His hands and feet. Most of his dentition."

"There enough to get a positive with those?" Jabbing the notebook toward Dr. Steiner's envelope.

"It's iffy."

"Iffy?"

"I have a total of three crowns."

"You know burned teeth when you see 'em?"

"Yes." Guarded.

A fraction of a pause, then the notebook slaps shut and disappears into a pocket. "You gotta go out there."

"No. I don't." I almost say "gotta."

"Doc Becknell would."

"I'm not Doc Becknell."

A moment of standoff silence. I break it.

"I have found something disturbing." Positioning the magnifier over the posterior right parietal, I gesture him to me.

Slidell circles the table, takes the lens, and brings the skull into focus. Up close, I see oily strips of scalp between the rain-parted hair. Smell drugstore cologne and stale cigarette smoke.

When Slidell finally speaks, I'm not sure what I hear in his tone. I know it's not good.

CHAPTER 4

"That what I'm thinking?" Slidell is sparking energy that wasn't there before.

"It is."

"You're sure?"

"Yes, Detective. It's a bullet entrance."

"How do you know?" He flips to a clean page in the spiral.

"The round shape, the radiating fractures, the beveling on the endocranial border."

Slidell's eyes come up and narrow in warning.

"On the inside of the skull."

"Where's the exit?"

"I don't know."

"Where's the slug?" The questions fire pepper-hot. I wonder if this could be Slidell's first homicide.

"It may have exited through an orbit, maybe the mouth or nasal opening. The face is too damaged to tell."

"Any way Millikin could have popped himself?"

"It's possible, but unlikely." I demonstrate by winging an elbow to point a finger to the back of my head.

"What else?"

"It puzzled me why Millikin's skull stayed intact. The bullet hole explains it."

Slidell twirls the pencil stub, impatient.

"It must have been an oven in that Airstream. At temperatures that high, liquids in the brain expand and the increased intracranial pressure leads to cracking, even explosion." An oversimplification, but good enough.

"The hole acted like a steam vent."

"Yes." Not bad, Skinny.

"So you're telling me some fuckbucket capped Millikin, then fricasseed his ass?"

"I'm telling you Millikin suffered a gunshot wound to the head. I don't know what killed him. If it *is* Millikin."

"What about those?" Indicating Dr. Steiner's envelope.

"I'm not a forensic dentist."

"I'm gutted. Just take a look."

Slidell watches as I remove a set of tiny X-rays and arrange them in anatomical order on an illuminator.

"Crap."

"What?"

"Millikin's dental work is all on the lower right. I don't have that half of the jaw."

"You think it's still out there?"

I shrug. Who knows?

Slidell makes a sound in his throat I cannot interpret. Shoots a cuff to check his watch. "Rinaldi radioed while I was on my way here. In twenty minutes, the arson boys start tossing that trailer."

I know that's a death sentence for fragile bone. Knowing I know it, Slidell hammers harder.

"By all accounts, this guy Millikin was Charlotte's

answer to Mother Teresa. You don't want to help catch the bastard that killed him?"

"That's your job."

"One day ain't gonna derail your life."

I know Slidell is playing me. I also know he's right. Conscience already booking a guilt trip, I cross to the phone. Check a list of extensions. Dial the other autopsy room. When Larabee answers, I explain the situation.

"We'll have to be careful with this."

We?

"How much are you missing?"

I tell him, then wait out a long, gaping pause.

"You think more teeth may have survived?"

"It's possible."

"Will you go out there?"

"I've never worked a fire scene."

"Suppose we do it together?"

I rearrange things in my mind. Take a look at priorities. Make another decision.

Millikin's Airstream is off Highway 49, almost at the South Carolina border. Too far south of Charlotte and too far north of Lake Wylie. Real estate that is cheap and untrendy. I pass few other homes along that stretch of two-lane.

I find the turnoff and make a right down a narrow track cutting through hickory, chestnut oak, and short-leaf pine. My wipers slap the windshield, fighting off rain. My tires spit gravel, struggling for traction. My radio pumps songs about angels and reindeer.

A quarter mile, then I reach barbed-wire fencing. Signs warn NO TRESPASSING in bold orange on black. The gate is open. I drive through and across a clearing.

The Airstream is a motor home, not the small bubble I'm expecting, silver with a bright blue stripe. The entrance is outfitted with an awning and makeshift wooden porch. On the porch is a green La-Z-Boy, stuffing sprouting from the seams like over-yeasted dough. The door has a square window with blinds covering the inside. Like the gate, someone has left it wide open.

I take a moment to assess. Behind the Airstream is a shed. Opposite the shed is a rectangle of dirt fenced in the same barbed wire that encloses the clearing. A triangle connects the three through soggy brown grass, gravel paths neatly edged with rock.

In the garden, stakes project from parallel mounds now devoid of vegetation. Rain pools between the mounds in long, skinny canals, brown-black and pockmarked by the deluge.

A truck is parked beside the Airstream, CHARLOTTE-MECKLENBURG PD CRIME LAB written on one side. A white Crown Victoria is parked beside the truck, a black Pontiac Bonneville beside that. I assume the cars belong to Slidell and Rinaldi. Not sure why. The Airstream must be towed by a vehicle. I ponder the whereabouts of Millikin's car or truck.

I pull in beside the Pontiac, kill the engine, and get out. Somewhere, a startled creature squeals. I glance around, banjos dueling in my brain. Seeing nothing sinister, I retrieve Becknell's case and the camera bag from the backseat, lower my head, and scurry to the trailer.

I enter what was once a kitchen. The air is damp and smells of smoke, scorched metal, and melted plastic. Everything wears a thick coat of soot.

My mind continues logging input. I note the burned-out hulks of a sink, stove, and fridge. Warped cabinetry. A blackened tube that probably supported a table. Pipes twisting inward from their points of attachment.

Slidell and Rinaldi are to my right, in what I assume is the living room. Wires dangle from the ceiling. Unrecognizable objects cover the floor and lie angled against walls or the denuded frames of built-in sofas or chairs.

Two arson investigators are present. One is taking photos. The other is down on all fours, making notes as he advances along a wall. I assume Slidell has told them the trailer is now a crime scene.

I set down the case and camera bag and start picking my way forward. Hearing movement, Slidell turns.

"Bedroom." Pointing toward the opposite end of the trailer. "Have at it. They've already shot pics."

I reverse, grab the equipment, and duck under toppled metal shelving, boots crunching on complicated stratigraphy involving a lot of broken glass. At the burned-out doorframe, a noxious element enters the olfactory mix. Gas or kerosene.

I stop dead, adrenaline zinging. Not the smell. The sight.

The room is small, maybe six by nine. Almost filling it is a jumble of charred rubble, blackened mattress coils peeking through. All that remains of a bed and bedding. To the right of the bed sits a scorched metal box, I assume the suspect space heater. Beside the box, a grotesquely distorted lamp. No bulb. No cord. No shade.

High up, on the trailer's rear wall, is another window covered with aluminum blinds. Bleak, rainy-day light oozes through the disfigured slats.

I make out footprints. Ash trails leading to objects stacked along the baseboards. The handiwork of the brothers Grimm. I realize it is pointless to try to reconstruct body position. To recapture information forever lost.

I step forward. Squat. See a chalky-white metacarpal. A talus. Moving ever so calmly, I open the case, pull on latex gloves, and drag my fingers through the ash. A molar crown rolls into the track, enamel brittle and checked by a latticework of spidery cracks.

I stare at the tooth, a funhouse of emotion whirling inside me. Can I do this? Unbidden, Slidell's taunt sounds in my head. *A charred stiff's a charred stiff.* Crude wording. But this morning I've learned it is true.

I shout, "I need light in here!"

Minutes later two battery-operated LEDs have the room blazing like a Hollywood set. Becknell's tools are laid out: trowels, brushes, strainers, tweezers, pipettes. I have marked the date, the location, and my initials on vials and evidence bags. I have prepared Vinac, a solution of polyvinyl acetate resin and methanol useful for preserving calcined bone.

I mask and go to work. Larabee arrives thirty minutes later. I explain the grid system I have devised for mapping the location of finds, then continue searching the east side of the room. He takes the west. We work in silence. I lose all track of time.

I'm dripping Vinac onto a crumbling incisor when I hear raised voices. Male. The words are muffled, but the cadence is clear. Both men are angry.

I look to Larabee. He shrugs, a bony move that makes me think of a turtle.

Cold and needing a break, I creak to an upright position. My knees are not happy with the new arrangement. I flex and straighten each to encourage circulation. Behind me I hear Larabee doing the same.

We are about to worm our way toward the kitchen

when Slidell appears in the doorway. He is tense as a cobra poised to strike. His face is the color of claret.

"You ain't gonna believe this."

"We've found most of the missing dentition." I think good news might prevent a cardiac event.

"We're busting our chops out here and who strolls in?"

"I'm not following." Larabee speaks for us both.

"The asshole himself."

Nothing.

"Jesus Christ. Do I have to spell it out? The dumb-shit doc."

"Millikin?" Simultaneous.

"No. Hawkeye Pierce."

Neither Larabee nor I appreciates the sarcasm.

"Turns out Mother Teresa's been partying south of the border."

"Millikin was in Mexico?" This is making no sense to me.

Slidell nods.

"Doing what?" Larabee asks.

"Muchachas and margaritas. Ain't they famous for it?"

"So who's this?" I arc an arm at the evidence bags lining one wall.

"Beats me." The LEDs cause a collision of shadows on Slidell's face. "But he took a bullet to the head and there's a shooter out there who's going down."

CHAPTER 5

It's after eight when I pull to the curb in a neighborhood just south of uptown. Like Millikin's rural patch, Elizabeth is far from hip. But rent is cheap and the quartier has a certain je ne sais quoi.

I kill the engine, hear the wail of an ambulance not far off. After six months, the sirens barely register. Presbyterian Hospital stands at the end of the block.

The rain has stopped, but water drips from live oaks spreading their branches from the parkway out over the street. The drops beat fat and erratic on the roof of my Bug.

Up and down both sides of Kenmore, primary colors twinkle on homes, shrubs, lawns, and trees. Here and there, electric icicles frame a window or door. At mid-block, a neon-blue palm beams its renegade Noel.

I'm cold, my clothes are sooty, and I smell like I've spent the day in a smoker. Though I've cleaned my hands as best I can, my nails are as grime-encrusted as Slidell's. My thoughts are focused on Pinot and a long, hot bath.

I lock the car and climb to the porch. Am triaging keys when my common-wall neighbor's front door opens. Artemis prances out. Mr. Speliopoulos follows on the other end of a leash. Artemis is a dachshund. Mr. Speliopoulos is a barber. We exchange Christmas greetings. Neither comments on my appearance.

I ease out of my jacket, drop it onto the stoop, and let myself in. A hammered tin mirror on the foyer wall reflects me dimly. My hair is a mess, my face speckled with ash.

Bowie and Jagger are singing about dancing in the street. I'm pleased to be spared more Magi or drummer boys.

Straight ahead, a no-nonsense staircase shoots to the second floor. The living room is to my right, the fireplace, mantel, and woodwork that seduced us into signing a lease. The dining room is toward the back, through a wide arch whose sliding oak doors are forever jammed in their eighty-year-old pockets.

Pete is at the table, a sea of law books and documents flowing around him. The Zamzow case. A limb lost as a result of a bungled diagnosis. So claims the plaintiff. At breakfast we discussed defense strategies. Mostly I listened. Breakfast seems a lifetime away.

"The archaeo-warrior home from the hill." Pete speaks without looking up.

"Sorry I'm so late."

"Long day."

"It was."

Pete's nose and upper lip crimp. I know the face. He's sniffed rot that must be tracked to a Ziploc or bin. Inserting a placeholder finger in the file, he looks up.

"Christ on a cracker."

I hang my purse on the newel post.

"What happened to you?"

"Bath first."

Pete gives me the full-on lawyer stare. I give him the full-on don't-ask-now stare back.

"Need a hug?" Sincere as a bookie at an audit.

"Many. After I've soaked."

The bath is all I hoped it would be. Bubbles. Lavender-peach shampoo and conditioner. The old claw-foot tub was also a draw.

Thirty minutes later, I descend smelling of Jo Malone Pomegranate Noir body lotion. I wear a long-sleeved T and flannel pajama pants, pink with sheep and white clouds. The sheep are either drowsy or drunk.

Wynton Marsalis is now playing low and cool, and Mount Legal has been relocated to the sideboard. A pizza box sits center stage on the table. Two places have been set, including mats, plates, utensils, napkins, and goblets. Pete is being thoughtful, even by Pete standards.

My husband and I agree on many things. The hilarity of *Catch-22* and *A Confederacy of Dunces*. Beaches over mountains. Woody Allen. Politics. Pizza is not among them. I like everything on my pie but blubber and ants. Pete is a purist—tomato and cheese.

I take my seat and open the box. Half-gloppy, half-plain. I relax a bit. Pete fills my glass with Pinot. I sip. I relax a bit more.

Though curious, Pete waits, all caring eyes and reassuring pats. He assumes something has gone very wrong at the university.

We talk of other things. His malpractice suit. Last

night's Tar Heels victory. The latest happenings on *Cheers*. Mr. Speliopoulos's taste in music. My comments tend toward the monosyllabic.

When finished, we uncork a second bottle and move to the living room. Pete lights a fire, then joins me on the couch. Wrapping my shoulders with one arm, he pulls me close. I lean in to his chest.

As the logs catch, we sit in a quiet made up of a hundred small sounds. The ticking of my grandmother's mantel clock. The muted *whoosh* of tires on wet pavement. Artemis's whining on the far side of the wall.

Despite the calming metronome of Pete's heart, the fire is a mistake. The crackling and popping trigger images in my overstimulated brain. Jarring, like slivers knifing under my nails. Sensing my disquiet, Pete doesn't push. Finally, three Pinots down, I unload.

Slidell and Rinaldi at UNCC. Keith Millikin, his street clinic, his mysterious disappearance. The fire at the Airstream. The discovery of remains by Louis Grimm and his brother. My finding of skeletal compatibility with Millikin's profile. The bullet hole. The missing dentition. My recovery efforts with Larabee. The startling appearance of Millikin himself.

Pete asks the obvious. "So who died in the Airstream?"

"A white male, five eight to six one in height, thirty-five to fifty years old."

"That rules out Tina Turner."

I smack Pete's arm.

He feigns hurt, then refills my glass. "This Slidell sounds like quite the character."

"He's an arrogant prick."

"Still, you liked it."

"Liked what?"

"Maybe *like* isn't the best word." Pete thinks, shakes his head. "I don't know. There was something in your voice."

"Pinot?"

"Not that." Again he hesitates, perhaps unsure, perhaps not wanting to offend. "An excitement I don't hear when you talk about your research. About archaeology."

"What you're hearing is terror."

"Temperance Brennan fears nothing."

I raise my glass in acknowledgment. He clinks my rim with his.

No one speaks as we consider what he has said. What I have said. Then he asks, "Terror of what?"

"Being wrong."

"You're never wrong."

"There was that one time. I thought I was wrong, but it turned out I wasn't."

Another clink. Another thoughtful pause.

"You're right," I say. "I was reluctant to get involved. But once in, I kept thinking about the victim. About who he was. Who he leaves behind him—kids, a wife, a girlfriend. I kept remembering that somewhere someone is missing him. And somewhere his killer is walking around free."

"And the terror?"

All day, I asked myself that.

"In archaeology I work with anonymous populations. I think in terms of demographics: males, females; juveniles, adults. No names or personal stories. My findings are discussed in print and at conferences—"

"Or ignored."

"My point is"—this time he gets an elbow to the ribs—"praised or disputed, my theories about the ancient dead impact no one's life. The opposite is true with forensic work. Evidence can be recovered or lost due to the competence of scene processing. An innocent person can be falsely accused. A guilty person can go free. Based on lab analysis, a family can find closure or continue to search. Based on court testimony, a suspect can be convicted or acquitted. It's a huge responsibility."

"No one reads a skeleton better than you."

"True. But knowledge of archaeology and osteology isn't enough for the cops or the coroner. I'm a rookie. I'd need to retrain big-time."

"Why do I sense that decision has already been made?"

"Even then. What if I screw up?"

"I'll represent you."

I roll my eyes. Which feel loose. "I'd need to work toward board certification."

"How long would that take?"

"The rest of my life." The Pinot is weighing in.

"We survived the bar exam."

"I'd need to apply for membership in the American Academy of Forensic Sciences."

"And finish your dissertation."

"And that."

Pete sets his glass on the table. Collects mine and places it beside his. Leans close and breathes hot in my ear.

I lean back and close my eyes, traveling with the sleepy-drunk pajama sheep. The fire is glowing warm somewhere behind Pete's back. I hook my arms around his neck.

The phone shrills. We both startle like kids caught in the backseat.

My eyes flick to Gran's clock: 10:42.

"Ignore her," Pete whispers.

"She could be in trouble." We both suspect my sister, who often calls in the wee hours. Or at dawn.

"Harry's always in trouble." Sighing, Pete draws back. "More wine?"

"Definitely not." I lift the handset and click on. "This better be good."

A short, startled pause. "For me or the guy got whacked?"

Now I'm the one taken off guard. Then the voice registers. "Excuse me, Detective. I was expecting a call from my sister."

"Sorry to disappoint." Clearly, Slidell isn't.

I say nothing. Pete rises to gather the glasses.

"Doc Larabee says you done okay out there today. So I got something for you." In a voice that kicks the apprehension back into gear.

Pete's cleanup has gone quiet. I know he's listening.

"Eddie and I got shit running our own MPs, so we spread out, floated some queries. Got a response from Gastonia." I hear rustling, picture Slidell checking his notes. "Russell Ingram. The wife reported him missing this morning. Apparently Ingram left for work two days ago, never came home. No one's been answering his office phone. When she went to check, it looked like hubby never made it in. You're gonna love this. The guy was a dentist."

"The nurse said nothing about his absence? The receptionist?"

"Ingram ran a one-man operation. Guess his patients weren't kicking up a stink about not getting drilled."

"How old is he?"

"Forty-two."

"White?"

"Yes."

"The height fits?"

"Yeah. He wasn't a hamster."

I ignore that. "Antemortem records?"

"We're about to roll one lucky dentist out of the rack."

CHAPTER
6

The next morning I rise at six, a move not popular with my frontal lobe. Pete is gone but has made coffee. I down a quart and eat a bowl of raisin bran. After filling my travel mug, I palm two aspirin and head to UNCC.

While driving, I realize that Slidell said zip about Millikin the night before. I wonder where the good doctor is now. If Slidell has questioned him. His story. His relationship to Russell Ingram.

I've been observing cremains for over two hours when the phone rings. Slidell has Ingram's dental records and will meet me at the MCME at nine-thirty.

I check my watch: 8:55.

I secure the collection and the lab and race uptown. Mrs. Flowers buzzes me in, and I hurry to the stinky room. It is empty. It stays empty for the next twenty minutes. Frustrated, I look for Larabee. He is nowhere to be found. I decide to make use of the time I'm losing by writing a report on ME1207.

After collecting my notes, I walk to the front, explain my intention, and ask Mrs. Flowers if a spare office and typewriter might be available. She fires from her chair as though on a spring-loaded hinge.

"You just come with me." Beaming like an over-permed deranged clown.

I follow her to a room beyond Larabee's office. It is small and claustrophobic and contains a single desk and chair. Beside the desk are shelves holding nothing but unused folders.

On the desk is a keyboard attached to a computer monitor. Between the two is a pair of cubes labeled DRIVE 1 and DRIVE 2. Each drive has a slot and a small red bulb marked IN USE. Neither bulb is lit.

On the keyboard is a brightly striped logo shaped like an apple, with **apple II** inserted into a missing bite. I'm pleased. Though far from experienced, during my grad training I've brushed elbows with Steve Wozniak's genius creation.

Mrs. Flowers explains the obvious. "It's a personal computer. New to us. Dr. Larabee hasn't even tried it."

"Do you need it right now?"

"Oh my heavens, no." She actually takes a step back in her little gray pumps. "I prefer my Selectric."

I thank her. She leaves, promising notification the instant Slidell arrives.

I press a button to the upper right of the screen. Drop into the chair. The processor whirs and the screen lights up. I'm relieved to see an icon for Word-Star, a software program I recognize.

In the desk's long center drawer, I find a pack of five-and-a-quarter-inch floppy disks. I insert one into a drive, open a file, and begin transferring information from my notes.

I've almost finished when Slidell shows up. It is ten forty-five. I ask Mrs. Flowers to send him to the stinky room, consider lingering to let him cool his heels. Reluctantly admit that such behavior would be petty.

Slidell is checking his watch when I push through the door. Seriously?

"Detective," I greet him.

He hands me a brown envelope, not big but larger than the one produced by Millikin's dentist. *Dr. Allison Martin* is scribbled across the flap. I wonder if being in the trade translates into better care. Or if Martin is merely more meticulous than Steiner about covering her ass.

I don't squabble about lack of qualification. To placate Detective Delightful, I agree to render a preliminary opinion but insist that a forensic dentist sign off on a positive ID. Or Larabee.

This time I use a tabletop illuminator that I've found in a cabinet. I plug it in, flip the switch, and arrange Ingram's bitewings on the top half of the glass. Below them, I do the same with the postmortem X-rays Hawkins has shot for the charred remains recovered from the Airstream.

The action is all on the lower right, and includes the following. An unerupted third molar sitting sideways in its socket. A root canal and crown in the second molar. Restorations in the first molar and first premolar shaped like Montana and Ireland, respectively.

The white blobs and spicules on the antemortem films superimpose perfectly atop those on the postmortem films. Every root shape is identical.

I have no doubt. The dead man in Millikin's trailer is Russell Ingram. Still, I take my time. Slidell's arrogance annoys me almost as much as his tardiness. Childish, I know. I'm not perfect.

Finally, I straighten and turn. "You'll need a forensic—"

"Yeah, yeah." He wiggles impatient fingers.

"*Unofficially,* it looks like a match."

Slidell is about to respond when the pager on his belt erupts in a series of jarring beeps. He yanks it free and reads the message. Crosses to the phone and dials. I hear his end of the conversation.

"Slidell."

Pause.

"Sonofabitch. When?"

Longer pause.

"Where?"

I collect Ingram's X-rays and return them to their envelope.

"Any chance of a visual?"

I do the same with the postmortem films.

"They need help out there? I'm with the anthropologist."

I pivot. Slidell's eyes are on me. I glare and shake my head.

"She ain't gonna like that," he says.

She? Me? Like what?

"Yeah. We'll hold tight."

Slidell cradles the receiver. "It's your lucky week, Doc. 'Tis the season for crispers."

"I don't work here," I say.

"Doc Larabee's at another scene, says he and Hawkins can handle recovery. He wants you to hang here and help with ID."

I picture the cremains in my lab. Know they're fated not to return to the lender institution on time.

"You want particulars?" Slidell asks.

"Sure. The suspense is killing me."

"This one's a car fire. Toyota Corolla, probably 1980."

I don't ask where or how. Or why the make of vehicle is important.

"They're peeling the driver off the wheel as we speak. It ain't going well."

"Just one body?"

"Yeah. The dumbshit hit a tree, then *blammo*." Explosion of fingers.

"There may be a medical explanation for losing control." I sound pompous, don't care.

"Yeah." Slidell snorts. "Or a pint of Jim B. rolling around on the floor."

Hawkins arrives at the morgue shortly past noon. That's when I get my first look at the "crisper."

When exposed to fire, muscles shrink and joints bend. In humans, this results in the pugilistic posture, or boxer's pose. This has happened to the ill-fated driver of the Corolla. Though baked and blackened, a shroud of soft tissue holds the skeleton together. The fingers, wrists, elbows, and knees are tightly flexed.

The body is lying supine, limbs up. Unbidden, my mind pops an image. A puppy rolled onto its back to play dead.

I understand why Larabee has requested my help. The face is a featureless mass above a mouth stretched wide in a hideous grin. No nose, ears, lips, or hair remain. The eyes rest like shriveled raisins in the lidless orbits. The genitals are toast.

I return to the wondrous Apple II to finish my report on ME1207. Hawkins completes full body X-rays and photographs by one and wheels the remains to the stinky room. They have been assigned case number ME1211. I spend the next two hours tweezing off remnants of clothing, soaking and stripping flesh, sawing free bone specimens needed to construct a bioprofile.

By three I've finished with everything but the two heaps of charred rubble that accompanied or came off the body. My head is pounding. Maybe wine, maybe lack of lunch. Maybe the unsettling truth I have found yet again.

I'm jotting my final note when Larabee comes through the door. He holds a small pink paper in one hand.

"Rinaldi called." The scrubs tell me Larabee has gone from recovery of the fire victim straight into an autopsy. From death to death. I wonder if I want any part of this world.

"The car was registered to a Mark Wong." Larabee sounds exhausted. "Chinese American male, age twenty-seven, height five foot six."

There's no need to consult my notes. "That fits."

"I'll have Slidell collect antemorts."

"Where is he?"

"Questioning Millikin. At headquarters. I think. I'm not sure."

"What's Wong's story?"

"He's an acupuncturist. Was. That's all I know."

"Look at this."

It unfolds as a replay of the previous day. I step away from the table and hand Larabee the lens. He studies the defect I've found at the back of the skull.

"That's a bullet hole." He turns to me, worry lines creasing his brow.

"It is."

"Like Russell Ingram."

"Yes."

"Same MO. Cap the vic, torch the body. Any link between the two?"

"Both are men. Both were shot in the head."

"That should crack the case wide open. I'll call Slidell."

When Larabee leaves I start examining debris. The pile on the counter contains the shreds of scorched clothing I've removed from the corpse. The pile on the gurney came in lying beside him.

Much is burned beyond recognition. Not all. I start with the gurney. Find the vestige of a leather sole. A lump of melted vinyl, probably from the car. A key. Not sure of the protocol, I begin an evidence log.

I'm working through the clothing when I notice a patch of denim with several metal studs. The thing is maybe two inches square. I figure it's a portion of the victim's jeans, from the area of the seat protected by his bum.

The denim seems thick. Too thick. I look closer, realize I'm holding two pieces stuck together. A remnant of a pocket?

Using tweezers, I gently tug the top layer. Grudgingly, it lifts. When I peel it back, my heart throws in a few extra beats. A fragment of something thin and pale clings to the underside.

The fragment is stained and charred on the edges. It appears to be paper. The paper appears to have writing.

I raise and lower the magnifier. The letters are faint and refuse to focus. Except for a few. When I read them my skin goes cold. What I see can't be correct.

Barely breathing, I try to decipher more. Fail. The ink is too faded.

I'm still trying when the phone shrills.

CHAPTER 7

"Whaddya got?" No salutation. I am learning the breadth of Slidell's charm.

"The bioprofile of the victim is consistent with that of Mark Wong. But you'll need—"

"Yeah, yeah. Wong's antemorts are on the way. I ain't spent this much time with dentists since I was nine. Anything else?"

"The victim was shot in the back of the head."

"Holy shit."

That summed it up well, so I said nothing.

"That what killed him?"

"Now that I've finished my analysis, Dr. Larabee will try an autopsy." Given the state of the body, I hold little optimism. I don't say that.

"You get the bullet?"

"None showed up on X-ray." Again, I mention the upcoming attempt at a Y incision.

"That it?"

"There is one other thing. I found a scrap of paper in what I think was the back pocket of Wong's jeans." Realizing my error, I correct myself. "The victim's jeans."

"Doc, I got a zillion—"

"The ink is faded, but I can make out some writing."

"What kind of writing?"

I tell him what I think I've read.

"You sure?" His tone says he's skeptical. But interested.

"No."

Slidell thinks about that for a moment.

"You got the thing?"

"Yes."

"You know how to get to headquarters?"

I tell him I don't. He gives me directions.

"Be in the lobby in half an hour. I'll call the document guy."

"I have to get back to campus, so please—"

Dial tone.

The Charlotte-Mecklenburg PD is headquartered in a big stone fortress at the corner of Fourth and McDowell. Though just blocks from the MCME, I drive, hoping to continue on to UNCC.

To my astonishment, Slidell is waiting as promised. Same corduroy jacket, but today the shirt is green and the tie is blue. On it is something that could be an emu.

We ride the elevator in silence, pointlessly watching each digit light up. Slidell stands with feet spread, thumbs hooked in his belt. Twice, he sighs deeply.

We exit on the fourth floor, turn right, and proceed to what appears to be the crime lab's administrative area. Doors bear plaques: CASE AND ADMINISTRATIVE FILES; CONFERENCE ROOM; DIRECTOR.

Beyond the director's office is a door labeled DOCUMENTS SECTION. We enter a room that is small and furnished with a standard government-issued metal desk, chair, and file cabinet. A small table holds equipment I assume is used for optic analysis and measurement.

Seated at the desk is a man on the shy side of medium. Five six, wiry, hair neither long nor short, blond nor brown. He holds an ear by one finger in a way that makes me think he's just been probing.

On seeing us, the man rises. He's wearing a lab coat with a neatly knotted tie in the V at his neck. We approach. Slidell greets the man as George. I'm unsure if that's his first name or his last.

Slidell introduces me as the anthropologist, nothing more. I hope George won't feel compelled to shake hands. He doesn't.

Slidell has explained in advance the purpose of our visit. George is expecting us and asks if I have the specimen. I produce the vial containing the illegible scrap.

George leads us out of the front area and down a corridor I find surprisingly quiet. I've envisioned lab-coated scientists hurrying to and fro.

We enter what is identified as the Photography Section and walk to the back of the room. A long table holds a setup that includes a desktop computer, cameras, a display screen, and gizmos about whose functions I'm clueless.

"Ever seen a Video Spectral Comparator?" George's vowels stretch even wider than Mrs. Flowers's.

I shake my head. Slidell says nothing.

"She's a pip."

Slidell and I look appropriately impressed.

"Know much about light?"

"High school physics." I suspect I'm about to learn more than I want.

"Light is a form of radiant energy that occupies the four-hundred-through-seven-hundred-nanometer range of the electromagnetic spectrum and travels in different wavelengths. When you see colors, your eye is actually perceiving those wavelengths. You with me?"

I nod. Slidell doesn't bother.

"When light is directed toward an object, one of five things can happen."

Slidell starts to speak. George raises and waggles a finger.

"All or most of the light can be reflected, making the object appear white or lighter. All or most of the light can be absorbed, making the object appear black or darker." He ticks points off on his fingers. "Part of the light can be reflected and part absorbed, producing colors in the visible portion of the spectrum."

Slidell clears his throat. George lectures on, oblivious.

"Light can be transmitted through the object." Pinky finger. "Light can strike the object, be absorbed, and then be reemitted at a longer wavelength, an event called luminescence."

George gestures at the VSC. "This baby uses a combo of cameras, lights, and filters to allow the examiner, *moi*"—tenting the fingers of one hand on his chest—"to produce each of these effects."

"We just want to eyeball some script."

"Some wavelengths of radiant energy aren't visible to the human eye." Clearly, George has his own agenda.

"Infrared and ultraviolet," I say, hoping to hurry that agenda along.

"Exactly. The effects I've just listed occur in both the visible *and* IR and UV portions of the spectrum. But there can be big differences. The same object that absorbed light in the visible spectrum and appeared black can transmit radiant energy in the IR spectrum and appear clear as glass."

Sensing Slidell's irritation, I try again. "So ink that's faded to invisibility can leave traces viewable using UV or IR."

"Precisely." Proud teacher to bright pupil.

"Can we just do this?" Slidell is out of patience.

Lips crimped in displeasure, George gloves, removes the scrap, and positions it in the VSC. A white rectangle fills the screen. I still can't read the writing.

George takes a seat at the table. "You're seeing what the camera sees. I'll now apply an IR filter to block all visible light. Only radiation longer than six hundred forty-five nanometers will be seen by the camera."

Slidell sighs and thumb-hooks his pants. Though the visit is his idea, it's clear he thinks the effort is a waste of his time.

The monitor goes green. The letters on the scrap luminesce like glowworms in an underground cave.

Slidell and I lean in, lime pixels highlighting our frowns.

A short, shocked pause.

"It's ballpoint." No one listens to George.

"What the fuck?" Slidell explodes. Straightens.

"Language," George admonishes.

Legible on the scrap are letters and digits. *K Mil ik AZ 364 8111*

"Where's the phone?" Slidell's eyes are bouncing around the room.

George points to a side counter. Slidell beelines, snatches the receiver, jabs keys, listens, face moving through a series of grimaces and scowls. Thirty seconds, then he slams home the handset.

"I need a copy of that." Hooking a thumb at the message shimmering on the screen.

"Of course."

George gives Slidell the original denim scrap and makes a print of the enhanced version. I say thank you as we hurry off. Skinny does not.

It's five. The lab-coated experts I'd imagined now crowd the floor. The wait for an elevator seems interminable. Inanely, Slidell thumbs the button again and again.

I don't expect Slidell to share intel on the investigation; still, I'm offended. Standing beside him, I seethe quietly.

Finally, I can hold back no longer. "It's the phone number at Millikin's clinic, right?" I keep my voice low and discreet.

Slidell adjusts his emu tie. Says nothing.

"Is AZ an abbreviation for Arizona?"

Slidell lets out a clip of a snort. "Yeah. The guy was a Suns fan."

I ignore the sarcasm. "Larabee thought you had Millikin here. Is he still in the building?"

Slidell's eyes flick to me. No response.

"You're heading downstairs to interrogate him."

Slidell jabs the button.

"I want to observe."

"No way."

"I'm an anthropologist. I have training in the subtleties of human behavior." Bullshit. But suddenly I'm on fire to see Millikin questioned.

"Look, Doc. I appreciate—"

"Ingram and Wong were both shot in the head, then burned. Ingram died in Millikin's trailer. I found the evidence you need to tie Millikin to Wong."

"What I need is for you to keep out of my way."

"So that's my response the next time you come begging for help?"

The elevator doors slide open. We enter. Are body-packed to the rear wall.

"Well?" I whisper.

"Jesus, Mary, and the Mousketeers."

The elevator stops on two. Slidell elbows his way out. I follow in his wake, heart plowing my ribs.

I wonder what the hell I'm doing.

CHAPTER 8

Slidell legs it so fast I find it hard to keep up. We blow by doors, signs showing the hornets' nest logo of the Charlotte-Mecklenburg PD.

Men move along the corridor in both directions, most in shirtsleeves and ties, one in khaki pants and a navy golf shirt featuring the intrepid wasp symbol. Some carry mugs or vending machine snacks. All pack a lot of firepower. I assume they are detectives.

Slidell thunders into a room marked VIOLENT CRIMES DIVISION. I thunder behind. The space is large and divided into cubicles housing desks, some solo, some in pairs. Each desk holds a phone, in- and out-baskets, the usual office paraphernalia. Flying by, I grab quick peeks of photos, sports memorabilia, sun-starved plants.

Some cubicles are occupied. From one floats a fragment of an argument about ballistics. From another, unrestrained snoring.

Greeting no one, Slidell weaves to a work space with two desks shoved together so the occupants sit face-to-face. Rinaldi is at one, receiver pressed to his ear with one hunched shoulder. He glances up. Looks mildly surprised.

Slidell half-turns, sees me. Something flickers deep in his eyes. Wordlessly, he drops into his chair.

I stand as Slidell ignores me and Rinaldi talks on the phone. It's awkward. I would rather be with my ancient cremains.

Slidell leans back, toes free a bottom drawer, rests one foot on it, and ankle-crosses the other on top. His socks are orange. I wonder if the choice is a fashion statement or simply bad taste.

Rinaldi wraps up his conversation and unfolds to get me a chair. I thank him and sit. He directs subtly lifted brows at Slidell. A poorly camouflaged question.

Slidell shrugs. "She tailed me from four."

My cheeks flame. He makes me sound like a puppy.

Rinaldi asks about our visit to the crime lab. Slidell describes the note in Wong's pocket. Maybe Wong. I don't correct him. He doesn't mention my role in finding it.

"So Wong knew Millikin. And Ingram was killed in Millikin's crib."

"Booyah," Slidell says. I don't know what that means.

"Finding Ingram's body in the trailer doesn't mean Millikin knew him," I toss out. "Or that he died there."

Rinaldi nods. Slidell asks him, "You get a prelim from the arson boys?"

"Both the trailer and the car fire were deliberately set. They found accelerants at both. Want to see the report?"

"No. What'd you dig up on Ingram?"

"Not much." Rinaldi looks down at his notes. "Ingram's office was shut down three years ago for failing to comply with health regulations. Got nailed on a random inspection."

"The state yank his license?"

The licensing body would be a dental board, but I say nothing.

Rinaldi shakes his head. "He was fined and reprimanded. But the media hopped on the allure of unsanitary conditions, ran the story a few days."

"Slime and drool always boost ratings," Slidell says.

Rinaldi digs a photo from a folder and hands it to me. "You asked about Ingram's weight?"

The man looks like an orange grove with legs. His hair, lashes, and brows are carrot, his skin, behind a blizzard of freckles, sunburn pink. He is seated in a leather chair, which he dwarfs, belly overhanging his belt and forcing his thighs wide. He holds a book low to divert attention from the unglamorous crotch. Or maybe he was actually caught reading.

"Ingram was a big guy," I say.

"Three twenty." Rinaldi returns the pic to its folder.

"Wife got motive? Insurance?" Slidell.

Rinaldi shakes his head. "She gets nothing. And without his income she'll have to sell their home. Ingram was in debt to his eyebrows."

"Tell me about Wong."

"Acupuncturist. His office shares space on East Boulevard with a couple of massage therapists and a hair salon."

"No one reported the guy missing?"

"He wasn't gone that long. A masseuse saw him leave his office around noon the day before yesterday. He said Wong bunched his appointments to avoid working daily."

"The home front?"

"Wong was single, lived in Dilworth with a roommate." Rinaldi flips a page in his notebook. "Derrek Hull. Hull sells hospital equipment and claims he's been in Florida the past five days. Says he has a list of clients can put him there. I talked to the employer and his story tracks."

"Any issues between Hull and Wong?"

"I checked for 911 calls to the address, complaints about noise, that sort of thing. Found zip. Canvassed. None of the neighbors ever heard yelling or saw them fighting."

I think this amount of digging is premature without a positive ID on Wong, keep it to myself. Less than a minute later, I'm glad. While Slidell is gone getting coffee, Rinaldi's phone rings. It's Larabee. He has the dental file and will be signing off on Wong.

When Slidell returns, Rinaldi gives him the news. Skinny shoots me an "I told you so" look. I think. Hard to tell since he's focused on unwrapping a Mounds bar.

"Either of these yaks have a jacket?" Slidell asks through chocolate and coconut.

"No," Rinaldi says.

A full minute crawls by. Around us, male voices, sporadic laughter, ringing phones. Finally, Slidell folds the candy wrapper and uses an edge to probe a molar.

"How 'bout you keep digging while I go at him?" he asks Rinaldi after irrigating the irritant tooth with coffee.

"Sounds like a plan."

Both detectives consider me. I feel my stomach tighten, my jaw clench.

Rinaldi shrugs. "She found the link to Wong."

Slidell eyes me so long I'm certain I'm about to get booted. Then his mug hits the desktop with a sharp crack. Not bothering to mop the spillage, he dials an extension and asks that an interrogation room be set up pronto. That Millikin be brought to it.

After downing the dregs of his coffee, Slidell glares in my direction. "You sit and say nothing."

I follow Slidell out of the squad room, down the hall, and into a tiny cell containing a metal table, two folding chairs, a speaker, and a phone. The floor is dull and scuffed, the walls cinder block painted puke beige. Centered on one is a rectangular window made of one-way glass.

Slidell motions me to a chair and leaves. When the door clicks shut my jaw relaxes. My gut doesn't buy in. I take a seat and place my purse on the table.

In minutes, the audio sparks to life in a symphony of hollow sounds. A rattling door. Footsteps. A scraping chair. The window lights up.

Millikin is at a table identical to mine. Behind him is a wall similar to those surrounding me. He's a skinny white guy wearing a cranberry sweater, plaid shirt, and baggy jeans. His hair is dull brown, side-parted and thin. Deep dark hollows underline his eyes.

Slidell sits opposite Millikin, looking like someone who eats kittens for lunch. An unopened folder lies before him on the table.

"Why am I here? A man died in my home. I've lost all my possessions. I should be under medical care for traumatic stress."

"Damn shame. How'd it happen?"

"What can I say? I was out of the country. I authorized no one to enter my trailer. I've no idea why Dr. Ingram was there. Or how he got in."

"You expect me to buy that?"

"It's true!"

"Why the junket to Mexico?"

"I needed a break."

"So you split without so much as an adios to your patients?"

Millikin's hands are tightly clasped on the table-top. He stares at them.

"Tell me about Ingram." Slidell isn't even trying for good cop.

"I treated him. We weren't close."

"Why would a dentist from Gastonia visit a street clinic in Charlotte?"

"I'm not at liberty to share that information."

"You gonna pull that patient-doctor crap on me?"

"Hardly crap. It's the law. And a physician's duty."

"Uh-huh." Slidell flips open the folder and studies a paper. I know it's a ruse. "Tell me about Mark Wong."

Millikin's face blanches and his fingers tighten. I notice they are trembling. I notice something else. A feature heightened by the newly paled skin.

A tumbling split second as the detail beyond the window collides with a recently stored image slapping into my forebrain. *AZ*.

"Holy crap!"

I fire to the adjacent room and pound on the door. As expected, Slidell is not pleased with the interruption. Before he can bluster, I pull him out into the hall.

"Millikin has AIDS."

"What the Christ are you—"

"The lesion on his nose."

"He's got purple crud. So what?"

"It's Kaposi's sarcoma. Millikin has AIDS."

Slidell looks at me like I'm batshit crazy.

"Even under infrared, the note in Wong's pocket wasn't fully legible. I think *AZ* was part of AZT, a

KATHY REICHS · 356

drug for treating AIDS. AZT isn't available in the U.S. yet."

It sinks in slowly.

"Can you get it in Mexico?"

"Yes." I overnod.

"Millikin was treating Ingram and Wong for AIDS. That's why Ingram hauled ass from Gastonia to Charlotte."

"It makes sense."

"Millikin was running AZT from Mexico. You think the sonofabitch was dealing through his clinic?"

"His lifestyle doesn't suggest that he was in it for the money. *If* he was in it."

A tight jerk of his head, then Slidell whips around and storms back in to the interview. When I return to my window, he's already grilling Millikin.

"—know you went south of the border to score AZT. How much were you nailing these poor bastards? A three hundred percent markup? Four? Five? Or am I thinking too small?"

Millikin doesn't respond.

"Or were you hoarding the stuff for yourself?"

"It wasn't like that." Barely audible.

"Yeah? What was it like?"

"These men live in shame. No one wants to treat them." All Adam's apple and black-sun pupils. "I try to help."

Millikin's next words make my heart rate gallop.

CHAPTER
9

"Dr. Ingram and Mr. Wong were both under my care. As I've stated, information pertaining to their medical histories is privileged."

Slidell starts to erupt. Millikin raises a hand.

"What I can tell you is that I am also treating a patient who detests both of those men."

"Why?"

"He believes that his"—Millikin searches for a word—"issues are due to interactions with Dr. Ingram and Mr. Wong."

"What issues?"

"I can't say."

"What's his name?"

"I can't say."

Slidell looks like he's about to throttle the guy. Instead he leans back, crosses his arms, and speaks in a voice made of steel. "You know I'm gonna get it."

"I do," Millikin says. "But not from me."

"I can make your life hell."

"You can."

"This patient. Is he heated enough to kill?"

"I'm not a psychologist."

Slidell draws a deep breath. Exhales. Pooches out his lips and rolls his eyes to the ceiling. Then he leans forward, elbows on the table. "Look. I want to help you, Doc. But you gotta give me something."

Millikin meets his gaze. His conscience allows, "This gentleman was also furious with a third party. For similar reasons."

"A patient?"

"No."

"Then a name's no problem."

"Nero Height. He goes by Nehi."

Slidell jots it on the file folder. "What's Height's story?"

"He's just a kid, a corner boy who also turns tricks."

"What's he deal?"

"Crack, H, speed, the usual."

"Where's he live?"

"I have no idea."

Slidell tosses down his pen and glares.

This time, Millikin glares back.

Thirty minutes later I'm in my lab at UNCC. Slidell has dismissed me and, grudgingly, agreed to keep me updated. I don't believe him.

I find it hard to stay focused on my thousand-year dead, I'm so jazzed on the events of the past two days. The fires in the Airstream and Corolla. The gunshot wounds to the skulls of Ingram and Wong. Millikin's AIDS. His excursion to Mexico to buy AZT. His story of an angry patient. Of the street kid, Nehi Height. Shortly after seven I give up and head out.

On the way home, I divert to Reid's and buy marinated flank steak, sweet potatoes, and asparagus.

Pete's favorites. On guilty impulse, I grab a miniature spruce trimmed with spiffy red bows and candy canes. Christmas is just a week away and our townhouse wears zip that is festive.

Surprisingly, Pete is home when I arrive. His case has settled. He has placed a plastic Santa on the mantel and hung mistletoe from the dining room arch. I show him my tree. We both laugh. I realize it's been a while since I've done that.

We vow to keep dinner a work-free zone. While cooking, we discuss our upcoming Yuletide plans with Harry and her new squeeze. Pete thinks he's Arturo. I go with Alejandro. We agree that the name is unimportant, since the poor chump will be gone by year's end.

The plates have barely hit the table when I mention my trip to police headquarters. Pete asks about Slidell. I tell him Skinny and I may run off together. He gives me a faux sad face, queries other developments. I fill him in on the day's progress. I think he'll comment on Wong's murder. He doesn't.

"Millikin's right. People with AIDS take a double hit. Not only are they sick, they're stigmatized."

I start to agree, but Pete hasn't finished.

"An AIDS diagnosis is a death sentence. There's no support system, no effective treatment, and society just turns its back on these people. Why? The public sees AIDS as a gay disease. There's an attitude that scum like homosexuals—"

"And IV drug users."

"—don't deserve special attention. Everyone wishes the poor bastards would shut up and die in private."

"Not everyone." I'm surprised by Pete's vehemence.

"True. But there's that element. Some say AIDS is

what homosexuals deserve, that they started the epidemic. That it was brought about by gay orgies, free sex. One genius has proposed tattooing everyone who's infected."

"That's insane."

"Can you imagine how it must feel? No one will kiss you on the cheek or let you hold their baby?"

"It must be truly awful."

"The problem is we don't know the cause."

"Ever heard of a nineteenth-century physician named John Snow?"

"He related to Chrissy?" Pete refers to the ditzy blonde on *Three's Company*. I ignore his quip.

"In the 1850s, Londoners were dying of cholera and no one knew why. Snow discovered that all the sick had drunk water from the same well. He didn't grasp the underlying mechanism but knew that pump was the link."

"And?" Pete, not seeing the relevance.

"He removed the pump handle."

"That stopped the outbreak?"

"It did."

"Your point?"

"Eventually the handle will come off the AIDS pump."

As we clear the dishes, attorney Pete hits the talking points for a theory coagulating in my brain.

"Wong and Ingram were Millikin's patients. Do you suppose he was treating them for AIDS?"

"Could be."

"Wong does acupuncture, a procedure involving needles. Ingram's a dentist nailed for running a dirty practice. Dentists also use needles and come in contact with blood."

"Yes."

"Millikin treats people with AIDS. Maybe his

angry patient also has AIDS. Maybe he believes
Wong or Ingram infected him."

"Ergo, the killings are about revenge." I finish the
thread.

A beat.

Pete asks, "Nehi Height is a prossie?"

I nod. We both understand the implication.

"Shouldn't someone warn the kid?" Pete asks.

"They're trying to figure out where he lives."

We finish our wine, watch the news, and retire. We
don't go right to sleep.

Five days pass. I hear nothing from Slidell or Rinaldi. Nothing from Larabee.

On the sixth morning, the phone rings as I'm
preparing to head to the university. I answer.

"The guy's name is Terry Flynn."

It takes me a moment to dial in. "The patient Millikin refused to name."

"Yeah." Slidell coughs, hawks something unimagi-
nable, spits, I hope, into a hanky. "Flynn's a banker,
which narrows it to half the suits in Charlotte. Lives
in Eastover, which means he excels at his job."

I hear voices, maybe drawers being opened and
closed. "Where are you?"

"Millikin's office. I've been going through files.
Dull reading unless you're into diarrhea and shit."

I doubt Slidell is aware of his pun. "You obtained a
warrant?"

"Nah, I'm going rogue. Think a little entrepre-
neurial zest might play well with a jury."

I muster the willpower to bite back a snarky retort.

"CSU found a boatload of AZT in the shed behind
Millikin's trailer. The doc was selling to his patients,
but charging only nickels and dimes. Except for one
lucky customer."

"Terry Flynn."

"Bingo. The fat cat was paying through the nose."

"Where's Millikin?"

"We had to kick him."

"Did you confront him with all this?"

"Yeah. He rolled. Admitted he piped the money to the clinic, used some to finance his trips south. Looks like his story's gonna have legs."

I wait out another cough. Then I share the theory Pete and I discussed a few nights ago.

There's a long moment of background noise.

"I'm going to talk to this fuckwit Flynn. Maybe you want to be there."

That astounds me. "Where's Rinaldi?"

"Height's sister lives in the Southside Homes. Nashawna." He elongates the second syllable unnecessarily. "Eddie's watching for Nehi, wants to give the kid a heads-up if he shows."

"Dumb question, but why are you inviting me along on this interview?"

Slidell does something in his throat I can't begin to interpret.

"Sorry?"

"You spotted Wong's memo, Millikin's gay cancer."

I let the latter slide and wait for further explanation. Slidell offers none.

"So, what the hell? Am I picking you up?"

"Sure." I give him my address. What the hell?

Slidell's Crown Vic is a rolling recycle bin. The day is cold, and a filthy sky promises it's going to get wet. The heater is pumping and the car's interior is over-ripe with smells. Old food. Sweat. Bad cologne. Stale cigarette smoke.

The drive seems endless. It lasts ten minutes.

Flynn's home is on Colville Road in one of Charlotte's caviar-and-Cadillac hoods. Circle drive, manicured lawn, house definitely not trying for subtle. The place is lit like a cruise ship on a holiday sail.

Slidell drives to the top of the circle. We get out and climb to a veranda spanning the entire first floor. Propped by the door is a toboggan that says MERRY CHRISTMAS, Y'ALL!

Slidell thumbs the bell. I hear a muffled chime that goes on longer than Wagner's *Ring Cycle*.

No one appears. No voice crackles from the little intercom box.

Slidell rings again.

No response.

Slidell resorts to the same battering tactic he employed with the elevator button.

Still nothing.

A window to our right throws slashes of light onto the brick at our feet. I step to it, lean close, and peer through the plantation shutters covering the inside of the glass.

The room is a library with floor-to-ceiling shelves holding hundreds of books. The furnishings have a decidedly masculine air. Carved mahogany desk. Large, angular sofas and chairs. A globe. Photos of sports figures on the mantel over a fieldstone fireplace.

Behind me, Slidell curses. As I turn, he kicks out at the sled. It sails, hits the wall, and ricochets onto the steps. The Y'ALL greeting wings off into a bush.

I cock a brow but don't comment.

We're walking toward the Crown Vic when the radio sputters. Slidell hasn't brought his portable, so he bolts for the car. By the time I slide in he's rehooking the speaker mic. He looks like he's just had a kick to the nuts.

"What?" I ask.

Slidell shifts and pounds the accelerator. We reverse so quickly my head snaps forward. He throws the engine into gear, guns down the drive, and cuts a fast left. I brace myself on the dash with both hands.

"What the crap?" I say with more feeling.

"A patrol unit spotted Flynn's Bimmer on Baltimore Avenue."

"And?" I don't know the street, the significance.

"It's parked opposite Nashawna Height's unit."

CHAPTER
10

The Southside Homes feel suburban to the extent that public housing can ever feel suburban— one- and two-story brick duplexes with small windows, small porches, and small front lawns that bleed into one another. Some units are fronted by shrubs, others by ragged dirt strips. Here and there, a window is edged with jingle bell lights. Not Chestnut Hill, but not the usual "government-bleak efficient" mode either.

Dumpsters sit at intervals along Baltimore Avenue. At one, a cat paws trash that has fallen or been tossed to the base. Its calico fur is matted and dull, its body cadaver-thin. As we pass, the cat's head whips up and it crouches so low its belly touches the ground.

Rinaldi's Bonneville is parked across from unit 8A, a short distance below the intersection with Griffith Street. He's in it. Slidell noses to the Pontiac's rear bumper and we both get out.

"Where's Flynn's ride?" Slidell asks.

"Gone when I got here."

"You talk to the sister?"

"Nashawna. She's not receptive."

"You clue her that Nehi's ass is in serious jeopardy?" Slidell is eyeing 8A. I'm sure Nashawna is similarly assessing us from behind the blue sheet draping the dingy front window. Suspect others are doing the same.

"I told her I was here to help."

"You say you're a cop?"

"No need. The lady's been through the system."

"She probably thinks you came to bust her brother."

Both detectives look at me.

Rinaldi says, "A unit's cruising, looking for Flynn."

"How 'bout you hang here while I chat with Nashawna?" This time Slidell has brought his hand-held radio. Not awaiting Rinaldi's blessing, he strides toward 8A. The Motorola looks like a brick in his hand.

I watch him climb the steps, ring the bell, wait. Open the screen and fist-bang the inner door. A series of dull thuds carries in the wintry air.

I notice a Weber grill beside the neighboring unit. A ceramic pot on a rusty tripod. A section of ankle-high picket fencing protecting both.

Thud. Thud. Thud.

I watch two small children coax a kite skyward in the area of common grass running behind the buildings. An old woman walking a pit bull that looks even older than she. Two geezers arguing, too far away for me to hear the point of contention.

I feel my fingertips turning blue. Think about gloves. Slip my hands inside my pockets.

Finally, Slidell pauses and his upraised hand drops. Though his back is to us, I see his shoulders angle downward and his head move in a way suggesting conversation. I assume Nashawna is listening to him through the smallest of cracks.

Slidell takes something from inside his trench coat. A beat, then he pivots and hurries to rejoin us.

"Christ. There's a brain trust."

"What did she say?" Rinaldi asks.

"She and Nehi ain't close. She hasn't seen him. Kiss my bony black ass."

"What do you think?"

"I think the kid probably has product stashed in her bedsprings."

"Now what?"

"Dispatch knows the situation with Flynn?" Slidell is scanning the block, not looking at his partner or me.

"Yeah."

"Tell them to find the dirtbag." Slidell's voice has that buzz again. "I'm going to drop the doc off, then swing back to Flynn's pad."

I don't protest. I'm not properly dressed and my toes are going numb.

We've gotten off I-77 south onto the John Belk Freeway and are approaching the Fourth Street exit when the radio spits something that snags Slidell's attention. He grabs the hand mic. As he thumbs and releases the button, I hear both ends of the exchange. Flynn's car, a black BMW 735i with tinted windows and North Carolina plate NNX-43, has been spotted heading south on Tryon Street toward Griffith.

"Tell them to stay on it."

"The unit is no longer in visual contact."

"Sonofabitch!"

We spin a U-ey sharp enough to launch me sideways into the passenger-side door. Slidell activates flashing headlights and a *whup-whup* siren and bulls his way across Fourth and onto Third. We're barreling back the way we came when dispatch again summons him.

"What?" Barked.

"A Nashawna Height just dialed 911 asking for you."

"What's she saying?"

"A man is parked across the street watching her place."

"What's he look like?"

Pause.

"He's white."

"Jesus on a jump rope. What's wrong with people? Old, young? Tall, short?"

Pause.

"She says he's a tall skinny white guy."

Slidell's scowl tells me the description fits Terry Flynn.

"Height calling from home?"

"A neighbor's phone."

"Tell her I'll be there in less than five. Keep her on the line."

"I'll try. She's pretty agitated."

I feel my heart beating way too fast.

Dispatch keys in again. "Height says she's watching the guy from the neighbor's kitchen window. Says he's out of the car and walking toward her building."

"Is her brother with her?"

Short pause.

"The brother is in the home."

"You got a unit en route?"

"Yes. Hold on."

Long pause.

"Height thinks the guy's armed."

"Tell her to stay where she is. I'm three minutes out, max."

Slidell runs a stop sign at the Remount Road exit. Drivers hit their brakes and their horns.

The dispatcher's voice reemerges from the static. "The caller says she's leaving to help her brother."

"Order her to stay put! I'm almost there!"

My heart is now racing as fast as the Crown Vic. I know we can't reach Nashawna or Nehi before Flynn gets to the door.

No response.

"What's happening?" Slidell demands.

"I lost her."

"What do you mean you lost her?"

"She hung up."

At Baltimore Avenue, Slidell makes a high-speed right turn and mashes the gas pedal. Halfway up the block a white panel truck pulls from the curb. Slidell slows a hair, swerves around it, and accelerates. In the side mirror, I see the receding driver wave a one-finger salute.

"Where's Rinaldi?"

"On his way."

In moments we squeal up behind Flynn's BMW. Slidell throws the gearshift into park. My whole body lurches forward. He is out before I can right myself.

"Ass on the leather!" he shouts, finger jabbing at me. He starts toward 8A, gun drawn and held low by his thigh.

My fingers are white on the dash. I push myself back. Realize I'm not breathing, and inhale deeply.

I look around. See the Pontiac but not Rinaldi. No cruiser. No Flynn. No Nehi. No bony black ass.

The kids are gone from the grass. The pit bull granny. The bickering men. I'm glad. Every instinct in me is howling danger. Adrenaline is pumping hard.

I lower my window and listen. Except for distant

vehicles, all is still. Just traffic and my hammering pulse.

Seconds pass. A full minute. I hear a scrape followed by a crash. My mind offers no picture to accompany the soundtrack. Then recognition. The tripod-urn has been upended and shattered.

I'm digesting that when a gunshot rips the cold morning air. Another follows. A third.

An image explodes in my forebrain. Slidell ambushed, bleeding out on the icy lawn. Maybe Rinaldi.

A man bellows. Another bellows back. The voices come from behind 8A. I can't make out the words.

I'm not good at taking orders. Never have been. I know I should stay where I am. That I'm untrained. That I shouldn't put myself at risk.

But I need to find out what's happening. And hiding in the car isn't going to help a damn.

I take a few calming breaths and slip from the Crown Vic. Do a three-sixty sweep, then, moving as discreetly as possible, diagonal toward the gap between 8A and its neighbor.

I see them as soon as I round the house. Slidell. Nashawna. Nehi. Flynn. I assume Rinaldi is near but out of sight. All are locked in a tableau of horror and shock.

Flynn has Nehi at gunpoint, barrel pressed tight to his throat, forcing his chin up at a painful angle. They are on the back stoop. The door has flown inward and is no longer hanging square on its hinges. Muddy footprints suggest Flynn has kicked it in. A trio of small holes explains the gunfire.

Nashawna is at the rear of the neighboring unit, hands pressed to her mouth, hunkered behind the Weber. Slidell is beside her, gun held two-handed and pointed at Flynn.

Flynn's body is little more than a skeleton shrink-wrapped in bruised flesh. His face is emaciated, the cheeks hollow, the eyes sunken, the nose a spiny beak sharply contoured by the underlying cartilage and bone.

"You didn't tell me, you twisted little prick!" Flynn's voice trembles with rage.

"Tell you what, man?" Nehi's words are choked due to pressure on his trachea and the unnatural thrust of his jaw.

"You killed me, now I kill you. Eye for an eye, *man*. Justice, *man*? The Bible tells me so."

"What the fuck you talking about?" Nehi is small and wiry with eyes like those of a terrified dog, deep brown and rimmed with way too much white.

"You signed my death certificate, you sick little bastard."

"You talking that gay immune shit? I ain't got that, man."

I hear an engine, tires, car doors opening behind us on Baltimore Avenue. The sputter of a radio.

"It's so wrong. You sell heroin and crack. You sell yourself. You're scum. I had so much to live for and you took it all away."

"I said drop your weapon!" Slidell shouts. I know he isn't firing, for fear of hitting Nehi.

Flynn jams the muzzle deeper into Nehi's flesh. Tightens his grip on the handle. Though Flynn is far taller than his prey, his posture is so stooped their heads are almost level.

Feet pound in our direction. I note the rhythm. Four.

"I'm telling you one more time!" Slidell yells. "Drop the gun."

Nehi is a scrapper. A survivor. And afraid for his

life. What happens next is a testimonial to that powerful trifecta.

Flynn's eyes cut to the sound of the approaching footsteps for a sliver of a second. Sensing the shift, Nehi twists, hooks one leg around the back of Flynn's knees, shoulder-shoves his chest, and strikes at the gun hand. Flynn goes down with a sound like logs striking a hearth. The gun flies free.

"Height! Back away!"

Ignoring Slidell, Nehi straddles Flynn's chest and presses both his wrists to the ground. It's no contest. Teenage street fighter versus middle-aged invalid. Though Flynn struggles, Nehi has him pinned.

The choreography is spontaneous and fast. Slidell closes in. Rinaldi steps from behind the unit to the north, gun straight out and aimed at Flynn. Two uniforms round the house, see the action, and draw their weapons. Nehi jumps free and scuttles sideways. Rinaldi scoops Flynn's gun from the grass. It is over in seconds.

Nashawna scrambles from behind the Weber. I run forward and wrap her shoulders with one arm. Tears stream down her cheeks. She is shaking and allows me to restrain her.

"He's okay," I say. "Everything will be all right."

"That man crazy," she says. "Nehi don't got no AIDS. His girlfriend made him get hisself tested."

Over her shoulder, I see that Flynn is on his feet. One of the uniforms cuffs him, reads him his rights. Nashawna and I watch him and his partner lead Flynn away. He walks between them, wobbly, limping.

I try but feel little sympathy for Flynn. He is dying, but murdered two men and tried to kill a third. I can forgive that he is angry. Confused. Distraught. I cannot forgive that he is vengeful.

And I cannot forgive that he is self-righteously judgmental. That he views himself as superior to Nehi Height. His life as more valuable.

Terry Flynn is an arrogant ass.

"Thank you," Nashawna says.

"Thank them." I indicate Slidell and Rinaldi. The cops who are folding Flynn into the backseat of their cruiser.

Nashawna lifts one shoulder in a noncommittal shrug.

Slidell is talking to Nehi, his bearing haughty, his tone brusque.

I think, You are arrogant, Skinny Slidell. But far from an ass.

Flakes are now swirling in indifferent eddies, not snow, not rain. I watch a few settle and dissolve on the grass.

Nashawna says something I fail to catch.

"I'm sorry?"

"Happy holidays," she repeats quietly.

I have forgotten.

It is Christmas Eve.

CHAPTER
11

Years later.
  Something brushed my shoulder, spiderweb-soft.

I opened my eyes.

A silhouette blocked my view of the screens, a dark cutout against the aquamarine glow.

"How are you doing?" Whispered, voice filled with compassion.

"I'm good," I lied.

Andrew Ryan smiled encouragement. I tried to smile back. Managed only a melancholy tightening of the corners of my mouth.

"You need a break?"

I shook my head.

"How's he doing?"

I shook it again, more slowly, not trusting my voice.

"Want company?"

"Sure."

Ryan disappeared, returned from the corridor with a second chair. Dropping into it, he reached out a hand. I took it. Held tight, overcome with a tangle of emotions.

Time passed.

The monitors paraded their bloodless peaks and valleys. Sounded their impartial pinging.

And then they screamed. And the lines went flat.

Ryan's eyes met mine, too blue, too wide.

Adrenaline snapped through every cell in my body. No!

The door winged open and Nurse V. Sule charged in and grabbed the crash cart, all stainless steel and bright red drawers. On top were a defibrillator and what looked like a tackle box.

Others raced in with her, color-coded in their scrubs. Faces grim, focused.

I got to my feet. Sensed rather than saw Ryan rise beside me. My eyes were fixed on the man in the bed.

Nurse V. Shule threw back the sheet, now motionless as the sea after a wild storm. Ripped open the gown covering his chest. Her eyes skidded to me as she positioned her palms, one atop the other, for CPR.

"Please." Tipping her head toward the open door. Arms already pumping.

Ryan and I hurried out into the corridor. Stood, not knowing what to say. What to do.

Feeling helpless, and needing to move, I crossed to the window and looked at the city spreading out eleven floors below. The day's first pale light was tickling the horizon. The skyline of uptown rose out of the gray, a grainy black-and-white version of its daytime self.

A barrage of memories unspooled in my brain, some immediate, some distant. His voice on the phone. His form bent over a shallow grave. His eyes taking in a ghostly white newborn. His hands traveling over a mummified corpse.

Guilt swirled in the mix. A sister was coming from Fort Worth. What else did I know of his personal life? There were no children. Had there ever been a spouse? Partners had come and gone. I remembered no names.

I pictured his goodbye wave the evening before. Casual. Unaware he was living his last day on earth.

The onslaught was dizzying. The recognition that we would have no final parting. That words left unsaid between us would remain unsaid forever.

It couldn't be true.

Footsteps sounded, heels sharp on the tile. Not the soft-soled tread of the hospital staff.

I turned.

Two men were hurrying in our direction. One was dressed all in black, save for a small white rectangle at his throat. The other wore a plaid sport jacket over a grease-stained apricot shirt. Polyester pants.

Slidell's hangdog gaze met mine. Our mutual stare lasted what seemed a very long time. Then, eyes downcast, he veered toward Ryan.

The priest took a chair, laced his fingers in his lap, and closed his eyes.

It was true.

Tim Larabee was dying.

I felt tears burn my lids. Fought them back.

Behind Ryan and Slidell, through the open door, I saw a nurse slide a clear plastic mat under Larabee's back as V. Shule tore paper packets, withdrew pads, and attached them to his chest. When she'd finished, both women glanced at the defibrillator screen. V. Shule's lips formed a single word.

"Clear."

Everyone stepped back from the bed. Larabee's

body arched. Arched again. Lay still. The other blue-clad nurse placed two fingers on his carotid. Checked the pulse in his wrist. The screens. Shook her head.

V. Shule began a second round of chest compressions.

Ryan and Slidell were speaking in hushed tones, heads bowed and close. I swallowed, inhaled deeply, and crossed to them.

"—hopped up on crank. The sonofabitch—"

Slidell stopped abruptly when I drew near.

"Larabee was out for a late run?" My voice was calmer than I'd dared hope.

Slidell nodded, sorrow making his face look older than its legitimate claim. And exhaustion. I knew he'd been working all night, searching for Larabee's assailant.

"He was a random victim?"

"Wrong place, wrong time."

How often we'd talked of the fickleness of life. Larabee had coined a phrase for its sudden, unpredictable cessation. Death by acute numerical assumption. The victim's number was up.

A casual goodbye wave. A late-night jog in Freedom Park.

Behind the men, a nurse in green injected meds into an IV line. A bubble of space opened around the bed. Larabeee lurched, lurched again. Then a nurse in blue checked for a pulse. A man in white made notes in a file.

"Who's the doer?" Ryan was in cop mode. Keeping his emotions buckled down.

Ditto Slidell. "A street kid name of Garret Hearst. A real piece of work."

"Meaning what?" I asked.

"Hearst's a tweaker with too few brain cells left to wipe his own ass." Angry. Harsh. "Who the hell mugs a jogger? What's he gonna do? Carry a wad in his shorts?"

"You're sure he's the shooter?" Ryan asked.

"Surveillance video puts him in the park around the time a wit recalls hearing shots. The dumbshit left the gun at the scene. His prints are all over it. Ballistics will show a match."

To the bullets that ripped through Larabee's belly.

"When was that?" I had to know.

"Eleven-fifteen."

"The dog walker discovered him just past midnight?"

"Yeah."

Our little group fell silent, appalled by the ghastly image. Horrified by the possibility that quicker intervention might have saved Larabee's life.

"Where's Hearst now?"

"In the can."

V. Shule was again pumping Larabee's chest. My mind had done the math. Two minutes of CPR, then a vitals check, followed by defib. I glanced at my watch. Thirty minutes had passed since Larabee flatlined. I wondered how long the lifesaving efforts would continue.

"Have you interviewed the kid?" Ryan.

"The little prick's too fried to know his own name."

As suddenly as it began, the desperate dance stopped. In the room at our backs, everyone froze.

Larabee lay unmoving. Like the mourned and unmourned dead he'd tended to so gently for so many years.

The man in white looked at the clock. Spoke aloud. Entered time of death in his file.

The priest rose.

V. Shule circled the bed and drew the sheet up over Larabee's face.

Goodbye, old friend.

And then the tears had their way.

Seeing my distress, Slidell stepped forward and wrapped me in a crushing bear hug. Our cheeks touched. To my shock, his were salty-wet like mine.

Standing awkwardly, off-balance, I realized something for the first time. Through all the years—the triumphs and failures, the sorrows and joys, the harrowing rescues and the heartbreaking deaths—Skinny and I had never once embraced.

I leaned against him and wept on the apricot shirt.

AUTHOR'S NOTE

An origin story. That sounded like fun.

As I began to write about Tempe's start in the lab, it made me think of my own beginnings in forensics. In the early 1980s I was on faculty at the University of North Carolina–Charlotte, focusing on bioarchaeology. The ancient dead. One day, a Charlotte-Mecklenburg PD detective asked me to examine bones discovered beneath a house. I was teaching courses on human evolution and skeletal biology, but had never worked with law enforcement. It sounded intriguing. I agreed to do the evaluation.

The remains were those of a dog. Case closed. The police brought me other skeletal material from time to time and I told them what they had. Then I got a call that would change my life. The detective spoke of a missing five-year-old girl named Neely Smith. He wanted me to visit the scene. To determine if the small bones could be human. If they could be Neely's.

They were. Her murder hit me hard. She'd been the same age as one of my daughters. I wanted justice. Didn't get it. The prime suspect, an eighth-grade dropout, was never charged. He's currently serving a life sentence for eight counts of child molestation and the murder of a ten-year-old girl who'd lived one block from Neely.

The lack of closure was frustrating. I resolved to contribute what skills I had toward the resolution of such crimes. After retraining and earning certification by the American Board of Forensic Anthropology, I began consulting for law enforcement, coroners, and medical examiners. ID. Manner of death. Postmortem interval. Anything to provide answers for families and to help nail the guilty.

People in towns that have suffered crimes against children remember the names of those victims for years. Charlotte, North Carolina; Soham, England; Praia da Luz, Portugal. All have been scarred by violence against the helpless. The innocent.

A sad but true fact is that, unlike in fiction, not every killer is caught. In Neely's case, her bones were identified but her aggressor was not charged. I carry the names of several such children in my memory, and I am burdened by the knowledge that there will always be new murders, not all of which will be solved.

While Neely's case propelled me into forensics, the majority of deaths I investigate are not those of children. The victims in *First Bones* are adult males. Their murders take place in the 1980s, a time when the country was facing a different type of killer. The AIDS/HIV epidemic. For those of us working with the dead, AIDS and HIV posed a new and real danger.

The human immunodeficiency virus (HIV) and related acquired immunodeficiency syndrome (AIDS) were little understood in the early 1980s. The disease was initially thought to affect only gay men. Few preventive public health measures were in force. The medical community was slow to appreciate the widespread danger and did little to guard against it. But as evidence about the deadly nature of AIDS accumulated, drastic changes in procedure were introduced.

Medical examiners, forensic anthropologists, and laboratory technicians donned special masks and aprons and goggles and gloves. We avoided unsafe contact with the bodily fluids of corpses. We followed strict new guidelines for the handling and disposal of blades and needles. The threat was real and we were taking it seriously.

Improved medical methodology has slowed the spread of the disease. Education of at-risk populations. Better pharmaceuticals—drugs a long time coming.

Though much progress has been made, we still haven't "removed the pump handle," as Tempe says to Pete in *First Bones*. According to the Centers for Disease Control and Prevention, roughly 1.2 million people are living with HIV in the United States, with fifty thousand newly infected each year. Only 87 percent are diagnosed.

In 1985, a small group of people conceived a project to commemorate those who had died of AIDS. Known as the Names Project AIDS Memorial Quilt, the blanket is a patchwork of three-by-six-foot panels, each recording the name of a decedent.

I first saw the quilt in the early 1990s, during a visit to Washington, D.C., to see my daughter. It stretched from the Capitol Building to the Washington Monument, inviting us to sit down and learn about the disease.

When I saw it again in 1996, rectangles representing over eighty thousand people covered the entire

Washington Mall. Today the quilt has more than forty-eight thousand panels containing names from all fifty U.S. states and forty-three countries. If laid end to end, they would stretch for miles.

It is the storm of illness-related emotions that drives *First Bones*. The daily anxiety of those with HIV. Their fear that the condition will progress to AIDS. Their worry that they may have transmitted the sickness to others. Their struggle with the duty to disclose. Far worse is the agony of those diagnosed with full-blown AIDS. Their heartbreaking knowledge that the virus will kill them. That the death will not be pretty. In my story, these feelings grow strong enough to result in murder.

I sometimes think of my own "quilt." The bones to which I could not put names. The victims of violence whose perpetrators remain unknown. Or unpunished. I try to keep my work separate from my personal life. Try to leave the stories at the morgue. Still, in unguarded moments, the unsolved cases break into my thoughts.

I take satisfaction in knowing that most Jane and John Does go home to their families. That most killers are caught. I believe in the power of science. To battle disease. To solve crime. I will continue to apply my expertise in forensic anthropology toward the pursuit of justice.

For more information on
the Names Project AIDS Memorial Quilt, visit
aidsquilt.org/about/the-aids-memorial-quilt.

ACKNOWLEDGMENTS

I owe huge thanks to Roger Thompson, the former director of the Charlotte-Mecklenburg Police Department crime laboratory. Together, we reconstructed how it was "back in the day."

ACKNOWLEDGMENTS
FOR *THE BONE COLLECTION*

Writing is a team sport. I receive a great deal of help from many people. Thus, as usual, I owe a tremendous debt of gratitude to those who contributed their knowledge and experiences to the stories in *The Bone Collection*.

First and foremost, I must thank my daughter and fellow author, Kerry Reichs. Her ideas and insights are pure genius.

My sincere thanks to my agent, Jennifer Rudolph-Walsh, and to my meticulous and skillful editors, Jennifer Hershey and Susan Sandon.

I also want to acknowledge all those in the industry who work so hard on my behalf. At Random House in the United States: Gina Centrello, Kim Hovey, Scott Shannon, Susan Corcoran, Cindy Murray, Kristin Fassler, Cynthia Lasky, and Anne Speyer. Across the pond: Rob Waddington, Aslan Byrne, Glenn O'Neill, and Georgina Hawtrey Woore. At Simon & Schuster, north of the forty-ninth: Kevin Hanson. At William Morris Endeavor Entertainment: Katie Giarla, Elizabeth Goodstein, Tracy Fisher, and Raffaella De Angelis.

I appreciate the support of my tireless aide-de-camp, Melissa Fish.

To my readers, thank you for continually putting off sleep, filling (and photographing) your shelves with the series, and taking Tempe along on your own adventures. I love that you make the effort to find me at my signings and appearances, visit my website (kathyreichs.com), share your stories on Facebook (kathyreichsbooks), follow me on Twitter (@KathyReichs) and Pinterest (kathyreichs), and tag me in your photos on Instagram (kathyreichs). Because of you, I continue to do what I love. Thank you!